THE GATEKEEPER!

That was what Lipitero was, one of the Ykx, the legendary keepers of secret technology on the all too well-hidden world of Mistommerk. And now Skeen, trader supreme, had won the aid of Lipitero in her quest to escape from Mistommerk back to the freedom of the spaceways. But between Skeen, Lipitero, and the Stranger's Gate lay a world full of enemies, deadly foes determined to take revenge on these two adventurers and all their stalwart companions for meddling in things no off-worlder was ever meant to discover.

And even if they won through to the Gate, could Lipitero truly work the Ykx power to defeat the peril of the Ever-Hunger and reopen the way to the worlds?

SKEEN'S RETURN

JO CLAYTON

DAW BOOKS, INC.
DONALD A. WOLLHEIM, PUBLISHER

1633 Broadway, New York, NY 10019

First Printing, June 1987

1 2 3 4 5 6 7 8 9

PRINTED IN THE U. S. A.

WELL, HERE WE ARE AGAIN; YOU'VE HAD YOURSELF A NICE BREAK, TIME NOW TO GET BACK TO OUR QUEST.
SKEEN AND COMPANY HAVE DONE SOME REORGANIZING AND SHE HAS FACED THE FACT THAT THE RETURN TO THE STRANGER'S GATE IS GOING TO BE AS LONG AND DANGEROUS AND TEDIOUS AS THE JOURNEY AWAY FROM IT.
or
WHAT I WOULDN'T GIVE FOR ONE OF FLITTER HINKEY'S RETREADS.

"Djabo's ivory overbite." Skeen pushed her fingers through her hair until it stood in dark spikes about her thin face. A dozen meters south of her and considerably more than that above her, near the elaborate Gate that led to the Min Temple Maze which filled the center of the Sacred Island, Pegwai and the sponsors from the Sydo Gather were in a noisy, arm-waving argument with the Island sacerdotes while Plains Min stood about looking superior. "Every argument we covered in the past five days."

She closed her eyes. Tibo, ah, Tibo you baster, where are you? what are you doing? where's my Picarefy? why did you dump me? Same old questions, same old nothing. No answers, no way of finding out anything, anything, anything at all. She glared at the shifting knot of Min and Ykx circling about Pegwai and the Sydo Remmyo. Fuckin' backassed world. Months! Months before I can get back to the Gate. Months while you're skittering Djabo knows where. I can't stand it, I. . . . No, Skeen. Cool, Skeen. One

5

foot after the other. You'll get there. Yes, you will. If you don't fall on your face. She sighed, clasped her hands behind her back, turned to Lipitero. "They have to go over everything again?"

Morning started out well enough. When dawn was still red in the eastern sky, a lakeboat beached on the sand below the Gather cliffs. Half a dozen Min Ykx from the Sacred Island in the middle of the lake lifted from the deck, drifted over and dropped to stand before the Sydo delegates and exchange ritual greetings with them.

Britt moved closer to Skeen. The guide's plushy fur roughed and his glands gave off an acrid stench as he watched the Islanders. He didn't like them or want anything to do with them. "They'll cut your guts out," he said. "All the gold on Mistommerk wouldn't change that. You keep away from them." He growled, a soft sound inaudible a step away. A strained silence for several minutes. He spoke again, "You can trust the Ykx, that's a plus for you. They're cunning gits and you'd better watch for bait-and-switch before the hand-shake, but after that, no worry. The last time I talked with Dibratev, he said everything was set. He said the boat would be there this morning, docking out to the Island." He extruded his claws, picked delicately at the fur on his arm. "Plains Min you can do business with. Get past the hostility and they play by the rules. They let me come and go as I please; they get more out of me that way. Yours is a one-shot, so maybe you should worry some. I hear when they go down to Cida Fennakin, what they buy most of is slaves, ones with skills they can use; they like Pass-Throughs because these know things most other Nemin have forgot. That's you, Skeen. Dih's a prize, too. And given I was pushed to it, I'd say they'd give a lot to twist what the Boy knows out of him. Min and Chalarosh mix like oil and fire. Chulji, well, I'd say he wasn't worth their trou-ble. Too young to know much, but there's the chance they'd consider holding him against the services of older Skirrik. Other hand, he's only Min Skirrik, they despise their kin who've put off what they call the True Min shapes and they wouldn't be sure how much True Skirrik might be willing to pay for him. Lifefire solo knows what they'd do to Timka, no, that's not something which wants thinking about. So listen," he drew his claws lightly along her arm, waking memories that made her shiver with pleasure, "listen, Skeen, you and Timka had better split night watch between you. And maybe Pegwai. For a Scholar, he's pretty shrewd. I'm not saying they'll jump you, they probably won't. Just be careful, that's all." He glared at the Island Min, growled again, then stalked away, disappearing into the mouth of the Guest Valley.

Lipitero shook out her flight skins, folded her arms so the skins draped gracefully about her body. "Don't fuss, Skeen. It's the nature of the beast. He was born to make trouble, that one, but it doesn't mean anything."

Pegwai was intermittently visible among the gleaming shimmering flight skins that shifted with every movement of Ykx and Min Ykx bodies, catching the light and turning it to liquid ambers and bronzes. Mixed among the True and Min Ykx were other figures, long and narrow, taller than both sorts. Plains Min. Bipedal. The sharply defined eyes of avian predators, melting gold irids hot and hungry. Long narrow hands, the number of fingers varying from three to seven. In a curious asymmetry none of these Min had the same number of fingers on their right and left hands; four fingers and three, seven and five or any other of the possible non-matching combinations. Their faces had a vague similarity to the Ykx faces, the malleable Min flesh reacting to the presence of the Nemin on their borders. Odd though, odd that they kept their original forms so completely. Timka's folk, the Mountain Min, were mostly Pallah in their pri-

mary forms and Min Skirrik, well, only the Skirrik
could pick out Min from True. These Plains Min were
more intransigent in every way.

And having noted that, what did it say about the
Islanders who were fully Ykx down to the ornamenta-
tion they chose for their harnesses? Was serving on
the Sacred Island as much exile as honor? A weeding
out of weaker flesh?

The troublemaker doing most of the talking was a
shining almost ghostly figure, creamy white all over
with no gradation in the color of his fur like the other
Min and True Ykx showed. The Ciece Kirkosh was as
vehement in his cold restrained way as Pegwai was,
dividing his diatribe between the Scholar and the
Speaker for the Sydo Gather.

Skeen watched the exchange, fuming. "What's taking so long? I've paid the gold, what more do they
want?" She kicked a pebble against a boulder, watched
it go bounding off, glared at the dusty splotch on her
boot, then started jigging about in small tight circles,
trying (but not too hard) to work off her temper.

Lipitero yawned, settled herself on a flat boulder.
"That spook thinks we're his pets and he gets his fur
ruffled when he sees outsiders coming between him
and us."

"Pets." Skeen mouthed the word like a worm
dropped on her tongue.

"Oh, yes. They all do. When they get too pushy we
have to slap them down, and things get tense for a
while until the Remmyo's cadre chat them into forgetting their snit. Look. The Remmyo's interrupting
Kirkosh. Shouldn't be much longer now."

"So now we're back where we started, all that time
and energy wasted."

"So it seems." She chuckled, her eyes narrowed to
slits and gleaming with a gentle mischief. 'You've never
had to wait through this nonsense before? Are folk on
the other side so reasonable and calm about things?

Do you tell me you've never had to sit and sit and sit to wait for idiots to talk themselves into doing something everyone including them knew they were going to do?"

"Oh, endlessly. Endlessly, Petro. Still, there's always the hope that it won't be necessary in some new place."

"Ever happened?"

"No." Skeen sighed. "But I keep looking; I'm as unreasonable as the rest."

Lipitero laughed, then shook her head; she sat silent for several minutes watching Skeen fidget about, working her body to bleed off the impatience and irritation that might warp her judgment come a crisis. With considerable relief, she interrupted a series of squat thrusts and pointed along the shore. "You can relax, Skeen. Look there. The riverboat has arrived; it's tying up at the dock end."

The long narrow ship rocked gently against the pilings. Black and sleek, with stubby masts and waterjets flaring from its stern, its hybrid shape was for Skeen a paradigm of the incongruities and anachronisms she found here on Mistommerk. The crew moved about on deck, keeping their backs to the land; some leaned on the railings watching the strangers with a hostility they didn't bother concealing. Skeen remembered Britt's comment about what the Plains Min would like to do to Timka; what she saw in those mean faces told her how right he'd been.

The Aggitj, who usually took little notice of pointless prejudiced hostility, were staying well away from the boat; they sat in a tight group on a tussock of coarse grass, the Chalarosh boy pressed up close against Hal's leg. He'd adopted Hal as a surrogate father after the young Aggitj killed the Kalakal assassins responsible for the slaying of his mother and father. Chulji squatted a short distance off, his tripartite eyes fixed on the Min crew, his forelimbs moving restlessly, his mouthparts snapping together with vigorous disapproval. He had budded into a happy family, spent his child-hood in a friendly and peaceful society, lapped in the warmth of a general approval, a society filled with immutable hierarchies that tucked every hatchling and every budling into a niche it would never quite break out of no matter what it did or felt, but also a society that accepted it without reservations, that cherished it and tolerated its rebellions, its idiosyncracies. On this long trip he'd grown accustomed to a similar accept-ance from outsiders and, more than that, to praise for his talents. He was angry at these Min for rejecting him without cause and, like them, made no attempt to hide what he was feeling. Some distance farther along the shore Timka sat alone by the water, her knees drawn up, her arms crossed over them, hands dan-gling; she stared out across the lake, lost in what looked to be unhappy thoughts.

Skeen strolled away from Lipitero and walked to the end of the dock where she stood inspecting the boat and ignoring the scowls from the Crew. The craft looked swift and efficient, good on the river but probably a heller to run out on open water. Djabo bless, since Chulji had mastered his waterform, none of them suffered from seasickness; even the short dis-tance across the lake to the mouth of the river was likely to be tricky on the stomach. Built like a spear-head with a knife for a keel, not meant for bulky cargo, that craft. Slaves, fah! Skeen stared into hot gold eyes with a hostility of her own and a comforting sense of superiority; she might be a Rooner raping the ancient histories of assorted worlds, but she drew the line at dealing in flesh. Nostrils flaring, she turned her back on them and walked away.

Kicking aimlessly at small stones, she wound through the sprays of large and small rocks along the stony shore and finally dropped beside Timka. "Hurry up and wait," she murmured.

Timka looked blank a moment, then smiled. "Are you that anxious to get back? Think about Telka and her minions waiting to skewer us all. That should fuel your patience a while longer."

"Pah!" Skeen wiped at her boot with the heel of her hand, rubbing away the dust from the stone marks. "Fuckin' right I want to get back." Gloom saturated her voice. "Telka? We'll fox her till she doesn't know which end is up. Thing is, no more gold left, just small stuff; I don't like being tapped out this far from a city."

"First time I saw you worry about money."

"It's a bitch trying to wring coin out of a bunch of rocks." She scowled over her shoulder at the barren shore.

"Our fares are paid; there shouldn't be any bother about funds until we reach Cida Fennakin."

"Yeah, but I've seen this kind of thing before. The only cure for such wounded souls is a slather of gold. Guess whose gold."

"The Ykx will provide; you've got them round the neck. Stop grumbling."

"It's something to do while that farce is going on."

"Why aren't you over there with Pegwai doing some shouting of your own?"

"Lipitero. She said I'd better leave the talking to him. Said I'd lose my temper and get us all skinned. Said I wasn't tactful when I was angry."

Timka giggled. "So right."

"I know. I know." Skeen passed her tongue across her upper lip. "What a lousy place. What do they do to pass an evening round here?"

"You asking or still muttering?"

"Still muttering. Never mind. Tell me what you used to do, come sundown."

"Mmmm." Timka gazed thoughtfully at the lake-water lapping a handspan from her toes. Truebirds fluttered past overhead, raucous cries each time one of

them stooped at the water and rose with a fish in its
talons. "When I was living at the hostel with Aunt
Carema . . ." her voice was muted, with a smile in it,
her words ambled along at a nostalgic gait, ". . . and
her six apprentices, they were all talented to earth and
rooted things. Not me, but Carema wouldn't talk about
my talents or let me boast either. Aunt Carema. She
was what you hope all aunts are like, big and shapeless
as a pillow and twice as warm. Not sickly sweet, no,
she had a tongue that could strip the bark off a tree at
twenty paces. She couldn't abide fools and let you
know fast when you were being a silly lackbrain. Evenings . . . evenings . . . mmm, some evenings Carema
would have friends over, older Min, some of them
reaching back so far they'd stopped shifting and spent
most of their time rooted deep and husked over; she'd
feed them hot worran nuts and apple brandy. And
they'd tell us about times that were legend to most of
the Min, even the busy-busies like my father. They'd
do chants for us, they'd tell stories of things that
happened when they were young or sometimes stories
other ancients had passed on to them in just this way."
A wistful sigh. "Sounds like it should be dull, but it
wasn't. They were very impressive . . . yes." She
smoothed her thumb across her chin. "Sometimes there
were healers and herb doctors from other Min groups,
sometimes travelers who were drifting about because
they were restless or involved with quarrels at home. I
liked these; I'd sit and listen to them until they were
tired of talking. They'd fly in and Carema would give
them courtesy robes for the length of their stay and
they'd try to tell us and other Min about the world
outside. But they'd give that up fast, except for me."
Timka moved her shoulders, grimaced. "Most of my
kin and kind don't want to hear about anyplace else or
anyone else. Might disturb their satisfaction with themselves. I don't know . . . I still don't understand why
they are so afraid of changing. In spite of everything

they do, things do creep in from outside, things do change. We've got Pallah and Balayar words not just in Trade-Min but in the home tongue. Balayar spices growing in our gardens, and hundreds of plants from the Skirrik. I could name a lot more . . . and Telka, miserable, meeching Telka. She and her Holavish seem to think they can stop that creep. 'Get rid of the Pallah,' they say, 'shut the Valley, then we can be True Min again.' " She laughed scorn at that. "The Holavish are laying up weapons and recruiting followers to do that thing. Fools. When I was with the Poet he knew all about them. His brother the Byglave knew. The Besar Casach knew. I didn't tell them. How could I? I didn't know anything about Telka's maneuvers until the Poet told me. He enjoyed letting me know how Telka was using me to stir the Min up, to make them afraid of the Pallah; he'd laugh like a fool and I'd feel a handspan high. Oh, he liked that, especially when the Byglave was riding him about something he did or didn't do." She broke off, shook her head. "Sorry about the rant." She leaned back, looked up the hill. "They're breaking up. You'd better go see what Pegwai has committed you to."

Skeen sniffed, got to her feet, reached her hand down to help Timka up.

Timka shook her head. "Better not. They're touchy about stray Min. Send Chulji over to me. We'll play last on board."

Skeen frowned, glanced at the dark ship. "You sure?" She waited a moment longer in case Timka changed her mind, then walked away. She hesitated again as she came even with the Min Skirrik youth, then put her hand on his top shoulder. "Chul, Ti wants to talk with you."

"How come?"

"She'll tell you. I think you should go."

"It's those Min, isn't it. Stinking znaks."

"Talk to Timka." She moved on toward the dock.

Behind her Hal got to his feet, tall and lanky, the silvery not-hair moving softly about his head. He was excited but controlling it; he was the one responsible for the others; he was the oldest, generally the calmest. He urged the others up and went with them to stand behind Skeen as she met Pegwai near the shore end of the dock.

"How much?" An edgy tartness in her voice.

Pegwai flung his hand out in an angry angular gesture. "That misbegotten son of a corpseworm claimed we'd pollute the boat so it'd have to be burned, that he couldn't let it back in the lake. Either the Patjen and his crew should back out of the deal, or you should be charged the full value of the boat."

"Yeah, I expected something like that. And?"

"Dibratev tried soothing him. That didn't work so he put the squeeze on. The Ykx own a quarter share in the riverboat, and they're the ones who keep it running. Dibratev mentioned that." Pegwai grinned. "Dropped it into a moment of silence when Kirkosh was snatching a breath. The silence got a lot louder." Skeen matched Pegwai's grin; he chuckled, then turned serious. "The next thing he said was the Sydo Ykx weren't happy with the Islanders, too much interference and he was looking at Kirkosh when he said it. If that interference kept up, the Ykx might decide to withdraw from the Min-Ykx compact. He wasn't just throwing that on the scales. He meant it and it showed. The Patjen saw he meant it and turned on Kirkosh so fast it was almost funny. Fare was paid, he said, and if the Ciece wanted to fool with the deal, maybe they'd better call on the Synarc to adjudicate. The Islanders started whispering at Kirkosh and he spent the last half hour worming out of the mess he'd got himself in. Good thing we're leaving right away; give him a hint of an excuse and we'd be fueling bone fires."

Skeen rubbed at the back of her neck. "No extra gold?"

"None."

"When do we board?"

"Soon as the gear is stowed. Which I'd better see to right now."

Skeen watched him walk away, then glanced at the sun. Halfway to noon already. Might be slow, but I'm coming, Tibo. Enjoy yourself, you baster. When I catch you, I'll skin you slow. Maybe I will. Why'd you do it, you little . . . little devil? Why did you strand me? Why?

LOOK, LET'S NOT TALK ABOUT THE GLAMOUR
OF QUESTING. MOST OF IT SEEMS TO
BE KEEPING THE RAIN OUT OF YOUR
BLANKETS, FLEAS OR THEIR ANALOGS OFF
YOUR PERSON, FOOD IN YOUR BELLY AND
THE LOCALS OFF YOUR BACK. OF COURSE,
NO ONE CELEBRATING THESE EPIC JOURNEYS
PUTS IN ANY OF THAT—TOO DISILLUSIONING
AND WORSE, TOO BORING. SO LET'S SKIP
THAT TRIP DOWNRIVER. TAKE AS READ THE
UNRELENTING HOSTILITY OF THE PLAINS MIN
CREW AND THE DISCOMFORT OF THE
RIVERBOAT.
NO AMBUSHES, NO THREATS TO LIFE AND
LIMB, JUST DAY AFTER DAY OF COLD WET
JOLTING.
or
ARRIVING BROKE IN CIDA FENNAKIN.

Cida Fennakin was a rambling city of interlocking
compounds whose walls were an elaborate play of textures and colors climbing the small steep hills above
the ragtag working port. The higher the compound,
the more elaborate the stone dressing of the walls, the
more power the Funor inside had over the days and
nights, the lives and loves and general subsistence of
those who lived outside those walls. The Port itself
was a conglomeration of elbow to elbow structures.
Warehouses, taverns, half-ruined compounds turned
into shelter for the flotsam off the ships that were
continually arriving and departing—abandoned or run-
away sailors, escaped slaves, servants who had lost

their usefulness from age or disease or crippling accident, ruined gamblers, thieves, whores of both sexes and assorted kinds, beggars, street players, the mad and half-mad, druggers and drugged, hardboys collecting the sub-taxes for local thuglords, small traders, rag and bone men, cookshop owners, tailors, cobblers—a thousand other small enterprises that brought in enough coin to feed and clothe the families who ran them. A noisy, stinking, lively port, the streets so filled with folk that walking was like swimming in a powerful river. Cida Fennakin, the most important port on the western end of the Halijara sea, the last stop of most trading ships, the gateway to goods from the interior.

The Patjen brought the riverboat past the rubble at the outskirts of the port as the tip of the sun pushed over the highest of the compounds, a sprawling mass of stone whose broad towers were boldly black against the gray-pink sky. He nosed the boat up to a tottery wharf, the first in the long line of wharves that followed the bulge of the river, a dusty unstable structure long abandoned, its piles loosened by the working of spring floods and winter ice. Without ceremony, he put them ashore and dumped their goods onto the groaning planks, then took his ship back into the main current and hastened toward more propitious surroundings.

Skeen frowned at the ruins around her. Not a soul in sight. Nothing happening here. Silence, cool and damp. Almost no breeze, shadows with edges sharp enough to cut, the river a dull, sub-audible yet pervasive sound. Trickles of sand and eroded brick rattling down here and there. A hint of voices, far off, broken tones rising and falling, punctuated by an occasional shout. Smell of urine and excrement, of something dead not so far away, of rotten food and the dry rot in the planks of the wharf. The remains of a warehouse that had burnt out a decade ago, battered by the seasons, crumbling back to the soil it was built on, eaten at by fungi and weeds. And deserted. Even the worst off of Fennakin beggars found better shelter elsewhere. "Lovely," she said.

Pegwai stumped over to the pile of gear and rooted out his pack. He straightened with it dangling from one hand. "No point hanging about here."

"Noooh." Skeen clasped her hands behind her, turned her head side to side, scanning the draggled wrecks collapsing onto rotting planks. "Let's wait a while."

"Why?"

"Something I'm remembering."

"What?" He took a step toward her, leaped back as the plank started to collapse under his weight, dry rot turning the wood to dust under the lightest pressure. He glared at the plank, transferred the glare to Skeen. "Hardly the time to indulge in nostalgia, woman."

Skeen clicked her fingers impatiently. "Nostalgia? Nonsense. Listen, the place where I grew up was on a river like this with blights . . ." she waved a hand at the tumbledown structures on the bank, ". . . a lot like this, and whenever anything happened around those blights, we used to snake down there and see if we could make a dime or so out of it. Street kids can be useful, Peg, if you trust them as far as you can see them and know a little about how to take them. And right now we need one." She looked around at the others. Lipitero, her form and face concealed by a voluminous cowled robe, sat with her back against one of the old bitts, an anonymous lump, waiting and willing to continue waiting until Skeen was ready to move. Timka perched on another bitt, her eyes half shut, her face unreadable. Ders was jittering about, but that meant nothing. He seldom sat anywhere longer than five minutes at a time; she suspected he couldn't stay still any longer, that there was a switch in his brain that set him on PACE at predetermined intervals. Hal and Domi were immersed in a game of stonechess. Hart was talking softly to the Boy who was absently making the Beast sit up and beg for bits of raw fish.

Chulji squatted on his four hinder limbs while he preened his antennas with the hooks on his wrists. "Let's wait a while more," she said. "We might acquire a guide. Which is better than barging in and starting something we maybe can't handle."

A small skinny boy ambled down the cluttered alley, a pre-pubescent Funor, the knobs of his horns two gray velvet buttons poking through lank dirty hair whose original color might have been a pale reddish brown; it shifted with the wind and the quick darting moves of his head. He wore a ragged tunic of some thick coarse material rather like worn canvas, the armholes and sliced-off bottom blooming with cottony fuzz. He kicked casually along the coarse dirt, tickling weeds with a whippy stick, whistling through tooth gaps. After the first furtive glance at the strangers, he seemed to ignore them though Skeen's memory told her he was keeping a sharp eye on them.

She stirred. "Got a minute?"

The boy stopped (well out of reach, poised to dive away if it seemed necessary) and considered her briefly, then his dark eyes skittered from her to the others and back. Then he raised a small hand with three fingers, one excessively thin, the other two thick as the thumb. Thumb and thick fingers looked clumsy but that was probably deceptive. He rubbed his thumb across his fingers in a rapid flutter, a sign that had so far in Skeen's experience proved universal.

Skeen dug into her belt pouch (regrettably flat), brought out one of the broad coppers that served as small change on this world and held it up. The boy gave it a scornful look and fluttered his thumb some more. She shook her head. He turned to leave. She let him go. He took one step, then another, then looked over his shoulder at her. She held up two coppers. He drifted back, cupped his hands together to make a hollow. She tossed him one of the coppers, kept the second. "We want a place to light," she said. "Somewhere that's quiet . . ." she paused after the word, gave him a one-sided grin, "and the Keeper's reasonably honest, don't pitch the clients to the nearest slaver, and where the ale don't take the lining off your throat. You got that? Good. And cheap, young friend. We aren't silkers looking for delights."

For the first time, he gazed directly at them, one after the other, ending with Skeen, his mouth open, stupidity glazing his eyes; he picked at his nose, kicked one foot back and forth over the dirt, blinked slowly at Skeen, held up his skinny finger.

Ders snorted and would have said something, but Domi touched his arm before the words could spill out. "Wait," he murmured, "let Skeen work."

Skeen frowned, tossed the boy the coin she was holding, dug out another and showed it to him. "When we get there."

He stared at her a moment longer, then nodded and stopped looking quite so stupid. "Angelsin Yagan's Chek," he said. "Tain't much, but's a roof and walls." He turned his shoulder to them and sidled away. "Coom," he said, "coom, 's not far."

He led them through weeds and ruins, led them deeper and deeper into the slum quarter. As they wound away from the river, the crumbling buildings grew gradually steadier, stuffed with folk of all sorts, teeming with life, noisy, nosy and assertive, questions shouted at the boy in half a dozen languages besides the Trade-Min, most of which he ignored. The streets filled up with strollers, with porters carrying bulky loads at a trot, with beggars and street performers, singers, dancers, jugglers, magicians, shell and pea men, meat pie venders, water sellers, several women with goats who sold cups of warm milk, a pancake woman with a horde of small children dashing about delivering hot cakes and collecting coppers from those that bought them, dozens of other street venders sell-

ing everything from secondhand clothing to scrap metal
and rags, cutpurses (very wary because the street would
turn on them and stomp them if they weren't deft
indeed and choosy about their victims), hardboys who
swaggered along taking whatever they wanted, protected by their relationship to the secret ones who ran
the quarter. The boy trotted along without stopping
until a tinny drum sounded over the noise. He hustled
them into a back alley the moment he heard the tonk
tunk of that drum and warned them to stay put while
he nosed out what was happening.

Skeen grabbed him by the shoulder, swung him
around and demanded an explanation of his jitters.

"Eh, lemme go."

"A minute. Tell me about the drum, what it means."

"Chicklee turds, them. Guards. Thump you if ya
don't skip."

"Tell me 'bout 'em."

"All you gotta know is keep clear." He wriggled and
squealed with pain; she ignored that, knowing it was
playacting, and kept her clutch on his shoulder. "Lemme
go, huh," he whined. "I NEED to see what those
turds doin'."

"Drum's not moving that fast, there's time. Why do
we have to duck them? We're not making trouble now
and not going to either, so what's the scream?"

"They ben agitatin' round recent, pickin' up strays
like they figurin' on cleanin' out South Cusp. Mines
want hands, that's it, you keep ya head low when the
mines they want hands. Loose strangers, they get picked
up fast. You wanna spend ya life inna hole?"

"Do they go in the cheks?"

"Nuh-uh, 'cept taprooms say they hear fightin' or
they followin' some terp or they got a thirst."

"So they're not ferrets."

"Nuh-uh. They grab what they see."

"Won't come around here?"

"Prolly not, what I gotta see 'bout if you lemme
go."

She watched him trot off, stepped quickly to Chulji. "Follow him, bird's best. Get as much as you can about those guards and what they're doing."

Chulji gave her the wriggly Skirrik grin, shifted and took off as a hunting hawk, spiraling high and moving after the Funor boy.

Skeen touched Pegwai's arm. "You see? Nostalgia has its uses. We might have put our feet in something we couldn't scrape off."

"It's not seemly to say I told you so." He spoke with the austere dignity of a slightly pompous instructor of youth, exaggerating a natural trait as a pedantic sort of joke.

She chuckled, pinched his arm.

Ders fidgeted out of the hole where the boy had stuffed them, kicked about in the shadows that filled the littered alley, nosing into anything that looked a bit interesting. Domi swore under his breath and collected his cousin with more force than he usually showed.

Lipitero pulled her robe more closely about her and moved to the crumbling corner of their niche. (It was a boarded-up gateway in a high thick wall, deep enough to give them some protection from a casual glance along the alley.) "Do you think the child will return?"

Skeen nodded. "More likely than not; he's still got a copper coming and he's curious about us. And he'll get a commission for delivering us to Yagan's Chek."

Timka leaned against her and stared down the alley. "You grabbed him. Won't that scare him into running off?"

"Wouldn't have scared me when I was his age. He gets a lot more pinching and bruising from his friends than he got from me. No way for me to say anything for sure. He could be selling us to the Guard right now. That's why I sent Chulji to watch him. I'd bet a copper or two on him keeping out of sight and doing what he said, but I wouldn't trust our lives on it. Chul knows that; he'll be careful, let us know if we should jump."

The boy came sidling back a few minutes later. "Looks like they aimin' for Tes Silah's wharf; bunch of slaves comin' in and they after the Bohant's Levy. 'Nother squad, they comin' this way but not hurryin', sticking to Sukkar's Skak. We go careful, we can make Yagan's Chek without us gettin' close 'nough to smell the turds. Ya coom?"

He led them to a tall narrow structure, a building cobbled together from bits and pieces, old stones, bricks, wood beams plastered over with heavily strawed river clay, a surprisingly neat and well-built place, with a workmanlike finish to it that spoke of skill and pride. Skeen liked the look of it immediately, though she wondered about the cost of staying there. She wasn't ready to start prowling yet; the more she saw of Cida Fennakin, the more she wanted to know about customs and conditions before she lifted a finger. It had the smell of a dangerous place for a misstep and missteps were all too easy when you didn't know where to put your feet.

The main entrance was open, the door pushed back against the wall; it was built from massive planks crossed and recrossed by iron bands and had an equally massive lock. Skeen glanced at it as she followed the Funor boy inside and suppressed a smile. You'd need a picklock the size of a crowbar.

The room spread the length of the building, dim and shadowy, lit by the early morning sunlight trickling through parchment covering the windows. A small fire burned on one of the hearths but did little to cut the gloom. The Funor boy trotted across the room to the end of the slab of wood set on sections of pile salvaged from the river, a long wide bar with a polish on it that drew light into the depths of the wood. A thronelike

chair was built on a low dais at the end of that bar, a
huge Funor woman sitting silent in it. Not fat, just big.
If she stood, she'd probably be somewhere around two
and a half meters tall. Large bones, solid muscle
wrapped around them. Coarse reddish hair twisted
into a braid that hung forward over one shoulder, the
tassel at the end pooled on her broad thigh. Ivorine
horns rose like half crescents poking through the frizzled bands of hair drawn back past her ears. Her face
was a pale blur, her mouth a slightly darker blur, her
eyes velvety shadows with an occasional gleam in the
depths. A powerful hieratic figure. Skeen felt an ata-
vistic chill along her spine as she stood in front of the
woman and waited for her to acknowledge their
presence.

Their juvenile guide flopped onto his knees in front
of her, reached over and laid his grimy hand on the
toe of her shoe. "Angelsin Yagan," he said, "These
folk want a place to light where the host is sorta
honest and the ale doon't ream out their throats."

A rumbling chuckle. A deep rich voice. "Quoting,
Hopflea?"

"Yah, mam."

Shadow eyes glimmered at Skeen. "How long?"

"Say a fortn't. If we need longer, we'll talk then."
Skeen took out the third copper, flipped it to the boy.
"If we can agree on price."

The hawk tapped at the window frame. Skeen swung
it open and let Chulji flutter in. When he'd shifted
from hawk to Skirrik, she said, "You'll be bunking in
here with Timka, Lipitero and me. Took all my silver
to hire two rooms. What about the guards?"

Chulji scratched around until he was squatting comfortably on a hooked rug, a long oval put together
from soft rags in muted earth colors. "The Funor boy
climbed a wall and stretched himself out on a roof so
he could watch the squad tramp past. Weird how that

street cleared out in front of them. You remember
how busy it was, hardly room to breathe? Well, when
the guards came in view, wall to wall it was empty like
it'd been sluiced clean. Folk didn't look scared exactly, more kind of cautious. They faded into doors
and alleys soon's they heard that drum. Skeen, seems
to me it's dumb for guards to announce themselves
like that. Anyone they figured on catching would duck
when they heard the first tunk. I mean, that's what
happened, wasn't it? Why the drum?"

"If I was guessing, I'd say they leave the drum quiet
when they're serious about catching someone specific.
Other times, well, it's a winnower. The ones who
duck are homefolk, the ones who don't are outsiders
and fair game. Like we'd have been except for Hopflea.
The Funor boy. What'd he do when he came off the
roof?"

"He had a few words with some folk, an old woman
and two kids about his size. Then he scooted back
down the alley to you. I figured there was no problem
with him, so I stayed up in case the guards turned
round. They didn't. They went straight to a wharf
about a half a kilometer on and collected some men
in chains and marched off with them. I was flying high
enough so I could keep an eye on you all; that's how I
knew where to come." He grinned at Timka who sat
on a low stool, her back against the wall. "And once I
was close enough, all I had to do was feel around and
find the right window that way."

Skeen laughed, shook her head. "Min, hunh."

Timka gave her a slow smile. "Sometimes it's useful; nothing's ever a complete loss."

"I wouldn't bet a snipped-off fingernail on that.
Seriously, Chul, did you touch any other Min while
you were feeling about?"

"Well, there was the Crew and the Patjen, but they
were easy enough to screen out, being all lumped
together like they were. No mistaking them." His

mouthparts clicked together, his antennas twitched.
"I'm not sure . . . I wasn't really trying for anyone but
Timka . . . I think maybe I skimmed past some others
. . . two, three . . . I'm not sure . . . did they brush
me too? If there were really Min there. . . ? I don't
know, I couldn't even guess."

Skeen rubbed at the back of her neck. "And if you
go hunting them to make sure, they'll be sure about
you. Hmm. Keep your feelers out . . . sorry, you're
right, Ti, no need to tell you that. Hunh, Ti, what
would you do if your face froze like that? Chul, you be
thinking what you could do to earn some legitimate
coin, we're going to meet in here after the noon feed
to talk that over some. Maggí Solitaire won't be
here for another three weeks. We came downriver a
lot faster than I expected, so we're going to need some
eating money. I'm down to a handful of coppers and
some lint."

In the days that followed, the days while they waited
for Maggí Solitaire to show up, Skeen and the rest
scrounged for coin to keep and feed themselves.

Lipitero stayed behind in the room, bored but re-
signed to her confinement. She was myth made flesh
and would attract far too much attention if she showed
face and flight skins. Who wouldn't want to possess a
creature out of dreams? What a temptation it would
be to clip a dragon's wings and keep him always there.
In a culture where slave holding was an unquestioned
part of the system, no soul was safe from the slaver's
snare; the unprotected had little recourse but ducking,
dodging and generally keeping out of notice. In spite
of the skills and ferocity of Skeen and her Company,
they wouldn't be able to protect the Ykx from seizure
if anyone outside discovered who and what she was.
She spent her time carving small forms out of fragments of wood the Aggitj scavenged for her; she was
meticulous, taking great pains with each stroke of the

knife, putting one piece down and taking up another
when she tired of the first; it wasn't likely she'd finish
any of them in time to add to the Company's store of
coin, but the work kept her from perishing of boredom.

Skeen, Timka and the Chalarosh Boy worked together. Skeen played her flute and Timka danced,
then while the Boy and the Beast worked the crowd
for coin, she did some conjuring and patter to ease the
pangs of giving. (Nervous Finnakese were more generous than they intended when the Boy smiled winsomely
at them, exposing the twisted, grooved poison fangs,
and when the Beast sniffed interestedly at their ankles.) More than once street urchins tried some fast
poaching from the cash bowl, but backed off when the
Beast squealed and lunged at them or the Boy hissed;
Skeen'd told him he was responsible for protecting the
take and he didn't intend to let her down. When the
hardboys came to collect the Bosses' cut, intending to
treat themselves to most of what was left over, even
they kept their distance from Boy and Beast.

The audience faded with practiced ease the moment
they appeared, leaving Skeen to face the young thugs,
four Funor shorthorns with their cowls gathered in
folds about thick necks, their hair in tight brindle
curls, their faces blunt, flat, doughy, the features etched
into the dough as with a blunt stick, nostrils flat slits,
eyes thumbed deep and dull, mouths shapeless holes.
Big and ugly by birth and raising. Their timing was
miserable, she'd been about to send the Boy out to
collect for the performance; all that work for nothing.
She had to struggle to keep a hold on her temper as
she waited for the biggest to say what he'd come to
say.

Hardboy number one gargled at her in mangled
Trade-Min: "Street cunk gotta pay the Hussa a cut."

Skeen relaxed; she'd been expecting this, but she
didn't let that show. She tucked the flute into a pocket
on the cloak she'd improvised out of one of Lipitero's

robes; if she had to fight or run she needed her hands clear and she didn't want to toss the flute where it would get trampled or stolen. "How much, how often, how many bosses have to be paid?"

He opened his beady deep-set eyes as wide as he could. "Huh?"

Skeen sighed. "All right, one thing at a time. How much?"

He wrinkled his broad flat brow. The horns poking through the greasy brindle over his ears seemed to strain with the effort. "Uh. Half."

"Hah!" Skeen planted her hands on her hips and looked down her long nose at him, being as irritating as she could without coming flat out and calling him a lardhead. "Listen, you scrub, we might be new to these streets but that don't mean we don't know what's what. One in ten. That's the going rate and that's what we'll pay. One in ten. Every third day."

He rubbed meaty hands along his sides, worked his fingers. His herdmates behind him were getting restive and he knew if he didn't handle this business right, he'd be hooked in the belly before the week was out and one of them would be replacing him as top kicker. "One in ten," he blared at Skeen. "Yah, sure. Every day come sundown." He watched her warily; when she didn't seem about to object, he regained some of his swagger. "Collector be by. You have it or you don' work 'n you have it right. We got ways a knowin' the take."

Skeen made the cape swirl about her as she executed a magnificent mocking bow. "I hear and obey," she chanted.

He gazed at her with a touch of uncertainty, sensing dimly that she was making a fool of him, but the hints of rebellion in his mob had subsided and he didn't want to mess that up by pointing out what they hadn't noticed. He shouldered past her, made Timka skip away to avoid being trampled, but kept carefully wide of the Boy and the Beast.

Timka watched them stomp along the street and disappear down a side alley, then she turned to narrow her eyes at Skeen. "You gave in fast."

Skeen dropped to a squat, rubbed her back against a rough place in the wall. "No point kicking against that bunch. We won't be here long enough to make it worth the trouble." She smiled as the street began filling up again, the noise level rising to what it'd been before. "Djabo gnaw their toes, those gits chased off our audience." A yawn, a last scrape against the stone. "Ready?" She pushed onto her feet, ran her tongue over teeth and lips, inspected the flute, shook it out and began to play a plaintive tune.

Timka grimaced, wriggled her body and shook her arms, then she began to improvise a circle dance of graceful drifts and slow leaps.

Pegwai thought to set up as a street scribe, but while he was looking for an inkseller and the proper spot, he came across a Balayar trader who made Cida Fennakin his homeport, a distant cousin of his he'd known when he was a boy in the Spray. After a belly-burning lunch that made Pegwai momentarily nostalgic for cool nights on the sand and coals burning down over a buried porasbabash, Tilman Sang found him temporary work as tutor for the sons of another merchant with aspirations to importance; later he could boast his sons were educated by a Scholar from the Tanul Lumat and avoid mentioning how short his tenure was.

Over wine punch that night, feet up before a crackling fire, Tilman Sang turned to Pegwai. "Too bad I couldn't get you into one of the Funor Ashon households. I'd like to know more about how those old bulls think."

"Plenty of Funor outside the Keep walls. Study them."

"They're different. Oh, I won't deny there are connections, I only wish I knew how those worked, then I could avoid a lot of mistakes which could be bad for

the health of me and mine. My six boys and me, we
watch those outside Funor every chance we get, and
nine times out of ten, we can't make sense out of what
we're seeing." He shook his head, frustration visible
in the reddening of his round face. "It isn't just curiosity, cousin-isl; around the Funor Ashon, ignorance can
be fatal." He settled back in his chair, took a sip of
wine and stared at the stunted crawling flames. "Or
close enough. I tell you, cousin-isl, none of us knows
what will turn them cranky; it makes living here interesting, that I have to say. Not like in the Spray where
you know how everybody breathes. Keeps you perked
up if it doesn't kill you." He took a long swallow, then
sighed. "That's the trouble with this place, you just
get to enjoying things and the crazy Funor change the
rules on you. Are they that hard to get along with over
on Tanzik? No? I suppose your Funor kicked their
crazies out and they all landed here. Let me give you
an example what can happen. Terador Mil—yes, I'll
admit no Mil ever had the sense to walk in out of the
rain, but he's not a bad sort. Fussy and ready to go
overboard on rules and regulations, like to irritate the
skin off anyone who has to deal with him, but honest
as a Mil ever gets. So fill up your glass and let me tell
this.

Four, five years ago, old Dogbiter was the Faceman,
the Bohant's Mouth; he was the one who said hop and
the whole damn city twitched like a clutch of nervous
fleas. Deogabut ProCheng the Peakman, if you want
the formal of it. He seemed more reasonable than
most of them; if you were careful you could get a lot
out of him and be fairly sure the deal would stick. He
stayed on the highrope longer than I can remember
another doing and most of us otherWavers knew quite
well how to tickle him sweet. Day came when Terdi
Mil had to go see him about some trouble he was
having getting in a cargo of seeds from Istryamozhe.
He climbed the hill, dressed in his best go-to-meet-
the-Dogbiter clothes, the horrible pink and purple mix

old Dogbiter insisted on. He banged on the jakka
gong and when the Greeter opened the wicket, he
nearly turned round and marched back downhill. The
Greeter's badge was different—new colors, different
squiggles in the sections—no one but Funor Ashon
can read Funor writing. If he hadn't been Terdi Mil,
that's what he'd've done, turned right round and got
out of there, but he's a hard head, him, and he settled
himself down, went through all the contortions and
kowtowing the Funor make us go through before they'll
talk to us, the high and noble ones anyway. The
Peakman was the worst; if he was anything but Funor,
I'd swear he was playing games on us, sitting somewhere watching and laughing his fool head off at the
asses we were making of ourselves. Well, Mil banged
his brow on the ground for the last time, then he
asked to see Dogbiter, using his grand name and all
his titles, just like everyone had a hundred times. Far
as he could tell, up to then, everything was fine. But
before he finished with last title, the Little Gate banged
open, Funor swarmed out, stripped off every clout and
kicked him around the ring and beat him until he was
staggering, cursing him, spitting at him, using their
tonks on him until the only way he knew he was alive
was the pain. Until they didn't, he was sure they were
going to kill him, but they pointed him downhill and
started him off with a boot on his quivering ass. Well,
he's a tough old wart and he got himself home before
he passed out. Had to stay in bed nearly a month, but
he got over it. Took the rest of us traders a while more
to find out the Dogbiter had a stroke and that interrupted his dance long enough for him to get kicked off
the rope and finally strangled; there was a lot of maneuvering until there was another dancer firmly in
place and things finally settled enough so we could
stick our heads up and go back to trading. One hairy
time, I tell you; you never knew what was going to
happen. Folk you'd known for years turned up missing
and you never took notice of it because you were

scared it'd happen to you if you did. Well, that's over
now, but Lifefire only knows how soon it'll happen
again—when this Faceman falls, and we won't know it
until some other poor skuk will be goat for us all."
Tilman Sang grinned at his cousin. "You figure a way
to read them, Dih, and I'll work you a nice little
commission."

"It's an idea, cousin. I'll think about it." Pegwai was
bland and noncommittal, but Tilman expected as much
and only meant to plant the seed, a seed he'd manured
with the obligation he'd laid on Pegwai by getting him
the tutoring job. One way or another Pegwai would
clear the debt; that's the way things worked among the
Balayar of the Spray. Pegwai got to his feet and began
the long process of taking his leave.

The Aggitj came tramping down the stairs, arguing
vigorously in Aggitchan flinging arms about, letting their
bodies handle the mechanics of the descent. They
quieted when they reached the long taproom; the younger three hung back while Hal walked over to Angelsin
Yagan, not forgetting courtesy but not intimidated by
her massive presence. Ders jigged about behind Hart
(who stood stolid and disapproving, his arms folded,
his eyelids drooping, the corners of his mouth tucked
into the deep creases slanting from his nostrils and
dropping under his jawline) and Domi (who merely
looked impatient).

"Mamam Kai, by your kindness tell us where we
can find the Aggitj Slukra. We're hunting work by day
or week."

Angelsin leaned forward, moving her face out of
shadow, her deep-set eyes dark and unreadable, her
gaze uncomfortably searching. Hal kept his smile though
it took more effort than he was happy about. Ders
stopped whistling and moved closer to Domi, shivering now and then in a way he had when particularly
nervous. Domi put his hand on his cousin's shoulder,
closed it tight. Ders calmed, leaned against his taller

relation and watched from slitted eyes. Domi draped his arm over the boy's shoulder and waited for the woman to speak. He'd argued a good half hour with Hal about approaching her. She gave him chills in the belly whenever he was in the same room with her. We can live here and pay her for the privilege, he'd told Hal, but no more; we should keep as far away from her as we can manage.

"Why?" she said. Her voice was warm and creamy, her mouth soft, smiling. "I'll give you work if you want. There is more than enough lifting and carrying about this chek and I will pay better than anything the Slukra can find for you."

Hal forced a smile. Domi saw the muscles in his neck tighten and knew Hal the always-right had a flood of second thoughts. "Most kind, Mamam Kai." His voice sounded stiff though he was trying to speak naturally. "It's not just work, we want to greet our kind and see if kin have come this far. There's news to pass from Boot and Backland."

Angelsin Yagan settled back, her broad face once more in shadow. "That is natural," she said, the warmth gone from her voice. "But they're a nosy lot at the Slukra. My business is none of theirs; be sure you leave me out of your news passing. My offer is withdrawn. I would wish you fair going, but if you continue to ignore the blessings of fortune, you'll land in the slop and deserve what you get."

"Ah, Mamam Kai, don't ill wish us. We don't mean to offend, but we're a long way from home and blood means a lot. Where will we find the Slukra?"

She gave directions in a die-away exhausted voice and they left as quickly as they could without offending her further.

Ders trotted ahead, waited for them to catch up and skipped backward in front of his cousins. "If that one ever had children, I bet she ate 'em raw soon as they popped out."

Domi scowled. "Eat you if she hears you saying things like that, flea brain."

"Eh, Domi, who knows Aggitchan here?" He flapped his arms in wide awkward sweeps that almost decapitated a smallish Pallah whore who jumped aside just in time and sent a gush of curses after them, then went on her way muttering unfriendly things under her breath.

"Could be anyone, you chump. This is a trade port and a big 'un. Take the wheels off your tongue. We can't scoot for cover this time, not till, well, you know." He looked warily about, but no one was paying them undue attention. "Watch your mouth, cousin, or you could get us all skinned."

Ders dropped his arms and he pouted for a while, but his sulks never lasted very long; in a few paces his buoyancy had returned and he bounced along, whistling under his breath.

Within the hour they had work as day laborers along the wharves with the promise of plenty of jobs ahead, as much as they wanted as long as they wanted it. Here too, Aggitj extras were preferred workers. The Aggitj in the Slukra looked wary when they mentioned where they were staying, but said little, only a veiled warning. Don't get her mad at you. You won't like what happens. No, that's all. Do us a favor, forget we said anything.

Chulji found work outside town in the ring farms, transferring from one to another, dealing with plant disease and other problems; he didn't earn much, but got most of his meals from the farms, easing the drain on the common purse.

Skeen took some of the coin and went prowling the taverns, listening to talk, answering questions when she was recognized as a Pass-Through, trading yarns, her own told with a purpose, an indirect way of digging out possible involuntary contributors who'd fund her return to the Stranger's Gate. The larger streets were safe enough even in the gray hours before dawn, but alleys and indoors were something else; she stumbled into a few troubles, but fought her way clear with feet, hands and boot knife, paying for her inattention and less than alertness (all that ale that she told herself she was swallowing to oil the give and take that gave her the names she needed) with bruises, cuts, a three-day limp and an almost concussion that kept her ears ringing for another three days. But she was slowly, safely building up a list of the affluent but truly despised, intending here as in Oruda to pick a victim so wormish that he (or she, of course) was unlikely to spur fervent pursuit, a victim whose plight was more apt to evoke belly laughs and appreciative chuckles and a tendency to wish the thief well as long as it didn't involve any danger or discomfort to the wisher.

JUST ABOUT EVERYONE WHO TALKS TO ASPIRING WRITERS SAYS SHOW, DON'T TELL; GOOD ENOUGH ADVICE, BUT YOU DON'T WANT TO LOOK ON IT AS HOLY WRIT. AS SKEEN MIGHT SAY, HAVING A RULE IS SUFFICIENT EXCUSE FOR BREAKING IT. NOW AND THEN THOUGH, THERE'S A LOVELY, COMFORTABLE DELIGHT IN CONFORMING TO TRITE OLD RULES; YOU CAN FEEL VIRTUOUS AND ENJOY THE HELL OUT OF YOURSELF AT THE SAME TIME.

or

HERE'S ONE OF SKEEN'S STORIES, THE ONE THAT GOT HER THE NAME SHE WANTED.

Skeen says: Now I do not guarantee the truth of this tale. The man who told it to me was not one to confine himself to thus and so; he'd got a skinful, too, and oiled his throat so the words came sliding out like silky ribbons. Oh, it was glorious to hear and I am far from his equal, but I'll give it to you nonetheless.

Vitrivin the Slave Maker
and the Corbi of Tinkle's Thwart

Vitrivin was a snatch artist, so they say, the slickest fox who ever slid a chick away under a guard's long nose. Some slavers went roaring in, scooped up everything lively enough to walk about and went roaring out again, waiting until they were clear of chasers before they sorted out their catch. That wasn't Vitrivin's way. He was a cautious man. He was a careful man. He spied and spied before he went in; he would know the tongue and how folk greeted each

36

other, he would know the proper clothes and the way to wear them. He would know where he could hide and when it was safe to come out. And when it was safe to come out, he would go into a place as a trading man and the things he would sell were tiny sweet machines that could do wonders without half trying and what he would buy was whatever things took his fancy; he bought them mostly because folk would wonder about him if he did not. The treasures he sought were not such trifles, but the folk that swirled about him, laughing and loving, buying and selling, the living treasures. From these, he made his choices and marked his choices with metal burrs smaller than a dinka seed, metal burrs with silent voices that would cry out to the meatmen who followed him and swept the marked ones in the terrible black maw of the meatwagon. He chose the most charming of young children, though not too many of these (children clogged the auction halls). He chose singers, musicians, sculptors, swordsmiths and any other artisans with special gifts, as long as they were young and healthy. Three places he went, no more, then away to his ship to wait the return of the meatwagon and the sleepers stacked inside. Oh, yes, he was a cautious man, a careful man. And tasteful. A businessman who knew his markets and never wasted a snatch.

What did he look like, this excellent and dedicated slave maker? Like everyone and no one, a shadow man, a gray man, a man no man would notice in a crowd of two. His nose sat meekly in the middle of his face. His eyes were eye-colored, neither dull nor sharp. His mouth was neither small nor large, neither pale nor bright. His voice flowed along like stagnant water. He was a dim little shadow flitting past you, not dim enough or odd enough to catch your eye. And after he passed, one-two-a dozen-twenty vanished, swiftly, silently, forever, as if they had never existed. Mothers wept, fathers cursed, lovers searched, but the gone never returned and no trace of them could be found and the emptiness they left behind healed over like any wound. And Vitrivin laid up mountains of sweet gold, but no mountain was high enough to quench his thirst for more, so he took his ship and his meatmen and went out again and again and again, making slaves with no end to the making.

Until he came to a Lostworld that called itself Three-legged Crow. Which is an odd thing to call a world but the Flingers who settled worlds like that, worlds away and away from the empires and the commanderies and the commensalities, away away from the traderoads and the sweeplines, those Flingers were without doubt the oddest folk a sun ever shone on.

He crept up to TLC as was his custom, tucked himself behind one of the five moons and studied the folk below.

Spirals were what he saw where the population was thickest on the ground, ovals where there were fewer folk, the fields spread round in webs. Folk went about in huge wheeled carts pulled by pairs of horned beasts, but a larger web joined the smaller places to the spiral centers, monorails with light slipping along them like silver sparks. The two things didn't belong together; that sent a little chill crawling up his spine. He thought about leaving and trying elsewhere until he saw the images his spy eyes gathered for him.

The folk of Three-legged Crow were tall and handsome, gold-skinned blonds with eyes as green as the mammoth forests tucked round the fields and villages. They took joy in making things by hand and making each thing a wonder in itself, be it such a simple thing as a waterbowl for one of the small fuzzy beasts they kept as pets. Even the elders were handsome and vigorous. And the children were elfin charmers. His mouth watered at the thought of merchandising a shipload of these Crowmese. He told himself you're foolish old man, what can these backwoods know-nothings do against you? So he made his preparations and took his ship down. He couldn't sneak in this time; he was too short and too different and the villages were too small for him fade into, so he was just a wandering trader looking for someone who'd buy his machines and sell him local things he could sell somewhere else. A commonplace little gray man who wouldn't scare the spookiest child.

He walked away from his ship with his sample cases and started into one of the spiral cities. It was as easy as that.

The folk gathered around him, chattering like tuneful birds, bright and beautiful, open and friendly; he was nearly overwhelmed by the wealth of choice about him; he could have taken them all and profited from them so he marked none. Not yet, no, wait until you see more, he said to himself. Around the next corner there will be women more beautiful, there will be artisans more skilled.

In this spiral city on the coast he found a woman who played waterpipes with a poignance that brought tears to his eye-colored eyes. He found children who danced in strange circles whose meaning hovered just beyond his understanding. He found an ivory carver and a clipclap singer and a weaver and five beautiful women ranging from one joyous creature who'd just become a woman to the mother of five children who was radiantly female in so powerful a way that it reached even him though he didn't like women at all. He marked these and some others and took the monorail inland to a deep woodland village where he marked a pair of twins in their fifth year of life, and two woodcarvers and a viol maker and a blind herbalist who made wonderful perfumes, and three more women all very young, just emerging from their baby fat. All this he did in a single day and in the dark he took the monorail again to a steep walled cleft high in the mountains where miners and metalworkers lived. Tinkle's Thwart it was called.

He slept on the journey and had bad dreams, dreams of choking, of flying and falling, of endless pursuit by something he never quite saw. He woke in the gray light of dawn as the train slowed for the station at Tinkle's Thwart. He was sweating and more tired on waking that he was when he sank into that heavy sleep. He was afraid. As he hauled his sample cases onto the station platform and programmed them to walk beside him, he wanted terribly to get back on the train and race to the coast; he wanted to leap into his ship and get away from here. He hesitated too long, the train slipped away; he thought of the heaps and heaps of gold his cargo would bring in and told himself he was a superstitious fool to take dream warnings seriously. They probably were born in something he ate; though he was careful about his food and tested everything before he ate it whenever he was in a strange place, there was always the chance something sly slipped through. Only something I ate, he said to himself. Still, there was an oddness about the way these Crowmese looked at him after they'd been round him a while; their smiles retreated to the tips of their teeth. Ah, well, I am a stranger and they've had few of those round here. This has happened to me before. Forget it, old man, you're not going to be here long enough for that feeling to cause trouble.

Tinkle's Thwart was one of the oval settlements, a ring of houses and shops, a broad brick roadway, a central common; this was a carefully tended garden with velveteen lawns, clumps of lace trees, splashes of primary colors from the flower beds and a small noisy stream meandering through the middle of it all, singing its way over several short drops. A pleasant place just coming to life, high enough to be cold in the early morning in spite of the bright summer weather. There was a cook shop next to the platform and he ate his breakfast amid a bustle of young Thwarters going to work in the village food fields in a valley lower down; they were catching a last hot meal before the fieldwork began. He paid for his meal with a handful of local coins, then herded his sample cases out of the shop, ignoring the laughter that followed him as the Thwarters noted for the first time the hippity-hoppity progress of the cases on their dozens of short skinny legs and stubby feet.

A tall girl danced a silent circle about him, her hair hanging loose, so pale it was almost white, the ends frizzed and shifting in the slow breeze; she was all length and awkward elasticity, but her too-visible bones had a promise of everlasting elegance. Her eyes held a touch of blue, huge bright eyes that judged him coolly and found him wanting. "Hello," he said. "Lady, I thank you for your greeting." He bowed.

Her lips parted in an enigmatic smile, baring small chisel teeth and canines that dropped lower into dagger points. She said nothing but continued to stare at him for a long uncomfortable moment, then she darted away.

He wiped the sweat off his face, promised himself he'd

mark her the moment he got a chance; let her learn lessons of humility from better teachers than him. He tucked his kerchief away and stepped onto the bricks of the ringroad, heading for the first of the shops.

He bought and sold, sold and bought, moving slowly along the curve of the oval; the sun rose and shadows shortened and children came from everywhere to dance in rings about him, the rings changing each time he returned to the brick paving. They clapped their hands and chanted magic syllables at him; it was charming and annoying. He managed to ignore them and went patiently from shop to shop. By noon he'd finished two-thirds of the circuit, had tagged a dozen Thwarters and was near perishing of hunger.

He stepped from a silversmith's shop and stood irresolute, looking about for the nearest eating place. A long line of children wove toward him, dancing hand in hand. They swung about him, closed the circle and chanted:

> Fai nay, fai nay, kik lon doan
> Prauto, prauto, tris eh own

then they danced a high energy circle about him and chanted again:

> Fai nay, fai nay, kik lon doan
> Prauto, prauto, tris eh own

the circle whizzed about him a second time and they chanted a third time:

> Fai nay, fai nay, kik lon doan
> Prauto, prauto, tris eh own

and a third time the circle wheeled, but this time, as soon as the circuit was complete, they broke apart and darted away in a dozen directions like drops of split mercury, high wild silvery giggles bubbling out of them.

One child remained at his side, a young boy, shy and lovely as a faun, his crystalline eyes the pale green frozen

into pure ice. Vitrivin knew he should get on with his rounds
and finish his tagging, ignoring all this nonsense. Kid games,
nothing more, he told himself, forget it. His intuit alarms
were throbbing but he ignored those. It was almost done, he
was almost on his way back to the ship; his meatmen were
out and working by now, he'd soon be gone from this
spooky world. He took a step, then turned to gaze down at
the boy, a forced smile stretching his lips.

The boy watched him with grave and disconcerting interest.

"What was all that about?" he said.

"Oh, it's just a game we play," the boy said.

"Ah, well, that's fine. What is the purpose of the game?"
he said.

"We catching you," the boy said.

"Oh." Vitrivin thought about pushing it further, but decided
not to. "Where is a good place for the noon meal that's
close by so I won't waste time?"

"Memo Julso sells sammitches and salads. They good,
um um." The boy rubbed his belly and made a large gesture
of licking his lips. He caught Vitrivin's wrist and tugged.
"Down along two steps. You buy me a bratta, huh huh?"

"What would your mum say to that, eh, boy? You shouldn't
take things from strangers." He spoke with heavy jocularity,
a distilled essence of adults talking down to children, adults
who had forgotten how to be children, adults who had forgotten childhood so completely they couldn't remember how
to be alive.

"Memo IS ma mum," the boy said. He grinned at Vitrivin,
patted his wrist. "Come, come, one sniff will tell you I've
said true, even if it is my mum."

Vitrivin let the boy pull him along into a half-walled garden
that opened onto the brick roadway and looked across it at
a tree-framed section of lawn and a small tumble of water.

About halfway through his sammitch he heard bells and
looked up. That skinny girl was back. She came dancing
onto the grass, carrying strings of silver bells that rang when
they bumped together, and dropped lightly on the center of
the patch of grass, facing west, and began unthreading the

bells from their carry cord. He chewed stolidly and watched with greedy interest as she set the bells about her knees.

She lifted the largest, rang it briskly, chanted: An draa po disss tis a a a koo ayyy ye an drup o diss ti yess hem oh hem all a gay. . . . There was more, much more of that and winding through it the singing of the bells.

The sound itched at him, lovely as it was. He hurried up his chewing and when he finished, wiped his lips with the napkin Memo Julso gave him and put it neatly by his plate. The boy sat off a bit, chewing on his bratta. Vitrivin beckoned him over. "Her," he said and pointed. "Who is she?"

"Oh, her. She is the Corbi and she's tolling."

"It is a strange but charming performance," he said, with the same heavy artifice he'd used before. He was not certain he should venture further, but a mix of fear and curiosity dissolved his prudence. "Why is the Corbi doing that?"

"Because that's one of the things Corbis do."

Before he could ask what tolling was, Memo Julso came out and called her son to her. Vitrivin's prudence congealed again. He got to his feet, gave the Julso a ponderous bow and a clumsy compliment and before he was half finished, she was smiling and relaxed. The boy leaned against her thigh and put his hand on the hand she laid on his shoulder and then he smiled lazily at Vitrivin, his ice crystal eyes shutting to slits. With a chill in his gut though he didn't show it, Vitrivin chirked his sample cases into a hasty shuffle and herded them out. The tolling bells and the Corbi's chant followed him eerily as he went back to his selling rounds.

Children came from nowhere and danced around him.

> Skooo ah nair sko ah nair
> Braay fuss bro tair

Over and over they chanted that, over and over till they broke and ran and other children came to dance round and round him

> Oy da tis ay glow ka nair oy da di o ti enthay
> Pag gi day so sko a nair, ap pa tay

So sou tis ay
Glow ka nair sko ah nair, day oh say
Fai nay, fai nay, kik lon doan
Prauto, prauto, tris eh own

He continued to ignore them and moved from shop to
forge to shop, his gut in a gelid knot. He didn't hurry, but he
didn't linger either; he no longer tagged anyone, he simply
wanted to get out of here and let the meatmen begin their
harvest.

Day oh say, sko ah nair—so the children sang.

Air ka par ah Corbi-me, air ka, air ka, tris an dris—so the
Corbi sang and mingled magic syllables with the tintinnabu-
lation of her singing silver bells.

He walked slower and slower; his feet seemed to stick to
the bricks and pulling them loose took more and more of his
energy. His thoughts moved slower and slower, but the chill,
driving terror in his gut snapped them loose and the beast
that lived within went round and round struggling to escape.

The children danced round and round him, chanting at
him.

Somewhere behind him, the Corbi rang her bells, chanting with them.

And he finally understood what they were saying, from the
first of the circle chants; he understood what they were
doing to him.

Weave weave the bind-   That the children sang.
ing ring,
About him thrice, three
times around.
Slave   maker,   listen,   That the Corbi sang.
slave maker hear us.
Shadow man, shadow   That the children sang.
man
Baby eater
I know who you are,
gray man, I know why
you're here.

I will trap you, shadow
man, I will trick
You, I will so.
Gray man shadow man,
I am binding you
Weave weave the bind-
ing ring
About him thrice, three
times around
I am binding you   That the children sang.
Come to Corbi, come,   That the Corbi sang.
come
Come oh come, you tear
making men

His body stopped completely and stood like stone on the
bricks. He felt more than saw a shadow pass overhead,
heard the whine of the meatwagon. He knew then what the
Corbi tolled because the meatmen weren't due until he left
and signaled them. The beast within shouted in fury and
frustration, trapped inside stony flesh where no one and
nothing could hear him.

The whine groaned down to a subsonic growl. The bells
rang louder, the rhythms more jangled, the sound reaching
deep and deep, stirring things in him he didn't want stirred
up; he fought but the music was far stronger than him, he
was meshed in a web from which he couldn't break loose.
Other voices joined the chant, mature voices, deep and rich.
Over these he heard a dull steady shuffle.

The chanting came closer. The bells rang louder. The
Corbi danced around where he could see her. Her face and
her eyes glowed with a wild and burning light. The beast
within that was the real him quivered with a terror like that
his victims must have felt, something he'd never expected to
know. He was a careful man, he was a cautious man, he
was too good at his work. He had fooled a thousand tracers,
ten thousand guards; he'd dipped in and out of worlds no
other slave maker managed to penetrate and left no proof
behind that he'd ever been there; empires had mobilized to

catch him and he'd laughed at them. Yet here, now, a lanky
half-grown child had trapped him, prepubescent babies had
bound him fast. Had done it as easily as if he were a
brain-burned phlux head. Children! He would have ground
his teeth together if he could have moved his jaw. The beast
within raged at the Corbi and she smiled back, glowing with
triumph, arms, hands, body moving effortlessly through the
sacred dance.

His meatmen tramped around where he could see them.
They wore purple paper chains wound about and about
them and bowed under the imagined weight of these ephem-
eral bindings; their jaws bulged as they strained against that
weight while the gentle breeze sent paper edges scraping
lightly against their arms.

Slave maker, the Corbi sang at him. Slave maker shadow
man, the children sang at him. They knew. They all knew.
From the seaside spiral to this tiny mountain village, they'd
touched and tasted him; when he thought he was fooling
them, they were laughing at him for he was the fool.

Corbi danced before him and rang her silver bells; the
children wheeled round and round him, chanting, swung
round and round the line of meatmen, chanting. The adults
of the village made three sparse rings about them all, two
rings moving one way, the ring in the center opposing them;
they boomed along in their deepest tones, male and female
alike, while several sopranos and high falsettos performed
elaborate descants, weaving in and out of the song of Corbi
and the children.

Coldness crept up his legs and up his arms, his eyes
grew dim and dull, the sounds wheeling about him went far
away and when the light was gone out of his eyes and the
sound gone out of his ears, the beast within that was him
lay down and died.

The adults of Tinkle's Thwart levered the stone statues
from the middle of the road and took them down to the station
platform and left them standing there looking away along
the slick silvery rail. As the years slid past, new batches of
children replaced the paper chains with flower ropes, winding them around and over the gray chalk figures until these

finally wore away to shapeless pillars and everyone forgot what they had once been.

A drunken Pallah leaned against her, patted her shoulder; the fumes of the quatsch he was drinking mingled with her ale and made her head swim. "Lu like th tha story. Goo good stuff." He sniffed juicily, slapped at the bar, his hand hitting it obliquely and sliding. His elbow crashed down and he grunted, the knock on the funnybone breaking through the anesthesia of the quatsch, not enough to hurt, though it did get his attention away from her a while.

A pair of elderly Aggitj nodded and sighed. "Lurvlee," one managed. "Like Tilimai uss used to tell b b back. . . ." His voice trailed off; he lowered his head onto the bar and went to sleep. The other continued to nod a while, then brooded at a pool of spilled brandy gradually fuming dry. He cleared his throat, spoke slowly and with great care, his eyes fixed on that splotch. "I know   uhhhm   I know   some un here. Like that slaver st stink. You know un. . . ." He nudged his sleeping companion, eliciting a breathy snore but no further response; he went on as if he'd got a coherent answer. "Uh huh, you know un, Gresh Gresh   Gredgi. Stinkin snot. Hah! Nochsyon Tod. Got our Hixli. Li like to have that Corbi h h here, yes I would. Turn ol' Toad into chal chalk. Hoptoad chalk." He started giggling. "Chalk Toad. P p pizz ul on im. M melt im in to mud. Dir ty mud. Mud. Mud." Lost in giggles, he slapped his companion on his back; the other Aggitj struggled upright and joined in though he had no idea what the laughter was about.

Skeen gulped down more ale, coughed and sprayed half of it out again as a rising giggle caught her in the throat.

The Pallah roared with laughter. "Piss on un. Melt un down. Do it, yah, me, I'd do it. Do it. Yah." He quieted after a while and glowered at the barrels piled up behind the bar. He produced some guttural mutters that finally surfaced into audibility. ". . . dirty sodding renegade smearing shit on all us Pallahs . . . somebody gonna get him. . . ." He clenched his fist about his glass, opened his eyes wide because he'd forgotten he was holding it; he gulped down the quatsch left in it, made a soft gargling sound and slid bonelessly off his stool, curled up on the floor and started snoring.

Skeen blinked down at him, shrugged and banged her glass on the bar, calling for a refill. She turned to the Aggitj. "What uh what happen to what's his name, um, Hizli?"

Heavy clank, metal sliding jerkily over wood, acting on her head like a dentist's drill, worrying her out of a stuffy, nightmare-ridden sleep.

Skeen started to lift her head, lowered it with extreme care as first her stomach then her whole body protested. She cracked gritty eyes enough to register the painfully bright morning light filling the room, snapped them shut and tried to swallow. She was hideously thirsty; her mouth and throat demanded gallons of anything wet, but her stomach felt delicate and stirred with a pre-nausea that was more a warning than an upheaval. There was a stink in the room she didn't really want to think about. The sounds continued, adding the slosh of water and the scratch-scrutch of a scrub brush. There was something she should remember, but her head wasn't working too well. So she worked her mouth. Djabo, I'm dry. Gahh, if my mouth smells like it tastes, I could lay out a dreegh. Another clank. Bucket, brush dropped into it. Skritching sound like a finger drawn across a slate. She shuddered. I'm going to have to stop this cruising the bars. Must be something in the ale. She took a long breath, spat it out. Sweet sour stench of vomit. Djabo bless. She squeezed her eyes tight shut and tried to think. Oh, Djabo, Djabo, I am not going to do this again. I am not going to do this again. Not, not . . . ah, Djabo, once an addictive personality, always . . . I am not getting into that. Oh, fuck, I haven't vomited on my-self since I was . . . I'm too old for this. . . .

The longer she lay breathing in the vomit stink and the harsh fumes of the lye soap someone was using to clean up after her, the worse she felt. She started remembering things she'd done; that didn't help. *On hands and knees, crawling along some street, slapping grumpily and ineffectively at small hands tickling over her body like lice.* She didn't need to check her belt pouch; whatever was in it left in those hands. *Feeling her way along walls until she crashed into the night wicket, pounding on it until the porter came out cursing her. He booted her inside, slammed the wicket, put the boot in a couple more times, then went grumbling back to bed.* She could remember being dimly surprised as she crawled painfully toward the stairs. He hadn't raped her; she wasn't particularly appetizing at the moment, but that hadn't stopped men before. *Angelsin looming large and pale in her chair at the end of the bar. Does she ever move from there? Groaning onto her feet, feeling a stabbing pain somewhere around her ribs. Nausea threatening. Angelsin would kill her if she messed in the taproom. Throw her out, anyway. Lurch-ing up the stairs, falling too many times, cracking her knees, her shins, her elbows, struggling to reach her room before voiding the burden hanging at the end of her throat.*

Head threatening to break off and roll away, gasp-ing with the effort, she untangled herself from the blanket and sat up. She clutched at herself, groaned.

Timka raised her head, a cold anger on her face, then she went back to scrubbing the floor.

Skeen smoothed her hands down her body. She was clean, even her hair. Naked but clean. She lifted her head. Her eddersil trousers and tunic were fluttering by the window, the morning breeze whipping out the last of the stink. The hooked rug was rolled up against the wall under the window. Doesn't look damp, maybe I missed that. She rubbed at her nose, watched Timka scrubbing angrily at the planks, and winced as snatches of last night came back to her, humiliating fragments of memory. Small strong hands wrestling her around, holding her, as she vomited. Angry whispers as Ti stripped off her soiled clothing. Towel's corner soggy with cold water dragged across her face, the roughness of a mother at the end of her patience with a fractious child. Hefted into bed over a narrow shoulder. Covers pulled up. A sigh. A small hand drawn softly along her face. A door shutting.

Skeen shook off those memories. She'd learned early on that thinking too much about the immediate past guaranteed a sour head to match the sour stomach she already had.

Timka dropped the brush in the bucket, sat on her heels, drew her arm across her face, pushing straggles of hair out of her eyes. She turned her head slowly, her arm still up, the soft black hair falling over it, and scowled at Skeen. "How many more times are you coming back like that?"

Skeen ran her fingers through tangled oily hair and couldn't remember the last time she'd washed it. "No more," she said absently. "I've decided which one to touch." She pulled her fingers loose and passed her hand from brow to nape. Timka gazed at her, saying nothing, her skepticism tangible. Skeen took a corner of the blanket and scrubbed it across her eyes. "I know what I'm talking about, Ti." She dropped the blanket across her knees. "I've been here before," she muttered, went on rather more hastily than she meant, "and I've pried myself loose before, it just sneaked up on me this time . . ." she dropped the blanket across her legs, touched her hair, grimaced, ". . . for a lot of reasons you don't want to hear about." She poked at the blanket, began twisting an edge, her hands working until it threatened to tear. "This fuckin' stupid world, run your legs off to your crack and get no place. Ahhhh, Tibo, WHY!" She started crying, hiccuping, swaying back and forth, clutching at the blan-

ket, her head aching, her stomach cramping, her mind
in confusion saying I don't do this kind of thing, I
don't do this, I don't cry, not even when I'm drunk, I
used up my tears twenty years ago, I don't . . . I
don't. . . .

Timka sat watching, cool and distant, only half-
believing what she saw and heard. She'd seen this
remorse too many times before, with Skeen and the
Poet both, not crying but near enough; she'd heard
both mutter promises it wouldn't happen again. And it
always did. And there were always reasons and the
reasons were always different and always meant the
same thing. She waited until Skeen's spasm was over
and the lanky woman had control of herself again.
"Lipitero and I, we finished the night in with the
others. I doubt anyone got much sleep but you."

Skeen dabbed at her face with the back of her hand.
"Sorry, I don't usually. . . ." She slid off the bed and
dug out clean underthings from the pack hanging from
a wall peg. "Enough said on both sides. I got the
name locked." She leaned against the wall, working
up the energy to lift her leg. "We can stop marking
time and start really working now." She pulled her
underpants on, cursing and wincing as she had to bend
to straighten a twist. "Nochsyon Tod the slaver. If you
agree, you can start the overflights tomorrow as soon
as it's dark. If there aren't any strange Min about.
Right? Right." She held out the undershirt and blinked
at it, felt about the neck to find the front, then jerked
it down over her head. And clutched at her temples.
"Dja bo! Never again. Never. . . ." She opened her
eyes and pulled the corners of her mouth down into a
painful, inverted grin when she saw Timka's disbelief.
She pushed away from the wall, headed for the window and the rest of her clothes. "Considering the coin
I got through last night, today better be a good one."
She unpinned the tunic from the curtain, turned to
frown at Timka. "You look tired. Want to catch some
sleep? The Boy and I can manage alone for once."

Again the inverted grin. "Though you're the one that loosens the purse strings."

Timka got to her feet. "Let me get rid of this slop and wash up. I'll be down by the time you've eaten."

"Food, yecch."

"Don't compound your idiocy, Skeen."

"You're saying I've got enough already without adding interest? You could be right."

Shaking her head, Timka took up the pail and went out.

The House of Nochsyon Tod was a rambling walled compound near the South Cusp of the meniscus that was Lowport. It lay a jump and a half from the river and was the last structure of any note on the Sukkar's Skak, that broad and busy thoroughfare that arched through the town from north to south. Though it was mostly surrounded by warehouses and traders' dens deserted come sundown for the livelier center, there was one great advantage to its position. It lay across the Skak from the Armory Guardhouse where the Funor guards and the mercenaries had their barracks. Gathering like fleas about the Armory were taverns and brothels, cookshops and tailors, knife sharpeners, armorers and metalsmiths of assorted skills; indeed, there were dozens of small establishments there to cater to any need the Guards might dream of feeling. Along there the street was never dark or deserted, or even quiet.

The outer walls of Tod's compound were eight meters tall and proportionately broad, made from field-stone, clay and timbers with a rubble fill; a crumbly sandy plaster was pasted over the outside and white-washed every month or so, more often in the rainy season. The whitewash flaked off at a touch and even under guttering torchlight, a sentry walking along street or alley could instantly spot the marks of any thief ignorant or stupid enough to go after a man who sent barrels of ale across the Skak every minor feast day and donated prime female slaves at the Spring Sarmot for the entertainment of the Guards.

The walls enclosed a space roughly a square and were, very roughly, a hundred meters to a side—they bulged and buckled like a green plank abandoned to rain and sun. A squat watchtower rose at each of the corners and there was a smaller one by the northside Gate where all but the most favored buyers came to inspect Tod's stock. Cressets burned all night, set in a ring about each of the towers and the guard on watch there had little to do but keep them burning. One sentry paced along each section of the wall, moving through the towers and along the ramparts from gate to gate. Three men sufficed for this since there were only three gates. By tacit agreement, they reduced their legwork to one circuit each watch, spending the rest of the time in the towers, taking turns sleeping on pallets they kept there or passing around jugs of homebrew. Having set up the system and considering it admirably efficient, Nochsyon Tod left it to run on its own and was at present quite unaware it had long since begun to run down. There was nothing to provide the tension it took to keep watchers alert when they knew full well their master was peacefully asleep.

Inside the walls. . . .

THIS COULD SWELL INTO A LONG, COMPLICATED AND NO DOUBT CONFUSING DESCRIPTION, SO LET'S DO SOME COMPRESSING. SEE SKEEN AND TIMKA TALKING LATE AT NIGHT, AN OIL LAMP CREATING EXOTIC SHADOWS THAT SHIFT WITH THE FLICKERING OF THE FLAME. SEE SKEEN AND TIMKA WORKING OVER A SHEET OF PAPER ADDING DETAILS TO A SKETCH MAP. SEE THE PLAN THAT FOLLOWS. IT SHOWS THE PHYSICAL DETAILS COLLECTED BY TIMKA DURING HER SEVERAL OVERFLIGHTS. SKEEN AND TIMKA BEND OVER THE MAP.

"I can go in over the wall there." Skeen touched the D tower. "Where there's that deep bay by the gate, it'll give me shelter going down."

Timka frowned. "Why not here?" She put her finger on the place where the thinner lower garden wall merged with the outside wall. "You're closer to the house, trees for shelter, which you won't need anyway once the guards are asleep."

"That's one thing you never count on, Ti, guards being asleep. There's always some snerk with insomnia or an overactive bladder. No, I want to keep as far away from the Skak as I can get. Besides there's the woffit pack."

"I can freeze those. You don't need to worry about the woffits."

"A dozen? And you told me they don't stay together, they go nosing off alone or in pairs. Besides, I

54

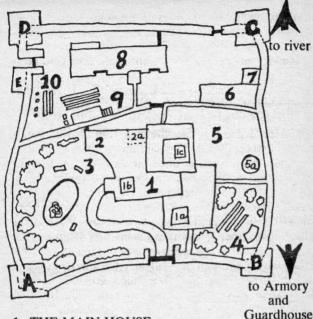

1. THE MAIN HOUSE
   la, lb, lc—watch towers
2. PARLOR with Vault Room (2a)
3. ELABORATE AND FUSSY SHOW GARDENS WITH ORNAMENTAL WATER
4. ARENA WHERE SLAVE AUCTIONS ARE HELD FOR THE EXALTED OR THOSE WHO CONSIDERED THEMSELVES EXALTED AND HAD THE POWER TO ENFORCE THIS VIEW ON OTHERS
5. KITCHEN GARDEN
   5a—deep well for drinking and irrigating water
6. BARRACKS OF NOCHSYON TOD'S PRIVATE GUARDS
7. CELLS FOR RAMBUNCTIOUS SLAVES
8. SLAVE PENS
9. AUCTION PLATFORM
10. WHIPPING POSTS AND VIEWING BENCHES

don't like that garden, gives me an itch. I want to keep well away from it." Skeen moved her shoulders, shivered.

Timka made a small impatient sound, but said nothing more.

"So. You're sure you can carry the darter when you're flying?"

"I have hauled heavier fish; yes."

"Right. Once you dart the guards in D, I'll go over the wall where I said. You said no one moves about in the slave block section once the sun's down. Mmm." She tapped a fingernail on the watch tower by the slave pen. "We'll need an exact schedule of guard changes here. This one's bound to be more alert; I suspect he'd be taking the place of any slave he allowed to escape. This wall will shield me from the rest of the guards until I go over here." She tapped the place where the garden wall met the one shutting in the slave pen section. "Dark here, go over fast and low and not even tower C could spot me." She frowned. "I want to let C alone if I can. Mmm. Worth taking a chance on one of the guards there being awake. I can keep close to the slave pen and the pen wall until I go over the garden wall." She scratched at the watch towers rising from the house roof. "Bothers me, these. You sure no one is in them?"

"I've been flying four nights now, late and early, and I've never seen anyone there. I took a look in the highest tonight, scared out some pigeons. Old nests, dung all over the floor, cobwebs, dead leaves, some very old mouse bones. Lice crawling over everything." Timka grinned. "I shifted to fish and took a swim soon as I got away from there. Don't know if I picked up company, but I sure didn't want to keep them if I did. Believe me, Skeen, even the worst sloven would at least sweep the place out before spending any time there."

"I hear you, but you'd better take a look again the night I go in. Just to be sure nothing's changed. Where was I? Oh. I go over the wall here, fast and low, slice the latches or bars or whatever on the kitchen door here, then I'm in and prowling."

Timka set her forefinger across her lips, looked thoughtfully at the sketch map. "You don't know anything about the inside of that house. How will you find where Tod keeps his gold?"

"Look for it. Believe me, Ti, it's easier than you think; no matter their kind, folk tend to hide things in the same places and there aren't that many of those places."

"Still, it wouldn't hurt if I went in and worked out the way the rooms run so you wouldn't have to waste time finding out what's where. And who's where. Woffits in the garden running loose, there could be more in the house. Wouldn't you rather know that before you ran into them?"

Skeen frowned. "Thing is, if you aren't careful, you could run me into a wasp nest, with guards behind every curtain waiting for me to show."

Timka nodded. "I see that. Listen. Let me sniff about a little and learn the woffit. Who's going to worry about seeing another woffit?"

Skeen ran her thumb along the table's edge. She found herself resenting Timka's persistence, her insistence on contributing to the plan. She found herself almost angry as she saw control slipping away from her, then was angrier at herself for her pettiness. She glanced at Timka who was beginning to fidget at Skeen's continued silence and was jarred by a sudden insight. Did I do that to you, Tibo? Oh, Tibo my heart's darling, did I treat you like a handsome little doll, did I take you out of your box when nothing was happening, did I pack you away when I was doing something I thought was important? Was it me that drove you into striking back? She stared past Timka at the wall and saw neither as she flipped through memory and found nearly every image accusing her now that she had eyes to see what she'd missed before. Aayii, Tibo, it's a wonder you stood me this long. In spite of what memory was telling her, she still could not believe that he had done what he must have done, she still could not understand why he had taken Picarefy and stranded her. Everything she thought she knew about him told her it couldn't happen. But it had. Did someone twist it out of him? She hadn't thought of that before and after a minute she knew why. She simply didn't believe it. He was tough and slippery and once he was onboard Picarefy, he'd have her help. It was him alone. He did it. Why, Tibo? What reason? You had to have a reason. I have to know. I have to know why.

"Skeen?"

Skeen blinked. She cleared her throat, rubbed one hand across the other. "Maggí Solitaire is due around the end of this sennight."

"What? I know that. We all know that."

"Yes, yes, but there is a point. What will the Funor Lords do the minute Tod screams he's been robbed?"

"Funor? I don't know. But if this was Dum Besar, the Casach would have all strangers gathered up and dumped in the cells . . . ah. I see."

"Too many hostages. You could get out, and Chulji, maybe Lipitero. The Aggitj and the Boy, they'd fight, kill a lot and get killed themselves. Pegwai would get sucked in. . . ." She spread her hands, sighed. "I want them on Maggí's ship headed out of here before I touch a wall."

Timka played with the sketch plan, pushing it about with her forefinger. "Aggitj aren't going to like going off without us."

"I know. Djabo, do I know." She rescued the plan; Timka was tearing bits off one corner. "Take all the time you need to learn the woffit, I don't want you going in until Pyaday . . ." she stopped herself, "don't you think?"

Timka chuckled, tapped the back of Skeen's hand.

"Pyaday's fine. You want me to hunt up a boat we can use?"

'You know anything about boats?'

"About enough to tell a mast from an oar, enough to know we want one that floats."

"Idiot."

"Seriously, I'd take one of the Aggitj, Hal or Domi for choice. Domi told me once he was crawling around in boats before he could walk."

Skeen slid back in the chair until her head was hooked over the top rung. She yawned, used both hands to scratch at her head, flutter her hair. "You'll have to stick pins in me to get me out of bed come the morning."

Timka glanced at the window. "Which isn't that far off. *The Balance* is up. Which by the way and don't ask me why reminds me about Angelsin. She watches us."

"She watches everyone." Skeen pushed up out of the chair and began stripping. "Her Ant Pack are all over. One or another of them watches us every day we perform. I figure she's one of the local bosses and is keeping an eye on the take."

"I think it's more than that."

Skeen hung her tunic on a peg, looked over her shoulder. "Why?"

"Don't know. Like you and the garden."

"Hm. I'll think about it. But if she's planning something, she won't have much time and she mightn't know that; I paid for another fortn't this morning."

"I keep thinking about Lipitero." Timka glanced at the still mound on the narrow cot pushed up against the far wall where the shadow was so deep the forms of cot and sleeper were only dimly visible.

"Petro hasn't said anything to me about snoopers."

"Nor me. But she's nervous, I can't be mistaken about that."

"Could be she's getting cabin fever shut up all the time in this room. No, no, I believe you. Soon as I have a spare minute I'll see what I can find out." She stepped out of her trousers, chuckled. "If you promise to clean up after me again."

"Skeen."

"No, no, I was only joking." She yawned. "Djabo, I am too tired to sleep, I think. Well, only one way to find out."

WHILE PEGWAI WAS COPING WITH THREE ADOLESCENT PALLAH BOYS WHOSE CHIEF DELIGHT SEEMED TO BE THINKING UP INANE TRICKS TO PLAY ON HIM, TRICKS SO BRAINLESSLY INEPT THEY SOMETIMES EVEN SUCCEEDED, WHILE CHULJI WAS IMMERSED IN RUST AND SMUT AND ROOT ROT, WHILE THE AGGITJ TOTED BALES AND HAULED BARRELS, WHILE LIPITERO CARVED AND SIGHED, WHILE TIMKA AND SKEEN PERFORMED BY DAY AND PLOTTED AT NIGHT, THINGS WERE HAPPENING ABOUT THEM THEY KNEW NOTHING OF AND ONLY GUESSED AT LATER, LOOKING BACK ON THAT HECTIC TIME.

or

SKEEN FORGETS THE WARNING AND TIMKA ACQUIRES THE RIGHT TO SAY I TOLD YOU SO.

This is how it might have been, what a fly planted on the cavern wall might have seen and heard.

"Hopflea, rub my knees," says Angelsin. This is one of those nights when boneache occupies her head until she finds herself losing track of the strings she must pull to keep her puppets dancing.

The small Funor boy brings over a footstool; with practiced ease he slides his hands under her instep (slimfinger curled to protect it) and lifts her foot onto the stool. He waits, kneeling, looking elsewhere until she slides her heavy skirt up to bare the massive knee. For some minutes he kneads the flesh around the misshapen bone, then he jumps to his feet with the celerity of his namesake and goes into the nearest of

61

the cells cut into the wall of the cavern. He reappears a moment later, rolling a gum-wheeled trolley with a deep bowl on it crouched amid coals, sending up clouds of steam. He positions it beside Angelsin, kicks a brake in place. He uses a wooden forceps to lift a folded cloth from the hot water, teases it open, holds it out so Angelsin can judge the temperature with a quick touch of her slimfinger. She nods, takes a hard grip on the chair arms and endures the pain when he spreads the cloth over her knee. After a minute he takes it away, replaces it with another. Angelsin's eyes go feral at this new pain. She half enjoys conquering it, half curses fate for cursing her.

Her deep voice gravelly, she says, "Has anyone managed a clear look yet at the one who never goes out?"

Hopflea looks quickly up, a flicker of apprehension on his soft face, then prods with delicate precision at the soggy cloth; when he speaks, the words come slowly, without much feeling in them. He gives the impression of shrewd but wholly amoral judgment. "No. I set the maids at her, but she keeps the door locked and has ears like a woffit's, so there's no surprising her. She sits with hood up and her back to the door." He goes silent while he changes cloths. "You want I should buy a couple of hardboys and have her stripped sometime the others are out?" They are speaking Funorish and he has dropped the mangled speech he uses to bolster his stupid act.

Angelsin's eyes are half closed, but she doesn't miss that flash of fear. It pleases her. Hopflea is her most valued agent and he knows it, but he knows too that if he slacks off or cheats her in any way, he's dead. And if he quits her, he's dead. He has made too many enemies in the long years he has worked for her. Given that the fly on the stone is reasonably percep-tive, he must have seen by now that the Funor Boy is no boy at all. Though his face has a dewy youth that neither his years nor the things he has done seem able to touch, the flickering light from the richly decorated oil lamps brings out a patina of age and hard usage that is more apparent to the mind than the eye. "Not yet," Angelsin says finally. "I want to know more about that clutch of misfits before I show my hand. The Pass-Through seems to be as much leader as anyone. You found out anything more about what she's up to?"

"She has not gone to the taverns in a while." He changes the cloth again, sits back on his heels. "Something about the others—the Min and one of the Aggitj, they've been looking at boats. Noserat wiggled close enough to listen. He knows some Aggitchan. They were talking about how seaworthy several fishboats were."

"Buying?"

"Not them."

"Settled on one?"

"Didn't show it if they did. They're not so green as that."

"That's enough heat on that knee. Use the oil. The Pass-Through. If she's stopped the drinking, she had a reason for starting it. What?"

"At first I think she a lush." He bends over the knee, rubbing and rubbing, kneading the hot distorted flesh, his hands slippery with scented oil; he speaks in short grunted packets of sound with hissing gasps between them. "She drink she talk make jokes 'n stories. After while hits me. All them stories all them 'bout bad things happenin' to slavers, money lenders, assassins, drug dealers, those types." He sits back on his heels and looks away as she pushes her skirt down. "And what she got out of that was stories about folk here in Fennakin or sometimes just names, when someone says something like that should happen to Eller that filth." He gets to his feet, frees the wheels and pushes the trolley to Angelsin's other side while she slowly, painfully, trades feet on the stool.

"What names?" she says.

"Esmerkop Eller, the moneylender on the Ditta Skak," he says, "the one who's always late with his tithe." He kneels and begins kneading and manipulating the second knee. "Plossung Mil who runs the baby shop on Jatter Way." He stands and uses the forceps to bring up a new cloth; he holds it out for Angelsin to touch, then lays it on her knee. "Nochsyon Tod. Hummerfig Tig who runs the front for Doodamsitirsabo, that Chalarosh tightfist who won't pay any tithe, you know, the one who cut up Tiilk and his mob. Kar hes Kituk, he's a drug dealer, works the North Cusp, stays out of our holding." He changes the cloths. Angelsin closes her eyes. Her lips press into a thin line. Breath snorts from her nose. "A couple more," Hopflea says, "but those're the important ones."

"And tell me, Hopflea, why was she going for those names?" Her voice is harsher than before, ugly with the effort she is making to control it.

"Thieving," he says. Again he changes the cloth, using the forceps to make sure the hot cloth is covering the whole area.

She cannot speak for several minutes, then forces out two words. "What more?"

He looks slyly at her; he is going to dance a dangerous game around her, counting on his knowledge of her to help him stop in time. "What more? What more?" He taps his head. "This, that's it, this clever knob, old lady." Thick white eyelashes flutter. "Guess, huh. Guess which one she picked. Guess how I know. I give you a clue about who. The craziest choice of all."

"Don't play stupid games." She sounds angry, but an instant later, she gazes thoughtfully into the darkness, smiling a little, amused, as she thinks over what she knows about those named. "Tod," she says finally.

He giggles. "Worm, he happens to see this big old owl come flying out a those women's window. He figures it is the Min going to do something she don't want no one knowing about, so he goes twisting after.

Moon's high, owl's big, flying low. Worm, he pick up
Chickfat and the Tump and they go slip slip after and
what do they see but owl flying round and round over
Tod's House, and it goes slip slip down, it sits on a
house tower, turning its head, looking and looking.
Then it goes flying off, back to the window and in
whoomp and then someone shuts the window, but the
light goes on burning for a long time. That same thing
happens four nights running until day before yesterday, then no more owl. Easy to see the Min is scouting
for the Pass-Through and maybe that other one and
the Aggitj, they're looking out a way to run so they
don't get picked up after the thing is done. Worm
swears neck and gizzard he sees everything he tells
me."

Angelsin shudders as he takes away the last cloth
and the cold air hits her flesh, then sighs with pain and
pleasure mingled as he pours the warm oil on and
begins rubbing it in. "Min," she says thoughtfully. "If
. . . no. Can't trust them. I wonder how the Pass-
Through managed to tame that one? It might be wise
to ask her that. Say you so, my Flea?"

"Might be."

"But first we find out more about this Min. Nose it
out for me, Flea; who is she, what's it about her
makes her different, why does she keep away from her
own? And do it fast, Hopflea. If she's looking at
boats, we have not got a lot of time."

The male Min follows Hopflea cautiously into the
chek and hovers nervously beside him as the Funor
taps at the door behind the empty chair. A deep rich
voice sounds through the heavy door, the young Min
winces, glances at the entrance to the taproom, obviously regretting his decision to follow what he thought
of as a Funor boy. "Come," the voice says and even
muffled by the wood, the single word is pregnant with
threat and power.

The room inside is huge, filled with so much satu-

rated color that it is an assault on the eyes, so much
intricate line work it is an assault on the mind, convo-
luted Funor writing scrawled in flaking gilt around and
around the walls, echoed in the looping swirls in a
crimson and gold rug worth a small fortune but spread
with careless prodigality over a floor of fitted hard-
woods. The Min blinks and shies, but Hopflea is waiting. He goes in feeling overpowered by it and by the
huge Funor woman sitting in another of her oversized
chairs. When he looks at her, she reduces that shouting room to a gentle background rustle.

Hopflea leads him to an armchair almost as large as
Angelsin's. The Min is a slim delicate-faced young male
whose primary orientation is avian; he looks and feels
like a child when he sits. His feet dangle and the dark
heavy chair swallows him, diminishes him. He is intensely uncomfortable. He doesn't like being here. He
is terrified of coming anywhere near Timka and her
lethal protectors; he knows every Min who tries to
seize or slay her becomes quickly and futilely dead. He
knows her sensing range is at least double his; he
has been told she will be gone all day, but he hates
and distrusts all Nemin and these more than most. Nor
does he trust Timka to do what she says she is going to
do. He is convinced she is vicious and perhaps insane,
that she hates all Min and wishes to see Mistommerk
cleansed of them by whatever means she can devise.
Nothing Timka could say or do would convince him
otherwise; his mind is sealed against her.

(That fly again, clever little insect; say it is perched
in the loop of gilt painted on the wall behind Angelsin,
a dot of black encroaching on the sweep of gold, our
metaphorical fly on the spot reporting to us.)

The young Min watches Angelsin and hates her and
fears her. Being so close to her makes him sick; he can
barely control his loathing and disgust. He fights the
feelings because they distract him when he knows he
needs his wits at full stretch. He is here because she
offers him a chance at the destruction of one he

KNOWS is a deadly enemy, without being destroyed himself. Only for this can he control face and gut sufficiently to stay quiet in that horrible chair and listen to that grotesque in the other chair. He holds his legs still, clasps his hands lightly over his cincture. His face he makes a mask, unsmiling, but also hiding the sneer he wears inside.

Hopflea crouches at Angelsin's feet, watching him.

Angelsin inclines her head, makes a minimal gesture that might have meant anything. "It has come to my ears that you seek a certain Min, a female outcast from her folk."

He licks his lips, his hand twitch. "Yes," he says.

She raises a brow, then sits waiting, using her silence to force speech from him.

"Yes, it is true we want the one called Timka." He moves uneasily, realizes what he is doing and forces himself still. "She escapes us because she is well protected by those with her; so far all we've tried has failed." He shuts his mouth, furious with himself for having said so much.

"Her protectors are scattered during the daylight hours." There is curiosity in her deep voice. She doesn't try to hide it, rather it is another pin she is sticking into him. As if to say—do this yourself, don't bother me.

He collects himself and for the moment declines to let her prod him into more revelations. "That means nothing, she stays on the Skaks. Would you take her there? Certainly not. You say you can deliver her for a price. Name it."

She smiles. The light from the many gold and alabaster lamps slides with buttery richness along her ivorine horns and touches her large pale face, deepens the shadows about her eyes.

He looks away from her, intimidated in spite of his loathing and his well-manured pride. If he could have killed with a look, she would be shriveling on the floor, but she terrifies him almost as much as Timka and those deadly Nemin with her. When his voice is sufficiently under control, he says, "How can I meet your price without knowing it?"

She bows her massive head. His fear grows when he sees how sharp, glossy, lethal her undecorated horns look. He feels his essence shiver and he knows without understanding how he knows it that this Funor woman has the Min secret, that she can kill him with one hook of those horns because she knows where to put them. Her large right hand caresses the base of a lamp that sits on a leggy table close beside her chair. That oil flung at him is his death too, if she chooses to act. He jumps as she speaks, his mask breaking up. She smiles. "For the woman," she says and pauses. Her voice is lazy, sensual. She looks like she is sucking on the words and getting pleasure from their taste. "For the woman, one thousand gold." She smiles more broadly. "For protection against her companions, a guarantee they will not interfere with your pleasure, another thousand."

"You mistake me, Fomirie Nemin Angelsin Yagan." He cannot help letting his bitterness seep into his voice. He has no authority to speak with her, emphatically none to dicker with her. He is supposed to be a forward watch, sent to observe only, expendable, little trusted, while the powers among the Holavish plot a trap for her in which he will have no part, will gain no renown; the ancients will not sing-chant his deeds into the dark of time. He does not lay blame on Telka or the other powers; they only follow their Necessity. It is Timka and her Nemin panders who have provoked Necessity. It is Timka and those with her that he hates for stealing away his fame. If he can snare her somehow, he alone, if he can slay her and take her S'yer back for proof, then who will be greater than he, who will need to know how he does the thing? If he can somehow meet this monster's price, this great cow with her posturing and petty menace . . . he says petty to himself again, trying to diminish her as he is diminished by her. "There is no need," he says, "to take the Min here and now. It is perhaps simpler and better to wait until she comes to us. For she will. She must. It might be worth something if we do not have to trouble ourselves. Something, Fomirie Nemin, but not over much. Say fifty gold for her, and let her familiars do what they will."

And so the bargaining begins That fly on the wall grows quickly bored because the young Min is painfully outmatched. Picture him rubbing his forelegs and preening his wings, doing his flydance to amuse himself, round and round the gilded loop as the unequal contest moves to its inexorable end. Angelsin turns the Min inside out though he is unaware of what she is doing. Unaware that she is extracting from him everything he knows or suspects about Timka and her companions. There is one break in Angelsin's smooth performance, enough to have warned him if he were not so blindly sure of his abilities. He lets slip his conviction that Skeen has somehow acquired an Ykx. The Pass-Through wants to reopen the Stranger's Gate and pass back to the place she'd come from. Angelsin is so startled by this that she lets her desire flare through her trading face; the betrayal is brief but complete. If he had been looking at her at that moment, he would have sprung from his chair and fled that room so fast he left his shadow behind. But he is not looking and he does not run and he continues beating at Angelsin's price until he drives it down to a bare two hundred gold which he is sure he can acquire one way or another within the three-day gap Angelsin specifies between agreement and delivery. He does not notice that the last part of the chaffering is perfunctory on her part, clear evidence that she no longer cares what price she gets for Timka's flesh.

The Min youth leaves, full of himself and his dreams, congratulating himself on his cleverness. Angelsin warns him to say nothing of the bargain until it is completed or it might come unglued. He quickly agrees with her;

he sees in his imagination the day he can walk up to the Powers of the Holavay and display the S'yer of Timka Minslayer.

Buzzing now in smaller circles, preparing to flit, the fly, could it speak, might have said to him: You have three days to live, Fool. Enjoy them.

After the door has closed on the Min, Angelsin smiles down at Hopflea. "It is almost a sin to play one like that."

"But he is too juicy to throw back."

"True." She shifts her feet, groans. "Have someone keep an eye on that idiot. He'll hint he's got something, he can't help it; if he starts talking too much, take him out. We don't need that kind of misery."

"You really going to give him the Min?"

"Certainly not. If he lasts long enough to get the gold, bring it to me; don't bother bringing him."

"I hear."

Angelsin gazes thoughtfully at a small black dot buzzing busily on her sleeve. It walks down toward her thumb. She pinches it between the thumb and a broadfinger of her other hand, then extends the hand to him. "Clean that. So. The shy one is Ykx."

Hopflea cleans the mashed fly off thumb and forefinger, then smooths a scented cream onto the soft pale skin. "Angelsin's luck," he murmurs.

She clicks her teeth, a sound of exasperation. "Word will get out."

"Not by me." He says that hastily with a touch of fear.

"Not by you. It's that Min. How many has he told, how many of them? We'd best be quick."

"Tonight?"

She frowns at a tall clock ticking loudly by the door. "It's early yet. That Chalarosh hanging around the Boy. . . ."

"Terp the Hole, he says the Chala takes care none of them see him." Hopflea says that, not as one providing information, but as one using a form of words

to show his agreement with an obliquely stated thought.
"Bring him?"

"Softly, softly, my Flea. So softly even the whores
don't catch you at it."

"I hear. After noon meal? Good." He bows quickly
and goes gliding out, leaving Angelsin to her musing.

The Chalarosh stalks in, gives the room a single
glance and ignores it thereafter. He also ignores the
chair and squats on the carpet far enough from her so
he doesn't have to look up to see her and can watch
Hopflea at the same time. Intransigence is writ indeli-
bly in the set of his neck, the spear of his spine. His
face is concealed behind a head cloth and mask made
from bronze links, supple chain mail fine as heavy
velvet. He sits saying nothing, the only movement
visible the sometime glitter of his eyes through their
slits. His aspect is that of one willing to wait forever.

Defeated, Angelsin speaks. "You want the Boy."

The only sign that he hears her is the flicker of his
eyes. He says nothing.

"This is not a matter of intruding into Chalarosh
affairs." She is speaking slowly, using her rich warm
voice to woo him out of his (as she reads it) pretended
indifference. "This is a trifle of commerce. The
Chalarosh want something, this one can deliver it."
She waits. Again she is defeated by the desert man's
impenetrable silence. "A simple matter of reaching
agreement on the price." Silence. Exasperated, she
says, "You are here, Chala. Why?"

The Chalarosh gets to his feet. He has Angelsin so
off-balance that she almost signals Hopflea to have
him stopped. She catches herself and is yet more flus-
tered at her narrow escape. The community of Chalarosh
exiles and traders is small and quarrelsome, but it
unites immediately and lethally when attacked from
without, and that touchy half-mad collection could
take offense at almost anything. She straightens her

back, breathes heavily, near strangling on the rage she dares not show to that corpseworm of a Chala.

He turns when he reaches the door. "The words are understood." His voice is soft, almost a whisper, almost gentle. "The intent of the speaker is judged. No injury is found to the honor of the Chalarosh in the words, for no nacarach has any idea of honor and will stray where the winds do blow it. Touch not the Boy. We will deal with him according to our honor." He turns to go.

"A moment." Angelsin speaks calmly, with effort. "What if the Boy threatens me and mine? What if I lock him away, gently and without doing him injury, until such time he can be loosed without harm to either?"

The Chalarosh stands silent, a tall thin man muffled in layered black robes, the painted mail mask swaying with his breath. "No price to loose him?"

"No price."

"Do as you will." The door swings silently shut behind him; Hopflea scrambles after him to see him out and set a watch on him.

When the Not-boy comes back, Angelsin is swaying in her chair, yielding to the fury that had been consuming her nearly the whole while that the Chala was there. A few years back she would have been pacing about the room, a whirlwind of rage, throwing whatever her hands touched, destroying anything fragile enough to break or be torn, but her affliction has made her immobile as a statue. And it has made her clever where once she was merely powerful, so the folk of South Cusp fear her far more than they did when she walked among them. Then they could run from her, hide from her, now there is no place to run; what her legs cannot do, her mind performs through the agents that come like flies to her hands.

She quiets when Hopflea kneels before her and sets his hand on her foot. She looks down at him. "It is time we were rid of these vipers, these Chalarosh," she says to him, "not today and not tomorrow, but soon." She smiles and her anger is gone and there is a new vigor in her gaze. "One by one they die, never knowing the agent or the reason. One by one death will come to them, one by one until there are no more Chalarosh in Cida Fennakin. Yes. Not today and not tomorrow, but soon. Oh, soon."

SO MUCH FOR SPECULATION. TIMKA AND SKEEN GO ON WITH THEIR PLOTTING, IGNORANT OF THE INTRICATE WEB OF ACT AND EYE BEING SPUN ABOUT THEM.

In her night owl shape Timka circled high over the compound watching the guards and the servants settle into their nightly somnolence. A fan of light spread across the lawn that sloped to the oval pond, the fringes of that light skipped along the wind-teased ripples on its surface. Beside the ceremonial door to the main house, also near the edge of the light, half a dozen Funor guards squatted over a grid chalked on a paving stone and played stones and bones in finger flickering silence while they waited for their Char to march them home uphill. Forbidden to speak on duty, they'd evolved the finger signs and honed them until they approached the level of speech. Six guards, all true Funor, no mercenaries. Whoever was visiting Tod was one of the uphill Funor, either important or desiring to seem so; two was the usual number even after dark.

Though Skeen would yell it was foolish (but who was Skeen to inveigh against rash acts?), Timka gave in to the prodding of her curiosity and spiraled down to an open window in one of the upper floors, smiling inside as she acknowledged the change in her since Skeen winkled her out of her comfortable prison in the Poet's house. She had resented that once, but no longer. She was alive as she hadn't been in a long, long time, not since she fled the mountains and Telka's spite, though she felt more pain now that the numbing was gone, felt the ache of being cut off from her kind. There were moments when she suffered a loneliness

74

that seemed more than she could endure. Such moments generally came late at night when she woke for some cause or other and lay staring up into the dark; they never came when she was actually with her own; then she was usually so irritated at the Min she felt more kinship to Skeen than she did to any Min, however close by blood and belief. Insular, rigid, fearful, ossified—loving, gentle, tied deeply to the land in ways even the Skirrik who came closest to that tie could not experience or understand. Like three rounds, one placed over two, bits of her overlapped the Skeen world, other bits of her overlapped the Min world and bits of her touched neither. That's my sigil, she thought, three mingled circles. She had begun to understand Skeen's restlessness, her need to keep busy; when she was busy with immediate concerns all that other business about having no place to call her own was something she could ignore. More than ignore. Forget.

She aimed herself through the window, snapped her wings out once she was inside and curved to a soundless landing on a carpeted floor. A bedroom. Empty now, though there were noises outside, women talking, one laughing. Huge room; the one she, Skeen and Lipitero shared wouldn't make a closet here. More voices, getting louder, the speakers coming toward her. She ruffled her feathers impatiently and peered about. Stupid choice, Tod's own bedroom. Stupid. Go out and start over? No fuckin' chance as Skeen would probably say. Unless I absolutely have to. She shifted to woffit and padded away from the hidden women. A door. Woffit's large ears up and swiveling. No sounds outside. She shifted to Pallah, needing hands, squeezed the latch and eased the door open. Lifefire be blessed, old Tod didn't like squeaks and kept his hinges oiled. She started to go back to woffit, then hesitated. Woffit eyes were dim, unreliable. Woffit nose was keen, but she needed to SEE. I'm going hunting, so I go as Hunter. She shifted to her cat-weasel shape, willing her splotchy fur high-summer dark, then went padding

down the wide hall keeping close to the side, blending
into embroidered hangings blowing gently in the drafts
that prowled the halls with her. Ears twitching, her
hunter's eyes searching, her nose tasting the air, she
teased out the pattern of the rooms. The big house
was mostly empty, no children in it as far as she could
tell, a few women. Slaves? Probably. From what she'd
learned about Tod, he'd want no one he couldn't
control anywhere near him. His slaves would be sufficiently cowed to offer no threat. She left the halls and
stood in the shadows at the top of a graceful spiraling
ramp, whiskers twitching, tail jerking back and forth,
irritation like heartburn in her middle.

In the Great Hall below servants were clearing away
the remains of a sumptuous feast and a pair of semi-
naked gauze-draped Balayar girls (they looked like
twins) were moving along the table, getting in the
way, helping themselves to tidbits off the plates, each
clutching at a decanter of wine and drinking from it
without bothering with glasses. The serving women
worked patiently on, ignoring them as if drunken twelve-
year-olds were a common thing in this place and perhaps they were.

Timka-cat fidgeted back and forth behind the elaborate grill that fenced off a sort of balcony that ran
along the wall giving a concealed view of the hall. She
could not go down to snoop on Tod and his guest as
long as those women were working. She glided to the
end of the balcony nearest the place where she could
hear snatches of glittery music, settled in a corner and
waited. Tinkly metallic sounds, pretty enough but irritating to her cat-ears. The soft clish-clash of the cleanup
below was pleasanter but she was happy enough when
it stopped. She crawled to the grill and looked down.
The women were lifting the sections of table, carrying
them to the edges of the Hall. They came back when
that was done, lifted up the sleeping twins and carried
them away. Ti-cat moved swiftly to the head of the
ramp, but waited before she started down it. Within
moments she was glad she had.

Two girls came back carrying a heavy tray laden with a steaming urn and etched crystal stemware. They crossed to the embroidered velvet arras that was pulled across the northwall of the Great Hall; the girl on the right carefully freed one hand and pushed the folds aside, baring an open archway. The music was abruptly louder. Moving with continued care the girls eased around the end of the arras, letting it fall into place behind them.

Timka dithered briefly, then darted to the ramp and oozed-down it as fast as she could without breaking silence. She flowed across the mosaic tiles to the west end of the arras, nosed it aside. Blank wall. Good. She dropped to her belly and edged along as if she stalked nervous rabbits in short grass until she reached a section of wall pierced and set with fans of stained glass. With the dimly lit Great Hall behind her and the heavy dark arras she felt safe enough to ease an eye past the edge of one of the fans.

Tod and his guest, a longhorn Funor, sat cradled in lounge chairs. Beside them a fire danced in the round throat of a free-standing hearth, its threads of smoke carried off by a funnel chimney hung above it. The serving girls were arranging the urn and goblets on a table between the chairs. The men ignored them as they watched torches being set on poles outside a long curved wall that was mostly glass. When the lawn was dancing with shadow and firelight, Tod clapped his hands. The musicians stopped their tinkle twang and filed out, all of them stocky Balayar women much older than the other servants. Or slaves. Whichever they were.

The serving girls moved on their knees to Tod's side and knelt there, mute and pliant, waiting for whatever he chose to ask of them. Timka had done the same herself with the Poet and thought little of it then. A matter of surviving with a minimum of pain and fuss. Now her tail twitched and her muzzle flattened in a soundless snarl. The fit was brief and ended with a burst of silent laughter as she mocked herself. It all depends on where you're watching from, eh, Ti? For those girls no doubt it was the same as it was for her. A bit of business in the art of surviving. No more than that. For all her understanding, though, a bad taste lingered in her mouth.

Tod sent the girls away with a flick of his hand. Timka edged her head under the arras and watched them stroll off across the hall and vanish into the back where the servant quarters were, stretching, rubbing at their necks, talking in whispers as they moved.

Ti-cat crawled nearer to the archway, flattened herself below the glass fans and pricked her ears to listen. Nothing. Her tail jerked against the arras with small thudding sounds. She raised her head. The men were looking out at the torchlit lawn, watching the musicians as they readied themselves. A few scattered notes, then a heavy driving beat from the drums, a fast hard counter from the cittern strings. A tall angular androgynous Pass-Through walked between two torch poles, took up the beat of the music, stamping in place on the grass, torso rippling, then began a splendidly barbaric dance.

"Oh, it's not authentic," Tod murmured, his peeping voice so very modest, "just a little entertainment I devised for your pleasure, Char Vassa Bassa."

The uphill Funor had laid aside his cowl. Ti-cat could see the back of his neck, one ear and a bit of face. His half-meter horns were polished until they gleamed a dark ivory; gold and silver wire were inlaid into the tough substance, intricate whorls that outlined cartouches where bits of jade and pearl and chips of amethyst and emerald and ruby were shaped into rayed designs. A glittering opulent decoration to an otherwise undistinguished form. Fat jowly head, very white skin flushed roseate with wine and lust. He leaned toward Tod. "That dancer, is it as agile on a mattress as it is on the grass?"

Tod shrugged. "Too old for my tastes, too bony. So

many more enticing come through here. . . ." A wave
of a limp hand.

"You live in a paradise most men only dream of,
Tod. Are there no men at all in your house?"

"Women are pliant creatures and adaptable," Tod
said. "They keep me comfortable, why not. My men
walk the walls and watch from the guard towers, why
should I have them here?"

Outside, the dance ended, the musicians and the
dancer collected their gear and vanished round the
side of the house.

"And woffits in the garden. No doubt there are
woffits where I sit once you have gone up." Vassa
Bassa sounded blearily envious. "And a peaceful night,
bedwarmers beside you, no fear your throat will be cut
before the dawn breaks. Sometimes I think I should
buy peace with that cow Pululvatit Grytta and go back
to the Funor Plain where I have kin who'd guard me
with their lives instead of spending those lives looking
for a way to bleed my veins dry." He gulped at the
tepid wine and his neck got a degree redder while the
ear that she could see was almost purple. "Heyya hai,
I'd do it tomorrow had I the blood price. Tod, you
Pallah don't know what greed is; just wait till you
come across a cow in spite, you'll find out." He grunted,
squeezed his nape into accordion folds and gulped the
lees of his wine, blew out a cloud of droplets, and
settled back muttering to himself. "Not my fault he
had air 'tween his horns. Every shorthorn plays rough
games. We played rough games, so what? Wasn't my
fault he tried to play Fool without the Tapping and
bashed the Ippy Lyta. Nearly got ME killed, that gimp
brain." He scowled uncertainly at the goblet, wrestled
himself up and refilled it at the urn cock. The effort
seemed to sober him. Head swaying, he peered at
Tod. Ti-cat read hostility and alarm in what she could
see of his face and the set of his body. Tod had the
presence of mind to have his eyes shut and to produce
a soft eeping snore. The Funor relaxed. He's either

dumb or very drunk, Timka thought; she watched him
settle back and changed her mind. No, Ti, you don't
make that mistake or you're the dumb one; maybe
he's not the brightest of the Funor, but he's cunning or
he wouldn't be alive. No. Tod was giving him a way to
save face and he took it because Tod's too useful to
him to throw away for such a little happening.

After a few more minutes of silence punctuated by
Tod's tactful snores, Vassa Bassa cleared his throat,
flicked a fingernail against his goblet's bowl, making it
ring loudly. "Tod!"

Tod opened his eyes and sat up with a thousand
apologies for his discourtesy.

Vassa Bassa brushed them off, showing his irritation, and turned the conversation to the reason he was
there. "Word is you've a shipment due soon."

"Not soon, Char. Tomorrow. The messenger bird
came shortly before you did. Your timing, as usual, is
impeccable, oh Char. Shipmaster Khorem will be tieing
up a short while after the noon meal if all goes well."

"Sent he a list of what he's got?"

"In general terms, Char. Twelve fives of young Pallah
studs, sturdy stock with years of work in them. And
this is a coup indeed—Khorem got his hands on nine
Skirrik dames old enough to be well-trained in their
arts but young enough for heavy work. And three
Skirrik pups guaranteed to be deft at sniffing out Min
spies. Twelve twos of tender girls, a mix of Balayar
and Pallah with three young Chalarosh bitches, defanged
of course. Something else, what, what . . . ah! a handful of Aggitj extras. He took those on because they
come from the orehills in the Backland and one is said
to be an ore-sniffer, but I truly doubt that because no
family would exile such an asset."

"Unless they happened to be a family of ore-sniffers
and too many of their kind would lessen their worth."

"So wise, oh Char, then the report might be true. I
will not guarantee it though, not without a trial of his
skills. And it will be important to keep the presence of

these Aggitj quiet. You know the Slukra, they squeal like rats and turn mean if they think you're fooling with their cousins."

Vassa Bassa snorted, gulped at his wine. "When will you be showing them?"

"I will have to polish them up a bit, settle the restive ones, work on them so they show well. No doubt I'll have the first presentation next Pyaday."

"Arrange a private showing, Tod. Next Tirday, no later." Vassa Bassa reached into his robe, fumbled about a bit, lifted out a heavy pouch. He loosened the thongs, emptied the coins inside onto the floor, a ringing, clanking shower of gold, a ringing rattling outrun as coins that fell on edge rolled away and toppled over. Before the noise was finished, Vassa Bassa was on his feet, pulling his cowl over head and horns. He didn't wait for an answer but stalked out. A moment later the ceremonial door slammed and he was bellowing his guard onto their feet.

The arrogance and ill will in that gesture didn't begin to touch Tod. He lay smiling a little, his hands clasped over his stomach, until he heard the guard marching off, then he got to his feet and stumped heavily to the line of long windows. Drapes were tightly bunched at both ends, stiff, hieratic, fold packed against fold. He shook his wide sleeves back from his wrists, found the pull cords and began drawing the curtains over the windows. They flowed smoothly shut, heavy and dark, blocking the view from the garden. Whistling tweedle-weedle he came back, dropped to his knees and began collecting the coins. He weighed each, right hand left hand, tested each with a thumbnail filed to a point, ran a thumbpad around the rims. He looked supremely contented handling that gold, caressing it, stacking coin on coin into solid little piles. Vassa Bassa's attempt to humiliate him hadn't touched him because he had nothing but contempt for that uphill Funor; the heavy shining gold was all that mattered.

When he had retrieved all the coins, judged them
and sorted them, he got to his feet and walked quickly
to the archway, passing less than a meter from Ti-cat's
whiskers. A moment later she heard bars slam into
their sockets at the ceremonial door, then he was back
again, carrying a small silver tray. He stopped short of
the arch. Again she eased her head under the arras,
wanting to know what he was doing. He moved to the
ramp, looked up it, made a circuit of the Great Hall,
snooping in the corners, then he walked briskly to the
arch, pushed the arras aside and was back in the
parlor. He transferred the gold to the tray and carried
it to a woven tapestry hanging on the east wall. He
pushed the cloth aside (its rings rattled loudly enough
for Timka to hear the noise and twitch at it), took a
key from round his neck and opened the steel door the
tapestry had concealed.

Timka watched him swing the door open, then she
was edging back along the wall, getting clear of the
arras. Lifefire alone knew how long he'd spend in
there fondling his treasure; it was time to get out.
She'd had all the luck she could expect in a single
night.

"Sometimes I think it's better to be lucky than smart.
That was not smart, Ti."

"It worked."

"So it did." Skeen looked grim, but couldn't hold
onto that sternness. She patted Timka in the middle of
her glossy black curls. "It's a good child, but if it does
anything like that again, it's going to get a spanking it
won't forget."

Timka shifted suddenly to cat-weasel and snarled,
then was Pallah again, giggling at the speed with which
Skeen pulled her hand away.

Skeen sighed and shook her head. "Well, don't
make a habit of being that rash. As a corpse you're no
use at all." She stretched out on the bed. "Djabo's
teeth, I wish Maggí would get here."

WHERE TWO PLOTLINES CROSS, LIFE CAN GET MESSY FOR YOUR HEROES AND VILLAINS BOTH.
or
HOW THE HELL DID I GET HERE?

Skeen woke. Head a fuzzball twice its usual size, two little men taking turns hammering at her temples. Stomach churning. Stink of old vomit and stale urine. Cold. Hard. Stone under her. How. . . . She flattened her hands beside her and pushed herself up, moving slowly, careful not to jar anything vital. How . . . where. . . . She shuddered as sudden terror flashed through her. If her mind was so far gone that she couldn't remember how she got here or where here was, if she couldn't remember what she was drinking and where, then . . . Djabo! Blackouts now. There was a time when she lost hours, days—once, a full week. She was shooting heavy pilpil then. That was after old Harmon died and there was no one she dared trust near her and the world seemed wide and cold and empty. It was far easier to drift in the warm arms of pilpil dreams. Her drift lasted until a shipment of pilpil was intercepted and the dealers she could reach went short. She came down hard and when she bounced, she got all too good a look at herself and the world she lived in. She looked and she said, this is it, no more. A long, long time ago that was, a warning of what could happen that she took seriously. She'd never lost herself again, not even in her Pit Stop binges. Well, reason enough for that, she was enjoying herself too much to waste those hours on unconsciousness. Something about this world that seduced her into excess. No, Skeen, not the world. You. Face it. You're terrified you'll find out Tibo and Picarefy really did get together and betray you because if that's true there's nothing anywhere you can trust. Not even yourself. Especially not yourself. And there's no way you can find out short of half a year. Months of slogging dangerous travel ahead. Months while you feel like you're trying to run in glue. Accept it, Skeen, it's not strange you're chewing your fingernails off to your elbows. All right, all right, I can live with that. But I don't remember, I can't remember drinking that much, I stopped drinking too much a sennight ago, why can't I remember? How did I get here . . . here? Where is here?

She looked around. A reddish gray light trickled into the cell through a long narrow tray slot about knee height, enough to give her the outlines of the place. Four walls, a ceiling and a floor. One door. Admirably understated. She grinned into the dark, that touch of humor like heat in her shivering body. A minimalist cell. She eased herself onto hands and knees (feeling a bit better but still very fragile), crawled to the door and peered out the tray slot, pressing her face close to the splintery planks. Frustratingly narrow field of vision, but off to one side she saw dark verticals close together and behind them a bumpy lump of blue-violet. She closed her eyes, digging back into foggy recalcitrant memory; the last time she could remember seeing Lipitero, the Ykx wore her blue-violet robe. She pressed closer to the slot, slid back along it to extend her view and saw a familiar pair of knees and part of a massive throne chair. With a sigh that had no surprise in it, she turned away from the slot and eased herself down until she was sitting with her back against the door. Angelsin. Forty devils gnaw her gizzard. How did she find out? Ah, why ask, you know how such things seep out; the only place to bury a secret and expect to keep it is in the heart of a sun, and even then if more than one knows it, forget it. It's going to surface, that's inevitable as entropy. Why should you think you could bag a secret as big as a mythic Ykx? Well, she hadn't really expected so much, she'd just hoped to keep the noise down until the Company got away. Maggí, ah Maggí, get your butt up the river, will you?

She pulled her legs up. Left me my boots. She prodded at the right boot. No surprise. Knife gone. She pulled the boot off and felt around inside. Smiled. Picks and spare blade were still there. Made of a non-refractive resin, they flexed with the leather but were as tough as fine steel, the knife had a blade with an edge that could cut a thought in two; it was thin, a delicate stiletto with a leather hilt; it could turn a steel blade in a fight and slice a throat with ease but it was whippy and treacherous and hard to control, not your general utility weapon. Belt was gone, with her tool kit and darter. Angelsin, you take good care of those till I come for them. The wire saw was nestled in the waistband of her trousers, they hadn't found that either. Well, it could stay there, no bars or chains to cut, at least not now. So. No blackout, Djabo be blessed, just Angelsin drugging us all. All? That's not right. Chulji was out with his farmers and Pegwai was eating with his cousin . . . eh! If it was last night she did us. She rubbed at her ringless hand; the chron was gone. Fuckin' thieves. How long have I been here? How long? How how how long? Body didn't know. Time snipped out, ragged ends spliced. She wiped her hand along the stone beside the door. Damp. Underground. Could be the middle of the day up in the streets. Or the middle of tomorrow night. Any tomorrow. No, no. She flattened her hand over her stomach. Not that long. Likely a few hours, no more. She passed her tongue along her lips. Wonder if they'd bring me some water if I yelled loud enough?

Lipitero sat in the cage and gloomed at the distant wall where the cells were.

Angelsin hadn't bothered drugging her, just sent in a swarm of children with a large net. When she was

tangled so thoroughly she had nearly strangled herself,
the children called a pair of Funor shorthorns; these
hauled her to the cavern and dumped her in the cage.
At a word from Angelsin, they slashed most of the net
clear and went out.

Angelsin stood outside the cage, leaning on a cane.
She watched Lipitero tear away the fragments of net.
"Take off the robe," she said.

Lipitero snarled, then started jerking the neck ties
loose. There was no point in refusing; Angelsin would
just call the hardboys back and have her stripped. She
pulled the robe over her head and dropped it to the
floor of the cage.

Leaning heavily on the cane Angelsin walked around
the cage making murmurous sounds as she inspected
Lipitero. When she was around in front again, she was
smiling. "Put on the robe," she said, then labored to
the throne chair that lost size and impact the moment
she sat in it. She clicked her tongue. Hopflea took the
cane, tucked it behind the chair, then scuttled around
to crouch by her feet. She gazed at Lipitero a long
time, saying nothing.

Feeling like a side of meat, not knowing what to do,
how to react, Lipitero looked away—then stiffened.
The cavern was a huge knobbly thing, filled with shadows; most of the torches were set up close about the
cage and the chair and very little of the light reached
as far as the walls, but she could see dark shapes
carrying in other shapes. She counted these new prisoners. One, two, four, six. Skeen, Timka, the Aggitj.
Chulji was spending the night out with his farmers,
Pegwai must be with his cousin. The Boy? She looked
around. Not here. She glanced at Angelsin; the huge
Funor woman was watching the parade with a brooding satisfaction. Lipitero closed her hands into fists, a
tightness in her throat, a deep ache between her shoulders. She sold him—that wombless mistake sold the
Boy to the Kalakal. Or killed him. She watched the
limp forms carried into the cells, one to each cell, the

doors slammed shut, the bars dropped into the clamps. She pulled her hands inside the robe and slid her fingers along her harness. Cutter. Lift field. Shunt. Stun beam. One by one she counted them off, the operations worked into the metal decorations that seemed only ornament. Tiny weapons, tiny aids, powerful but limited, Lifefire, so limited. She had to make a plan somehow. Had to free Skeen even if she couldn't free herself or the others. Nothing must stop Skeen finding Rallen and bringing Rallen Ykx to shore up Sydo Gather. To open the Gate, to free the Ever-Hunger if she needed the defense, Skeen didn't need her, only her harness. She squeezed her hand about one strap; the node there was modified so Non-Ykx hands could trigger it if need be, she'd insisted on that. She closed her eyes and visualized the flight of Ykx moving through the nights over Suur Yarik, shadows against the moon, heading for the Fellarax Gather caves near the Gate, caves abandoned millennia before when the Waves started coming and the turmoil in the Mountains made life too uncomfortable there. The Remmyo had arranged the flight because he couldn't in conscience agree to release the Hunger unless there were Ykx in position to corral it again before it devastated Mountains and Plain. Another reason for preserving Skeen, ten members of the shrinking Gather put in jeopardy, if Sydo lost them for nothing. . . . . Something, I have to do something. It was painful to realize how little she knew about the otherWavers and the Pass-Throughs. Until the desert Chalarosh had swarmed into Coraish Gather she'd lived a contented but circumscribed life, knowing nothing of the great outside, wanting to know nothing of the folk that lived there.

When the slaughter was over, she crawled from beneath a pile of bodies—dead Chalarosh, dead Ykx, dead adults, dead children—her fur matted with blood, feces, urine, stomach contents let out through slashes. For hours, dazed, too shocked to grieve, she hunted

through the dead for her children, for anyone at all
left alive. She found her children huddled in a wall
niche meant to hold a zocharin and a flower; her son's
head was smashed, his small body shattered, mingled
with the butchered body of her daughter. She touched
an arm; she thought it belonged to the boy but couldn't
be sure. Cold. The cold entered into her. She walked
away, no longer looking at the dead, no longer caring
if any besides herself still lived. She walked away and
went out onto the lip. For a long time she stood
staring out into the desert, then she sat and waited to
die. She expected to fade as Ykx had faded before,
separated from the Gather, staked out for torment in
Chala clanspace. She sat all day waiting for the fade to
start, but when the cold evening shadows crept over
her the only emptiness she felt was hunger. She scrambled to her feet and screamed fury and frustration into
the darkness, but there was no answer, not even an
echo. She flung herself off the lip, meaning to let
herself tangle in the downdrafts and crash on the stone
below, but a freak blast of cold wind swept over the
mountains, caught hold of her and automatically she
extended her flightskins and rode that wind on and on,
out over the desert, on and on. She was in a state of
shock, the only thing she knew was she could not let
herself fall here, could not give her life to the Chalarosh
as if she were ripe fruit falling into their bloody hands.
When the wind faltered, she exerted herself and spiraled up to catch the highwinds. On and on she went,
hunger a beast gnawing at her belly, occupying the
whole of her mind, or that part of it the thirst-fire left
free.

She soared all that day, strength draining from her,
a slow leaching that blurred her eyes until she saw
nothing but a blue haze surrounding her, that blanked
her mind until hunger and thirst were a distant thing
hovering about her but not part of her. The highwind
blew her on and on; she left the desert behind, she left
the rind of farmlands behind, she glided out over

water. Aware, she might have loosed that wind and
drowned, but she had left purpose somewhere in the
desert and was a leaf on the wind, mindless as any
leaf. Late in the afternoon on the second day the wind
turned capricious, dropped her, caught her, dropped
her yet lower, caught her again, then vanished al-
together. She plummeted toward the water. Shocked
out of her numbness, her body worked desperately to
save her; she felt the powerful drive of a will to live
she had not known was in her. But the long flight had
weakened her; she was too feeble to do more than
sketch at attempts to catch an updraft and rise again.
The water caught her trailing feet and pulled her down.

When she woke she was in a Balayar fishcanoe. The
young men working it had bathed her face and trickled
water into her, then the cordial all Balayar kept for
times when the boat was far out and there was no
wind. Drop by drop they got that rich sweet liquid into
her and coaxed the lifefire within from ashes to a
crackling blaze. She was alive and knew she was going
to keep on living; the time was past when she could
have killed herself.

They asked her no questions when they saw that she
would live; they went back to their lines and nets,
working with a noisy cheerfulness, a mixture of joking
and song that fed strength into her as surely as the
cordial did. They cooked her one of the fishes they
tumbled like oily silver rain into the well of the boat
and the youngest of them fed it to her bit by bit,
chatting without expecting any answer, telling her about
the girl who had him dying from love and exasperation
because she was a darling, a pearl among pearls, but
she would flirt with every cousin he had, even Jikki-
toh who was too young to have any notion what girls
were for. He didn't seem unduly alarmed about her
wanderings, nor upset by the distinct possibility she'd
choose one of those cousins over him. There was this
other girl a couple of islands over who could dance fire
into the blood; he didn't like her as well as Meromerai,

but maybe that was because he didn't know her as
well. He stroked the soft silver fur on Lipitero's arm,
taking so much pleasure in the feel of it and how it
changed color with the angle of light, that she could
not feel insulted or ashamed at being handled and
found herself seduced into an unexpected pleasure in
the durability of the body that had brought her so far,
a satisfaction with the shapes and textures of that
body. This astonished her. She smiled at the boy. He
laughed and handed her the bowl. You're fine, he
said, I expect you'd like to do this for yourself.

She stayed with the Balayar for two weeks, gathering strength of mind and body; they were a contented
folk, their lives at once simple and complex, changing
yet mostly the same, repeating patterns their ancestors
had repeated, the rebellious and the misfits going out
on the trading ships that came from the larger islands,
coming home and going out again. They found her a
wonder and pleasing to have around; Balayar babies
were delighted with her fur, they crawled over her
knees and cuddled in her flight skins; their sleek round
warm bodies comforted her and let loose her grief.
The Balayar gathered about her, patting her, listening
to her laments, singing wordless tenderness and understanding to her. They wanted her to stay with them
and she was tempted, but after those two weeks had
passed, knew she could not. She needed Ykx around
her for her mind's health, and she was honest enough
to admit that she did not enjoy living with the Balayar;
she missed the comforts of a Gather, the stimulation
of Ykx who talked about something more than fish,
sex and infants, and most of all she missed her studio
and workshop and the crafting of delicate electronic
gear for the use of the Gather and for her own pleasure. Sadly, but with that deep understanding of need
they had always shown her, the Balayar went with her
across a narrow strait to a tall island, a desert of stone
and ash; she rode in the canoe that had picked her out
of the sea, crewed by the same young men who brought

her in. These youths made a cradle for her out of cord
and climbed with her to the top of the cone (they
climbed as well as they swam, reading the stone like
they read water). They squatted and began singing a
farewell song they'd made for her that was a mix of
sadness and excitement. She hesitated, waiting for them
to be done, but after a while they waved their hands at
her, telling her to leave while they were singing. She
felt for the wind, took hold of it and leaped into it.
The sound followed her as she spiraled up and up.
During the last turn, she snatched a look at them.
They were dancing precariously on the lip of the cone.
Down below, the little boats that had come with her
were filled with Balayar waving energetically, singing.
Snatches of sound came up to her as she started the
long soar north and west.

The healing that was the gift of the Balayar babies
slipped away from her on that endless increasingly
desperate flight across the ocean; even the Balayar
cordial could not keep her blood stirred to a living
heat. She retreated as she'd done before, shut off
mind and let body carry her; if it wanted to live, it
would get her to the Sydo Gather with life enough left
to power its engines.

Arrive she did, a ghost with flesh. For a terrible
while, she existed in a half-life where turn and turn
about either everything about her was unreal and she
couldn't touch it or she herself was a nightmare drifting through things that couldn't touch her. She made
everyone around her uneasy, unhappy, uncomfortable,
but the Sydo Ykx would not put her out of the Gather;
that was not their way.

After an especially depressing day, she left the intricate caves of the Gather and went to the rim of the
cliff above the mouth, sat where she could look out
across the lake. I can't continue like this, she thought.
I should go away; they won't make me go; I should
take it on myself to go. She felt a powerful revulsion
drive up through her body and knew she couldn't

make herself leave; if she left she would surely die. At the front of her head she wanted that surcease; she was a walking wound with the kind of pain no one ever got used to. At the back of her head, though, where her will was, where her body spoke, she clung with an equal determination to life.

Sometime near dawn a cub came climbing up the scratch, went past her without seeing her and went scrambling up a clump of boulders dangerously close to the lip of the cliff. He stood teetering on the top-most rock, flapping his soft little flight skins. Chewing her lip to keep fear from spilling out, moving as silently as the ghost she'd been, she eased onto her feet and crept up behind him. He crowed with delight as the sun peeped up behind the lake, waved his arms and tottered precariously. She snatched him off the rock and cuddled him against her chest; she was trembling with relief but the cub was loudly indignant. He screamed with frustration and fought against her hold. The hot hard-rubber body, all knees and elbows, banging into her broke a hard thing inside her; she didn't realize this at first, just kept on soothing him, cooing calmness into him. When he was quiet she took him down the scratch into the Gather. His mother was darting about searching for him, turning out the whole Gather with her cries of grief. She was very young for having a cub that age, her youth and inexperience intensifying her grief at losing her baby, her joy when Lipitero gave him to her. She bubbled with a wordless gratitude, then turned and ran away, shouting out the cub was found, he was all right, the naughty boy was found and fine.

Lipitero watched her vanish around a curve. She touched her lips, outlined them with the tip of her finger because she was astonished to find herself smiling. The dawn outside was slipping down the mirror ways and turning the Grand Round into a bright warm soup that dripped into her veins. Yes, it felt like that as she suddenly knew with a clarity which matched the clarity of that light that the cub was her child, that the cub's young mother was her child, that every Ykx in the Sydo Gather was her child; she was buoyantly, extravagantly, indescribably happy. The glow didn't last, but the half-living half-dead state she'd been drifting in was gone forever—unless that monster Angelsin destroyed Skeen and with her, Sydo's hope.

Angelsin was talking at her, something about why she was traveling with the Company, was she a captive, that sort of thing, but Lipitero let the noise wash over her without listening to it. Skeen. Ah, Skeen, what do I do? Wake up, Skeen, do something. She slid down one of her magnifiers, sacrificing some of the light to bring the far wall closer and sharpen her focus. Twelve doors. Twelve cells cut into the stone. Twelve cells, the farther cells filled, but who was where?

A shout. An Aggitj. Ders, poor boy, waking up alone and in a panic. The four shorthorns acting as guards gathered outside one of the cell doors, third along from the end; they yelled insults in at Ders, banged on the door. A quieter voice cut in, soothing, comforting. Domi. Yes. As usual, busy calming his nervous cousin. Two of the shorthorns starting cursing him and pounding on his door also, second from the end.

Something was happening at the door to the sixth cell from the end, behind the backs of the guards. A dark serpent's head came through the tray slot, then about a handspan of body; the head swayed, the tongue flickered at the noise. A moment later the serpent oozed with smooth deceptive speed through the opening, its chin touched the cavern floor and it began gliding away, its mottled coloring so close to that of the stone Lipitero had trouble following it. More and more snake emerged.

A spate of whistles, rapid bursts of unintelligible speech, laughter. Lipitero whipped around. Street urchins, Angelsin's Ants, were running from several of

the side holes, the cave chamber magnifying and repli-
cating their noise until they seemed a hundred, but
when she counted them, there were only a scant dozen.
As they passed her they flashed her a bouquet of
gestures; though she was unfamiliar with this particular language of the hand, she was comfortably certain
the signs were the most obscene in their vocabulary.
She snapped thumb against midfinger, flung her hand
away and up to show them her contempt. Forgetting
her enhanced eyesight and the distance to the cells,
she waited tense with anxiety for them to notice the
serpent; she kept her head turned resolutely away
from the cell, although she couldn't resist a few rapid
glances that way and a plea under her breath for Ders
to keep up his clamor. When the snake's tail flicked
out, she had to stiffen herself against her relief, then
duck her head to hide the smile she couldn't stop
spreading across her face.

Ders quieted. The Funor guards milled about for
another few minutes then went back to their desultory
pacing in front of the cells.

Lipitero pushed her hood back a little and watched
Angelsin. The Funor woman leaned into the armrest
and bent her head so one of the ragged boys could
whisper in her ear. The others squatted on the rich
furs spread about the foot of the great chair, waiting
their turn to climb its side and whisper their reports.
Lipitero risked a longer look toward the shadows
beyond the line of cells; the serpent was out of sight;
even with all of her lenses in place she couldn't see
anything but the forests of stalactites and stalagmites,
the irregular bulges and hollows of the walls wherever
they were visible. Timka had gotten herself into hiding
quickly and thoroughly, though what she was going to
do now. . . . Lipitero sighed with frustration, huddled
in her robe, fingers moving restlessly over her weapons; all she could do was wait and be ready to back up
Skeen or Timka when they acted. She looked from
Angelsin to the cells and back. Stay alert, she told

herself. She scowled at Hopflea who was prowling
about the chair; he vanished behind it and apparently
settled on the furs there because he didn't appear
again. Wait, she told herself, I should be good at that,
I've done so much of it.

Timka woke sick and sore. Automatically she shifted
to cat-weasel, then to rock leaper and back to Pallah,
losing the nausea and bruises along the way. "If this is
what Skeen feels like, I wonder she ever. . . ." Drugged.
We were drugged. Angelsin. Using her fingertips and
the faint bleed of light from the tray slot, she explored
the cell. A bare box chiseled from stone. No way out
but that heavy plank door. Nothing in here but me,
not even fleas. Me and a stink. Must be older than
me, that stink. Annoyed, she moved to the door and
dropped to her knees by the tray slot. Directly across
from her, about a hundred meters off (she could see
details that far away because of lamps bound onto
setpoles, a double handful of them burning with vigor,
placed at several different heights so there were no
spots of concealing shadow) she saw a cage with a
blue-violet lump inside. Lipitero. That explains some
of this. Furs on the stone to the left of the cage.
Hopflea crouching beside another of those giant throne
chairs, Angelsin's feet and knees, one forearm with
attached hand. What a mess. A dark blur moved past
the slot. She blinked, then realized there were guards
pacing back and forth in front of the cells; when she
listened for them, she could hear the scrape of their
feet, their voices as they exchanged grunts or strings of
words she couldn't understand because the echoes mangled them too badly. All of us? No. Not Chulji.
Angelsin's reach covers South Cusp, she wouldn't go
beyond, not when she has an Ykx in her hands. Chulji's
loose. Until he comes back. Due in tomorrow night. If
we haven't got away by then, Lifefire! Pegwai? Depends on how long it's been since supper. She sighed.
It doesn't matter, Ti. If one gets out, we all do. She

drew back, sat on her heels and scowled at the tray slot. She could get her arm through it up to the shoulder. She stretched out her arm and looked thoughtfully at it. When she was a child running the forest like a wild thing, she'd handled a lot of snakes but she'd never thought of learning the serpent shape, too slow for one thing. She dropped her arm, closed her eyes and tried to remember.

Ders began to howl. The Funor guards converged on his cell, yelling, cursing, kicking at the door. Domi called out, his voice soothing, repeating familiar words over and over as he struggled to calm his cousin. Again Timka couldn't make out the words, but she didn't need to. She blocked out the noise and concentrated more intensely. In her desperation, she achieved a serpent of sorts. She didn't know how to move, even simple breathing required immense effort, but eventually she got her head up, her ribs working and crawled to the door. She managed to get her head and a bit of body through the slot, then discovered that her serpent eyes were incapable of resolving forms more than a few paces off and color was a vague memory. However the pits above those feeble eyes were giving her an astonishing amount of information about the location and distance of live bodies, their heat like a shout against the cold of the stone and her flicking tongue brought her messages of fear and anger along with the sour stench of unwashed bodies. She took a while to start processing the data pouring into her receptors, but she grew rapidly more proficient and in a short while acquired enough confidence to start wrestling herself through the slot. The snake was growing easier to handle, but she hadn't the time to let herself sink into it and learn it thoroughly, she had to get out before the guards came back and caught her. She'd never tried such a slapdash shift and was in a state of mild panic that intensified when her mid-section, her thickest point, nearly jammed in the slot. At the same time the waves of anger, the vibrations of the shouting and blows were all decreasing in intensity, a warning that the guard could come back any minute. At the cost of burning pain and a feeling she was suffocating, she muscled herself free, then moved as quickly as she could along the stone.

After a few seconds of awkward exhausting crawl, she hissed with disgust at her stupidity and shifted to cat-weasel, then padded rapidly toward the deep shadow beyond the end of the cells where (Lifefire be blessed!) wasp-waisted columns and stone teeth were thick as the roots of some monstrous tree, stalactites and stalag-mites in grotesque and garish profusion. She slid into the shadow with a flood of relief that turned her bones to jelly, stood shivering while the clamor at the cells died away as Ders settled into a (probably tempo-rary) calm and the shorthorns went back to their des-ultory pacing. When she recovered, she moved silently through the teeth and columns until she found a rea-sonably dry niche behind some waxy looking stalag-mites; she settled herself so she could see Angelsin and her chair and beyond her the cage where Lipitero crouched. Fine, she told herself. I'm free. What now?

Angelsin was busy with a clutch of her Ants; one by one they climbed the side of the chair, clung to the arm and whispered for several minutes in her ear. Working her shoulder muscles, her claws, in a physical expression of her satisfaction, Timka watched the ex-change, the intent faces of the children. Her slither through the slot had gone unnoticed . . . she broke the thought as she saw Lipitero's head turn, then twitch round again. Looking for me. Lifefire grant she's the only one who saw something. What now? Yes, what can I do . . . at any minute Angelsin could finish with the Ants and send for one of the prisoners—a touch of what Skeen called Mala Fortuna and it would be Timka she called for. Timka shivered and started to panic when the Funor woman lifted her head and looked around; the lamplight turned her horns to butter ivory and the points looked dagger sharp, her arms were big around as a man's thighs and as powerful. No sag, little fat. Lifefire!

Hopflea wandered into sight, moving through the children crouched on the furs. He came around behind the chair (it was set about two meters from the cave wall on a natural dais that was the driest place in the chamber), reached out and flicked Angelsin's cane into a lazy swing, then vanished around the other side. A few minutes later he was back among the children. He drifted over to the cage and stared at Lipitero. He seemed to whisper something, but the Ykx made no sign she heard him. Another moment's fidgeting, then he ambled off toward the cells.

Timka went back to watching Angelsin.

Another child had pulled himself up the rungs set into the wood and knelt on the chair arm, leaning intimately against Angelsin as he whispered; furtively he stroked her arm and shoulder as she inclined her ear, a familiarity she tolerated with monstrous maternalism. The Ants were her children whom she protected and consumed. Like the cat-weasel whose form Timka wore and knew so well. The female had a short but furious heat. At the end of it, exhausted, she snarled the males away from her and made ready her den; with her fearsome clever forepaws she scythed down swathes of grass and mouth-carried them to line the hole. Then she went on a killing spree, burying what she couldn't eat in the dirt of the den. Her litters were born into that miasma released as she dug up and ate the putrefying meat—huge litters—fifteen, twenty, sometimes even thirty. Gradually, as the days passed, operating on some logic or trigger that no Min studying the beast had ever fathomed, she began eating her kits. One by one, she chose the discards from among the mewling squirming mass of hot fur. One by one she ate them until after a month, two kits—three at the most—were left. If two, one was always a female, one always male. If three, two would be female and the third male. Always. No matter what ratio of male to female existed in the original litter. Timka wrinkled her blunt muzzle and twitched her whiskers in a rapid flash of humor. Hopflea was Angelsin's remnant, her cherished one. Who'd be the next in that brood? You are my chosen ones, you are my favored until you disappoint me, unless you disappoint me, be careful not to disappoint me. Walk warily but not too warily, obey me in all things, show initiative and wit, but not at my expense. Too much dependence and I will eat you up, too much independence and I will cast you out to be eaten by the wolves. Dance on the highwire, my poppets, keep me sweet with your capers and beware, the time will come when despite your pretty ways you please me no longer. A time will come when you must be ready to run or be eaten. Look about you. Are you the oldest of the Ants? Then beware, my pretty, protect yourself, my love.

She let the Ants pat her and stroke her and she gave them silver bits and taffy and smiled at them and told them how clever they were and sent them chattering, giggling out of the cavern.

Hopflea came ambling back, his arms full of Skeen's gear; he settled behind the chair, sitting cross-legged on the furs piled there and began exploring the pockets in the belt, fiddling with the contents until Timka wanted to scream. She didn't know what those things were, but was sure they were dangerous and probably fragile. Skeen would be furious if that idiot broke them. He tucked everything back where he found it, began playing with the darter. He shook it, frowned as it sloshed. He fished out one of Skeen's picklocks and began prying at every crack. Timka locked her teeth— stupid little twit, you'll wreck it—breath hissed through tight nostrils, claws scraped over stone. He put the pick away, shook the darter again, peered down the front end. Timka tensed, but the slideplate was clicked home over the sensor spot and he never managed to dislodge it. He set the darter aside and began fiddling with the cutter; the cover over its firing sensor defeated his prying fingers, though he did manage to get the cap off its business end. He peered into the aperture, tried to get at the jeweled lens that glittered inside, then threw the enigmatic little cylinder onto the furs and picked up the money pouch; counting the coins inside was obviously a more satisfactory experience. He fondled them, piled them onto his thigh, counted them again and with evident reluctance slipped them one by one back in the pouch.

The last child she could see climbed from the chair and pattered away into the dark mouth of the nearest out-passage, the sound of his feet fading swiftly. Angelsin stirred, sighed, turned her head; she said something but the echoes scrambled the words so badly Timka couldn't catch a single syllable. Hopflea gathered up Skeen's gear, set everything where he'd found it, searched out the cutter and tucked it away, climbed up the chair's side and dumped his load in Angelsin's lap. She began picking through them much as he had, murmuring to Hopflea, raising her voice to push questions at Lipitero, questions the Ykx ignored. Lipitero sat silent, huddled, the silky blue-violet cloth draping in graceful folds over her body, pooling around her on the floor of the cage.

Timka curled into a knot, tail wrapped around her muzzle. The cold of the stone was seeping into her in spite of her heavy belly fur; she thought she felt it chilling her brain, she couldn't decide what to do now that she was loose and able to act. Skeen wouldn't dither about like this. She seemed to know this sort of thing as if it were imprinted so deeply in her bone and blood she didn't need to think. How comforting that must be, how simple. Timka found herself starting to boil with resentment, envy, a sense of futility; she closed her eyes, locked her forepaws over her face and struggled to calm down. I'm fighting with ghosts I've created for myself. Ghosts. Her envy of Skeen's competence and her despair at her own ineffectiveness were distortions of a far more complex reality. She

was laboring against years of conditioning and doing
not so badly at it. Stop biting your own tail, Ti, get on
with some positive thinking. You don't have to depend on anyone, even Skeen. You've proved that.
You're wasting time you haven't got. Think! She lifted
her head, yawned, flared her whiskers, opened and
closed her eyes and kneaded at the stone, these small
actions stirring the sluggish eddies in her brain as she
began assessing the difficulties ahead of her.

Four Funor shorthorns, clumping about before the
line of cell doors, were too far off to be an immediate
problem, especially if she could get hold of the darter,
but they'd have to be taken out fairly soon. The children were gone. For the moment. Lifefire solo knew
when they'd be back. Hopflea. Treacherous, yes, a
nasty fighter. Take him first? He's the most mobile,
the most dangerous. Angelsin. She looked formidable,
well, she was formidable, but she couldn't move fast
. . . no, no, can't count on that. She stretched her
mouth in a cat grin. As Skeen would say. If Angelsin
was angry enough, who could guess what she would
do.

Hopflea listened, his body limning the intensity of
his concentration; he nodded, climbed down the chair
and started toward the cells.

Timka came onto her feet in a quick and utterly
silent surge. She hesitated a second longer to make
sure he wasn't headed for the passages. No mistake.
Going for one of the prisoners. She went leaping from
behind the stalagmites, covering the distance to the
chair in great silent bounds.

A shorthorn yelled.

Timka gathered herself, leaped and landed in Angelsin's lap. Claws retracted, she slapped at the Funor
woman's face, then doubled up and closed her teeth
on the belt with the holstered darter.

Angelsin's arms whipped around her, surprising her
with their crushing monstrous strength, frightening her;
before she could react, she was nearly dead, Angelsin's

steel fingers digging into her body, driving for the S'yer that held her life, the master control of her malleable body. Pain. She was burning. She squawled and lashed out with claws and teeth but she couldn't get any purchase or put any power behind her blows; she did some damage to the massive arms. She could smell blood, but not enough, not nearly enough, most of the time she was clawing air.

Sound like cicada scrapings. So odd and unexpected it got through to her though she paid little attention; her life was burning out of her; Angelsin's hands were digging deeper and deeper. Cicada scrapings. Louder.

Angelsin's arms went slack. Her hands fell away.

Timka rolled off her lap, fell onto the furs piled up around the chair. She didn't wait to catch her breath or discover what had happened, but shifted immediately to her Pallah form and scrambled frantically until her hands closed on the belt. She whirled onto her feet, ripped the holster flap open and caught hold of the darter's butt. With a continuation of that movement, she swept her arm in a whipping arc that flung holster and belt off the barrel's end, flipped off the cover plate and put darts into the shorthorns running at her, bellowing; they fell away and she darted Hopflea before he could skitter into more solid cover.

She stood a moment holding the darter stiffly in front of her, then she dropped to her knees as her legs lost all strength; shaking with relief, she let her arms drop, the darter fell cold and heavy on her thigh. Her fingers had the strength of wet paper; they opened and let the darter slide away; it fell onto the fur without a sound and lay tilted against her foot. Lipitero was yelling at her, her name over and over; the Ykx sounded distant, weak, as if she was so far away her voice barely reached Timka. She was rattling the bars of the cage, that sound penetrated the haze, made Timka's head ache, but she couldn't raise the energy to do anything about it.

Cicada scrapings. She twitched, moved a hand; her

shoulder prickled, arm and hand went numb, for one startling moment it seemed to her a part of her body had vanished; she straightened up, fighting the lethargy that was like chains wrapped around her. Something heavy fell against her.

Gradually her shaking stopped and the heaviness began to flow away. After a few deep breaths, she lifted her head. There was a solid weight pressing into her side but she ignored it as she gazed blankly at Lipitero.

The Ykx was busy at the cage door. With a soft exclamation filled with satisfaction, she pushed at the bars and the door swung open. She came swirling out, her robe fluttering in the local breeze about her vigorously moving body. She brushed past Timka who smelled the sweet bite of her fur and the subtle soapy aroma of the fluttering silk. She scooped up the darter, stepped back so Timka could see it. "How does this work?"

Timka moved her shoulders, pleased and rather surprised to find her strength returning. "Point the long cylinder, touch the dark glassy spot near your forefinger."

She watched as Lipitero lifted the weapon, held it at arm's length and put two darts into Angelsin. The big woman was bleeding sluggishly from the scratches on her arms and her skirt had a few rips in it, but overall, Timka had done very little damage despite her frantic struggles. She stared at Angelsin, thought about the cicada sound. "What happened?"

Lipitero didn't answer her. She's good at not answering, Timka thought. The Ykx turned a rapid circle, scanning the cavern, as much of it as she could make out, then faced Timka. "Can you move?" Impatience sharpened the words.

Timka sighed and lurched onto her feet. One of Angelsin's Ants fell past her; she'd missed seeing him somehow. She blinked, touched her toe to the fingers frozen about a short ugly knife. Lipitero stepped around her, put a dart in the boy. "Nice weapon," she said. "How long will they be out?"

Timka rubbed at her arms, shivered; it was cold and dank in this huge chamber in spite of the heat put out by the lamps and she regretted the loss of the cat-weasel's thick fur. "At least an hour, probably longer. What was that noise? You got them off me. Thanks."

Lipitero tapped at her chest with a long thumbnail very like a claw and produced a muffled metallic click. "Stunner," she said. "Fast but only a short time relief, enough to catch your breath. The effect passes off somewhere around five minutes." She looked over her shoulder at Angelsin. "Short range too, I didn't know if I could reach her; Lifefire's blessing I did. If you're feeling shaky now, I probably clipped you with the spray from the beam."

"Doesn't matter, she was killing me."

"Formidable, that one."

"Eh, Petro, I've never been so scared." Timka sneezed, shivered. "Let's fetch the others and get out of here."

Lipitero nudged the darter's barrel up and down the side of her face as if she scratched an itchy thought. "Complications," she said slowly. "We've got to decide. . . . Get your clothes and let Skeen and the Aggitj loose, I'll keep watch here." She tapped the darter against her thigh. "Ah . . . it might be a good idea to hurry, I'm feeling. . . ." She didn't finish the thought and didn't need to.

Skeen stood with hands on hips, examining Angelsin. A half-smile lifting one corner of her long mouth, her yellow eyes laughing, she turned to Timka, raised her right eyebrow.

Timka tugged nervously at her blouse. "She had the darter in her lap with the rest of your gear. I thought I could get it and get away." She rubbed a fold of cloth between thumb and forefinger, embarrassment mingling with a remnant of resentment. "I didn't think she could move that fast. Petro stunned her or I'd be dead." She stared at her feet and felt like an inept child.

Skeen laughed. "That's one of the great secrets, Ti, having good backup around for the times you screw up. Me, I'm pleased as hell you and Petro did all the work getting us loose." She turned slowly, her laughter fading as she surveyed the dozens of dark holes pocking the arching sidewall between clusters of stalagmites and stalactites. "Djabo! What a maze." She stamped around and scowled at Angelsin. "Do we have to wake her to get out of here?"

Lipitero held out the darter. "That's not important; if we get lost, Ti-cat can nose our way up." She started kicking about in the furs. Looking for the belt, Timka thought; she frowned, trying to remember where it had flown to. "Seems to me this puts a knot in our plans," Lipitero said. "Ah." She scooped up the belt, stood holding it in one hand while she fluttered the fingers of the other at the comatose Angelsin. "Otherwise we've got to do something about her. I haven't the vaguest notion how to handle her, Skeen. She's got too many ways of striking at us. I strongly suggest we get away before the mountains land on us. Any ship going anywhere."

Skeen chewed on her lip, scowled at Angelsin. "Another port I might agree. I could always leave a message with the Aggitj at the Slukra, they'd see Maggí got it. But. . . ." She glanced round at Lipitero.

Timka recognized the half rueful, half sassy look Skeen got when she was about to say something possibly hurtful and certainly true.

"Truth is, you're the problem, Petro. You're the one puts the rest of us at risk. Here anyway. This slaveport. Look what happened where we've at least got maneuvering room—on a ship, well, I don't want to put that much temptation on someone I don't know. No. We have to wait for Maggí."

Timka looked round at the shadowy spaces of the

great chamber. Maneuvering room for sure. Echoes
murmured over every word spoken here; it was getting
so they murmured over and around the words in her
head. The long difficult night was turning eerily unreal; she was tired, she was filled with a low-grade
anger that only time would bleed away, she was getting more and more impatient with Skeen and the
silent Aggitj who stood a short distance off, waiting
with that amiable patience of theirs for someone to
decide something. For the first time she doubted Skeen's
ability to deal with the mess they were in; for the first
time she was painfully aware of Skeen's tendency to
alternate between terrifying rashness and an irritating
obsession with safety where she fussed for endless
moments, even hours, overproviding emergency exits
in case something went wrong. Timka wanted to shout
at her, *get on with it, Skeen;* she didn't because she
didn't quite know how to do that getting on.

"Well," Lipitero said, "that being so, what do we
do?" She held out the belt, took back the darter for a
moment while Skeen buckled it on.

Skeen clipped on the lanyard, stood a moment,
hands on hips, looking around at the fallen, finishing
with the huge slumped figure of the Funor woman.
"Hal."

"I hear you, Skeen ka."

"You think you and your cousins could lift her," she
nodded at Angelsin, "back up to the chek?"

Hal wrapped his hand about a lamp pole, shoved at
it, nodded with satisfaction as the tough wood resisted. "Cut us two of these and let Lipitero lend us
that robe, we could make a stretcher." He grinned.
"Be some heavy, but . . ." he flexed his biceps, "we
got practice hauling barrels of saltfish."

Ders giggled. A quick skipping step took him to Angelsin's side. He lifted her meaty arm, let it splat down.
"Yip-yip, can't carry her, we can always roll her up."

"Why bother." Hart's voice was gruff, his words
clipped. "Cut her throat. Save a lot of trouble. You

don't want to do it, I will. Scum like that shouldn't be let live."

Skeen opened her mouth, closed it, made the tight little sign with her left hand that Timka read as *don't bother arguing, he won't understand you and you haven't got the words to convince him*. She'd seen that sign several times before when Skeen had given up on her; what brought it on now was something Timka couldn't answer. She agreed with every word Hart said, it seemed to her the best solution would be to cut that massive throat and hide the body for the short time they'd have to wait. What was Skeen doing? Did she have some weird idea she should defend this monster? Timka got a strong feeling that for a brief moment she and the others were on the far side of a glass wall that had come down between them and Skeen, that Skeen was seeing all of them as enemies, though why she felt that she didn't know. *I'm so tired I'm hallucinating*, she thought.

Abruptly Skeen relaxed. "Bad idea, Hart. I take it you've never seen what happens when a boss like Angelsin either vanishes or is killed. Soon as the news got out—and it would, my friend, the moment her lines of command went slack and that wouldn't take long—there'd be at least half a dozen contenders for her place. In that kind of war there aren't any neutrals allowed. You dance with one side or another and hope you pick the strongest. And there's more shit could land on us. She's got uphill connections, Hart; what if they decided to close the port and wipe out the Cusps?"

"Why should they? For something like that." A stubborn growl in his voice.

Skeen sighed. "Think a little, Hart. She's too open about what she is, what she does, like she's flaunting herself in their faces. She might be outlaw but she's not out of touch. She runs South Cusp for them, keeps order, collects taxes, lets them keep their hands clean while they make a juicy profit from her acts. Hai!" She slapped her forehead. "No rants, Skeen, this ain't

the time." She dug into her tool kit, took out the
cutter and knelt by one of the taller lamp poles. "Be
ready to catch, Hal." She sliced the cutter beam through
the wood close to the stone, watched him steady the
pole. "Angelsin can't move fast." Timka made a sound
in her throat, Skeen grinned over her shoulder at her.
"Not on her feet, you'll admit that." She moved on
her knees to another long pole. "Ready for the second, 'ware the hot oil." She leaned into the pole,
cutter ready, waited until Domi was there to catch it,
then sliced it loose. "And she's vulnerable; let someone get the idea she's being mauled about and having
to take it, she's done. Depends on how good she is at
keeping her temper, but maybe we've got a thin chance
there." She cut the lamp off the first pole and set it on
the stone beside the furs. "If we can maneuver this so
no one knows what we're doing to her, if we can make
her believe all we want is to get the hell out without
getting burned, then maybe, just maybe we can keep
the lid on long enough for Maggí to show up." She
dealt with the second lamp, then stood back and
watched as the Aggitj cut strips from the tough blue-
violet silk and bound Lipitero's robe of concealment
onto the poles. "It's going to be a nervous few days,
that's for sure." She slapped her forehead again.
"Djabo! I am not thinking. Time. Time. What time is
it? Anybody got an idea?" Not waiting for an answer,
she started feeling in her belt pockets, then poked
about in the pouch. "Ah." She slid the ringchron onto
her finger, glanced at it and smiled. "Well. Not too
bad. About two hours past midnight. That gives us
plenty of time to get set before we have to face the
world."

"Skeen, aren't you forgetting something?" Timka
nudged the Ant with her toe. "This one. Hopflea. The
shorthorns. What do we do with them?"

Skeen made an impatient gesture. "You want to do
some throat cutting . . . No!" she shouted as Hart
started toward the boy. "I was joking. Put them in the

cells, we can let Angelsin deal with them later. Yes, I
know, probably comes to the same thing, but she'll be
happier if we let her handle things like that. Believe
me. Better she doesn't think she's completely helpless.
No. It is not good tactics to make her desperate. We
want her to cooperate, not dig her hooves in and
decide to take as many of us with her as she can. Of
course she'll be plotting the minute she wakes up; I
want that. It'll keep her from doing something precipi-
tate, like ordering her Ants to swarm us, calling in her
hardboys to back them up; she won't do that unless
she's pushed into it. I think I'm shifty enough to
thwart her, for a while anyway. Um. Bring Hopflea
over here. We'd better have him up there too; he
might be missed. He shouldn't weigh much, you think
you could carry him, Petro? I'd like Ti-cat running
scout ahead while I guard our rear. Good. Well, let's
get moving. Sooner we're settled in, the better I'll like
it."

They found the Boy curled up with the Beast, both
deep in drugged sleep, locked in a small room that
opened off Angelsin's bedroom.

Angelsin was laid out on the bed like a corpse for a
wake except that her long three-fingered Funor hands
were placed one over the other on her diaphragm and
rose and fell with each breath. In this huge and gaudy
room only one lamp was lit, throwing most of it into
shadow. Skeen and Timka sat without talking on a
plump bulging backless sofa pushed against one wall.
Out of sight, moving in and out of the other rooms,
searching them, poking through Angelsin's secrets, hunting out the hidden exits from this fortress suite, Pegwai
and the Aggitj had slipped into wild humor and made
the silences ring with laughter and jokes and shouts of
discovery. The thick walls were eaten into termite lace
by the secret ways Angelsin had gouged in them,
evidence of the value she placed on her hide.

* * *

"Tell me something, Skeen."

"Hmmm?"

"When Hart wanted to slice Angelsin, you nearly exploded. Why?"

Skeen was silent for several more minutes; Timka began to think she didn't mean to answer. Finally the long thin woman stirred, lifted a hand, let it fall. "That word," she said, "that attitude. *Scum*. Not even people. Us. Well, maybe not Chulji or Pegwai." She spoke slowly, pausing frequently to dig out the word she wanted. "I suppose the Aggitj don't feel it either. Their people threw them away like trash, but they're . . . um . . . accepted well enough out here, though if they went home . . . I don't know, that could be different too . . . when Hart said that, it cut at me. . . ."

"Skeen! There's no comparison between you and that . . . that eater of filth. She's a monster. She's evil. A beast. This world would smell better if she was wiped off it."

"Of them all, I thought you might . . . um . . . see what I'm saying, Ti." Skeen's voice had a dull sadness that Timka found oppressive and to a large degree incomprehensible. Skeen passed her hand across her eyes, slapped it down against her thigh. "It's like . . . um . . . choosing sides in a game, Ti. My style might be different, but Angelsin and me, we're on the same team. The Scum Team. The ones respectable types sneer at and stomp when they can. When you say wipe her away because she is what she is, then you're a hairline off from doing the same to me." Her hands were working, her tongue flicking out to follow the line of her lips as she struggled with what she'd not put in words before. "Pit Stoppers aren't a sweet bunch, Ti; to say true, we're a godsawful collection of misfits, murderers and thieves. The excrement of the universe." A small tight grin, not much humor in it. "You take 'em as they are, or take yourself off. You

ought to know there's lots worse than Angelsin sitting
in seats of power—think about Telka—Angelsin at
least takes care of her folk and she doesn't expect
them to kiss ass for it. Pegwai calls her a monster and
I suppose she is, I don't know . . . I don't know. . . ."
She moved her shoulders uneasily, got up off the sofa.
"I've heard of saints, but I've never met any." She
walked with quick short steps to one of the barred
windows, pushed aside the heavy lace curtain and
stood staring out at the night sky.

Timka frowned at the stiff erect back. For her, the
difference between Skeen and Angelsin was broad and
glaring. A chasm. And she was indignant at Skeen for
implying there was a tie between her and Timka and
that creature. Lifefire, she confuses me, she thought.
There has to be some order, some rank of values. I
can't live in the kind of chaos you imply, Skeen, and I
don't believe in it. No. She smiled. Haven't I seen you
despising and loathing this, that and the other? No
universal acceptance in you, graverobber my friend.
Hmm. It's that word. Scum. That's what bothers you.
The dismissal in it. So easy to . . . yes, I think I see.
What Telka's trying to do with me, that's why Skeen
thought I'd understand, turning me to a beast that
other Min won't fuss about hunting, slaughtering. Still,
me and Angelsin? I'll never accept that. But I begin to
see the other thing. What Skeen didn't quite manage
to say. I deserve to live because I desire to live. I
deserve what I'll never be able to command as my
right. I deserve to exist simply because I do exist. The
attack on Angelsin is an attack on me. Timka pushed
up off the couch and moved to the foot of the bed
where she stood for several silent minutes contemplat-
ing the sleeper. Her lips twitched. She started laughing.

Skeen swung around. The curtain fell in place behind her. "What's that for?"

"I've been thinking about what you said." Timka
stretched, rubbed at her back. "And I've been thinking about the dead along our back trail." She hitched

a hip over the footboard and laughed again. "Wouldn't it be lovely if she woke up and came charging at us and gave us a really satisfactory reason for removing her? No fuss about words, no fuss about worth, just she lives or we live. A nice clean uncomplicated choice. Pop! and it's over, all settled."

Skeen nodded, her face drawn and grim. "It'd settle a lot of things. Us, for one." She moved along the bed until she stood gazing down into the Funor woman's broad pale face. A swift bend, a thumb lifting an eyelid, then she swung around to face Timka. "She's still under, but I don't know for how much longer, there's a lot of meat laid out there. Djabo's weepy eyelids, I'm about done, I need some sleep. Ti, go hunt out Pegwai and see if the two of you can come up with some stout rope, or something else strong enough to hold that much muscle. And take Hopflea and stuff him in a closet somewhere. Be sure it's not one with a trick exit in it; better tie him too." She yawned. "Have Domi do the knots. You said he's a sailor, he should be able to thwart that ancient baby's tricks. Remind him Hopflea's got lots of experience squirming out of tight spots."

Dawnlight filtered through the heavy lace curtains. Timka dozed in an oversize armchair, her feet tucked under, mind and body relaxed, drifting in that twilight region where nightmare and strokes of genius lived. Skeen's slow breathing went on for several minutes until her breath caught in her throat; she blinked slowly, then pushed up and looked around. She brushed at her face, swung her legs around and slid off the couch, started stretching and bending, moving quietly, the only sound the soft brush of the eddersil against her body. Timka roused, watched her sleepily without bothering to move, blinked in time with the whispered grunts as Skeen swung through her exercises.

Angelsin snorted, shivered, tried to move, went still as she understood the pull of the ropes that tied ankles and wrists to the bed posts. She lifted her head, looked venomously at Skeen, but said nothing.

Skeen kicked at the footboard, made it boom. "Some things I want to make clear. One. You made a bad move tackling us, now you pay for it. Two. You know better than me how many down here would go for your throat if they thought you'd sprained your wrist a bit. Three. You try going for us all out and what you'll get is a bloody mess. You won't do us and you'll announce to the world how we've done you. Four. You're not going to have time to get organized. We'll be out of here in a day or two. Five. If you're reasonably intelligent, you'll keep your temper on a low simmer and let it off kicking ass once we're gone. That way you won't lose anything you think is important. Six. I want to buy a temporary peace and the coin I plan to use is your life. I won't off you unless you make me and I won't let the others touch you. Seven. You push us and you're dead. The minute it looks like we've made a bad bargain, you go. That's it. Keep quiet until I've set out how we're going to handle the logistics of this mess. When I'm finished, then you can have your say." She grinned tightly. "Yelp all you want, but don't waste my time too much."

A LITTLE GAME FOR THE GENTLE READER.
PLAY OUT THE BARGAINING IN YOUR OWN
HEAD. YOU SHOULD HAVE A FAIR IDEA NOW
OF THE TEMPERS OF THE TWO WOMEN AND
WHAT STRICTURES AND LIMITATIONS THEY'RE
OPERATING AROUND. IF YOU WERE ANGELSIN
ABOUT TO BE HELD PRISONER ON A FAIRLY
LONG LEAD, HOW WOULD YOU WANT TO SET
THINGS UP SO YOU'D HAVE A CHANCE AT
STOMPING THIS GNAT WHO IS DRIVING
YOU CRAZY? NOTE: THERE'S SOMETHING
SKEEN HAS NO WAY OF KNOWING; THERE IS
A RITE ANGELSIN WILL NOT DARE BE
ABSENT FROM COMING UP IN FOUR DAYS
(more about this later; read ahead if you
want) SO SHE HAS A LIMIT TO HOW PATIENT
SHE CAN BE. IF YOU WERE SKEEN,
DRIVEN BY A NEED TO MAINTAIN THE LID ON
THIS SITUATION FOR A MINIMUM OF TWO
DAYS, IF YOU SUSPECTED THAT THERE WERE
A LOT OF UNKNOWNS THAT COULD BLOW
YOUR PLANS TO ASH, HOW WOULD YOU
SET THINGS UP, WHAT SUSPICIONS WOULD
YOU HAVE, HOW WOULD YOU WORK TO
LIMIT THE DAMAGE ANGELSIN COULD DO
YOU? REMEMBER, YOU WANT HER
COOPERATION. TO GET THAT, YOU WILL HAVE
TO KEEP THE SURVEILLANCE INCONSPICUOUS.
ANGELSIN HAS THE ADVANTAGE OF HOME
GROUND, SKEEN HAS THE ADVANTAGE OF
EXPERIENCE AND FIREPOWER.

**ME, I'D SAY SKEEN HAS A SLIGHT EDGE. HER
NEEDS ARE SIMPLER. IN TIME, THE FORCES
SHE IS HOLDING DOWN WOULD EXPLODE
UNDER HER, BUT WITH A LITTLE LUCK, SHE
AND THE OTHERS WILL BE GONE BEFORE
THAT HAPPENS. THE BEST METHOD FOR
SURVIVING A VOLCANIC ERUPTION: BE
SOMEWHERE ELSE.**

Images:
Angelsin silent and brooding in her chair at the end of the
bar, a boiler with the valve locked down, pressure building,
building. . . .
Usual crowd for the early evening hours, drinking, playing
with the House Gamer, watching dancers caracoling along
the bar or twitching from table to table, their musicians
trailing after them. A lot are eating. Angelsin's cook is cele-
brated in Lowport, South Cusp to North Cusp; Uphill also,
so there are as usual several older bulls slumming for the
night, their jeweled horns glittering in the smoky light.
Sitting somewhere with an unobstructed view of Angelsin:
Skeen or Timka or Pegwai, depending on whose watch it is,
armed with the darter, alert, ready to down the Funor
woman the moment she gives them half an excuse. Also
present, guarding the watcher's back and sides, two of the
Aggitj; the other two patrol outside (with the Boy and the
Beast along for added security). Chulji spends most of his
time in hawkform, eyes searching for anything that might
mean trouble; sometimes, though, he takes a short jog
down the river to see if he can spot Maggí's ship.

The Schedule:
First hour after sunup. Wake Angelsin, untie her, let her take
care of her body functions and dress. No privacy allowed.
Pegwai and the Aggitj are on guard again. They take her

downstairs, get her settled in her chair. The cook brings breakfast to them all, Angelsin included; she eats from a tray
clamped to the chair arms. Two of the Aggitj settle at a table
and continue their unending game of bones and stones.
Pegwai takes the morning watch, then goes upstairs about
an hour before noon to catch some sleep; Skeen takes over
from then till suppertime; then she naps and Timka watches.
The Aggitj pairs switch stations and continue their backup
watch. They snatch what sleep they can during the night,
they don't seem to need much.
One hour after midnight: The Funor woman is roped to her
bed. Pegwai and two of the Aggitj stand guard for the first
part of the night. Skeen and Timka take over for the rest
with the other two Aggitj as backup.

"Eh, Skeen, you drop inna hole or somethin'?" A
schooner of ale in each battered hand, a big rough
Pallah pushed through the noisy crowd gradually filling the room. After a moment of blank surprise, she
remembered him from several of her more drunken
forays. He set a schooner in front of her, pulled over a
chair and dropped into it. "Hey?"

She gazed into the deep rich gold of the ale, breathed
its bitter perfume. One wouldn't hurt, she thought.

The Pallah nudged her with his elbow. "Hey?"

"Can't do it," she muttered and repeated the words
louder when he cupped a hand about his nearside ear.
"Got me in the gut," she yelled and pushed the schooner away. "Sorry, friend, that'd light too much fire."
The real regret thickening her voice brought a sharp
look, but shut his mouth.

He drained his own schooner and ambled off, after
livelier company. She looked after him. Friend or
shill, who knows.

She glared at the heavy glass beaded enticingly, the
liquid inside flowing with gold fire, whispering temptation to her. One won't hurt, just one. Her throat
closed up. She swallowed several times. Finally she
got to her feet and snagged a passing waiter. With

considerable reluctance and several attempts to mis-
understand her, the Funor mossyhorn took the ale away.

During the last two hours of her watch, one after
another of her drinking buddies ambled over to the
table, tempting her with just about anything that poured
out of a bottle. She grew increasingly edgy as these
incidents rubbed at her never wholly stable temper, but
the suspicion that it was all contrived and the massive
presence of Angelsin reminded her continually of how
important it was for her to keep hold of her appetites
and her head. She stayed dry and she stayed cool
enough, but when she went upstairs, she exercised for
hours before she tried sleeping. She slept without dreaming, going so deep the chek could have burned down
about her without waking her.

That was the first day.

While Skeen and Timka slept, during Pegwai's morning watch, several small bands of shorthorns came
winding toward the chek. Chulji screamed a warning,
the Aggitj and the Boy raced about threatening first
one then another, but when one of the skirmishes
spilled into a Skak, the tunk tonk of a guard drum sent
both sides scurrying into the alleys and the attack was
abandoned for the day.

When Chulji was aloft again, ready to spot for them,
Domi sent Ders inside to report to Pegwai.

". . . and they disappeared like they were Min Shift-
ers," Ders finished.

Pegwai glanced at Angelsin, but the woman's broad
pale face had no more expression than it usually did.
If she knew what was going on, if she'd planned that
sniping, she showed no sign of regretting the failure of
her ploys. "How serious were they about wiping you
away?"

"Domi says they testing us. Would a got us if they
could, but they never pushed it very hard and they
backed off fast when it looked like the guard would
stick its nose in." He shifted from foot to foot, doing a

nervous dance, anxious to get back to his cousin but too polite to hurry Pegwai.

Pegwai drummed his fingers on the table, his dark eyes darting about the room as if he sought answers there he couldn't find elsewhere. He gazed at the staircase a long minute, shook his head. There was no point waking Skeen. I'm not wholly inept. I hope. "Tell Domi if they come at you again, they'll be serious about the attack; the two of you and the Boy get back in here and I or whoever is on watch will have a little talk with our hostess.

Ders giggled, flashed an obscene sign at Angelsin and slouched out of the room.

The second day passed. Angelsin increased pressure on them though she did nothing overt. No sign of Maggí yet. Again Skeen exercised for over an hour, trying to drive the maggots out of her head. She slept as heavily as before, but this night she dreamed, all the old sores opening again, playing over and over, with the new humiliation mixed in—Tibo's betrayal. She woke as tired as when she lay down.

The third day. Angelsin was showing strain. Her bones were paining her because she wouldn't give her warders the satisfaction of seeing her tend her joints. Her calm was brittle from the moment she woke on the morning of the third day; she snarled at the Aggitj who watched her void her bladder, wash herself and dress; she spewed invective on them which they ignored with that amiability that could be more irritating than curses. Her face was blotchy with temper as she struggled downstairs and into her chair; she could no longer sit with massive intimidating stillness, but fidgeted with her sleeves, moved her hands along the chair arms, traced the cuts of the carvings, turned from side to side, moved her feet. Dark glitters shone in eyes sunk so deep in their sockets they were usually lost in shadow. When Skeen came downstairs, she walked into a glare that sent chills along her spine.

Maintaining her calm though it took considerable

effort, she turned her back on the Funor woman, ambled to Pegwai, dropped into a chair beside him. "My my," she breathed. "If looks could kill. . . ."

Pegwai rubbed red eyes. "Skeen, we are so close to losing hold of this thing," he broke off his whisper, shook his head. "If the ship isn't here today, you'd better come up with some other way of getting out of this place." He swallowed a yawn, knots of muscle punching out beside his mouth. "I'm played out, haven't been sleeping well; I've got to sleep, but I don't know if I dare close my eyes."

"Eh, Peg, you might as well. I hear you and yeah, you're right. Don't worry, I'll come up with something. I've been in tighter pinches before and I didn't have you all round to help me out."

"Help, hunh." He closed both hands over the edge of the table and started to push away, then changed his mind. "Skeen, there's a young Pallah who keeps coming in, fidgeting around, watching Angelsin all the time. She pays him no mind and he drifts out again. I don't think he's Pallah. I think that monster made a deal with the local Min for Timka's hide and the boy's here to collect it." He pushed heavily to his feet. "Hopflea followed him out the last time. I don't like that. I've been debating whether to get Timka down here and see what she says." He straightened his back, looked round the room a last time. "I'm going to wake her; she can decide what she wants to do." He stumped off toward the stairs.

The room was almost empty; the buffet table had a plate of raw greens and some stuffed toast on a long tray, nothing like the usual spread of delicacies. A Pass-Through of the tentacled variety, indeterminate as to species or sex, was slumped bonelessly in a chair near the fire, a half consumed mug of ale on the table beside him. Another customer slouched on the far side of the hearth, his shape mostly lost to shadow. Even the noises off the street were hushed and hurried, scurrying footsteps, voice murmurs, the whistle of a freshening wind, nothing like the raucous vigorous blare of most days. Skeen listened to the wind and wondered if it was blowing north or south; between the delta marshes and Cida Fennakin there was a long stretch of the river that ran almost directly north/south through a mile wide canyon that funneled winds at any ship attempting to traverse it. Bona Fortuna grant the wind was coming out of the south, blowing Maggí to them, though that could turn into a problem if they had reasons for getting away fast. When she couldn't stand the wondering any longer, she went to the door and looked out.

The street was almost as empty as the taproom; a few bits of paper and dead leaves, a scatter of feathers and some mattress flocking scudded along the cobbles, moving south to north; she leaned against the door-jamb where she could watch the street and Angelsin both by turning her head a bit. "I've never seen the place so dead," she said, raising her voice to be heard over the whine of the wind, "What's happening?" She watched Hopflea come running along the street, head turning continually, his small body shouting excitement and apprehension; any unexpected noise and he'd be off down a sidestreet so fast he left his shadow behind. He was hugging a heavy pouch to his ribs. When he got close enough she could see a smear of drying slime on one sleeve. Goodbye, boy Min, she thought. I'd say we don't have to worry about you any more. Hopflea ducked into the alley alongside the chek and Skeen moved back inside, settled herself at her table. "What's happening?" she repeated, the snap of command in her voice.

"It's the eve of a season-change Moondark," Angelsin said, resentment harshening her vowels and biting at the consonants; Skeen almost expected the words to squeal as they slipped between those broad chisel teeth. "The first Moondark of the Dying Quarter. The Pallah are on the hilltops outside the city." The Funor woman started to relax, as if she was grateful to have something to take her mind off her own problems. "Each Pallah clan has its own hill; they stack wood higher than a house and crown the pile with the bones they save from the flesh and fish and fowl they eat between fires. They wind paper chains about the wood and stuff paper charms in the cracks between the layers." She curled her lips in a faintly contemptuous smile. "They're clever with those five stiff fingers, useful sometimes. I've hired Pallah dancers now and then and they've made paper birds and beasts for me for some extra coin to decorate the private dining rooms upstairs. They'll be spending the night out there, the Fennakin Pallah, drinking some foul concoction they call possel, dipped so hot from the possling kettles, you'd think their gullets were lined with copper. Capering the night away and coming back so draggletail they're no use for a fortn't after." She moved heavily in the chair; Skeen decided her bones were bothering her more and more and she couldn't find any comfortable position no matter how she shifted. "The Balayar now, they like their comforts too much to spend a cold night getting bit by chiggers; they've been cooking for a week now, all of them—man, woman, child. They've hired a warehouse up in North Cusp and packed everyone in it to eat and drink and do whatever else it is they do to celebrate the end of the storm season; that's what this Moondark means to them. You won't get a smell of them for at least three days. Too bad your friend is tied up here. He's missing an orgy of eating and tupping. The Aggitj? Who knows what the Aggitj are doing. Who cares. The Chalarosh—they're probably in some cellar somewhere torturing something." She spat. Skeen suppressed a shiver; Angelsin had a hate so big for the Chalarosh she didn't bother to hide it, knowing there was no way she could avoid showing what she felt. The Funor woman turned her glare on Skeen. If she saved her ultimate hate for the Chalarosh, she had a lot left over for an interfering

Pass-Through. Remind me, Skeen told herself, I should
never ever pass through here again.

Hopflea was in the chek somewhere, but he hadn't
showed his face in the taproom. Skeen went back to
standing in the doorway. The street was empty. She
sighed, and wondered if they were going to have trouble with the local Min. Domi strolled by, talking with
Ders; they threw her a wave and went on with their
untroubled patrol. She looked up. Chulji must be
downriver again. She rubbed her back against the
doorjamb, listening to the snores of the sleeper by the
fire, the soft voices of Hal and Hart as they tossed the
bones and moved the stones about.

She strolled to the bar, hitched herself onto the slab
and sat gazing thoughtfully at Angelsin, ignoring her
angry hiss. "Pallah, Balayar, Chalarosh, Aggitj," she
murmured. "What about Funor Ashon? How do Funor
celebrate the Moondark?" She raised both brows.
"Well, Adj Yagan, are you supposed to be somewhere
tonight?"

"Yes."

"Tell me about it."

"No."

SECRETS. SOME ARE WORTH A LIFE, SOME ARE SILLY, SOME ARE BOTH. THIS ONE TILMAN SANG WOULD HAVE PAID A LOT FOR; IT WOULD HAVE CLEARED UP HIS CONFUSION IF HE COULD HAVE SEEN THE FOOL BEHIND THE FACE OF THE FACEMAN. IF HE COULD HAVE KNOWN THAT THE HIDDEN FUNOR FEMALES HELD THE REAL POWER, NOT THOSE GLITTERING SWAGGERING MALES HE SAW WIELDING THAT POWER. HERE'S WHAT ANGELSIN YAGAN WOULD NOT TELL SKEEN: EVERY SEVEN YEARS (AND, TOUCHED BY MALA FORTUNA'S NOT SO BAD HAND, THE COMPANY HAD LANDED IN CIDA FENNAKIN ON A SEVENTH YEAR) THE FIRST MOONDARK OF THE YEAR'S LAST QUARTER MARKED THE TIME OF TAPPING. EVERY FEMALE FUNOR ABOVE PUBERTY RETREATED INTO PREPARED ROOMS AT THE CALL OF THE HORN, JOINING HER SISTERS IN RITES THAT INITIATED THE GIRLS WHO'D REACHED THE PROPER AGE INTO WOMANHOOD AND PERFORMING OTHER ACTS THAT SOLIDIFIED IN THEM THE SENSE OF THEIR POWER. WHAT THOSE ACTS WERE ONLY A FEMALE FUNOR KNEW AND EVEN THE OUTCASTS NEVER TOLD; IT WAS A MYSTERY, IT REMAINS ONE IN ALL THE DEEP OLD TERRIBLE SENSE. A DAY AND A HALF AFTER THEY RETREAT BEHIND LOCKED DOORS THE FEMALES BURST FORTH INTO THE HALLS OF THE UPHILL KEEPS, SHOUTING

THAT DEEP HOOMING CRY THAT FREEZES
EVERY MALE IN EVERY HOUSE. THE YOUNGEST
AND THE ELDEST LEAD THE WOMEN,
THE YOUNGEST HOLDING THE SIMMRAEL
STAFF THAT WOULD TAP THE NEW GREAT FOOL
INTO BEING, THE ELDEST WHISPERING TO
HER, DIRECTING THE CHOICE OF THE FOOL.
THE MALE THE ROD TAPPED WOULD BE THE
SECOND MOST POWERFUL FUNOR IN CIDA
FENNAKIN; HE WOULD BE THE COMMON
PROPERTY OF ALL ADULT FEMALES, SERVING
THEM IN EVERY WAY THEY REQUIRED, YET
HE WOULD HAVE AUTHORITY OVER ALL
MALES AND FEMALES BUT THE BOHANT, THE
FIRST AMONG WOMEN, THE LAWGIVER, AND
ONLY SHE COULD COUNTERMAND ANY OF
HIS ORDERS. THE GREAT FOOL WAS THE
FACEMAN, THE FORM THROUGH WHICH THE
BOHANT SPOKE TO THE OUTSIDERS IN THE
CUSPS OF LOWPORT AND THE TRADERS FROM
EVERYWHERE. HE MIGHT SERVE THE WHOLE
SEVEN YEARS OR HE MIGHT SUCCUMB TO A
FOLLY REAL RATHER THAN CEREMONIAL (THE
FOLLY OF THINKING THE POWER HE WIELDED
WAS HIS OWN, NOT SOMETHING BORROWED
FROM THE WOMEN THAT HE WOULD HAVE TO
SURRENDER TO THEM AT THE END OF HIS
TERM). MORE THAN ONCE THE WOMEN
HAD TO UNMAKE WHAT THEY HAD MADE AND
CHOOSE A SECOND FOOL TO FINISH THE
SEVEN OUT.
ANGELSIN YAGAN WAS DUE IN A HOUSE
UPHILL THIS VERY NIGHT, DUE TO ANSWER

THE CALL OF THE ELDEST OF HER HOUSE
OR BE CAST OUT. DEATH WAS THE ONLY
ACCEPTABLE EXCUSE FOR ABSENCE FROM THE
RITES AND EVEN THAT WAS SHAKY; IF THE
DEATH WAS JUDGED SUICIDE, THE BODY WAS
EXPELLED FROM THE COMMUNION AND IF
THE WOMAN WAS REBORN AT ALL, IT WAS
AS A LOW-CASTE MALE, NOT A FATE TO BE
DESIRED. ANGELSIN MUST NOT ALLOW SKEEN
AND COMPANY TO HOLD HER AWAY FROM
HER HOUSE, NOR WOULD PRIDE OR THE
OATHS SHE SWORE AT HER OWN PUBERTY
ALLOW HER TO EXPLAIN ALL THIS TO SKEEN.
HER BRAIN IS TEEMING WITH SCHEMES FOR
HER ESCAPE; SHE IS GOING TO HAVE TO
CHOOSE BETWEEN WEAKENING HERSELF,
PERHAPS FATALLY, DOWN HERE IN SOUTH
CUSP OR DESTROYING HERSELF UPHILL. OF
COURSE, SHE HAS NO REAL CHOICE; SHE
WILL BEND HER PRIDE A LITTLE, COMPLAIN OF
THE PAIN IN HER KNEES AND ASK SKEEN TO
LET HER RETREAT INTO HER OFFICE WHERE
HOPFLEA CAN PUT FOMENTATIONS ON THEM
AND EASE THE ACHE A LITTLE. SHE IS
REASONABLY SURE SKEEN WILL PERMIT THIS
THOUGH SHE IS EQUALLY SURE SKEEN WILL
KEEP A SHARP EYE ON HER. SHE IS HOPING
FOR A DEGREE OF OVERCONFIDENCE, SHE IS
HOPING THAT THE AGGITJ WILL BE LEFT
OUTSIDE THE OFFICE, SHE IS HOPING THAT
HOPFLEA HAS MANAGED TO GET HOLD OF A
NAGAMAR DAGGER DART AND HIDDEN IT ON
THE STEAM TABLE WHERE HE COOKS THE

TOWELS. ONE TINY SCRATCH FROM THE POISONED TIP OF THAT TINY DAGGER AND GOODBY SKEEN. ANGELSIN SITS AND STARES OUT THE DOOR AT THE EMPTY STREET AND RUNS HER PLAN OVER AND OVER IN HER MIND, SEEKING FOR EVERY POINT OF WEAKNESS SHE CAN VISUALIZE.

"Maybe you could convince me to let you go."

Angelsin stared at her a long minute, then looked away, saying nothing.

"If you want to be like that." Skeen slid off the bar and went back to her seat at the table. She fished in her belt pouch, pulled out the bit of wood she'd cadged off Lipitero and began working on it with her boot knife. As the hours passed, the quiet inside and out intensified and with it, Skeen's uneasiness. The sleepers by the fire woke, looked around, went out. Angelsin stopped fidgeting; she was stone now, not even her eyes moved.

Midafternoon. Domi came sauntering in with a hot meat pie in each hand; he gave Skeen one of them and settled beside her to eat his. "Chulji dropped down," he murmured, his voice so soft it almost seemed he hadn't spoken, that the movement of his mouth was due to his chewing. "Maggí's ship is about an hour away downriver."

Skeen forced herself to keep chewing steadily. It was a while before she could trust herself to speak. "He is sure it's her?" She kept her voice as soft as his. "An hour?"

"He talked to her. Less than that now."

Skeen swallowed, closed her eyes. For a moment she felt events rushing out of control and panic urging her to do something, anything, to release the tension that threatened to overwhelm her. She took a bite of the pie, chewed with careful stolidity and swallowed the mouthful before she tried to speak. "Did he tell her about this mess we're in? Give her the chance to back away?"

Domi wrapped both hands about the remnant of his pie, mischief sparking in his eyes, his whole body laughing at her.

She glared at him, wanting to throttle him, which he guessed and which amused him even more.

"She sent you a message," he murmured. "She said, 'Don't be an idiot, Skeen. Do what you have to, then get on board.' "

"Ah."

"And she says she's sorry she's a day late, but the wind turned contrary and she couldn't start up the Slot till this morning."

Skeen rubbed her hand across her mouth. "Less than an hour." She frowned down at the ring chron, then looked round at Angelsin. The Funor woman was watching them; she had to know something important was happening. Maybe it was a good thing those Funor rites were going to absorb most of her attention. Still, I have to hold the lid on till after dark, or do I? She ran her hands through her hair, shook herself as if that would settle the uncertainty in her mind. "Um . . . less than an hour, yes . . . Domi, fetch Ders and the Boy, then you go upstairs and wake everyone and see our gear gets packed." She looked over her shoulder at Hal and Hart, who'd stopped their game to watch her. "Um . . . we'd better stay here on guard, the three of us, until you get things ready . . . um . . . have a word with Chulji, tell him to warn us the moment the ship is tied up so we can clear out of here fast. Ti and me, we'll find a place to lie up until we can go after Tod's gold. We'll take that boat you and Ti decided on and follow after."

"Will do, Skeen ka, but I'll wait with you." Laughter in his eyes again, he said, "You need someone to sail the boat."

"I've done a bit of that now and then here and there."

"Here and there. Oh, sure you have, Skeen ka. How many of those boats went by wind alone?"

She wrinkled her nose. "You've got a point, my friend. Um . . . not Ders too, he's a lovely boy but . . . um . . . fidgety."

"And I'd rather have him safe away from here. Yes. And you'll have to sit on Hal a bit. He'll want to be the one, he'll never admit I'm better than him with boats."

"I hear. Stop by Hal and give them the news. And be careful, Domi; I've seen too many folk get killed a hair before they're safe. They relax too soon."

"Yes." He got to his feet, set the pie end on the table. A glance at Angelsin, a shudder, then he said, "She scares the stiffening out of my bones; I won't feel good again until we're out of the reach of her horns."

Shadow crept toward the door. Angelsin began shifting position again, grunting, opening and shutting her hands. At first Skeen thought it was jumpiness like her own nervous fidgets, but as the show went on she began to wonder whether it was pain or plot. Though the grunts and grimaces got on her nerves, she ignored them and continued chipping at her block of wood.

After a half hour of this with no reaction from Skeen, Angelsin gave up. "Pass-Through," she called out, a whine of pain in her voice, "I need to retire into my office to apply fomentations to my knees. If you'd call Hopflea to me, I think he must be in the kitchen."

Skeen swung around, beckoned to Hal. When he reached her, she said, "Take a look outside and see if Chulji's somewhere about. If he is, I'd like to talk to him."

Hal nodded and marched out. Hart sat at the table fingering the gamepieces, his eyes shifting from Angelsin to Skeen.

Angelsin clutched at the chair arms, her breath coming in hoarse pants as she fought to retain control of the rage in her. She'd slashed her pride raw to maneuver Skeen into what could have developed into a trap with a little luck. Now it seemed that scarifying exercise was useless.

Skeen sat with her hands clasped in front of her, watching the shift of Angelsin's features, wondering how far she could push the Funor before the situation turned irretrievable. Not much farther, from the look of her. Yes, yes, calm down, woman, Djabo! "Give me a minute, Adj Yagan. A little patience and," she watched the door but slipped quick glances at Angelsin who had slid into a steady-state simmer, "we can ease apart, both sides still whole." She kept talking in that vein, her voice quiet, soothing, but not so soothing Angelsin could mistake care for condescension.

Hal came back with Chulji-Skirrik tick-tocking along behind him.

Skeen leaned forward, whispered, "It's getting late. Where's the ship?"

Chulji clicked his mouthparts; his antennas shivered. "My mistake, Skeen. I forgot about the current in the river. She took longer than I thought to make the distance. She's tying up now."

Skeen sighed, gripped the edge of the table, fighting against the effect of the sudden rush of relief. She pushed the chair back and stood up. "Hal, get the others down here; make sure they've cleaned out the rooms, we don't want to leave anything behind." She glanced at Angelsin, then at the door. "I'll keep the lid on until you're all out. Take Hart up with you. Chul, flit over to the ship, tell our friend we're on our way."

Angelsin was panting again, her face working. She wanted to throw Skeen onto the floor and dance on her bones. Yes, she wanted to hook those horns into her flesh and worry them about; Skeen didn't have to mindread to know all that. She waited, tense and wary, to see what the Funor would do. If she had to, she'd lay Angelsin out right there, but she'd prefer to keep the precarious peace intact; this wasn't her homeplace but she had no wish to bring down a power struggle on it.

Angelsin sucked in a long breath, snorted it out as she gripped the chair arms harder, the muscles defining themselves in her arms when she put pressure on her hands. She grunted onto her feet and got down from the chair. Ignoring Skeen she circled to the door at the end of the bar and pulled a bulky key from her pocket.

Skeen moved closer, stopped just beyond the reach of the massive arms that had given Timka such a bad time. As Angelsin pulled the key from the lock and started to push the door open, Skeen said softly, "Move slow, my friend. Try shutting that door in my face and I'll put you out so fast and hard you won't move for a sennight."

Angelsin stiffened; her broadfingers twitched, her slimfinger coiled into a knot. Saying nothing, she pushed the door wide and walked with difficulty toward her masterchair. She grasped the arms, muscled herself up and around, dropped heavily onto the seat. Skeen pulled the door shut, moved a few steps into the room.

"Call Hopflea," she said. "I want him where I can see him."

Angelsin smoothed her hands over her thighs. "You'll have to fetch him."

"No, I don't think so. You have a way to reach him from here; don't try to tell me you don't."

"What you think doesn't change what is. Do what you will, I can't call him." She blinked slowly, stubby white lashes glinting. "Send the barman."

Skeen frowned at her. Sounds logical, but I'd have to go out and leave you here alone; I don't think so. She moved closer, circled round the chair, looking it over as minutely as she could while staying beyond the woman's reach. She came round again, scanned Angelsin's face. The Funor had decided to be stubborn about this minor point. Well, so be it. One last thing. "How soon do you have to leave to be in time to make your duty uphill?"

Angelsin pressed her lips together. Her hands opened and closed, opened and closed. Nothing she could do about the situation as long as Skeen kept away from her; the ache in her bones that slowed her to a crawl denied her that satisfaction.

"Look, Adj Yagan," Skeen tried to cram all the reasonableness she could into her voice, "I'm going out of my way for you. It's a long, long story why—so don't ask. Tell me. Sundown, moonrise, midnight, what?"

A sharp jerk of the big head, the ivorine horns jabbing, then Angelsin sighed, snapped out a single word. "Midnight."

Skeen risked a glance at her ring chron; sixth hour from noon. If she put a single dart into the woman, Angelsin would wake with at least an hour clear. "See you never," she murmured and touched the trigger sensor.

She slipped from the office, pulled the door shut, locked it with the key she'd taken from Angelsin's pocket. Domi and Timka were waiting for her "They are cleared out?"

"On their way." Timka flicked fingers at the door. "The Yagan?"

"Out of it. Domi, stand watch here; Ti, come with me, we've got to find Hopflea."

Moondark. Scuds of clouds obscured most of the stars, hanging low enough to be stained with pallid reds and golds from the bonefires burning in a ragged arc to the south of Fennakin. The streets were empty and silent except for the dank wind that wasn't especially cold but nonetheless bit to the bone. Timka-owl flew over the roofs, crossing and recrossing Skeen's path, a dark silent shadow lost in the fog beginning to thicken the already stygian air.

Skeen swung along covering ground without seem-
ing to hurry, her senses at their widest outreach, though
she kept her body relaxed and seldom looked behind
her. The matte-black eddersil tunic and trousers absorbed what little light there was and with her black
boots and black gloves and near black hair and leaving
aside her pale face, she was close to invisible; a long
black knit scarf was wrapped about her neck and over the
lower part of her face, its presence amply justified by
the temperature of the ambient air. She carried a large
leather bag, one gloved hand holding it against her
side, the shoulder strap taking most of its weight.
Several times she met other Cuspers out on nocturnal
errands (she suspected these were similar to her own),
passing them without interference or interfering.

When she was within a few minutes of Tod's House,
she moved off the Skak and plunged into the maze of
narrow winding alleys and byways no wider than a
deerpath through thick brush. Here near the river the
fog was denser. She slowed, groped along, one hand
brushing the walls of the warehouses and shuttered
shops that backed onto these smelly lanes, stopped
now and again to run over once more the route she
and Timka had laid out in their planning sessions, to
check on touchmarks. A brick wall, the bricks in an
intricate pattern of verticals and horizontals. A plank
with a hole in it half the size of Skeen's fist shaped like
a pointed oval. A rickety fence of scavenged lumber.
A dump of fish offal that never seemed to get larger
or smaller; no need to touch that, it announced its
presence a dozen meters away. And so on. Past shuttered windows and blank walls. No one about, not
even a drunken derelict sleeping in a sheltered corner.
Grope along and hope to get it right. She let herself
sigh with relief when she saw the fuzzy reddish glow of
the torches on Tod's watchtowers. Another interval of
groping, mercifully brief, and she was standing in the
mouth of a narrow alley looking across a broad cleared
stretch at the tatty whitewashed walls that shut in

Nochsyon Tod's house and business. She took the
darter from its holster, unsnapped the lanyard from
the loop in its butt and drew the ring across the stone
wall at her side making a small grating sound. She
repeated that twice more, then stood waiting.

Ti-owl dropped out of the fog, flew low over her
head, swept up, circled and came round again. Skeen
held out the darter. With a powerful delicacy the owl's
talons closed on it and lifted it from her hand, then the
bird powered up until it was an indistinct blur in the
fog.

By straining her eyes and knowing where it was
going, Skeen could follow the blur to the tower. It
hovered a moment outside one of the high narrow
unglazed windows, then drifted on out of sight around
the bulk of the tower. She waited, tense, until the dark
blotch appeared again and settled gently onto the wall
where it shifted into a larger different shape and vanished into the tunnel walkway where the wall met the
tower.

Skeen pulled up her tunic, unwrapped from around
her waist a length of light rope knotted at intervals for
quick climbing, an iron claw tied on one end, the
metal warm where it had rested against her skin; she
stripped the leather pads off the claws and dropped
them into the lootbag, smoothed her tunic down, re-
settled the shoulder strap and waited.

A long shape eased out of the walkway and stood a
moment at the wall's edge. Skeen held her breath, but
there was no alarm. Timka was having trouble managing the darter; she went squat and broad into the owl
shape, left the weapon lying on the wall and launched
herself into the air; she swung round the watchtower,
swept down, snatched up the darter and flew off, the
fog closing about her as she moved deeper into the
slaver's hold.

An eternity later the owl swooped down, hooted a
warning and dropped the darter into Skeen's reaching
hands. It landed in the alley mouth and shifted.

Shivering as the cold air hit her bare skin, Timka
grinned at Skeen as the Pass-Through dug into the
lootbag and found the fur cloak they'd lifted off
Angelsin. Timka wrapped it round her and sighed with
relief. She kicked the end under her to get her feet off
the damp icy cobbles and managed to stop shivering.

"Well?"

Timka's grin widened. "So easy it was almost shame-
ful. The wallguard and the towerwatch were wrapped
in blankets snoring by a brazier; they'd split a jug of
homebrew between them and wouldn't have noticed
anything if I'd stepped on them. I put a couple of darts
in each just to make sure and went for the pen tower.
There was just one there, a Pallah with a royally juicy
head cold; I was doing him a favor putting him out of
his misery for a while." She pulled the cloak tighter
about her. "And I took a last swing around the grounds,
the housetowers were empty like always, the woffits
are out and prowling like always; maybe a handler
somewhere about, but I didn't see anyone. I still think
I should go in with you; if there are surprises anywhere it'll be in the house."

"I thought we settled that a week ago. Inside's my
job; I don't want anyone but myself to worry about.
You keep the guards off my back and make sure I
have a way out if I run into trouble I can't handle."
She slid her arm through the coil of rope and moved
off, heading for that section of wall where she'd decided to go over.

Skeen whipped the claw loose, pulled the rope
through her hands and caught the grapple before it hit
the hard-packed earth. She looped the rope and thrust
her arm through the coils, then ghosted along the wall
to the narrow end of the slave pen.

Though she had planned this for days, though she
had done this sort of prowl a thousand times before in
circumstances far more demanding, she was nervous
as a ferg in a high wind; this was so easy it was actually

frightening, she felt as if she were being pushed into something before she was ready. As she moved along the pen, she decided the feeling came mostly because she wasn't used to depending so much on others; Timka had done all the scouting and a lot of the planning, Angelsin and Maggí had determined the timing. She didn't like this. No, not at all. She turned the corner of the pen and moved along it, fingertips slipping along the stone.

The walls of the slave pen were thick and there were no windows in them, but she felt vast groans issuing from the stone, groans impressed into it by decades of misery. Not much rage. Those who spent their days and nights in there had long ago exhausted their capacity for anger.

Her fingers slid off the stone. An arched opening. She hesitated, moved into it. A door. Built from massive planks held together with iron straps and studs. She explored the lock. The opening was large enough to admit a forefinger to the last joint. I haven't time for this. Djabo's throb, I've got things to do. She knelt by the lock, took out the sturdiest of her picks and began working; throwing the wards took more strength than skill, the lock was disengaged a few breaths after she began. She got to her feet, scowled at the door. Inside locks. No. After I clean up the strongroom. She smiled at the thought of Tod waking to find his gold gone and a good part of his slave shipment. Yes. That's good.

The claw bit into the inner wall with a satisfying chunk-unk. She waited a few breaths to see if the noise had alerted anyone, froze as she heard a coughing bark, but it was some distance off, muffled by the intervening greenery. She looked up. Ti-owl dipped a wing, signaling all-clear. She went up and over the wall in a swift silent glide and found herself in an open-air scullery. Sinks and buckets, brooms and mops, sponges and pumice stones scattered about, dropped when the staff was done with them. The pavingstones

were clean enough and there was little smell, well,
that was easy enough to explain; you can't confine a
stink and it meant trouble if a wandering stench reached
the master's nose. She walked warily through the clut-
ter and stopped before a well-worn door, the wood
splintering, disintegrating from dry rot. She pulled on
the latch. With a small click it moved down and the
door swung open, pressing against her hand, catching
her off guard; she nearly stepped into a bucket, caught
herself before she clattered like a rank amateur. Eh,
Skeen, get serious. Want to or not, you've got to go in
there. Settle down, or you'll get yourself scragged and
wouldn't that be a shame. She eased the door open
enough to slip through into the kitchen and pulled it
shut behind her, tugging on the latch until she heard it
clunk home. Well, old Tod, maybe this will be a
lesson to you. Check your arrangements at least once
a purple moon and you'll save yourself nasty surprises.
    The darkness in the kitchen was stiff with smells;
bread was rising somewhere, the yeasty odor dominant over damp stone and old food and ash from the
banked fires; a kettle of soup simmered in a warming
hole, adding warmth and a rich meaty aroma to the
mix. Skeen sniffed and sighed with pleasure, then
shook herself. Eh, old girl, you're sliding again. Business, business, do get on with it. She dipped out
several pinlights, attached them to her sleeves and
powered them up, then moved quickly across the kitchen
and passed into the servants' refectory and workroom.
The furniture there was made of some tight-grained
wood, knocked together by someone with little taste
and less skill but it had a certain charm in its utilitarian
simplicity and the wood was heavy, polished by long
use into a mottled smoothness that took the light like
tortoiseshell. She touched the table with appreciative
fingers, remembering all too well the synths that fur-
nished her uncle's house, gaudy, tawdry pseudo-
elegance; she gave the table a final tap and moved on
to the door that led into the main part of the house.

No latch or anything this side, nothing but a hexagonal iron boss about chest high. She flattened her hands on the wood and pushed gently. About half a centimeter's give, then the door bumped against an obstruction. Bar. Right. Wouldn't want lovey's sleep disturbed. She slipped the cutter from its nest, shorted the beam to three cm and took out a plug; the beam seared the green wood as it cut and there was the smell of hot resin. Skeen sniffed, wondered if the woffits might smell that and gather round. She listened but heard nothing, then held a pinlight close to the hole. Not quite through. She cut a bit deeper, checked again, pursed her lips in a silent satisfied whistle. She readjusted the beam, swept a smooth arc across the door, cutting a slot a finger wide in the heavy tight-grained wood. More stink. New door, well, he's not completely hopeless; he takes good care of his fine pink skin. She switched the cutter for a tap awl, screwed it into the wood of the bar; silent whistle going again, beginning to feel like she was really working, she raised the bar to the vertical and started to push the door open. No, no, Skeen. We listen again, don't get sloppy. She gripped the awl's handle to hold the door shut, set her ear to the slot.

Nothing. Nothing. She started to straighten, froze. Click-scratch of claws on hardwood. A woffit. Moving closer. Only one. Skeen held her breath and thought: *moonlight playing on gently moving lake water.* Click-scratch, brisk, steady as a metronome, coming at a trot. *A wandering breeze ruffling the water, the plop of fish leaping. Butterflies circling in sunlight over the sand.* The trot slowed, the tock of the claws grew confused. The sound of panting, a soft whine. The door moved slightly as the woffit scratched at it. *Flowers swaying like dancers, soft bright green grass rippling like lakewater.* No other sounds but the whines and the scratching; the woffit was alone. *Woffits curled sleeping in the sun, intricately intertwined brown and gray fur.* The tocking of the nail clicks speeded up,

steadied, moved away. Skeen listened until she couldn't
hear the sound any longer; around her there was only
silence that was made yet more silent by the nearly
subliminal creaks and groans of the resting house. She
unscrewed the tap awl and tucked it away, pushed the
door open and stepped into a long, bare hallway. The
pinlights showed her rough plaster walls, a pale splintery wood floor with a narrow hessian drugget down
the middle. Right. Now we begin.

Down the hall, following Timka's instructions. Djabo
whip her with wet noodles for being so miserably good
at this business. A right-angle turn, the drugget changing to a thick soft carpet that glowed mulberry red in
the pinlight beams. She stopped a step away from the
heavy lined hanging that was drawn across the end of
the hallway. What Timka said, draperies all over the
place, hardly a wall without its hanging. Cuts the
drafts, she said. Tod's got this thing for covering walls
and doorways, she said, with fancy work that probably
blinded generations of weavers and embroiderers. A
yellowish unsteady glow crept under the bottom of the
drape. Skeen tapped off the pinlights and pushed an
edge of the hanging aside.

A few night candles in wall sconces, burning in tall
glass cylinders, shed only enough light to thicken shifting shadows into impenetrability. The Great Hall
looked, smelled, felt empty. Skeen waited several
breaths longer, then slid into the room. She drifted
along the walls, avoiding the light patches about the
candles, dipped into the shadow under the balcony,
reached the black arras without stirring up any guards—
either four-legged or two. She glided along the hanging, stopped outside the arch and listened again.

What she heard and felt was a stifled stillness. According to Timka, it was a much smaller, odd-shaped
room, ceiling half the height of the Hall so it was hard
to judge the difference in the feels. She frowned,
tapped the pinlights back into service, edged the arras
aside.

A weak red glow from the cylindrical fire basin, reflected down at the floor by the polished smoke funnel; a slight draft slipped past her, moving from the Hall into the sitting room, stirring the air. She could smell the smoky musky odor of woffit, hot ash, stale brandy fumes, the cold food she saw congealed on plates left sitting on the edge of the fire basin. She unfastened the holster flap, tucked it behind her belt, made certain the lanyard was securely clipped to the butt ring on the darter, then she shouldered the arras aside and stepped into the room.

Three paces in she stopped and darted the pinlight beams about. The fire basin. The two long chairs Timka mentioned, a few cushions and backed benches scattered about, nothing more. Across the room she saw the dark blotch that was the hanging Tod used to conceal his strongroom door. She started for it, moved past the long chairs—

A weight landed on her, driving her off her feet, a meaty arm slapped round her neck, squeezing, studded leather straps and hard round breasts pushing against her back. A curse in a hoarse contralto as she hit the floor and her attacker's elbow banged against the wood. Quick shift of large strong hands. She saw black spots swimming behind her eyelids. The breath had been knocked out of her, she was strangling, going out fast. Heavy thighs squeezed her, meaty buttocks bounced on hers, waves of stale sweat, woffit musk and oiled leather rolled over her. She grabbed at the woman's hands, found the little fingers and twisted. Hard. The woman howled, yanked loose, slammed an elbow into the back of Skeen's head, driving her face into the floor. Skeen locked her jaw against the pain and bucked wildly, trying to dislodge her rider before she could use that elbow again or get another grip on her throat. Woffits were growling and snarling around her, tearing at her; she kept her hands clear and ignored them, trusting boots and eddersil to keep their teeth out of her until she could deal with them. The

darter jolted out of the holster, bounced against the
floor as the lanyard jerked it about. Still humping,
twisting, scrambling, Skeen flailed about for the lanyard. Woffit teeth slashed along her hand, nearly tore
her thumb off. Their handler was slamming her fists
into Skeen's neck and shoulders, squealing with pain
and belting out broken curses. Skeen got her mangled
hand about the darter's butt, twisted it round until it
was pointing over her shoulder, went suddenly limp
and touched the sensor. And touched it. And touched
it, swaying the darter back and forth only by luck
missing her own head.

The cursing broke off, she heard a half-cough, then
a ton of dead weight fell onto her shoulders, pinning
her to the floor. Using her legs to power her, she drove
her body into a twisting scramble and dumped the
handler off her back. Growling, Djabo bless, but not
barking or howling, the woffits flung themselves at
her. She spun about, leaped onto one of the benches,
spun again, kicking out at them while she clumsily
switched to sprayshot and spat darts in a wide circle
about her at images her pinlights picked out for her.
Hating eyes that flared red as the beams sliced across
them, snarling mouths with dripping yellow saber teeth,
lean gray-brown sides working like bellows, whimpy ragged tails straight and stiff behind powerful hind legs—
ghostly feral forms leaping, curvetting, catching and
rejecting the light in a frightening dance of death.
Round and round she spun, spraying darts at them,
kicking at them when they leaped too close. Round
and round until the darter hissed, clicked, the reservoir empty.

Chest heaving, she lowered the weapon. In a silence
that seemed somehow more threatening than the noises
a moment before, she lowered herself warily from the
chair and picked her way through the comatose woffits
to stand over their handler, gazing down at her. A
Pass-Through, not one of the Wavers. She didn't recognize the species. Square body, mammalian to the ex-

tent of having breasts, each mound equipped with
three fingerlength nipples, brawny arms, thin legs,
broad flat feet. Round ball of a head, flat features
squeezed into a ludicrously small area, leathery pointed
ears, large and mobile as a bird's wings, toothless
mouth pursed into an eternal pout. Dark droplets fell
on the woman's skin. Skeen blinked, tried lifting her
torn hand and was startled to realize how weak she
was getting. The adrenalin high receding, she grimaced
at the pain in her hand and a number of other places,
fumbled for the darter and made a tourniquet of sorts
from the lanyard. She was dizzy, not thinking too
clearly, though it struck her as strange no one had
heard the noise they'd made; at the moment it seemed
to her the fight'd been noisy enough to wake the dead.
The dangling darter knocked against her thigh. Empty.
Got to fill the reservoir. She stumbled across the room
to the archway and pushed past the arras into the
Great Hall; moving seemed to help, at least it cleared
some of the fuzz out of her head. Kitchen. Water
there. She looked at the blood still oozing from her
hand; the flow had lessened considerably thanks to the
lanyard's pressure. Clean dishtowels. Yes.

She forced herself to move quickly across the Hall,
down the corridor and into the kitchen. Dimly she
remembered the woffit that had nosed at the door, but
there was no sign of him. Possibly he was one of those
stretched out in the sitting room.

Without bothering with neatness or too much quiet,
she pulled open cabinets and drawers until she found a
stack of cloths, old, stained, but clean and worn soft
with much usage. With the help of her boot knife, she
tore several of them into long strips, folded another
into a pad and made a crude bandage for her hand,
pulling knots tight with her teeth and her other hand.
Every moment made the pain more insistent but she
ignored it as she refilled the reservoir with water from
a large crock sitting in a corner away from the ovens.
Dizzy, half-fainting, she leaned against a worktable

and tried to think. Apparently the fight hadn't been as
noisy as she'd thought; otherwise there'd be guards
pouring in by now. She looked at the hand. No way
I'm going to be climbing ropes with this. Well, a bit of
luck—eh, Bona Fortuna, you're overdue this night,
what about dropping in for a visit, just a look-see,
well?—I can get through the gates. She thought about
the slave pens and nodded. No way am I going out
without finishing there. She smiled at the thought of
Tod's consternation and the pain retreated before her
pleasure. Or mixed with it? Djabo, am I going to be
inviting this kind of nonsense from now on? Ah ai, I
need to have a long talk with Picarefy. She's sorted me
out before. . . . Another sort of pain, a loss like a rip
down her heart. Picarefy—ah, I can't believe . . . he
must have tricked you somehow. She shook off the
ugly thought and straightened. Get to work, Skeen.
Timka is going to be throwing triple fits if I don't get
out of here fairly soon.

Dragging down on the hanging so the rings wouldn't
rattle on the rod, Skeen pulled it clear of the iron
door. She took out her cutter and sliced through the
lock's tongue; inelegant and humiliating to be so crude
about such a silly lock, but she hadn't the time or
energy or dexterity now to tickle the lock open and
pander to her pride in her work. She tugged the door
open and stepped in.

The pinbeams flickering about showed her shelves
from floor to ceiling, a chest at the far end. She fished
out a stickum from her kit, clicked it onto the wall
near the door and touched it on.

Boxes on boxes, undecorated simple forms all made
of wood rubbed to a high gloss—some flat like jewelry
cases, some standing higher like miniature chests—they
filled many of the shelves. Bibelots, glittering, gleaming, filled with sliding glows—gold, silver, bronze, shell,
crystal, grown work from the Skirriks. Several swords
and some knives. Rolls of canvas, probably more wall

hangings, ones he only put out for special occasions. All of it made her tingle with wanting, but most was too delicate, too complex or too heavy to take along. She moved to the chest. Another lock. She squatted beside it, knocked her wounded hand as she lowered herself. For several breaths she clutched at the chest with her good hand, cradled the other on her thighs and wept with pain, shock, dizziness.

The worst of the shock passed off; she pulled herself together and cut through the lock. Grunting with the effort, she pushed the lid up and looked inside. She smiled. The cavity was filled with small canvas bags, tied neatly at the neck with heavy cord, the knots sealed with red wax, a sigil stamped into the wax. She sliced one open and dumped out hexagonal gold coins, the Lesket Perpao mintage that wide-ranging Balayar traders had turned into something like universal exchange counters. She gathered them up and dumped them into the lootbag. One by one she opened the bags (not trusting Tod in any way, she needed to be sure she knew exactly what she had) and dumped the gold after the first coins. When the lootbag was three-quarters filled and about at the limit of her ability to haul it around, especially now when her strength was so depleted, she shut the chest and got unsteadily to her feet. Her knees went watery and she collapsed onto the lid. Djabo's weepy eyes! Come on, Skeen, so you've got a bad hand and a throat so sore suffocating would be a pleasure, you've been through worse. Lost a little blood, so what. She passed her good hand across her face, surprised herself with a jaw-straining yawn. Oh fuck, it's stimtab time, you know it, woman, you just don't want to admit it. Willpower won't do it, that's obvious by now. So you pay for it later. Later's when you've got the time. She dug out a stimtab, glared resentfully at the small gray-brown pill, tossed it to the back of her throat and swallowed it; she sat for several breaths waiting for the pill to act, then got to her feet and began inspecting the contents of the

boxes. Jewelry. Some was fairly standard, diamonds
and gold, fussy stuff; that she discarded without bothering to evaluate it; its weight wasn't worth what it'd bring
on the far side, too much floating about just like it. In
one large flat box she found a massive gold chain, odd
dullish stones set in every third link; each of the
ungemmed links was engraved with a fantastically con-
voluted line, many of the details too small to make
out, even when she moved a pinlight close and scanned
the shadows. She clicked the lid shut and tucked the
box into the lootbag. The bag's flap couldn't be buckled down over it but she ignored that and went on
searching. Another box held triangles of jet, Skirrik
work; someone had killed an old male and pried loose
his jet inlays. Each piece was intricately carved, low
relief, semi-abstract plant forms. They felt warm, vi-
brant, as if the life of the old Skirrik had passed into
them. She closed the lid, hesitated, but put the box
into the bag. They were lovely things and she knew a
buyer who'd salivate over them. Very tempting to take
them and keep quiet about it, but the one rule she
never broke was don't hit on your friends; in spite of
the compromises life forced on you, real friends were
rare and to be cherished. And you had to live with
yourself. The Skirrik hadn't harmed her; no, they'd
gone out of their way to help her; besides, she liked
Chulji, he was a good kid. Bona Fortuna/Mala Fortuna,
she wasn't leaving this with Tod the Creep. Chulji
could have it and do what he wanted with it. She
opened one of the thicker boxes and stopped breathing for a minute. Ancient Min work, drawn silver
brooches and rings set with ovals of crystallized resin
that glowed blue then green then purple and released a
subtle scent when she warmed it with her hand.
Sweetamber. She recognized it for she'd got a tiny
flawed piece of sweetamber set in a stab pin of a ring
brooch as part of her pay for extracting Timka from
Dum Besar and the Poet's bed. Feeling a little light-
headed, she grinned down at the treasure in the box

and made the warding circle, a tribute to Bona Fortuna
and an attempt to chase away the bad vibes that sniffed
about her gifts. She clicked the lid down and shoved
the box into the bag. Mala takes, Bona gives—almost
like it was a payment for sticking to principle and giving
up thief's right to the jet. She looked around at the
unopened boxes, sighed. The bag was full and there
was some question about whether she was going to be
able to haul it out. It was heavy, yes, heavy was the
definitive word. She sat on the chest, got her unin-
jured arm through the strap and heaved. With considerable effort she got the strap over her shoulder and
managed to stand. She giggled; there was a pronounced
list to the left. She collected the stickum, clicked it off
and put it away. Forcing her bandaged hand to work,
she got out the darter and held it along her thigh.
Anything that came at her she'd have to deal with at a
distance. Not much fight left in this poor old body.

She glanced at the woffits and the handler as she
went past. The darts would hold them for two, three
hours more. Probably. Anyway, long enough for Domi
to get us well away from Cida Fennakin. She pushed
past the arras and cut across the Great Hall, moving as
steadily and quickly as she could; already the strap
was biting into her shoulder and every time the bag
tapped into her hip, it jarred her whole body, starting
new waves of pain out from her wounds and bruises. It
offended her sense of herself to be so slapdash; ordinarily she would have closed and locked the strongroom
door, drawn the curtain over it; ordinarily she would
have taken time to close and rebar the refectory door,
but she couldn't spare the energy or the time; she
slipped out the kitchen door and stepped into a thick
swirling fog, couldn't even see her own feet. She crossed
to the wall and the door that led from the private
quarters into the guards' quadrangle. It was barred on
this side, but it had no lock. She slid the bar out of its
hooks and pushed cautiously at the door.

For all her care, the hinges squealed; she stopped

being careful, shoved the door open and ran through, counting on the fog and the darkness to conceal her; the only concession to caution she made was to stay close to the midwall where the shadow was thickest until she reached the watchtower by the slave pens; Timka had reported that the guards passed into the auction section through the tower, matched doors standing open during the day. Skeen sliced her way past both locks and stood trembling in the corner where the tower met the pen.

She slipped the loot bag off her shoulder, worked arm and shoulder to get some feeling back in it; she was faintly sick and wholly drained; she leaned against the pen wall and wondered how she was going to get going again. She touched the bag with her toe. I should really get the hell out and not bother with fancy flourishes. That's the sensible thing to do; those gits in there probably wouldn't thank her for interfering. No doubt they'd be a lot worse off it they were turned loose—starve to death or freeze. Trouble was, none of that changed her determination to cut them loose and goose them out of their security chains; she was doing it for that angry hurting child that lived somewhere down in her gut, she was doing it because she wanted to kick Tod where it hurt, she was doing it because . . . fuck all that, she didn't care why, she just knew it was something she had to do.

Faint susurrous, flutter of air across her face, Ti-owl landing in front of her, shifting to Pallah. "You all right, Skeen?" Timka moved closer, sucked in a breath as she caught sight of the bandages, a small sharp sound that made Skeen wince. "I knew I should. . . ."

Skeen cut her off with a quick irritable wave of her good hand. "I'm fine, Ti. Don't fuss." She spoke in a low mutter that made Timka lean closer so she could hear. "I made some noise coming out. You notice anything, anyone stirring?"

"No. I heard woffits howling a while back, but things have been quiet since."

Skeen rubbed at her throat. "Must have been when I put their handler out."

Timka sniffed. "Looks like he nearly put you out."

"She . . . what am I doing arguing gender? Ti. . . ." She straightened, swayed, flattened her good hand against the wall to keep from falling over. "Shit, I'm weak as a five-minute cub. Ti, the wickets in the gates over there, get them open, will you? I know they're locked, here." She fished out the cutter, gave it to Timka, showed her how to operate it. "Bring that back here when you're finished."

Timka came swimming from the fog, held out the cutter. "Open." She shivered. "Miserable night. I'm going to put on some fur."

"Wait." Skeen bent over, biting back a groan, lifted the bag. "Take this out first, put it somewhere you can keep an eye on it; better wrap Angelsin's cloak around it. I don't want her tied into this, she's too close to us. I'll be along in a minute or so."

"What? Let's get out of here now, there's nothing more we can do."

"Scat. I'm going to turn the slaves loose. No, don't argue, waste of time." Skeen started walking away along the wall, moving toward the entrance she'd unlocked at the beginning of this bungled business. She smiled as she heard Timka sputtering, then a sigh, a scrape of feet as the little Min accepted the inevitable.

Skeen's head swam; chills were beginning to travel along her bones. Fuckin' woffits, filthy mouths. I should do something about this; she fumbled at her belt, leaned against the wall, closed her eyes. Got to get through this first, yes, I'll worry about my hand soon as I have some real time to deal with it. She pushed away from the wall, tugged the door open and stepped into a broad, bare, very clean, lamplit corridor. Very little stench; that surprised her. No, no, old girl, you're thinking of contract labor depots, there it doesn't mat-

ter what the carks look like as long as they can stand
up and move the proper fingers or other appendages.
This world might be primitive, but don't go thinking
the folk here are stupid; they know healthy livestock
when they see it and clip the price otherwise. Wrought
iron lamps hung from black chains attached to a heavy
iron grating high overhead Smell of heat, burning oil.
Doors marched down both sides of the corridor, planks
bound with black iron, square air holes high up in
each door with their own smaller grates.

Skeen swung along the corridor trying to ignore the
various ills that elbowed about under her skin. The
stim tab was working hard. She was jittery and in
between the shakes got jabs of energy that unfortu-
nately ran out of her almost immediately. Like I got a
hole in my heel. Body's leaking, that's what it is.
Yeah, for sure, got a leak somewhere. Leak in my
hand, oh shit, it hurts. Forget it, Skeen; think about
Tod's face tomorrow when reports start coming at him
from all over. She stopped before the last door on the
right, sliced the cutter beam through the bolt and
tugged it open.

Skeen, Skeen, get your head together; she'd expected to find slaves chained hand and foot and laid
out on cold bare stone. Remember, this is prime stock,
meant to bring in the gold Nochsyn Tod loved to
fondle. She shivered as icy cold air slipped past her.

Seven Aggitj extras stretched out on clean straw
spread on shelf cots a good meter off the floor. The
floor was another grating, like animal cages she'd seen,
meant to let wastes drop below. That was where the
cold air came from; she could hear the muted sound
of water flowing down under it, how delightfully hygienic.

The boys were sitting up, the one on the cot nearest
the door smoothed down his kilt, then passed his
hands over his silvery not-hair. He blinked at her.
"Who?" The word was heavily accented, almost garbled.

Skeen felt a chill sinking that had nothing to do with
the wind that slid around her. Maggí said lots of

Backlanders never got near Min or otherWavers and
had at most a few words of Trade-Min; Djabo's nimble tongue, what if she couldn't talk to him. Her jaw
started quivering as much from tension as cold. "B-Bona
Fortuna," she stammered. Her lips felt stiff, hard to
control. "Come to k-kiss your hand. Lifefire, Aggitj,
who the hell could I be, looking like this coming this
time o' the night?" Running off my mouth like this,
she added to herself and shut her teeth on the flood of
comment gathering down her throat. Djabo bless, look
at the boy grin, I think he's got it, at least he's not ear
to ear ivory.

'Unfriend to Tod?' Again the words were fractured
by his accent, but she could understand them; that was
all that counted.

"You might say that." She swayed. In spite of the
heroic efforts of the stimtab she was beginning to fade
in and out, better get done with this. "Listen," she
said, "I'm going back along this hall here and I'm
going to slice open all the locks. Then I'm going out
the gate, the one they maybe brought you in through."
She straightened her shoulders, tried to chase the fuzz
from her head. There were things she had to say; in
her mind, somehow, these slaves had turned into an
omen of her own success or failure. If they won loose
and stayed loose, maybe so could she and there'd be
some simple happy explanation for Tibo running off
with Picarefy and leaving her stranded; Djabo's kinks,
this is ridiculous—no meaning, no omen, no whatever.
She forced herself out of that muddle and came close
to snarling when she saw the concern on the young
Aggitj's face. "You'll be clear, you Aggitj, once you
make the local Slukra. From what I hear even the
Funor don't mess with it." She closed her eyes, swallowed, propped herself against the jamb. "The others,
tell 'em . . . tell 'em to keep low and get the hell out of
here, don't wait around for Funor guards to come
looking for them. Y'unnerstan? Good. Good. Best
way's south along the river. North you got farms, they'll

turn in runaways there. South's best long as you stay
away from the mines." She yawned, a jaw-cracker that
sent her sagging against the jamb.

The Aggitj nodded.

"Um . . . one thing more, do me a favor, huh? Wait
a tick or two before you come out. Lemme finish with
the locks." She rasped her tongue over dry lips. "'N
keep back. Follow me close 'n I get nervous, might do
something, you catch?"

"I hear you, Bona kai Fortuna." He swept her a
graceful bow.

"Aggitj," she muttered and started off. Because she
didn't bother opening the other doors, the job was
done in a few minutes; she went out the entrance, a
murmur of voices getting gradually louder behind her.
She hesitated before leaving the shelter of the en-
tranceway, but there was little to see and less to hear.
Shudders passed in waves along her body while her
hand was so hot she feared the bandage would start
smoldering. Fuckin' fine fever, she told herself and
giggled at the alliteration.

A shadow in the fog, coming at her. She fumbled
for the darter.

"Skeen." A murmur soft as the pulse beating in her
ears; she slumped, her knees went liquid, she cursed
under her breath (which seemed to help a little). A
small hand closed around her arm. She heard a soft
gasp as Timka felt the heat in her.

"You finally ready to go?" There was more than a
touch of acerbity in Timka's voice.

"Ready. Ready." She grimaced, forced herself to
take one step, another, another. The hand left her
arm and the shape beside her changed, a cat-weasel
padded beside her, long and lithe and lethal. And
voiceless, something she was happy about, she wasn't
interested in hearing Timka's views on her shortcom-
ings. She pulled the wicket open and sent Timka through
ahead of her with a quick jerk of her hand.

The cloak-wrapped lootbag was leaning against the

wall in the short area between the gates. Timka trotted on through the second wicket and waited outside
in the street while Skeen knelt, slid the strap over her
shoulder, then began the effort to get on her feet
again. When she was up, she wiped the back of her
good hand across her forehead; she thought vaguely
about shooting some amvarban into her swelling hand,
but Timka thrust her head back through the wicket
and growled at her. She forgot about the shot and
stumped out after the cat.

Timka trotted through the alleys, looking over her
shoulder every few steps at Skeen; the tall woman was
moving easily, without obvious trouble, but Timka
grew increasingly worried as they neared the wharves.
She could hear Skeen muttering to herself, a rising
falling thread of sound; she couldn't distinguish the
words, but they weren't Trade-Min; the intonation
told her Skeen was chatting animatedly with herself;
she wasn't here but off somewhere in a world that
existed inside her head.

They moved down an alley between two warehouses
and came out on a wharf; the fog was thicker here.
Ti-cat trotted more slowly, stopping at intervals to
peer around and sniff at the planks. The hair along her
spine was pricking straight up, her belly was up and
tight. Nothing obvious, nothing she could smell or see
or taste, not even a stray Min about who might mean
trouble, but she sensed danger around, ahead, above,
she didn't know which, maybe all of them. She
ti-tupped along on the tips of her claws, head swinging, tail erect, the tip twitching like a metronome; she
heard feet scraping behind her, the continuing thread
of mutters.

A warbling whistle. Ahead, to the right. Hard to say
how far off, judging distance was chancy in this fog.
Timka mewed deep in her throat, heard Skeen's feet
stop, the mutters die off. Lifefire be blessed, she wasn't
wholly out of it. Timka glided in a tight circle about

Skeen. The Pass-Through had her darter out, she looked alert and dangerous, never mind she was cumbered with that heavy bag. Timka hissed with relief.

A horde of children came swarming out of alleys, off roofs, up from under the wharf, whooping and hooting, poisoned needle stilettos in their small fists; they swirled around Timka and Skeen, feinting, diving at legs and any other target presented. Eddersil turning the points, Skeen moved in small tight circles, darts spraying over the attackers; she couldn't move fast and she didn't try. She also wasn't keeping track of Timka. Timka had to duck and weave as she slashed at the Ants, doing her best to avoid their knives and sweep them off the wharf into the water. Several times she shifted to rock-leaper to shed the effects of the poison; the cat-weasel's fur turned most of the points but not all; she used the rock-leaper's horns and razor-sharp hooves on the Ants, then shifted to cat-weasel when the knives got through the leaper's long white hair.

The Ants began thinning as Skeen's darts and Timka's claws, horns and hooves got rid of them; slowly, painfully, they worked their way toward the boat where Domi was using his saber to keep the decks clear.

Skeen stumbled, almost went down; her eyes were glazed over, she was shooting wildly, missing more than she hit, as much danger to Timka and Domi as she was to the Ants. Timka roared and raced around Skeen, shouldering the Ants off their feet, slashing at them, driving them off into the fog. She roared again and Domi came leaping off the boat. He scooped Skeen up (she was about to fold into a heap on the wharf), grunted with surprise at the weight of the bag. With Timka wheeling and snarling as rearguard, he ran breathing hard to the ship, jumped down onto the deck. He slid Skeen down, wheeled and yelled, "Ti-cat, the chains, can you do them?" He didn't wait for an answer but jumped from deck to rail to wharf and stood panting beside her. "I'll handle these rats."

Timka mewed, switched ends and landed beside
Skeen. She shifted to Pallah, dug out the cutter and
managed to reach the stern without falling overboard
though the boat rocked wildly under her; she twisted
the cap off, flicked the sensor cover aside and slashed
the beam through the metal; the chain clanked against
the side of the boat as she loped to the bow and cut
through the chain there. Once again she wondered at
the power in the tiny cylinder and felt apprehensive
about following Skeen through the Gate into the universe that made such things. "Loose," she cried. "Let
them rot."

Domi jumped onto the deck, moved to the stern
with an easy grace that made her want to spit at him.
He settled there, took the tiller. "Push off," he said,
"the current will take us."

The boat edged out from the dock, moved faster as
it touched the fringes of the strong current in the main
channel; it slid off one boat's side, banged into another, slid along it, broke free. Impossible to see anything in this mess of night and fog, hard even to see
your own hands. Which was why Domi wasn't raising
the sail yet. The current gave him enough way to steer
the boat, but wasn't pushing it fast enough to damage
it or the boats it knocked against.

Timka knelt beside Skeen, brushed the spiky black
hair off her brow; her skin was hot and tight, she was
breathing heavily, moaning. Domi hadn't had time to
be careful, he'd dumped her on her mangled hand and
she'd lost consciousness immediately from the shock
to her system. Timka straightened her out, put the
hand on her chest. The bandages were sticky and stiff
with blood, the flesh puffed between the strips of
cloth. It didn't seem like flesh; touching it made Timka
feel nauseated. She put the cutter in its pocket and
snapped the flap over it, sat on her heels and frowned
at the belt. There were medicines in some of those
pockets, but only Skeen knew which and how to use
them. She lifted an eyelid, smoothed it down; Skeen

wasn't going to be giving directions for a good long
time. She worked the lootbag off Skeen's shoulder,
unwrapped Angelsin's fur-lined cloak, spread it over
Skeen. She tucked the edges under her, folded one
end around the battered boots, pulled the other end
tight about Skeen's head, leaving her only space enough
to breathe. She sighed; that was all she could do for
the Pass-Through, except hope she'd wake up enough
to help herself.

"How is she?" Domi's voice, just loud enough to
reach her, tense, filled with anxiety.

"Not good." Leaving Skeen in her fur cocoon, she
moved back so she wouldn't have to raise her voice to
be heard. "Woffit tore her hand; they've got dirty
mouths, almost worse than poison. Nothing I can do
right now. When we're downstream far enough, I'll try
bathing her face, see if I can get that fever down some;
the water here, it's so foul, it'd probably kill her."

"She going to lose that hand?"

"I'd say that was a fair bet, unless she's got something to kill that strong an infection."

Domi squeezed his long graceful fingers about the
tiller bar, sighed. "Better than being dead. I suppose."

They scraped by a mid-sized merchanter moored
out farther than most. A bleary looking Balayar popped
his head over the rail and cursed them in half a dozen
tongues; he beat on the rail in time to his cursing and
started to pull himself up so he could jump into their
boat and beat on them. Timka went cat-weasel and
roared him into a fast sweaty retreat.

As the merchanter vanished in the fog behind them,
Domi stretched his legs, moved his shoulders, grinned
at her. "You're handy to have about, Ti-cat."

"Hunh." Timka crawled over to the gear, found
shirt and pants and pulled them on. When she was
back by Domi's knees, she said, "I just wish I could
keep the fur and talk at the same time."

"Hm. That's something I've wondered about, Ti.
Seems there's dozens of shapes you can take if you

SKEEN'S RETURN   155

count all the variants of the basic ones. How come you
can't mix them and come up with some sort of
composite?"

"It just doesn't work that way. . . ." Her voice trailed
off as she gazed into the darkness. "Shapes have integ-
rity . . . or so I've always thought anyway . . . try to
change part and nothing can work . . . no one ever
tried to . . . that I heard about . . . and I would have
heard if . . . everything came to Carema's, though she
might not tell me. Lifefire singe your toes, Domi;
you've started me on something and I don't know
where it'll end. Ahhh, forget it. Something else. How
soon before we sight Maggí's ship?"

"Hard to say. Can't tell much about the time without the stars to measure it."

"Ah, wait a bit." She crawled rapidly to Skeen,
found her good hand, checked the ringchron. After
tucking the cloak into place again, she touched the
back of her hand to Skeen's face. No better, and
Lifefire be blessed, no worse. She left Skeen lying in
that near coma and went back to Domi. "About two
hours before dawn."

"Right, then. According to Chulji, who got it from
Maggí, the Chute is a good half day from Fennakin,
upstream, that is. Downstream, it might be less time,
but our loa, ah, that's length more or less, Ti, isn't a
third of Maggí's, so we're a lot slower. I'm not going
to raise sail as long as there's this much fog. It's too
dangerous. There's a good channel mostly snag free,
and long straight stretches of river between some easy
bends, but if we hit a sand bar too hard, that's it, Ti;
you want to try carrying Skeen on foot? Remember
there's hill country south of us. And mines. I'd rather
keep a long distance between me and any mine guards."

"So?"

"So, some time round midafternoon, maybe even as
late as sundown."

"Lifefire!"

"I know. Nothing we can do to change it either."

*   *   *

Hours slid one into the other. The sun rose and the fog burned away. Skeen alternated between a frightening lethargy and an equally frightening delirium that at times turned violent. Timka had to exert all her strength and the entangling effect of the cloak to keep her from throwing herself overboard or capsizing the boat.

As Domi had hoped, the wind swung around shortly after sunup and sent them slicing along, lines humming, sail taut, boat singing—bubbling, staccato, even cheerful noises. Laboring over Skeen, Timka was feeling far from cheerful. Skeen was sinking deeper and deeper into unconsciousness. Timka worked off the eddersil tunic, rolled it into a pillow for the Pass-Through's head and used the undershirt as a sponge, bathing Skeen's face and torso with cold riverwater, tryng to convince herself that she was doing some good, that she was indeed keeping Skeen's temperature from soaring out of sight, but she grew more and more frustrated with the little she could do. The flesh of the mangled hand looked worse, the cloth bands cut deeper and deeper as the swelling continued; she thought about taking the bandage off, but she had nothing on board to replace it and she was afraid to expose the torn flesh to contamination and what could she do if the wounds started bleeding again? She chewed on her lip and tried to think.

Domi looked her way now and then but most of the time his eyes were fixed on the river ahead and the sail as he rode a narrow balance between speed and stability. He whistled snatches of song time and again, but was mostly silent, not even asking how Skeen was doing.

Clouds scudded past overhead, high and thready, not threatening rain but keeping the day gray and muggy and cooler than Timka liked. Cida Fennakin was far behind now; they were passing through wild country, nothing impressive, fold on fold of scrubby barren hills that sent the river into long serpentines and kept Domi constantly adjusting sail and tiller.

There were scattered groves like clumps of hair on a mangy dog; they had a gray, stunted look Timka found depressing; even the water was beginning to take on an unhealthy grayness. She stopped using it to bathe Skeen, tucked the cloak back around her and settled into a cross-legged slouch as she watched the land slide past. They were coming into a peculiarly lifeless section of hills; a few birds flew in lazy spirals high overhead, slipping in and out of the clouds, but she saw no signs of beast life on the ground, not even the omnipresent squirrels that had made her home forest noisy and full of rustling life, swift impressions of darting leaps tree to tree, brown streaks along the ground. She could see puffs of steam rising from vents in the hillsides; at first she thought it was smoke from campfires, but there was no smell of smoke, only a vague rotten-egg unleasantness when a gust of wind caught one of the closer plumes and blew it into rags that fluttered around her. Except for the hooming wail of that wind, the soft brushing of the water and the small talk of the boat, they slid along in an eerie silence. Dead lands, drear lands. Was Skeen going to die? How much longer before they got to Maggi? Pegwai, he was a Lumat Scholar, wouldn't he know more than anyone about how to treat otherWavers?

That was the thing that bothered her the most; she knew quite a lot about treating Min ailments; at one time when she was considerably younger, she had tried using that knowledge to treat members of the Pallah families she lived with and it was only luck that kept her clear of total disaster. She learned then that there was no correlation between what worked for Min and what eased Nemin ills. She touched Skeen's face. Hot and dry. She sighed. Skeen looked diminished. Like the dead, diminished. Not dead yet, how long?

She slipped her sandals off, got warily to her feet. "Domi," she called.

His face and voice carefully neutral (she suddenly remembered how very young he was) he said, "Trouble?"

"I'm not going to wait any longer. I'm going to fly
ahead. Maybe Maggí or one of the others will know
what to do." She watched his face muscles fight his
control, aware he was terrified of being left alone with
Skeen and the boat; well, he had reason enough.
Lifefire knows a thousand things could happen he
couldn't handle alone. But there was no help for it,
she had to go. "I'll climb high," she said quickly. "The
winds up there blow faster, I'll be back before you
notice I'm gone."

"Ti . . ." He cleared his throat, giggled suddenly,
surprising both of them. "You're not seeing something
staring at you. Tell Maggí to up anchor and come
meet us, that'll make things move a lot faster. You
know you can't carry much when you sprout feathers."

"Hai!" She slapped her forehead. "Stupid. You're
right." She grinned at him as she started undoing her
trousers. "Never you mind my feathers. Medicines
don't weigh all that much, I'll bring back something
to start on. Hm. I haven't the least idea how long this
is going to take. Expect me when you see me."

She fought her way up the wind layers until she
found a southbound stream; it was faster than any she
remembered trying to negotiate and more turbulent. It
frightened her, but she cast herself into it; battered
and disoriented, she beat herself straight and went
sweeping south. When her initial dizziness passed off,
she looked for the river, tried to locate Maggí's ship.
She was flying above a layer of clouds; what she saw
most of the time was a thready whiteness though she
caught glimpses of the land through scattered small
breaks in the cover; unhappily, she passed over them
too quickly to see more than a few blurred details.

It was stony, barren country, with sluggish streams
and shallow ponds matted thick with ancient layers of
algae, meager scrub, grass like hair on an old man's
head, thin, patchy, drained of color. Off to the right,
where the hills swelled into mountains, she caught

glimpses of ugly gray structures. Mine works. Except
for those, it was an empty land. Nothing moved on
those hillsides but the plumes of vented steam.

Without warning the windstream turned east, straight
away from the river's course. Uttering an irritated
squawk she dropped and began casting about for a
new southflow where she could save energy and glide
along faster than she could fly. When she was stabi-
lized again, she started looking for the ship with hopes
this time of finding it.

And nearly lost her hold on the wind. It was directly
below her, swinging slowly about its anchor lines, bare
masts swaying to the tug of the wind. Giddy with
relief, she spiraled down to land on the quarterdeck
beside Maggí Solitaire.

Shifting from hawk to cat-weasel, she growled deep
in her throat, rubbed past the Aggitj woman's leg and
went bounding down the steps to the deck. She dropped
her hindquarters to the wood, growled again; tail tip
twitching like a metronome, she rose, stalked below,
stood waiting at the door to the Captain's cabin.

Maggí pushed past her, opened the door and went
inside. She turned to face Timka who had shifted
again and was pulling on the robe Maggí kept for her
on a hook behind the door. "Trouble?"

Timka smoothed the sash ends down, sighed. "One
thing I like about you, Maggí Solitaire, you don't need
long explanations. Skeen got her hand mangled by a
woffit and she's laid out with a fever. I need help." She
allowed herself a brief smile. "Domi says it'd be a
good idea if you upped the anchors and came to meet
him. Us. I'll be flying back in a minute, after I talk
with the others. By the by, you wouldn't have any
ideas how to break that fever?"

Maggí scowled past her, chewed on her lip. "Ah
. . . I'd be a bit nervous about trying. . . . A minute,
I'll be back." She circled the long table and vanished
into her bedroom; Timka heard her rummaging about
in there, heard a chest lid crash down. Maggí came

back with a roll of bandage and a jar of ointment. "Fever I don't know about, but this mess seems to work on all sorts of flesh. I've used it on close to everything that walks on this world." She smiled at Timka. "I even had occasion to use it on a Min once." She looked from her burden to Timka, frowned. "Lifefire, how are you going to carry this? Think it would be too heavy if I put it in a sack and tied it around your . . . um . . . foot?"

Timka giggled. "Be just fine." She sobered. "Leave room for whatever Pegwai or . . . well, anything I need to fly back to the boat."

Maggí set the bandages and jar on the table. "I hear you. I'll have one of the crew sew you up a sack. And I'll send the rest of your company down here. You want the Boy too? He's playing with my daughter."

Timka collapsed into a chair. "No, don't bother him. But you could stir up the cook and send down some hot sweet tea and a bun. I haven't had anything to eat since I don't know when and flying back's going to be harder work."

"I hear you." Maggí went out walking quickly, the soft patter of her bare feet faded almost before the sound of her last word.

Timka folded her arms on the table and rested her head on them. She was tired, hungry, afraid that whatever they tried would be too late. And angry with herself; Lifefire be blessed, Maggí had offered what she hadn't thought to ask for, the fresh bandages and the antiseptic. Stupid, stupid, Timka. This is the second time I've missed the obvious, my brain must be rotting.

Pegwai came in on a rush of words. Timka lifted her head but didn't try to sort them out until he calmed a little and settled into a chair. He flattened his hands on the table and sat staring at her. "What's wrong?"

Before she could answer, the three Aggitj came tumbling in; Ders ran at her shouting in Aggitchan; he caught hold of her shoulders, shook her. He was frantic, almost weeping, spitting in her face. Hal and Hart pulled him off her and got him settled in a chair. Looking almost as disturbed, Hal stood beside him, patting his shoulder to keep him from exploding again.

"Domi's fine," she said, "it's Skeen. . . ."

Lipitero came through the door in a whirl of silk and excitement almost as frantic as Ders'. "Skeen? What about Skeen?"

Timka sighed. "Hart, pull the door shut, will you. Thanks." She rubbed at her eyes. "Listen a minute, you all can ask questions later. Like I said, Domi's fine. He's taking care of Skeen and the boat right now, which is too much for anyone to handle alone, so I want to get back as fast as I can." She blinked. The ship was rocking. Lipitero stumbled against Pegwai, caught his shoulder with a grip so hard he grunted with pain. Timka smiled, relaxed a little. Maggí was getting underway, Skeen would have the help she needed, Bona Fortuna willing, as she'd say. She leaned forward, elbows on the table, fingers laced. "A woffit chewed up one of Skeen's hands; it's a dirty wound and she wasn't able to tend it for a lot too long, so right now it's a mess and she's laid out with fever." She nodded at the bandages and the small crock of antiseptic ointment. "Maggí came up with that for the wounds. That's good but what bothers me most is that fever. I want to get it down. Can any of you help me?"

A knock at the door. Hart opened it, let in Chulji and the cook who was carrying a tray with a pot of tea and some sandwiches. The cook stared around at the stiff faces, raised his brows at the ominous silence hanging about like smoke; he produced half a smile for Timka, gave her the tray, looked round again, sniffed with disdain and waddled out without saying a word. Timka reached for the teapot, stopped with her hand outstretched when Pegwai pushed his chair back and stood. "Let me look through my kit," he said. "I remember several antipyretics that work across species."

Lipitero caught hold of his arm, stopped him. "The

Balayar cordial, do you have any of that? It put strength in me when I was very close to dying." She looked anxiously at him, fingers trembling as she waited for his answer.

"Yes. I hadn't thought of that, you're right." He edged away from her, almost ran through the door as Hart opened it for him.

"Skeen mustn't die," Lipitero whispered. "She must not die."

The intensity in the Ykx's voice made Timka uncomfortable. She gulped nervously at her tea, looked with distaste at the sandwiches. She could feel the tremble of hunger in her arms and legs, her head was too heavy on her neck, but the thought of eating made her a little sick; she forced herself to bite into a sandwich, chewed unhappily at the meat and bread and washed it down with large drafts of tea. Pegwai was away an eternity, or so it seemed; he came back at that eternity's end with a stoneware flask of the cordial and a purplish brown syrup in a small glass vial.

He set these beside the roll of bandage. Hand on the flask, he said, "The cordial. It sits easy on the stomach; get as much down her as you can, at least half a cup before you try giving her this." He moved his hand to the vial. "The antipyretic. Give her no more than two drops an hour." He frowned. "If it's going to work at all, you might see signs of change before the end of the first hour." He examined his palm as if expecting to read the answers there. "I wouldn't worry too much if . . . ah . . . if you saw nothing happening for an hour, even two. After that, well, I don't know. Skeen. . . ." He shook his head. "I don't know."

"So say we all." Timka sighed. "If it does nothing more than bring her awake long enough to answer a few questions . . . Lifefire grant that happens. Pegwai, take these things up to Maggí; she's having a bag run up so I can carry them back to the boat. Chul, will you fly with me? I want to make sure nothing happens to that bag."

HELLO. DECISION TIME AGAIN. HERE WE HAVE
A MAJOR PLAYER AT A TURNING POINT.
HOW WOULD YOU DEAL WITH SKEEN AND
HER INJURIES? IF YOU WANT TO BE NASTY
AND NATURALISTIC, YOU COULD PULL A
WILD CARD OUT OF THE PACK AND KILL HER
OFF, LEAVING THE ENDS OF HER LIFE
DANGLING, NO ANSWERS TO ALL THOSE
QUESTIONS PLAGUING HER; AFTER ALL,
LIFE IS LIKE THAT; MOST FOLK WHO DIE
SUDDENLY DIE IN THE MUDDIEST OF MUDDLES;
MALA FORTUNA DOESN'T WAIT TILL THEY
TUCK IN THE DANGLES. THIS OPTION WOULD
CREATE SOME INTERESTING DIFFICULTIES
BOTH FOR YOU AND THE OTHER PLAYERS
IN THE STORY; IT WOULD TURN THE ACTION
INTO A RADICALLY NEW DIRECTION; WITH
A LOT OF SWEAT AND APPLYING RUMP TO
CHAIR, FINGERS TO KEYS, YOU COULD MAKE
IT WORK.

SECOND OPTION: YOU COULD HAVE PEGWAI
OR ONE OF THE OTHERS DO SOME PRIMITIVE
AND PROBABLY DANGEROUS SURGERY
AND CUT OUR HEROINE'S HAND OFF. NOW
THERE'S A FINE OPPORTUNITY TO DRIVE SKEEN
BACK TO DRINK AND COMPLICATE HER LIFE
CONSIDERABLY. SHE'D HAVE TO GET USED
TO A NEW BALANCE. AND IT'S HER RIGHT
HAND, AND SHE IS VERY RIGHT HANDED. AND
HOW IS SHE GOING TO TIE KNOTS, AND
THINGS LIKE THAT?

THIRD OPTION: YOU COULD KEEP THE HAND WHERE IT IS BUT GIVE SKEEN RECURRING BOUTS OF FEVER AND DELIRIUM; MAKE IT WORSE, HAVE THE FEVER BROUGHT ON BY STRESS. THINK ABOUT THAT ONE. YOU COULD LOOK TO ONE OF THE MARTIAL ARTS CLAIMS AND DO THE DRUNKEN BOXER BIT, HAVE HER BODY BE GLORIOUSLY EFFICIENT WHILE HER MIND IS OUT IN NEVER-NEVER LAND. THAT MIGHT BE INTERESTING TO WRITE, BUT YOU'D HAVE A TOUGH TIME KEEPING IT REASONABLY CREDIBLE; IF YOU HAD A FEEL FOR HUMOR THAT MIGHT DO IT. QUITE A CHALLENGE THERE.

FOURTH OPTION: YOU COULD SAY, WELL, SKEEN'S TOUGH AND LUCKY OR SHE WOULDN'T HAVE LASTED THIS LONG; THIS ILLNESS IS A TRYING INTERLUDE, BUT SHE RECOVERS AFTER SOME FINE AND LOVELY SUFFERING. IT'S HAD ITS USES; SHE HAS BEEN SCARED INTO TAKING THIS WORLD MORE SERIOUSLY AND PUTTING HER MIND TO WHAT SHE'S DOING, HER COMPANIONS HAVE BEEN SCARED INTO REALIZING THEY ARE TOO DEPENDENT ON HER AND SHOULD START DOING SOMETHING ABOUT THAT AND LET'S GET ON WITH THE GETTING ON.

WHEN YOU TURN THE PAGE, YOU WILL SEE WHAT CHOICE I MADE. WHY NOT KEEP YOUR OWN STORY RUNNING ALONG WITH MINE, SEE HOW FAR THE TWO THREADS DIVERGE?

Lipitero sat on the bunk, Skeen's gear held in the rough diamond space between her legs; a stickum was pasted on the wall giving her a steadier light than the oil lamps that flickered with the motion of the ship. She lifted each tool from the kit, examined it with delicate care, trying to decide without activating it just what it might do; she was not having much success at that in spite of her intimate knowledge of her own instrumentation; alien technologies tend to be incomprehensible to the eye, it's what they do that provides insight into what they are. If Skeen didn't come up enough to do some explaining, she planned to take the things on deck where she had room to provide for accidents. For the past several days Pegwai and Timka had been laboring over Skeen, trying infusion after infusion on her; several seemed to work—for a while. Skeen would sweat, grow restless, come close to cooling off; she surfaced twice during those frantic days, but was disoriented, rambling. They couldn't understand her or she them; she seemed to have forgotten all the Trade-Min that Telka had given her. Lipitero put everything back in the kit, clicked the flap shut with a sigh of frustration and began on the belt pockets. The infusions worked for an hour, a day, once two days—but the fever always came back triggered by the festering hand. Nothing they tried worked on the hand. Timka washed it, changed bandages several times a day, cut away dead flesh, cleaned out the suppuration. And Skeen kept getting worse, rotting hand and draining fever reinforcing each other. Lipitero lifted out a squat cylinder, eased the cap off and frowned at a smaller cylinder with a pinhole in one side.

Timka knelt by Skeen's head, held it up while Pegwai pried her mouth open and dropped a new concentrate on her tongue. He pinched her nose, held his hand over her mouth until he felt her swallow. He nodded to Timka, took his hand away. Timka lowered the head back onto the pillow. He moved down, bent

over the bandaged hand; the strips of cloth were taut,
the puffy flesh bulging, mounded up between them.
He slipped a scalpel under a strip, began cutting the
bandages off. Timka rubbed her hands up and down
her thighs, chewed on her lip, distressed by what she
saw. "Worse again, still worse," she said.

Pegwai touched the red streaks climbing toward
Skeen's shoulder. "We can't wait much longer."

"I know."

"She's not going to say anything more, too weak."

"I know. Petro hasn't found anything she thinks
could help. Which of us is going to do the thing?"

"I might as well." He grimaced. "I've done rough
surgery before when I was traveling around on my
Seeker journeys. This one will be easier, we've got
Skeen's cutter. Do a fast cut and cauterize at the same
time." He backed away to give Timka room to tend
the hand. "That's a tool I wish she'd leave behind
when she jumps the Gate."

"First we get her across the Halijara. If she's alive
when we reach Rood Saekol and Sikuro, then we can
talk about the Gate. Bring me the bowl, will you."
She swallowed, rubbed at her nose. "Hai, it stinks."
She began swabbing at the slashes, washing loose the
putrid matter. "Tomorrow for sure." She took the
scalpel from Pegwai and began cutting off the worst of
the rot. "Should do it now; I don't know about you,
me—I've got to work myself up to handling the idea.
My stomach is saying forget it."

Timka wrung out the cloth, folded it and laid it
across Skeen's brow. Lipitero had finally fallen into a
restless sleep. She was curled up in her flightskins on
the bunk across the room, her head on a folded blanket.

Timka listened to the breathing of the two women,
on one side light and fluttery on the other an increasing struggle; Skeen's labors made Timka's diaphragm
ache as if she were using her own muscles to keep
those lungs working. She hugged her arms across her

breasts and began nerving herself to try reaching deep
into Skeen's head. When she fled the mountains and
Telka's spite what seemed centuries ago, she'd suppressed her inreach. It was dangerous among the Pallah
to know too much about how they thought or felt; far
better to let them feel sorry for her and pleased with
themselves for helping her than to make them afraid
of her because she knew too much and couldn't tell
them how she knew it. So many years since she'd done
the exercises, so many years since she'd tried to remember what Carema had been teaching her. She
stroked her fingers down the side of Skeen's face. The
fever was coming down again. Maybe this time it'd
stay down. Once the hand was gone. Yes, Pegwai was
right about that, it had to go. She sighed and wondered how Skeen was going to take losing her dominant hand. She was used to her body doing whatever
she asked of it, that was obvious. She acted without
having to think about how she was going to do what
she wanted to do. It was going to be awkward, couldn't
get away from that. Skeen's temper was chancy at the
best of times; not that she meant to irritate other folk
when she was in a fuss, it just happened. Too bad they
were confined to the narrow quarters of the ship.
Room to maneuver. Something Skeen said down in
that cavern when Angelsin was getting ready to sell
them all. No room to maneuver on a ship, you kept
bumping into everyone you wanted, no, needed to
avoid.

The window was open. She could smell the swamp,
rotting vegetation, the acrid odors of the half-submerged
trees. Overhead a Nagamar must have been leaning
on the rail, one of their obligatory pilots; the hissing
call came in clearly, the answering whistle from the
raft drifting ahead of the ship. Pegwai had stretched a
fine netting across the opening. They needed the air in
here but not the flying biters that swarmed into every
corner of the ship. Tomorrow morning they'd be out
on the open sea. The Halijara. Three days, five days,

somewhere in there, and they'd be dropping anchor at
Sikuro. Not enough time for Skeen's stump to heal.
Without understanding quite why, Timka suddenly and
fervently wished Maggí would consent to take them
straight to Oruda. No stopping for passengers and
cargo, no. . . . She nodded. No stopping in ports where
Skeen would be surrounded by all the things that were
so very bad for her, things she'd be so vulnerable to
with an itchy aching stump instead of a hand, when
she was bound to be clumsy and uncertain and she was
sure to hate being clumsy and . . . and dependent.
Couldn't tie a knot, couldn't even get dressed without
help, at least, not until she'd worked out how to do it
and the stump had healed enough so she could use
what was left of the arm.

Timka touched the cloth, turned it over, patted at
Skeen's face. She dropped the cloth into the waste
bucket, took a fresh one, squeezed it out, folded it
and smoothed it onto Skeen's brow. Maggí would
have to throw the bedding out when the ship got to
Sikuro. It was already starting to grow mold, the drip-
pings from the damp cloths and the sweat off Skeen
whenever the fever broke enough to let her sweat
were keeping the mattress and pillow continually damp.
Timka leaned against the wall, pulled her legs up and
draped her arms over her knees. Face it, Ti, you're
just putting off failure, yes, admit it; Skeen knows
what should be done for her, she just can't tell us. It's
up to you to go in and pull it out of her. It's possible;
remember what she said about how Telka gave her the
Trade-Min. If Telka could reach her, so can you. Or
you could have if you hadn't let that part of your brain
atrophy. Like trying to walk after staying in bed a
decade or two. You were right to run. Telka would
slaughter you. Without Skeen's help. Lifefire, I can't
face her now. My twin sister, a match in everything
but temperament. We were a match, but not now, no
more. She kept driving, studying, practicing and I
rooted out, I am no more fit to face her now than a

fledgling for flying. She contemplated her situation for
some minutes more but broke off when she heard a
moan. She swung swiftly onto her knees and bent over
Skeen. The Pass-Through was moving weakly, drenched
with sweat. The cloth had fallen to one side. Timka
shook it out and patted gently at Skeen's face, hair,
pulled the blanket down, wiped her body dry; a futile
operation, by the time she'd finished more sweat had
beaded up. Skeen's eyes cracked open and she started
muttering. Timka tucked the blanket around her and
got a new cloth. She bathed Skeen's face again, spoke
soft soothing words, hoping her voice would pull the
other out of her haze, at least for a short while.
"Skeen, ah, Skeen," she murmured, "listen to me, we
can't help you, tell us . . . tell me how to help you."
The coated, flaking lips moved, but Timka couldn't
persuade herself Skeen had heard her. She bent closer,
tried to make out the mumbled words, but after a
moment she sighed and went back to patting at Skeen's
face, washing the crust from the corners of her mouth,
the cracklings from her eyes. Never the easy way, she
told herself, always complications. I'm going to have
to try. You won't help me, will you. Stand on
your own feet, decide for yourself what you want to
do. Hah! I remember once . . . yes, back in Oruda,
you asked me what I wanted out of life. Remember
what I said? Someone to take care of me, I said,
someone who'd provide silk sheets and scented baths
and day after day of ordinary days. You didn't like
that, did you? I remember how your face looked then,
Skeen my friend. You listened to my tirade, you didn't
say anything but I knew what you were thinking. I was
scared then, Skeen, I'm scared now. Scared? No. Terrified. Ashamed of myself for being so lazy, so. . . .
Well, there's no point in beating myself for what can't
be helped. She set the cloth aside, flattened her hands
on the sides of Skeen's face, slid her fingers up until the
tips were pressed against Skeen's temples. She closed
her eyes and tried to feel into the brain beneath the

bone. Her own brain creaked, it felt like an ancient
wooden clock, nothing broken but all the gears frozen
into immobility by an accumulation of grease and dust
and disuse. The gears moved a little as she applied
pressure. She began to see/feel ghost fragments, no
doubt fever dreams too pale and broken to recognize,
whispers tickled her ears but she couldn't bring them
clear enough to understand them. Even if I could, she
thought, I probably couldn't understand them . . . ay!
maybe I could, maybe. . . . Telka gave her Trade-Min,
why wouldn't that work the other way? Her head
began throbbing, lines of pain shot up from heels and
hands through her spine and exploded at the base of
her brain, exploded again and again. Gradually, as she
persisted, the force of those explosions lessened, she
got closer to her fingertips, finally felt as if she resided
in those fingertips; still she persisted. She battered
against the barrier as strong as bone that tried to deny
her. The heat and drive grew stronger, she grew frightened at what she'd started, tried to pull back, but the
thing that throbbed in her wouldn't yield; the barrier
shattered, she was in Skeen, she was Skeen. She
drowned in fever and pain, she struggled to hold on to
a thread of consciousness, but the pull of being Skeen
was strong, so strong. . . . Frantic, turned vicious by
fear, she clawed her way free, fell shrieking to the
floor.

When she was again aware of things around her,
Lipitero was holding her head, dripping Balayar cordial into her mouth. She grimaced, pushed at the
Ykx's hand; the cordial was cloying, unpleasant, as it
combined with the sour taste of stomach acid. Lipitero
set the flask aside, helped Timka to sit up.

Timka coughed, swallowed. A flash of memory
started her struggling to get up. "Skeen. . . ."

Lipitero restrained her gently. "Not worse, not better," she murmured, "What happened?"

"Help me up." She stumbled the two steps to the
bunk leaning on Lipitero's arm, dropped to her knees

and peered into Skeen's face. The sweat was gone, her
face was hot and tight again; like so many times before, the infusion's effect had worn off after a brief
respite. She cursed under her breath, lowered herself
until she was sitting on the floor, resting her arms on
the bed. After a minute she looked up at Lipitero. "I
was trying the Min inreach, I thought I might be able
to pull out of her some way of . . . of using something
of hers to fight this." She touched the blackening
hand, shivered. "Pegwai's going to cut it off tomorrow, today, I mean. I wanted. . . ." She lifted a hand,
let it fall.

Lipitero squatted beside her, stroked the straining
bandage. "Did you get anything? Even a fragment
might help me."

Timka closed her eyes, but all she saw was blackness; she couldn't remember anything but overwhelm-
ing terror. "No," she said. "Maybe after some sorting
out. . . ." She sighed, dropped her head on her arms.
"Hai, Petro, I'm tired. Too tired to think, I think."
She giggled, then started crying.

"Yes, I see you are. Come." She slipped her hands
under Timka's arms, tried to lift her. Timka fumbled
with arms and legs, but finally got herself together
enough to help. Lipitero got her across to the other
bottom bunk and eased her down. With a weary sigh,
Timka stretched out, smiled up at Lipitero as the Ykx
tucked a blanket around her and fluffed a pillow for
her. She closed her eyes, sighed again, and plummeted
into profound sleep.

Timka sat on the bunk, Skeen's head in her lap. She
swallowed, looked away as Pegwai brought over an
empty bucket and put it down beside the bed. "Do
you think you'll need that?" she muttered. "I thought
you said the beam will cauterize. . . ." She couldn't go
on.

"Think, yes—be sure, no. Besides, there's the hand;
should be something under it to catch it."

"Oh."

"Ti, if it bothers you that much, let me get the Mate in here. You don't have to watch this."

"I know. Has nothing to do with logic or even feeling, Pegwai. I just have to be here. And don't tell me Skeen wouldn't ask it of me, I know that. That doesn't matter either."

"She won't feel anything, it will happen so fast. . . ." He saw Timka's face and broke off, grimaced. "I'm not all that happy about it either. Still, it has to be done. Otherwise Skeen is going to die and soon."

"Stop nattering and do it."

"Hold her arm out and steady. I'm making the cut about halfway to the elbow." He turned pale, but stepped around the bucket and waited without comment as Timka slid around, lifted Skeen's arm and extended it so the hand was centered over the mouth of the bucket. He continued to wait until the arm was steady and still, then he positioned the cutter (Lipitero had set beam length through trial and much error at about a meter, long enough for ease of handling and a clean cut, short enough so he wouldn't carve holes in the side of the ship) and waited for the ship to drop and start its climb up the side of a swell. They'd left the river not long after sunup and were several hours out on the Halijara. He sucked in a long breath, exploded it out and brought the cutter down through the arm—swift, neat, precise in this as he was in most things. With a smooth continuation of the motion, he brought the beam back and placed the flat of it against the raw flesh until the cabin was thick with the stench of roasting meat and the gush of blood was stopped. He touched the beam off, tossed the cutter onto the bunk and reached for the pile of bandages and pads laid ready. The beam had sealed the blood vessels as he had hoped, but there was still some leakage. He knew he should have left a flap of skin to fold over the end of the arm, making a neater stump, but he hadn't the skill for that, nor did anyone else on the ship.

Maggí Solitaire acted as ship's doctor when there was need for one, but her training was even cruder than his. He stroked on some of her ointment, pressed the pad in place and began tying it down with strips of cloth. When he was finished, he looked at the arm with considerable dissatisfaction, shook his head and stepped back. Timka settled the arm on Skeen's stomach, averting her eyes from the bucket.

"Shouldn't you do something about the veins, sew them shut or, well, I don't know." Her fear and frustration shrilled her voice.

"You know as much as I do, Ti."

"That's not saying a whole lot."

"If you had objections, why didn't you voice them before?"

"You were so sure of yourself, Scholar." Timka slid off the bunk, settled Skeen as well as she could; still not-looking at the bucket, she gave Pegwai a tremulous smile. "Don't mind me. That was nerves talking."

"I know." He held out his hands. They were shaking. His face was a greenish gray, his eyes glazed. "Lifefire curse and claim the Funor Ashon. They know so much we've forgotten or never knew; if I could have taken her to one of their medical centers, well, none of this would have happened. They grudge the Lumat every scrap of knowledge from their store, though they're greedy enough to claim what we get from everyone else." He squeezed his eyes shut, pressed a fist into the space below the spring of his ribs. "I've got to get out of here. Ti, you able to stay until I can send someone?"

"Yes." Involuntarily, her eyes flicked to the bucket. She wrenched them away, gazed into the beam of brilliant light coming through the window. "Don't be too long. Sending someone, I mean."

For the next dozen hours Pegwai and Timka kept watch, alternately hoping and despairing as Skeen's fever bobbled up and down; the red streaks began to

fade after the sixth hour and after that the peaks of
fever were each lower than the one before. Timka fed
her cordial and clear soup, changed the bedding with
Pegwai's help, bathed Skeen and collapsed near tears
when the fever broke shortly after midnight and left
Skeen cool and peacefully asleep. Pegwai helped Timka
across the cabin to the other bunk. They sat side by
side and watched Skeen, not yet willing to trust this
change. They'd been suckered before by one of the
infusions when the fever dipped close to normal; the
thing that kept hope simmering in them both this time
was a small difference. Before, the hand didn't change—
if anything, the swelling worsened; now, the hand was
gone, the ominous red streaks were gone. One hour
passed. Another. Timka turned to Pegwai. "It's over;
she's going to make it."

More cautious, Pegwai hesitated before he answered.
Finally, he nodded. "I think so, but I'll be sure if she's
still improving come the dawn."

Shortly after noon, Skeen stirred, moaned, opened
her eyes. "Wha. . . ."

Timka bent over her. "Skeen?"

Skeen produced a thin smile. "I'm not too sure of
that." She lifted her head, tried to pull her arm along
and raise herself on her elbows; the pain in the stump
stopped that. She grunted, tried to raise the arm high
enough so she could see it, but she was still too weak
for so much effort; she lay back. "Things have been
happening."

"We had to take your hand off. I'm sorry, Skeen,
there wasn't anything else we could do—I'm sorry,
yes, but you're still alive. We used the cutter, you
needn't worry about that, the cut was clean."

"Pah! Timmy, don't babble on like that, you make
my head ache." There was a weary fretfulness in her
voice, pauses between the phrases. "If you expect me
to scream at you, you're being stupid. And don't worry
about the hand. Once I make the other side, I can drop

into a Tank Farm and have the flesh sculps regrow it
for me good as new." She drew her tongue across her
lips. "Think I could have some water?"

Timka brought her a cup of water, lifted her head so
she could drink. When she was finished, Skeen lay
back looking exhausted, great dark smudges under her
eyes, so little flesh under the smooth white skin her
face was uncomfortably like a skull. Timka knelt holding the cup and wondered not for the first time just
how old Skeen was; she'd muttered about ananile
shots which kept age at a comfortable distance. Cutter
beams, drugs that stopped aging, Tank Farms where
you could grow back missing parts; that otherside world
sounded more frightening the more she heard about it.
Pit Stops, world ships, stars that are suns, suns thick as
islands in the Spray. . . .

Skeen yawned, muttered, "Gonna sleep a while, my
gear. . . ." The mutter sank into inaudibility as Skeen's
breathing went deep and slow.

Timka waited long enough to be sure she wasn't
going to wake soon, then she went out.

She stood a moment blinking in sunlight she hadn't
seen for days. The Aggitj came running and swirled
like windblown leaves about her, even Hart excited
and babbling. "Yes," she said, "Skeen was awake for
a little. Yes, she's going to be all right. Yes, you can
see her in a little, but she's sleeping now, she's very
weak. Where's Petro?"

"Up there, still playing with Skeen's tools." Hal
waved a hand at the quarterdeck rising over them.
"Where she's out of the way. You want me to fetch
her?" He leaned toward her, his thin face eager. The
Aggitj had been passionately concerned about Skeen;
they had tried to help tend her, but Timka sent them
away. They couldn't control their reactions; they shared
Skeen's every pang and developed sympathetic fevers
that rose and fell with hers. Once they were back in
the light, with the crew and the scatter of passengers,

they recovered some of their ebullience, but nights were still difficult; they took mattresses off their bunks and put them on the floor, slept huddled together in a pile of warm flesh.

"No," Timka said, "I'll go. I need to talk to her." She squinted into the brilliant cloudless sky; the light made her eyes water. She blinked. "When Chulji comes in, let him know, will you?" She turned toward the stairs. The Aggitj parted for her. They watched her climb, wanting (she knew) to ask more about Skeen and why she wanted Lipitero; they were teeming with questions, but they said nothing, not even Ders. Aggitj tact. Lifefire bless them.

Maggí stood in her usual place watching the smooth operation of her crew; she came striding over and met Timka at the top of the stairs. "Skeen?"

"Fever's gone, I doubt it'll be back. She's sleeping now. If you could send down some soup in about an hour? I'm going to feed her a little every hour. She's pretty dehydrated in spite of what we managed to get down her the past week."

"Does she know about the hand? How did she take that?"

Timka laughed, shook her head. "She wasn't impressed. Do you know what she said? You'd never guess it. She said, 'Don't fuss, I'll just take myself to a Tank Farm'—whatever that is—'and have them grow me a new one.'"

"What? Never mind, I heard. Are you going through the Gate with her?"

"I think so. I haven't much choice, you know what's after me."

Maggí rubbed at her nose, looked thoughtfully at Timka. "Folk who give advice annoy me." Her mouth twisted into a tight rueful smile. "Keep as many roads open as you can. I don't know your people or your sister, but from what I've seen you could give her one fancy fight if you took a notion to; it might be worth trying. Skeen's world scares the stiffening out of my bones and I'm not ashamed to admit it. If I had a choice between going home to the Boot or following her, I'd take the Boot and you know enough about Aggitj to know what that means."

Timka smiled, but shook her head. Without saying anything more she started for the cloaked figure tucked away at the bow end of the deck.

Lipitero heard her before she got close, turned, stiffened.

"Skeen is starting to recover," Timka said hastily, she squatted beside Lipitero and eyed the array of enigmatic objects spread round the Ykx's knees. "Found out anything more?"

"A few hints." She lifted a squat cylinder. "This seems to have a measuring function, something to do with forces and numbers." She set the cylinder back where she'd got it. "How soon can I talk with her?"

"I'm waking her to feed her some soup in about an hour. She's very weak yet. Don't push her too hard."

"No, of course not. Does she want her gear? That why you came hunting for me?"

"In part, yes. She's very calm about the whole thing, even her hand. I can't really understand that. Even if she does think she can get the hand regrown once she's on the other side. There's a lot of pain right now; she's going to have problems with just about everything until she gets used to being without that set of thumb and fingers. You saw what she was like when we were stuck back there in Cida Fennakin, how she hated to have anyone help her with anything. Well, that's going to be a lot worse now. That's another reason I'm out here talking to you. You're going to have to help me with her, Petro. Especially when we reach port. She's going to be wild, I know it. If you could contrive some way of tracing her, so I wouldn't have to follow her around, we can give her the illusion of freedom and still be able to protect her if we have to."

"Ti, I don't see how I could do it without her

knowing; in that place of hers, well, they know a thousand times more than I do about that sort of thing."

"But we're not there, Petro, don't you see? She won't expect such a thing here. And it's only for a little while, till the stump heals and she's able to take care of herself."

"Yes. We have to make sure nothing more happens to her." Lipitero bent forward, began gathering up the instruments and tucking them away. "I'll see what I can do." She smiled over her shoulder at Timka. "I brought my tools; like Skeen, I'm not comfortable without them. I'll start working right away, I still want to talk to Skeen, though. An hour, you said? Good. I'll bring Skeen's gear when I come. Want to make sure everything's in its proper place."

Skeen was still too weak to object when Timka insisted on feeding her, but it was obvious she wasn't going to put up with that for long. Her arm was paining her, but she refused to let Timka give her some of Pegwai's drops. "I have to keep my head straight," she said. She raised her arm, rested it on her stomach. "You and Pegwai did your best," she said, "but I'd better add a thing or two from my own pharmacopoeia. Djabo bless you used the cutter. That will make things a lot easier for the flesh masons. Where's my gear?"

"Lipitero has it. She was looking through it to see if she could find something to help. She'll be down in a minute; she wanted to talk to you, I told her to come."

Skeen closed her eyes. "And the others? Everyone's here, safe?"

"Here, yes. How safe it is. . . . You'd have to ask Maggí that."

"You paid her? I don't want her thinking. . . ."

"I paid her the afternoon we brought you onboard. Don't fret, Skeen."

"That's good. I don't want her wondering how much we're taking her for. How is she? Peeved about not opening another market in Fennakin?"

"I saw no sign of that. She's got her daughter on board now. Tall skinny girl, looks a lot like Ders, poor thing, though that doesn't seem to bother her. Always got her nose in a book, except when she's playing with the Boy or talking to Pegwai about the Tanul Lumat. He's agreed to get her in there, says he'll arrange with the High Mother Ramanarrahnet to sponsor her once we hit Istryamozhe. Maggí is miserable about losing Rannah, that's her name, the daughter's, I mean. Same time she swells up near twice her size with pride every time she thinks about it. Let me warn you, don't tease her about Rannah; she's got no sense of humor at all when it comes to that girl. I suspect she'll be looking in on you the next time Domi brings the soup along here." A knock on the door. Timka got to her feet, went to open it. Lipitero came inside carrying Skeen's backpack and belt.

She put the gear on Timka's bunk, crossed to stand looking down at Skeen. "We worried," she said.

Skeen snorted. "What am I supposed to say to that?"

"That you won't do it again." She started to say more but thought better of it, and pressed her lips together.

"Hah! Tell that to Mala Fortuna, then jump back before she dumps on you." Skeen sighed, closed her eyes; her face was strained, weary. She seemed too fragile to support the spirit that had showed itself a moment before. "Bring my pack over here, if you don't mind."

"You should rest." Lipitero hugged her arms across her flat chest, scowled at Skeen. "There's no hurry now, is there?" She couldn't keep the anxiety out of the last two words.

"You want me to rest, bring me the fuckin' pack. This thing hurts, or can't you understand that?"

Lipitero turned to Timka. Timka spread her hands. "She won't let me give her any of Pegwai's concoctions."

Skeen produced a tired snarl. "I'm not about to get

addicted to primitive painkillers. Scares the shit out of me when I think of the glop you two poured down me before."

"Oh. I hadn't thought of that." Lipitero brought the pack from the bunk, held it dangling by its strap. "What do you need?"

"I need someone to help me sit up." The irritation was back in Skeen's voice. It's starting, Timka thought, and it'll get worse. She hesitated, shifted her weight from foot to foot as she tried to make up her mind what to do. With an angry spitting sound, Skeen drew her elbow higher and tried to lever herself upright. Hastily, Timka dropped beside her and supported her shoulders. When she was settled to her satisfaction, Skeen said, "I want something that looks like a disc about the size of your palm, Petro, and a cylinder— squat, gray, like the cutter but twice the diameter." She inspected the bandages on her stump. "Go into my right boot, feel around, you'll find a roughish spot about halfway up; fiddle with it until you work loose a thing that feels like a flat strip of cartilage, pull it out, but be careful. The business end of that thing can cut a thought in half. That's all for now, at least, that's all I can think of." She was leaning heavily on Timka. The Min wanted to suggest Skeen lie down until Lipitero was finished, but she didn't quite dare.

The disc was made of some gray smooth material; it might have been metal, but it was none Timka recognized. There was a knurled knob in the center and a small round hole near the rim on the opposite side. Skeen reached for the disc, then swore with weak fury as she realized she couldn't work it with one hand gone. "Hold it up so I can see into the aperture," she said. "Yes, that's good. Now put your thumb on the knob and turn it. Good. Keep turning until I say stop. Yes, yes, stop." She made an effort and held out her mutilated arm. "Press the disc against the inside of my elbow, aperture down, then . . . um . . . you see the edge of the knurling, put your thumbnail under there and lift. Right. The knob flips up when you hit the right spot. Ah. Good. When you've got the disc in the proper place, touch the sensor once, and keep holding the disc against my skin until I tell you to move it." She caught her breath as Lipitero followed her instructions with neat-fingered precision, allowed herself to smile when the job was done. "You can take it away now," she said. "Antibiotic, that was, clean out the blood." She closed her eyes for a minute, let herself lean more heavily on Timka, then she shivered, sighed and gave more instructions to Lipitero. This time the Ykx touched the disc to the end of Skeen's shoulder. Skeen sighed with relief. "That one kills the feeling in the arm. Now, we start work. Ti, cut off the bandages will you. Petro, you should look for a pair of dumpy gray cylinders. I've got several, I know that, hold each up so I can see it. Ti, use the thing that looks like a glass knife. Be careful with it. It's flexible enough to fool you and it'll cut to the bone before you know what's happening. Yes, I know it's been in my boot. Trust me, it's the best thing to use close to the wound."

The stump was ugly with ooze and suppuration, the blood vessels leaking blood with a freedom that prophesied disaster if nothing was done to check the blood loss. Skeen examined it with an eerie detachment that upset Timka more than the appearance of the arm. "Give me one of those pads." Skeen's voice was brisk though weakness produced a few breaks in it.

"Skeen, why don't you let me do that." Timka suppressed a shudder and reached for the pad Lipitero was holding. "I've cleaned your hand, I can clean your stump."

Skeen started to protest, then she scowled and nodded, a tight, grudging dip of her head. "Petro, hold that righthand cylinder with the pinhole thing facing the cloth, push on it for a second, let it go. Timmy, hold the cloth steady till the spray wets it." She gave Timka a sour smile that told her she'd meant to be irritating, using the nickname Timka despised.

Timka ignored that bit of byplay and cleaned the stump, then Lipitero sprayed it with a generous coating of the antiseptic; at Skeen's bidding she also sprayed the skin of the arm up to the elbow. By that time the arm was shaking and Skeen was near exhaustion. Her eyes looked glazed, her jaw was trembling, she was leaning most of her weight on Timka. "The other cylinder," she said, her voice slow and wavering. "Uncap it and spray it over the stump, cover all of the exposed flesh, bring the spray around and do the same for the arm skin, about two inches from the end. That should do it." By the end of this long and difficult speech, her voice was a thread that Lipitero had to lean close and flare her mobile ears to catch.

The second cylinder produced a film that immediately hardened and went opaque; it was tough and flexible as a layer of real skin, porous enough to let air reach the healing flesh. Skeen gazed at the grayish film, sighed. "Help me down. I'll sleep now."

For two days Skeen let them keep her in the cabin—well, it might be better to say she hadn't the energy to argue. On the morning of the third day, she got out of bed and gave herself a thorough sponge bath, ignoring Timka's protests. If she sat rather heavily on the bunk when she was finished, she ignored that also. She managed to pull on the tunic and press its closures the way she liked them, a little open at the neck, but she had to let Timka help her with the trousers, something that snapped her temper into shards. When she was ready to leave, she wouldn't let Timka hold her arm, and when Timka tried to walk beside her, she hurried ahead. The ship rolled over a swell, she overbalanced and smacked her arm against the side of the corridor, crashed onto her knees. When Timka hurried to help her up, she swore fluently in at least a dozen tongues, pushed Timka away and staggered on toward the rectangle of brilliant light where the deck door stood wide to facilitate the flushing of old air in crew and

passenger quarters. Gritting her teeth, resolved to endure what she knew was going to keep happening,
Timka followed her out. She hesitated, then climbed
to the quarterdeck and stood beside Pegwai and
Lipitero, watching Skeen greet the Aggitj, who danced
in circles about her, laughing, throwing questions at
her, hardly waiting for her answers, noisy enthusiastic
energetic mob of four masquerading as four dozen.
Maggí joined the mob, her Aggitj heritage overcom-
ing her usual calm; she whistled Rannah to her, shooed
the boys away and introduced her daughter to Skeen.
Chulji came swooping down, winged in wide circles
over Skeen's head, screaming a seahawk's greeting,
getting a wave and shriek from her before he sailed off
to return to his highwatch duties.

Timka watched Skeen take a step, misjudge her
balance and fall sprawling before any of those around
could catch her; she made a joke of it, exaggerating
her clumsiness, made another joke out of accepting
help back onto her feet, got those around her laughing
with her. Timka sighed. Not so bad as she thought it
might be; Skeen had plenty of experience protecting
herself, but bad enough for me and anyone else she
knows she can't fool. Me and anyone else who has to
help with the things she can't yet do for herself. Two
days till Sikuro? Three? I suppose I can last that long
without—she smiled grimly—killing her or myself.
Pegwai coughed, touched her arm, startling her as he
seemed to read what she was thinking. "I imagine it's
not so funny for you, Ti. Give me a whistle when it
gets too bad."

"What makes you think she'd let you do for her?"
Timka heard the bitterness in her voice with its tinge
of jealousy and bit down hard on her lip. Lifefire, do I
think I own her? She remembered some things she'd
surmised about the relationship between Skeen and
Pegwai and had the grace not to question him further.
"Don't mind me—that's irritation speaking. Thanks.

I've got a feeling I'm going to need a respite now and then."

Nightmares. That night, then the next and the next. Timka had sucked more than language out of Skeen.

A compacted darkness inhabited the back of her head. Images peeled off it. Each dream pared it away a little. Gradually it was being absorbed into her consciousness. As she had momentarily become one with Skeen's body, the dreams were making her one with Skeen's history.

Images of Skeen's appalling uncle, her scarcely less appalling aunt whose capacity to not-know surpassed anything Timka had ever seen even among those champion not-knowers, the Mountain Min. Image of a skinny battered child murdering the man and with that image a volcanic rage that terrified Timka. It was beyond anything she'd experienced before; she was unsure she could hold it inside her skin. It passed off and left her feeling gray and lifeless as a handful of ash. Image of Skeen and the old man Harmon, affection binding them, but so twisted and strange Timka could hardly recognize what it was. Skeen being punched out when Harmon was drunk or drugged or feeling destroyed by circumstances so impossible it seemed impossible anyone could endure them. Harmon also taking endless pains with Skeen, protecting her from dangers Timka could only half understand, in the end giving his life for her. Image of Harmon dying. With that scene, a grief so shattering that it could not be endured; Timka was catapulted out of sleep, sobbing, tears flooding from her eyes. Image of Skeen as an unwilling laborer in a fish cannery, one of a cohort of street teens swept up by an amorphous and much hated authority and thrust into indentured servitude that was supposed to train them and give them a means of making a living other than thievery, begging or whoring, though the authority was careful not to educate them beyond the mechanical motions needed to complete their assigned tasks. Reading was far too unsettling, numbers made a pauper uppity and contentious. When she woke from that dream, Timka understood far better what Skeen was groping to express when she spoke of Angelsin and herself being on the same team, the Scum Team. She still couldn't agree with Skeen's self-assessment, but she understood better why Skeen felt that way. As if to counter the dark images of the first spate of dreams, she lived with Skeen her first flight in Picarefy, shared with her that transcendent joy. The other dreams on the days while they were crossing the Halijara were ranged somewhere between the misery of the childhood scene and the joys of her flights in Picarefy, her intermittent happiness with an assortment of lovers, the other sort of happiness she found in her work. Timka felt something of a voyeur, but she met sleep eagerly those nights, wanting more and more of Skeen's life spread before her.

The dreams did more than narrate through sometimes grotesque images and symbols a sketchy history of Skeen's life. They started Timka reassessing her own; she'd thought herself unhappy, but compared to what she was seeing most nights her childhood had been close to idyllic. Except for Telka. She considered Telka and the Holavish, went over what she and the Poet knew of them. A small group, cohesive and fiercely determined to impose their views on the rest of the Mountain Min, a group far more diffuse and disorganized, without much leadership and generally unhappy with what the Holavish intended. They needed someone willing to stand up to those twisters . . . I've got to go back. The thought startled her so much she exclaimed aloud the single word *back* without a hint of a question to it. No. No. That's nonsense. Didn't they drive me out, at least, let Telka nearly kill me without defending me from her and do nothing, nothing at all, to stop me when I ran? Even Carema didn't try to help me stay, only to help me run. No, no, be fair, Timka, I wasn't ready then to face Telka and her lot.

She knew that, she knew it was better to get me away
until I grew up enough to protect myself. Took my
time about it, didn't I. No, no, it's absurd, I can't go
back, I don't belong there, not any more. Lead them?
They wouldn't follow me to a mating feast, what hope
they'd follow to a fight? No, forget that. There's another life waiting for me on the other side. I'll see that
before. . . . Before I make up my mind? Lifefire, it's
ridiculous.

During the day she called Pegwai to his promise and
retreated into a corner of the main hold where she
meditated and practiced the ancient skills of the mind
duelist for the clash she expected at the Stranger's
Gate. Telka would be waiting there, no doubting that.
Surprising how soon the skills came back, how quickly
the creaking in her brain subsided. But she had no
illusions about the outcome of a duel between her and
Telka. A few days of practice and contemplation could
never compete with years of discipline and experience,
no matter how great the raw talent. And there wasn't
that much difference between her and her sister. She
was a little quicker, a little more fluid in her thinking,
had a broader range—that was all. In everyday living
that might be an asset, in the more specialized world
of the duelist, it was a weakness, a diffusion of forces.
Were there mind duelists in Skeen's world? If you ask
her, Telka will know. Somehow she'll know. Sometimes I think the wind itself breathes news of me to
her. Better she doesn't know I'm trying to train, better
she keeps despising and underestimating me. I don't
understand her, I never have. She despises me, she
knows she can wipe her feet on me, but she's so afraid
of me she won't let me alone. I don't understand her.
Go back? Nonsense.

WAITING FOR WIND IN SIKURO, ROOD SAEKOL

Sikuro was a city set in a temperate paradise, a small-ish sunny valley cradled between two sets of cloud-raking peaks, cultivated by folk who managed three harvests a year, with three separate crops grown from the same earth. This is how it is: start with a reed-like plant (upper level) that produces a silky tough fiber they sell mostly to the sedentary Chalarosh for their world-renowned looms; in the same mound plant a berry vine (midlevel) for jams, cordials and brandy, and a tuber vine (ground level) that is a nitrogen fixer and produces a tuber with sweet yellow flesh that can be baked, roasted or fried, whose peels can be fermented and distilled into a colorless alcohol smooth as white velvet and strong as a simoon. On the mountainsides the Sikurose ran herds of rock leapers and wiry mountain cattle; they made cheeses from their milk, sausages of their flesh, tanned their hides, spun the leaper hair into worsted they dyed and knitted into bulky sweaters, most of which they kept for their own use. The valley was a quiet peaceful place; the different Waves who lived there kept more or less to their own areas but maintained comfortable relationships with each other. The mountains protected them from land raiders (if there were Mountain Min here, they kept very quiet and only the herdsmen and women knew they existed), and the long sinuous neck of the harbor took three days to traverse and was so narrow in places that any ship traversing it was completely vulnerable to attack from the cliffs that hung over it. There were small stone watchtowers built at each of these narrows, with signal arms on each raised high enough to be seen from the next. Each ship that

entered the Neck was announced by a staccato leap of
jointed arms along the neck and the Five Families who
ruled Sikuro and Sikuro Valley prepared for the visitor. Should the visitor be a known person, that too
could be flashed from tower to tower; the Families
liked to know who they dealt with. There were the
standard bribes to be solicited, the perquisites of each
office, there were the official fees to be collected—and
there were merchants to be notified. The Families
gave as well as took; they kept the peace, often by
drastic means, they facilitated contacts for the captains
of the trading ships that called at Sikuro, they arranged dinners and other entertainments and they po-
liced their merchants; a Sikuro tag on an item meant
top quality. Their name was a valuable asset and they
meant to keep it that way.

Maggí set down her wine glass and looked around at
her guests. Skeen, Timka, Pegwai, Lipitero, the four
Aggitj, The Boy (Beast curled sleeping at his feet),
Chulji, and her daughter Rannah. "We will be lifting
anchor shortly before dawn if the wind's on time.
We'll be tying up at Sikuro's wharves before the morning is half over. You know Sikuro, Pegwai? Good.
You can add your voice to mine. Lipitero, I'm sorry to
say this, but you'll have to stay aboard and keep off
the deck, even robed and even at night. If you thought
the Funor of Fennakin were hard to get on with,
believe me, they're children compared to the Families
when they want something. These aren't exiles—they
left home because they had too much energy and
intelligence to be comfortable there. A more ruthless
set of bastards you'll not find on Mistommerk, and I
don't except the desert Chalarosh or a Nagamar sha-
man on a vengeance quest. But if you don't stick
temptation under their noses, they'll contrive to ignore
it for the long term advantages they get out of not
antagonizing each other. They won't want to compete
over who gets you, at least, I think not, if you don't

flaunt yourself." She cleared her throat, took a sip of wine, waited a moment, but there were no questions. "Next thing, winds. Even with a favorable tide flow, the current isn't strong enough to carry a ship the size of my Goum Kiskar against a fairly heavy wind. You'll remember, I hove to outside the Neck waiting for sunup before starting into it. It's early autumn here south of the equator, that's the best time to catch a good wind; five days out of six morning winds blow south, evening winds north, it's something you can usually count on. There's something you should be prepared for, though. A few years back I was stuck at Sikuro for a full month waiting for a steady wind blowing the right direction. When the wind did blow, it came out of the north, the other days we had useless . puffs. That was autumn too. It's something to think about. I'm planning to be here four days. Chances are there'll be no problem leaving when I want, I just catch the evening blow and ride it north. But. . . ." She spread her hands.

Skeen gulped at her wine, put the glass down clumsily. She was having trouble using her left hand for anything but the simplest actions. "Families? Which Wave?"

"Five families, five Waves. Balayar. Pallah. Skirrik. Funor. Chalarosh, mostly sedentary, though there are a few cells from the desert tribes; these are tolerated until they do something fatal, then they're stepped on. The Waves get on fairly well. There's a general council with representatives from the Five and a city manager who handles everything but conflicts between two or more of the Families." She turned to the Aggitj. "One thing, don't you go job hunting here, no outsiders are permitted to work. Enjoy yourselves and pay your debts without arguing. It's an expensive port. Things will cost two to three times what you're used to, but the Sikurose won't be trying to cheat you. You can haggle in the markets, but not in the taverns or eating places. Streets, even back alleys, are generally

safe no matter what the hour. If a city guard tells you to
do something, you do it then, there, and without arguing. They don't argue, they'll just kill you. They
carry wrist slingers that use small iron shot they can
send through a solid inch of oak. And they don't miss.
They generally travel in double pairs, one pair visible,
the other acting backup so even if you take out one
pair the other will get you. No, no, don't look like
that." She chuckled at the consternation on the Aggitj
faces, "Be your usual cheerful friendly selves and play
as hard as you want, you shouldn't have the least bit
of trouble. They like the trading ships here in Sikuro.
They understand crew and passengers kicking up their
feet after being confined so long to a ship's deck."

Skeen used her napkin to wipe wine off the stem of
her glass; she didn't see Maggí's pained expression as
the dark red wine stained the snowy cloth. "We can
take rooms onshore?"

"If you want. There are plenty of Inns in the Port
quarter. And no curfew. Just remember what I said
about the city guards."

Skeen shrugged, dipped her left forefinger in a drop
of wine and began drawing awkward designs on the
wood.

Timka watched her, scowled, then turned to Maggí.
"Are there Min living in Sikuro?"

"Not supposed to be." She glanced at Chulji, lifted
a corner of her mouth. "I'm not as certain about that
as I would have been a year ago." She thought a minute. "This time of the year five to six ships a day tie up
at Sikurose wharves, could be Min on any of them. If
these Min don't know Sikuro, I suppose they could
consider having a try at you; if you're attacked, you
can defend yourself, but that'll mean trouble for both
sides; everyone the guards get their hands on will be
thrown in the nearest cells, and you'll stay there until
I'm ready to leave. Maybe longer. Better to avoid
trouble if you can manage that. Should you find some
stupid Min going after you, dive for cover and yell for

help. Guards should be here fast. Even if the Min abort the attack and vanish, you'll be showing your peaceable intentions. Once you explain, chances are the manager will give you a Skirrik bodyguard for the rest of your stay. If they've got half a brain apiece, most Min should know that so they won't bother." Maggí frowned at the Boy. "Which reminds me. My young friend, you'd better stay on board with Lipitero. Ravvayad assassins don't care if they're caught or not. I know it's boring, but you don't want to endanger your friends, do you?" She smiled at his downcast face. "Hal, there are always magicians and acrobats in the markets and I can remember several funny puppet shows. You look around for something you think the Boy would like, I'll pay the fees, you bring them on board. One a day, I think."

The Boy grinned. Hal nodded gravely. Domi lifted his glass, his eyes laughing. "And you don't need to worry, we'll be careful who we choose, no sinister strange robed figures or animal acts whose beasts are more than they seem," he said, laughter moving from eyes to voice.

The four days passed with little change in the activities of Maggí or the company of questers. There were no attacks by stray Min or fanatic Chalarosh. The Boy reveled in the little luxury of having his own shows and he graciously allowed the Aggitj, Rannah and any of the deck passengers who happened to be hanging around to watch with him as the acrobats, conjurers, or puppeteers performed. Maggí stopped to watch too whenever she was onboard the Goum Kiskar, but most of the time she was onshore, dickering with merchants, especially those who had fully tanned fur pelts trapped during the winterdeep on the high peaks. Because of Skeen's gold, she could afford to tie up more of her working capital in these furs than she usually did and she was in an ebullient mood most days.

Skeen flung herself onshore as if released from prison.
She didn't grudge Timka or the Aggitj the gold to pay
their way, no, she ladled it out with a generous hand.
But with a crackling intensity in her voice, a sharp
abrasive edge to her words, she told them to keep
away from her, play their own games and leave her to
hers. Lipitero had done her best, producing a tiny
burred beeper that Timka tried to hook onto the back
of the eddersil tunic; Skeen discovered it immediately,
as if even here in a world where such things weren't
supposed to exist, her nervous system was so sensi-
tized to electronic snooping she felt the burr like the
princess felt the pea. She pulled off the burr, ground it
under her heel and said some bitter unforgivable things
to Timka and Lipitero before she left the ship.

After she acquired a room in a midlevel tavern near
the wharves, she wandered aimlessly about, drifting
from market to market, tavern to tavern. Grimly determined, Timka-owl flew overhead, following her that
way, anxiously examining her walk as she left each of
the taverns, wondering if she was going to stumble
onto the downslide she'd begun in Fennakin, but
Skeen didn't stay long in the taverns. She seemed to
be on an orientation ramble, finding out which places
she liked, which she'd rather avoid. She began to
acquire company, male and female, until she was in
the middle of a small clot of folk who strolled along
laughing, exchanging toppers, shouting ribald comments to acquaintances they passed, enjoying themselves in a loud but comfortable way, under no pressure
to perform for each other. It might have been interesting if Timka had been one of them, but flying overhead she found the whole thing intensely boring. And
it went on and on, past sundown, past midnight. Skeen
finally went home with one of the men, her step still
steady, her hilarity subdued. Timka perched on the
roof of the tavern, wondering how far she should go to
insure Skeen's safety; should she slip down and see
what was happening in the room? Everything in her

resisted that. On the other hand, Skeen was more vulnerable than she'd ordinarily be, her ability to defend herself radically diminished by the loss of her dominant hand. She'll kill me dead if she catches me snooping like that, Lifefire! I'd kill me dead. Timka stayed up on the ridgepole and dozed until dawn. Stretched to the limit of flesh and spirit, she told herself Skeen wasn't likely to be out and away for some hours; she flew off to her own room to snatch some sleep.

Still the dreams came—daymares now—stealing from her the rest she needed; she didn't try to fight them. They led her deeper and deeper into Skeen's life, teaching her why Skeen had grown so restive and hostile. It wasn't so much the loss of the hand and the pain that went with the amputation as an accumulation of irritations from the whole of the trek. Skeen didn't deal well with people, at least not in long stretches; she needed solitude like most folk needed air to breathe. She hated being responsible for other lives, she shucked that responsibility as soon as she could with a skill acquired from much experience; her problem with the Company, us, that's different, there's no way she can ease herself free of us, not till we reach the Gate. Really, not even then. There's Lipitero and me on the other side as well as this; she knew that and it grated on her, exacerbating the small irritations that living in such close quarters was bound to produce. She was easiest around Chulji since the Min Skirrik boy spent the least time with her. She needed a lot more time than four days free of them all to flush out her system; where before Timka had dreaded the time in port, now she welcomed it. She found herself almost hoping that the wind would abandon them, forcing Maggí once again to spend a month tied up here. It seemed a secure enough place, stray Min weren't likely to attack, the Boy was safe onboard the Goum Kiskar, Lifefire help any Chalarosh stupid enough to try anything there.

I thought I was a solitary being, I thought I kept

myself apart and preferred life that way, I thought it
gave me power to be secret and sly and share nothing
and take nothing but those things that kept my body
comfortable. Now, looking into the mirror of a true
solitary, she understood how greatly she had misread
herself. Looking back at those years in Dum Besar,
she saw that though she hadn't let herself recognize it,
she'd been happy; looking back at the Poet, she found
a deep fondness for him—and a degree of respect—that
she hadn't at all expected. There were a lot of Pallah
she'd like to kick in the butt, the ignorant bigoted
bastards who'd gone out of their way to make her life
a misery; yet there were a lot more who'd treated her
well enough, they couldn't help doing stupid irritating
things because they understood nothing about her.
Even so, there were good hearts under the bumbling.
She'd seethed with resentment at the time, but a lot of
those times were almost funny now. And she didn't
want to see them slaughtered. And she didn't want to
see her own people slaughtered either, caught up in a
futile, vicious war. Telka and the Holavish were driving toward that, willing to risk all Min to rid the world
of the Pallah, the warhawks among the Pallah land-
holders displayed an equal fervor for wiping out the
Min. Each of these forces had to be defeated. She was
beginning to have a glimmer of how that might be
done, a vague notion involving Carema and her web of
friends, the Poet and his along with the unspoken and
generally overlooked good will that existed between
Pallah and Mountain Min along the border between
them after years of barter and the commonplace ex-
changes of emergency aid when children or livestock
were in trouble. She went back and back to that idea,
refusing each time to associate herself with it. I'll work
it out and write it down and see it gets to Carema. She
can take over from there. Yes, that's it, that's what I'll
do. Work it out, write it out.

Every morning the wind blew south, every evening
the wind blew north. The days were bright and clear,

with a gentle nip in the air. The hills around the city
were laced with reds and oranges, golds and brilliant
browns, the water in the Gullet danced to the wind,
sparkling blue like broken glass. The ships coming and
going showed off the fine details of their rigging even
when they were far enough off they might have been
toys. The markets were lush with fruits and nuts, with
cheeses and ropes of sausage, with wools and hanks of
fibers raw and dyed, with bottles of all shapes, with
jugs and barrels heavy with homebrew and cordials,
booths and pavement heaped and overflowing with the
good things the Sikuro valley produced. Musicians
played; acrobats leaped and whirled; dancers swayed,
leaped, tantalized; puppeteers played their dolls; beggars whined and displayed their sores (though beggars
here had a ruddy health that even their dramatic skills
couldn't quite hide). Day was swallowed by day, each
the same, a pleasant, comfortable, comforting sameness.

Maggí finished her cargo and spent the early half of
the fourth day getting it stowed. Cabin and deck passengers were coming aboard all day, checked against
the Mate's list before they were allowed up. The Aggitj
loitered on the wharf for a while, but they weren't
allowed to work and got bored. They drifed back into
the city to spend the last of the money Skeen had
given them. Pegwai had vanished among the Balayar
on the first day and hadn't been visible since. He came
dragging onboard a little after noon, looking a dozen
pounds heavier and so tired he barely managed to
move his feet. Maggí tried teasing him, but he de-
clined her openings, telling her his brain had been
asleep since morning and he wouldn't be a worthy
opponent for her wit for at least another three days.
He went into his cabin and collapsed on one of the
bunks. Chulji played on the quarterdeck with Rannah
and the Boy.
Midway through the afternoon, clouds began thickening overhead. The wind blew strongly out of the

north with no sign of dropping. In its usual pattern, it
turned erratic about this time of day and finally sighed
to nothing before rising again in the south, the sundown wind that blew ships back up the Neck on their
way to the Halijara. Clouds bumped and boiled and
turned black and ominous, while jags of lightning walked
through the gloom. The heavy air smelled cold and
burnt. Flurries of huge cold raindrops came slapping
down. Maggí cursed and got her ship snugged to the
wharf with extra lines, then hustled her passengers
onshore for the duration of the storm (Lipitero, Chulji,
and the Boy excepted). The city provided snug hostels
for these little emergencies. She routed Pegwai out of
his blankets, and sent him to find Timka. "Tell her to
stay where she is. And Skeen. No one's going anywhere until this storm clears out."

The clouds blew off by morning and the wind dropped
to nothing, dainty puffs that barely dimpled the surface of the broad lake. Maggí took a look round,
recognized conditions and didn't bother swearing. One
day, a dozen, Lifefire solo knew how long the calm
would last. She slapped the rail, turned to the Mate
who was standing beside her looking morose. "Tell
the crew they can draw against their shares if they
want, but remind them we don't know how long this
tikkush will last. I want a five-man guard aboard all
times, especially watch out for Chalarosh, stop any
that try to come aboard. Crew couldn't stop a guard
double pair, but should that happen, send a runner for
me fast if I'm not here. They'll be after our flying
friend, should that happen."

Houms grunted. "Saw Yiatch's brat yesterday. Counting the load, I think. You'd better see the Guard
Capo. If there's going to be Haamitti in the water, I
want to issue crossbows to the crew."

Maggí watched the brief shudder of a pennant, sighed
when it went limp. "I'd better get on it, then. Have
the bows ready." She cursed softly, Houms made soft

agreeing sounds. "I particularly didn't want to draw Family notice this time," she muttered. "Particularly not this run." She straightened her shoulders, gave him a tight smile. "Try not to shoot anyone before I get back."

The calm hung about. Air began turning foul, smoky, bitter with the stink of human and animal wastes; tempers grew frayed, even the Aggitj turned sour. Timka expected Skeen to grow more tetchy and difficult, but she didn't. She drank and sat around tavern fires exchanging wild stories with whoever'd listen, ended each night taking one or more of her companions back to her room with her. She was relaxed and amiable and showed it in her walk; she had learned a new balance, her stump was healing nicely, without complications, she could dress herself without needing help. Timka watched this, amazed.

Two days of calm. Three. Four. Five. High roostertail clouds began gathering above the haze. The air stirred, there was a faint hope the wind would return, the city began emerging from its lethargy. Six days. Seven. The clouds lowered, darkened, the haze began to smell of rain. Crews on the ships got busy again, checking the rigging, working with more energy at the unending maintainance that ocean-goers required.

Timka dozed on the ridgepole above the window of Skeen's room; she didn't quite know why she was there. Habit, she supposed. She dropped through the doze into sleep until a series of odd sounds broke through to her. She woke, blinking, looked dazedly about, then down.

Robed Chalarosh were lowering Skeen from the window. She was trussed in a webbing of rope, arms and ankles pinioned. Not dead, unconscious, or they wouldn't take such trouble with her.

Timka squeezed the ridgepole with her talons, not sure what she should do. Get Maggi? Pegwai? The

Aggitj? Or call the city guard? Two more Chalarosh
slid down the doubled ropes, collected them, lifted
Skeen over the shoulder of the largest and started off
at a quick trot. Follow them. Yes. That's best. For
now. She sidled back from the eaves until she was
near one of the many chimneys, then powered herself
into flight. She climbed as high as she could and still
see the streets through the soupy air.

The Chalarosh abductors stopped beside a two-
wheeled cart, dumped Skeen roughly over the tailgate
and climbed in after her. The driver flicked the reins
on the rump of the stolid vo and the beast started off,
the cart creaking along at a slow walk. They wound
through the waterfront streets until they were out among
the hovels that grew like mushrooms around the edge
of the city. Then they started up into the hills, following a woodcutter's road. Timka flew after them though
she was more and more unsure that she'd made a wise
choice; if they were coming all this way to avoid the
attention of the guards, wouldn't it have been better
to get those guards after them in the first place? The
problem was Skeen. She was in no position to defend
herself and Timka had a strong notion that the
Chalarosh would have killed her at the first threat to
them. Well, there was no turning back now, she was
committed to following them; if they showed signs of
. . . signs of . . . she almost giggled though an owl has
few facilities for giggling . . . murderous intent, she'd
have to take a hand, no—not a hand—a paw well
armed with claws.

The cart turned off the road (well, more like off the
ruts, it wasn't much of a road), circled north then
south about a pair of knolls covered with grass, old
stumps, and some flourishing brush; it dipped into a
dusty hollow with a miniscule stream and an abandoned charcoal burner's hut. The hut had a new roof,
bundles of twigs roped in place atop the crumbling sod
and wattle walls. Timka flew to the top branches of a

mossy ancient, one of a thick, cluttered stand of trees
that began three hillocks behind the hut.

Two out of the eight Chalarosh got down from the
cart and waited while the others muscled Skeen down
to them; they carried her into the hut and stayed in
there with her, apparently taking the place of the two
new ones who came from the hut and climbed into the
cart. The driver slapped the vo into motion, turned
the cart and started back for Sikuro. Torn between her
desire to rescue Skeen and her need to know where
the cart was going, Timka dithered in the tree, opening and closing her talons, doing a nervous dance on
the branch. She hooted softly, took off and swept a
circle high over the cart, gliding through wisps of fog,
shaking the fog out of her head. *It took them more
than an hour to get out here. I could catch them
before they got too far into Sikuro. If I can work
things right. Not a good idea to hurry, get careless, I
could get Skeen killed. Or me. Borrow some of Skeen's
fussiness, Ti, a bit of foresight never hurt, nor a little
patience.* She watched the Chalarosh bumping along in
the cart, now and then exchanging a few words; *they've
got the world by the tail, so they think. Let them think
it, they'll find out. I hope.* She swung back over the
hollow, inspected the hovel. *No windows, lots of holes,
but they can't see much out of those. I could land off a
bit, but what's an owl or two out here.* Her soft
feathers muting the sound of her passage through the
air, she slanted down, landed close to the hut, got
herself properly balanced, then shifted.

Ti-cat crept along the wall, belly to the ground,
nearly invisible as her camouflage blended with the
browns and grays of soil and sod. Near the door she
flattened herself and listened. Sketchy indistinct sounds
as someone moved about, creaks and scuffs. A few
words in guttural Chala. She didn't understand these,
didn't much care what the men were saying. As far as
she could tell, there were only two guards inside. She
didn't understand why they were doing this; they had

Skeen, what was the point of keeping her? An intriguing puzzle, but she didn't bother fiddling with it. That was for later, once this thing was done. She gave herself half an hour of patience, hoping she wouldn't have to charge inside and chance them slitting Skeen's throat before she could reach them. The dust was gray with ancient ash; it had an acrid tickling odor as small riffs of wind lifted it, flung it against her muzzle. There was an electricity in the damp air, the hair along her spine stood stiffly up; if she moved it would be in a haze of crackles and tiny worms of blue white static. Storm coming. Lifefire grant it marks the end of the calm.

Finally she heard what she was hoping for, feet moving toward the rough hole that served as a door. One of the Chalarosh pushed the sacking aside and stepped out. Timka lay very still, waiting to see if he'd turn toward her. She was on his left, chances were strong he'd turn to his right; he was holding a waterskin, chances were very good he'd turn right, the stream was over there. He threw the skin down, hitched up his robes. As he began to urinate against the wall, she came silently onto her feet, gathered herself and leaped.

She killed him swiftly, silently and left him lying in the dust.

The Chalarosh inside heard some of the small sounds she couldn't avoid. He called out, got no answer, called again, irritation in his voice. When he still got no answer, he whipped the sacking aside and charged out. He saw Ti-cat an instant before she struck, managed to twist aside, got his knife half drawn as she bounced off the wall and was on him again. She raked his knife arm with her hind claws, took off his face with her foreclaws. She leaped off him, scratched at the coarse earth to wipe off most of the blood, then went padding toward the sacking.

She listened a moment, then shouldered the sacking aside and went in; for a moment she stood blinking, half in half out, her eyes adjusting to the gloom. She made a soft spitting sound as she saw two bound figures, not one. They'd got Pegwai before they went after Skeen. Busy little gits, aren't they. Satisfied there were no more Chalarosh, she shifted and hurried to Skeen's side. The Pass-Through was still out and seemed likely to stay that way for some time, but her pulse was strong, her breathing natural.

"Timka!" Pegwai's voice had an urgency that brought her quickly to his side. "Go after them," he said, one word tumbling on top of the next, "They're going for the Aggitj. They want to trade us for the Boy."

"I hear you." She tugged at the ropes about his ankles. "Knife, I need. . . ." She jumped to her feet and ran out. The guard she'd defaced was still clinging to life and groping weakly. She wrenched the knife from his hand, slashed it across his throat, then ran back inside. She cut Pegwai's hands free, dropped the knife beside him. "Take care of Skeen. When I get a minute, I'll send transport for you."

In the short time she'd been on the ground the winds had strengthened and the clouds thickened; the threatening storm was no longer threatening but on them. She switched from owl to sea eagle and fought her way north after wasting several minutes trying to find a stratum of contrary flow; battered, tossed about like a rotted leaf, she struggled toward Sikuro, flying a lot faster than the vo, but far slower than she wanted. Unless she missed them when she passed through the fringes of a cloud, they were already in Sikuro. Though the gusts of wind and rain were dangerous, she dipped almost to roof level so she could find her way in the confusing maze of the Quarter.

A too-familiar cart was tied up outside the tavern where the Aggitj were staying.

Timka dived for the second-floor window of the Aggitj's room. She clipped her wings tight, plummeted through, snapped them out and shrieked a warning as the door ghosted open and the Chalarosh came sweeping in.

The Aggitj tumbled out of their quilts, caught up their weapons before they were fully awake and were immediately in a silent but vicious battle.

Scuttling to get from under trampling feet, Timka managed to reach a free corner of the room where she shifted to cat-weasel. Before she could start peeling the attackers off the Aggitj, a Chalarosh landed on her back, got a sinewy arm about her neck and began squeezing; his other hand drove into her side, probing for her life organ. A flash of wonder, why not a knife? and she was struggling frantically. This was worse than the time Angelsin had her; the way he was positioned (by luck or planning) she couldn't get at him; her limbs were too stiff, too awkwardly placed, the loose tough cloth of his sleeves baffled her claws; her brain was burning, her lungs were on fire, she could feel life slipping from her grasp. Grasp. Hands. Need hands. Need—need—need—in her desperation she did what she thought was impossible; the seed planted days before by Domi's question ripened to fruition. Her paws swelled into broad strong hands, her neck shortened, thickened and resisted the pressure on it more effectively. Using a skill she'd never learned, a skill that came into her mind and body from Skeen's memories, she drove her thumbs into the nerve plexus of his elbow. When the crushing hold loosened, she twisted around, got hold of his little finger and snapped it. As he screamed and sought harder to dig his hand into her body, she got her hind paws on the floor and pushed off, breaking free to switch ends and clap both hands hard over his ears; using another move that flashed across her mind's eye, she drove a handspear into his throat.

Leaving him crumpled on the floor, she leaped onto the back of a Chalarosh attacking Hal, jerked his chin up until his neck snapped, bounded away. Movement was a little awkward in this hybrid shape, but that

wasn't much of a problem. She didn't have to run any
races and the powerful hands combined with the skills
transferred from Skeen were a deadly addition to her
natural strengths.

The fight was fierce, but short. Movement stopped.
The noise died except for the scrape of harsh breathing. Hart spoke, the single word shocking as it broke
the silence. "Light." He went into the hallway outside
the room, came back with a lamp. He took the chimney off and lit the lamps in the room. Timka shifted
from hybrid to Pallah, sighed with pleasure as she
resumed the more familiar form. She was astonished
by what had happened but not ready yet to think
about it.

The floor was littered with Chalarosh bodies. Timka
started counting them. One. Three. What? A slim
white form among the robes. She dropped to her
knees beside the Aggitj boy, lifted his head, turned it.
Domi. Very gently she laid his head down and felt for
his pulse. There was none; she didn't expect to find
any, not with the loose boneless way his neck moved.
Hands trembling, she got to her feet. Hal came to
stand at her side, clutching a ragged gouge in one arm.

"Domi?" The word cracked in the middle. "Domiiii!"
It was a wild shriek. Ders flung past her and threw
himself down beside the body. He lifted its head,
shook it, wailing in unrestrained grief. He wrestled the
body around and lifted it into his lap like a mother
holding a sleeping child, rocked back and forth, sobbing and babbling in Aggitchan. Looking grim, Hart re-
claimed his knife, and began moving from Chalarosh
to Chalarosh. Not all of them were dead; he dis-
patched them with a quick neat pass of the knife. One.
Three. Five. The sixth was conscious enough to spit
his corrosive poison at Hart who twisted aside and
jerked up a fold of man's robe to block the flight of
the spittle; he jerked more of the robe up, wrapped it
around his fist, shoved it in the Chalarosh's face and
drove his knife up under the man's ribs. He wiped the

knife on the robe, got to his feet and stood watching Hal trying to quiet Ders. He cleared his throat. "Ti, that all of them? Six."

She rubbed her arms. "No." She shivered. "No, there were eight of them. Ahhh. . . ." She closed her eyes, did a rapid report of what she'd learned, why she'd coming winging in just in time to wake them. "Pegwai is waiting out there. I expect Skeen's still under." She looked over her shoulder at the window. "If you could get that cart and the vo. . . ." She permitted herself a small tight smile at the feral grin on his square face and gave him directions for reaching the hut. "It's a bad night out there; I imagine they'll head straight back, they think they've still got Skeen and Pegwai to bargain with, you were just insurance." She crossed to the window, grimaced at the solid curtain of rain, that was going to be a misery flying through. She shifted and backed off so she could get a running start. Behind her Hart was bending over Ders, shaking him, talking to him in a low voice, a flow of Aggitchan that interrupted the boy's sobs and brought him to his feet. Without a word he dashed out the door. Hal and Hart rushed after him. Timka looked around at the carnage, clicked her beak and shifted back to Pallah. She pulled the door shut, dropped the latch bar into its hooks. Better to keep the curious outside. From what Maggí had said the Families tolerated private feuds as long as they were kept private. You didn't do it in the street and you got rid of the garbage. She shifted, took a run and wafted to the windowsill; she balanced there a moment, got herself ready, then launched herself into the turbulence of the storm. After some hard labor and treacherous dips, she climbed into the clouds above the rain and began racing for the hut.

Skeen came awake in her bunk on the ship. She sat up, yawned. The ship was jerking about, resonant with groans, creaks and thumps. The storm plug was still down, but the parchment was drawn tight over the window, all the cords tied with double knots. Lightning flashed intermittently, the wind howled and hoomed and made a singing gourd out of the ship, heavy lines of rain beat with the steadiness of a stream in spate against parchment and shipside. Lipitero sat on the lower bunk opposite, working with delicate care on a small carving, timing her cuts to the movements of the ship.

Skeen swung her legs off the edge of the bunk and sat up. "What happened? We leaving in the middle of that mess?"

Lipitero dropped her hands to her thighs, the knife blade catching gleams from the swaying lamp. "What do you remember?"

Skeen rubbed at her temples, ran a hand through her hair. "I need a bath," she said absently. She plucked a fragment of dead grass from her hair, sat frowning down at the yellow-gray brittle strand. "What do I remember . . . um . . . I was coming back with Kut'im." She blinked at Lipitero. "Kut'im?"

"We found his body in your room, put it into the Gullet. We didn't want the Families nosing in."

Skeen stroked absently at the film over her stump. "Too bad, he didn't deserve that." She closed her eyes. "I unlocked the door, there was a bad smell . . ." she reached behind her head, probed through her hair, "ah, I can feel the knot. Don't remember anything after I opened the door." She grinned wryly at Lipitero, "That's happened before when I was hit a good crack. Who?"

"Chalarosh. Ravvayad Kalakal, we suspect, though it's a little late to ask them. They collected Pegwai, then you, then they went after the Aggitj. They figgured Maggí being Aggitj, she'd be more willing to ransom other Aggitj than a gaggle of otherWavers, however friendly she was with them. Timka was still keeping watch over you. Yes, don't blow up, I know what you said, but think a minute. She didn't interfere, she was just there in case something came up you couldn't handle. And a good thing too, she saw the Chalarosh lowering you out your window and followed them. They took you to a charcoal burner's hut in the hills south of the city. Apparently some of them were locals, at least that's what Maggí thinks, they knew how and when to move to avoid the city guards. They were being very careful, doing a little bit at a time, it seems, taking Pegwai first, getting him clear, going after you, getting you stowed." Lipitero looked down at her hands, set the knife and the chunk of wood on the blanket beside her. "They went for the Aggitj next," she said, her voice a whisper almost lost in the storm noise. "Timka got back in time to warn the boys, but. . . ."

Skeen jerked forward. "What?"

"There was a fight. Domi was killed."

"Ah." Skeen folded over, clutching her stomach, breathing hard. After a minute she swung her feet up and lay back, staring at the slats of the upper bunk while she cursed in an aching whisper until she ran out of breath, tears slipping silently past her ears to soak her pillow. She sank into an unhappy silence for a while, hearing vaguely the ticking of the bits of wood Lipitero was chipping off and the dull storm noise outside. Finally she turned her head. "The Chalarosh?"

"Timka killed the two guarding Pegwai and you and left them to the maggots. Six of them were killed in the fight or shortly after, there in the Aggitj's room. Ders, Hal and Hart ran down the other two. They piled the Chalarosh corpses in the cart, Timka flew watch overhead, and they dumped them in the Gullet. Timka remembered you had company when you went back to the Tavern and figured they'd probably have to clean up there too. They found another place to put your friend into the water, thinking his bones would rest easier if they didn't have to lie beside the Chalarosh leavings." Lipitero cleared her throat. "That's about it. Hal brought Ders onboard and Maggí gave him a

draft that put him to sleep. Hart and Timka went to
pick up Pegwai and you. I don't know what the
Chalarosh used on you, maybe it was something to do
with their poison, but you were limp as a squid and no
one could wake you. We were worried, we were going
after Chalarosh if you didn't wake come morning."
She smiled, her crystal eyes glowing in the shifting
light. "I am delighted we weren't forced to try that. I
have a feeling we wouldn't have learned much."

Skeen hesitated, licked her lips, rubbed her hand
nervously across her stump. "Domi?"

"They brought him onboard. Tomorrow Hal and
Maggí are going to see the manager for permission to
build a pyre for him. They've asked Timka to scatter
his ashes in the mountains. Maggí's anxious to leave
once the wind is right, but she's agreed to stay for
that, as long as the Aggitj need."

Skeen laid her arm across her eyes. For several minutes she said nothing, wrestling with a guilt she couldn't
talk herself out of. If she hadn't let the boys come
along, because they were useful, because she liked
them about, because . . . oh, a thousand reasons and
most of them accusing her now, if she hadn't neglected
to take care of them like she should, Domi wouldn't
be dead now. Out whoring around, trying to forget
they existed. Djabo's pointy teeth, she knew there
were desert Chalarosh here, she knew they'd never
give up until the Boy was dead. Ah, now, Skeen,
what's the point of this? If you're going to be guilty
about anyone, try Kut'im. The Aggitj knew their danger and stayed, they didn't have to stay; Kut'im was
an innocent bystander if ever there was one, got the
usual wages of the innocent. She tried to feel something for him but couldn't dredge up more than a
vague regret. She licked her lips again, wanting a
gallon of ale to smother the ache in her. Domi, why
did it have to be the best of them? Domi. Fuckin'
brain, doesn't know what to forget. Images of Domi
sharp as tryptich photos. Domi—face grave, eyes laugh-

ing. Domi gentling and calming Ders. Too many images. She tried to shut off the hurt, but she couldn't.
She rolled on her side, face to the wall, and wept for
Domi, for Ders who needed his cousin so desperately,
for herself, most of all for herself out of guilt and hurt
and loss.

LOSE A HAND, LOSE A FRIEND. OF THE TWO THE HAND IS EASIER TO DEAL WITH. ON EARLIER OCCASIONS DEPARTURES HAVE BEEN FILLED WITH EXCITEMENT AND HOPE. NOT THIS ONE. THEY LEAVE SIKURO LATE AT NIGHT, THE DARKNESS IS NEAR COMPLETE, THE MOON AND STARS ARE COVERED BY A THICK LAYER OF CLOUDS; THOUGH THE STORM THAT THREATENS HOLDS OFF UNTIL THEY ARE OUT FROM UNDER IT, THE WIND IS HOWLING MOURNFULLY BEHIND THEM, SHOVING THEM AWAY FROM THE CHARRED FRAGMENTS OF DOMI'S PYRE. THE AGGITJ HAD GATHERED THE BONE FRAGMENTS AND ASH AND GIVEN THEM TO TIMKA WHO FLEW THEM INTO THE HILLS AWAY FROM THE CITY, OUT WHERE THINGS WERE WILD AND FREE AND RELEASED WHAT WAS LEFT OF DOMI TO THE WINDS AND THE GREEN EARTH AND THE GRAY OF EARTHBONES. APPROPRIATE SEND-OFF, THE EARTH AND SKY AND SEA WEARING BLACK MOURNING GARB.

THREE DAYS LATER, THEY EMERGE INTO THE HALIJARA SEA ON A BRILLIANT DAY, THE SKY SHIMMERING LIKE THE INSIDE OF A SAPPHIRE, THE WATER GLITTERING LIKE BROKEN GLASS. THE AGGITJ HAVE LOST THEIR CHEERFUL EBULLIENCE, BUT THEY DON'T FLAUNT THEIR GRIEF; THEY ARE SIMPLY MUCH QUIETER THAN THEY WERE BEFORE AND KEEP TO THEMSELVES

209

MORE. IN A VERY REAL SENSE, THEY ADOPT THE BOY AS A KIND OF SURROGATE FOR DOMI. HE'S THE ONE WHO QUIETS DERS NOW WHEN THE AGGITJ BOY'S EMOTIONS THREATEN TO GET OUT OF HAND, AND HE'S THE ONE WHO PROVES TO HAVE MUCH THE SAME ACERBIC GOOD SENSE. HE BRINGS HART OUT OF HIS DOUR SILENCES AND PUNCTURES HAL'S HIGHFLIGHTS WHEN HE STARTS TAKING HIS RESPONSIBILITY FOR THE OTHER THREE TOO SERIOUSLY.

AH, WELL, THESE THINGS HAPPEN EVEN IN THE MOST MAGICAL OF QUESTS. THE GOOD DIE, THEIR PURPOSES UNFULFILLED. LOSE A HAND, LOSE A FRIEND. OF THE TWO, THE HAND IS EASIER TO PART WITH.

Supper in Maggí's cabin. Skeen, Timka and Pegwai are there. Rannah, the Boy and Chulji are eating with that portion of the crew off-duty for the moment. The Aggitj are still in their mourning fast, taking only a little bread and a few mouthfuls of water.

"It would be faster," Skeen said stubbornly, "and we wouldn't run into the traps and trouble bound to be waiting along our backtrail. If you're worried about your profits, well, name your price. Peg's maps say the ocean west of the Halijara is reasonably narrow a degree or so above the equator. We could come at the Gate through the Backlands. Chances are we'd miss Telka and her Holavish completely; they wouldn't expect us to come that way."

Maggí sighed. "If it were only so simple. Everything you say is true and everything you say is impossible.

Think about this, have you heard of anyone crossing Okits Okeano?"

Skeen ran her fingers delicately along the stem of her glass; she thought about the stories she'd heard in the past few days. "No," she said. "Doesn't mean a whole lot, but no."

"I thought not. There are a lot of liars around but none who'd expect you to believe they crossed the Okits and lived to tell the story. Consider this, you came along the Spray with several Shipmasters. Did any of them leave the island shallows and cut across deep water?"

"You've made your point. What's out there?"

"Sea Min and their pets. Stick the shadow of a mast in what they call their waters and they'll take ship as well as shadow."

Skeen turned to Timka, raised her brows.

Timka spread her hands. "Don't ask me. I know there are Min who live their lives out there, but they don't like Land Min all that much either. We meet maybe once a purple moon. And I only know that because I'm one of the few who talked with the travelers stopping with my aunt Carema. Fifteen, twenty years ago that was." She frowned at her hands as she searched dim memories. "Seems to me I heard there were factions growing in them too, one group wanting a limited trade with Nemin as long as the Nemin kept off their waters, another wanting to slaughter any Nemin who came within sniffing range, and the biggest lot of them wanting the other two lots to back off and leave them alone. I have to agree with Maggí, Skeen. Cross into their waters and they'll forget their factions. Sorry. It was a good idea, but it just won't work."

"Eh, Peg," Skeen tapped his shoulder, waited till he turned round, "give me a hand, will you?" She chuckled at his groan. "Seriously, I need a sparring partner who's good enough so that I don't have to worry about him."

He hitched a hip on the rail and examined her. "You're going to try switching your style left-handed?"

"Try's the word." She held her hand out, wriggled the fingers. "I've got strength enough in this, that's no problem, but it's about as functional as one of Timka's cat paws. Means knocks for me and my partner," she gave him a half grin, "mostly me, I expect."

"Staff or hand first?"

"Staff. My feet have got to learn a new balance. I can work on fine manipulations later." She rubbed her stump down the front of her tunic, looked at it. "I can use this to help control the staff. I think."

"We'll have to see, won't we. You talked to Maggí about practice space?" He looked round the busy deck. "No room down here. You'd give lumps to half the crew and more of the passengers."

"She says the quarterdeck's ours as long as we don't swat her. I put the staffs over there by the stairs."

The Goum Kiskar skipped along the coast of Rood Saekol, flitting from port to port, none of them near the size or richness of Sikuro. Every day Skeen worked with an intensity that startled Timka to regain her one-time fighting skills, practicing feints, wheels, thrusts, every conceivable move and combination of moves with the staff, and when she was tired of that or had done as much of it as she thought her body could absorb for the day, she changed to the sort of exercises Timka had watched dancers doing as they got ready to perform for the Poet. They had that trick of repeating movements over and over until they were temporarily satisfied with how they did it.

With hard work and discipline Skeen quickly reacquired a degree of competence—first with the staff, then the openhand drills she practiced with Pegwai or under his eye, but even Timka could see how labored her movements were, how different from the easy flow before she lost the hand. Skeen plateaued at a place where she could do most of what she wanted but none of it as well as she wanted. Timka watched, fascinated, as she began defining where her greatest weaknesses lay, then used her long experience at surviving to work out ways of compensating for those weaknesses. That hard-edged discipline and those long hours of exploration threw new light on parts of the Skeen-dreams Timka had thought distorted, projections of Skeen's wishthink.

Most of the lump of material she'd sucked in from Skeen's mind was digested now, part of her conscious and unconscious self. She seldom dreamed that sort of dream these nights, only the old anxiety ones: she shifted to smoke and was torn apart by the wind no matter how she struggled to reassemble herself, she ran and ran from some shapeless danger, her legs melting from under her; she was caught in a universal Choriyn shifting endlessly, unable to stop. . . .

One night when witchfires danced along the masts and the wake was a phosphor furrow, she found Skeen leaning on the rail watching dolphins dance in the white fire. "You've been working hard."

Skeen chuckled, echoes of the fire dancing in her eyes. "Didn't think I could, did you?"

"To say truth, no."

Skeen smiled at her and went back to watching the dolphins and the flying seabeasts who'd come to join them, bits of iridescent shimmer shapeless except for the rayed fans they glided on. The ship grumbled and chattered about them, the wind blew cold drops against them. Skeen's hair glittered with the droplets caught there that trapped and refracted the light from the waxing moon. Off to Timka's right, Saekol was a low black line on the horizon. The night air was so clear she could see the flicker of the surf breaking on the rocky shore. Skeen stirred beside her. "Someone taught me once," she said, "get it right tight and solid in the beginning and you won't have to mess with it later."

Old Harmon, Timka thought, but said nothing about

that. She felt vaguely guilty about knowing so much Skeen most likely wouldn't want anyone to know about her; at the same time she couldn't help enjoying her secret understanding. "I see," she said.

"You've been busy too." There was a lazy curiosity in Skeen's voice, an invitation to confide if she wanted, be silent if she didn't.

Timka leaned into the rail, feeling the movement of the ship deep in her muscles, feeling a quiet pleasure in the tranquility of the night. Up and down the ship went with a soothing periodicity, up and down in a harmonic web of sound, merging seamlessly with the flow of the night. "Old lessons," she murmured. "Trying to remember things I've let slide a long time. Too long. Too too too long. Ahhhh."

Skeen rubbed her body against the rail. "I know." She shook her head sharply, scattering the mist clinging to her hair, sucked in a long breath and let it trickle out. "I was in a lovely velvet rut when all this started happening. I suppose Mala Fortuna couldn't help sticking her long nose in. She won't leave anyone comfortable for too long."

Timka watched cold fire slip along the side of a dolphin leaping through a cluster of shimmering fliers. "Velvet rut. Are you going back to that once this business is finished?"

There was a long silence. Timka remembered then the glimpses she'd got of a sore Skeen couldn't keep from tonguing like an aching cavity in a back tooth. The shadowy little man who meant what? lover? friend? betrayer? Flickering images of something never seen clearly that had to be Picarefy the ship, an eerie amalgam of woman and machine. Man and ship wreathed about with pain and painful questioning. She wondered if Skeen was thinking about those two. She couldn't ask.

"This business. Sometimes I think I'll never be rid of it." The sleeve of the shortened arm had come unrolled and was dangling. Skeen rolled it back as neatly as she could with one hand. Stroking two fingers over the gray film, she gazed up at the moon's fattening crescent. "Depends on what I find when I get back." A long sigh. She shook her head again, pushed strands of damp hair off her face. "Time to worry when I get there."

Maggí paced the quarterdeck, volcanic energy barely controlled, eyes darting without cessation from sailor to sailor scurrying about taking care not to call down the Captain's wrath and flaying tongue on themselves, moving from these to the deck passengers settling in for the crossing, a worried speculation in her gaze as she examined each of them.

Skeen and Pegwai came up to watch the departure, took one look at Maggí and the swirling chaos on the deck and found a back corner where they'd be out of the way. Skeen brought her head close to Pegwai's. "Our Captain's been like a bear with a sore foot since she came back. I didn't smell anything over there," she nodded at the cluster of buildings that made up Efli Baq, "to explain it. You?"

"No . . . not exactly." Pegwai frowned. "A cousin of mine is tied up a couple of ships down."

"Djabo's hairy gonads, Peg, how many cousins do you have?"

"It's not that there are so many of us, it's just that we get around a lot."

"So, your cousin said. . . ."

"Nothing direct. He wanted me to transfer to his ship. He didn't give any reasons for it, but he kept on at me to switch. The only thing he'd say when I pushed him was that the Min had vanished, gone to ground in the hills, he thought. When I asked him what difference that made, he said if I wanted to be a fool that was my business. Wouldn't say a word more, just hoofed me off his ship."

"Hm. Ti said something about a faction of Sea Min that wanted to trade . . . no!" A snort of laughter.

"Peg, no, not trade, the good old fashioned pay-off scam. Look, I'm operating on a barrel of guess to a drop of fact, but I'd say this is an enterprising bunch of Sea Min. They made a deal with their dry cousins to sell the dirty Nemin safe passages across the Halijara." She giggled. "Djabo's greedy gullet, I wonder how old that racket is. Do you understand? You pay their fee and they see you get across with no holes in your hull. How long has your cousin been . . . never mind, it doesn't matter. Maggí's been sailing these waters for more than twenty years." She sobered. "Of all the fuckin' times, Peg; you know what your cousin was telling you?"

"I very much fear I do."

"That . . . Telka, I'd like to feed her inch by inch to the Ever-Hunger."

"You think her reach is this long?"

"I think she either bought them off or scared them shitless. I think somewhere in the middle of this bright blue sea we're going to get thumped."

"Tell Maggí?"

"Think we need to?"

"Skeen!"

"I didn't mean it like that. What I meant was, she knows. Look at her."

Pegwai watched the Aggitj woman stride about, listened to her shout orders, a growl like a hungry cat in her deep voice. "We'd better wait until she's not so busy."

Skeen chuckled. "Better."

"Your sister's been busy." The cook and his helper had cleared the table, leaving behind stemmed crystal and a cut glass decanter filled with rich ruby wine. The meal had been an uneasy one, none of them wanting to bring up the subject haunting them, at least those who knew and cared what was happening. The Aggitj and the Boy sat together around the foot of the table, the Aggitj still drifting, uncertain about where they were going, the Boy curious, interested, annoyed because he couldn't read the undercurrents he could feel swirling about the table. Chulji crouched beside him, subdued; he'd eaten his greens and soup with a listlessness foreign to him. His antennas quivered when Maggí broke the silence, he folded his forearms tight against his body and waited for her to go on. Timka dropped her hands into her lap, raised her brows, but said nothing. Lipitero watched, withdrawn, waiting. Skeen and Pegwai exchanged glances.

"Twenty years I've crossed here," Maggí said. "The only trouble I've had was jitsibays raising the fees. Twice a year every stinking year my Goum Kiskar noses out of here, dues paid, and goes sweetly across the Halijara without a smell of trouble other than the storms that shag down on you all the time out there. Twenty years and it's never happened that I go slipping into Stira's Court and find the shuping place empty. Not a jit there, just a few tinks trying to sell old metal. And they look at me like I'm crazy when I ask them about Kyalay and Lavan and half a dozen others. Gone home, I get told. Home? Where's that I ask. I get a shrug and an eyeroll. I go hunting for Captains whose ships I see tied out here either side of mine. Idiko Dih. Ximinarallan. Zehlen Papayesa. They don't know or won't say more than one day in middle of some dickering a jit came around and gathered up all the jitsibays and went off with them Lifefire knows where. Ordinarily this isn't something I'd mention and, my friends, I'd be obliged if you didn't say anything about it outside this room, not even to each other. Pegwai Dih, forget you're a Lumat Scholar and don't pass this on. It gets out, you'll mess up a lot of lives." She looked round at their faces, spent a bit longer examining Skeen and Pegwai. "Hai Lifefire, it looks to me like my fire's drawn already. Never mind, call it a favor to me, don't talk. Jitsibays are Min go-betweens. The Sea Min clans who live in these waters aren't such bad sorts, you can do a deal with them as long as you don't make a noise about it. Been profitable on both sides. We get weather news and a clear passage, they get . . . well, what they want. No point in talking about that. I certainly wouldn't mind doing some more direct trading with the Fish, but they don't dare be that open. It would get them fried in their own grease. They've got nasty neighbors down there. I repeat, every jit in Efli Baq has vanished. Ti, that sister of yours has got to them some way. I doubt if our Fish will be in on the attack, they're too slippy for that; they'll disappear down there like the jits did up here. No, she's done a deal with the sharks alongside and let our Fish know they'll have to back off, join the sharks or get stomped. Lifefire send her rootrot and rheumatism, if she keeps those shtupyens stirred up, she's going to make my life one stinking mess."

Skeen fiddled with her napkin. "You could avoid these waters until things settle down."

"I could."

"And you could dump us. That would make a smaller mess."

"I could." For a moment Maggí's face was stern, but there was a touch of warmth and humor there. She broke the mask with a laugh. "I won't. Know why?"

Skeen lifted her glass in a silent salute. She sipped at the wine, set the glass down. "One," she said, "if you can send those sharks running, you'll have the local Fish in your debt. I doubt you'd put much weight on gratitude, but a little fear's a healthy seasoning to any deal. The next time you negotiate your passage fees, you'll have that good will and fear working for you. Two. If ever you had a chance of fighting off a Sea Min attack, it's now with Ti and Chul to fly watch, with Petro and me on board," she grinned. "Not that we're so much in our persons, it's what we bring with us. So you're throwing the dice and hoping they come up winners."

"Well?"

"I'd say it depended on how many come at us.

Unless you've got sources you haven't mentioned, I can't see that we have any way of knowing that. So it's play or leave the table. You've got the most to lose, it's your choice."

Maggí nodded. "Ti, what about you? Can you add anything to that? Or you, Chul?"

They both started talking; Timka broke off, signed Chulji to finish what he was saying. His antennas flattened out and back as he ducked his head, embarrassed. "It's nothing much, just what I can remember about some stories I heard when I was a nidling. One of the nurses was an unmated female. Min Skirrik but you'd never know it by the way she acted, except when she was telling my sisters and me about the places she'd been. She'd been everywhere," his squeaky voice went even higher on the last word. "She told us about the gunja and the Pochiparn." He looked round at the uncomprehending faces. "None of you ever heard of those? Not even you, Ti?"

Timka closed her eyes, dug into her memory. "No, Chul. Neither one."

"Triffakezaram said the gunja were like the great, great, great grandsons of tattolits."

'Ah. Those I know about." Timka swung round to face Maggí and Skeen. "In the elder days before the Gate was opened, Min were collected in nokaffari which were loose groupings of clans; the clans were loose groupings of families who shared kinship and were usually neighbors." She laughed at Pegwai's eager face. "No need to take notes, Scholar, I'll go over this with you later when we've got the time."

Pegwai nodded. "I'll hold you to that, Ti."

"Patience, Skeen, this does have a purpose. You've got to have a little background to understand about Tatts. Nokaffari were almost always fighting about something; we were a contentious folk, bound to take offense at fleabites. But if we wanted a reasonably good life for our children and other dependents, we had to trade. So there were the truce fairs in early autumn and there were the zecolletros. These, what shall I call them, these aggregations of Min, these guilds, they reached beyond family, clan and nokarif. If your family or clan or nokarif was warring with some other group and one of the enemy made a zecolletro sign at you and it was your zecolletro, it was a call to truce. You couldn't ignore it. Both sides in the war would turn on you." She cleared her throat. "Which meant unless your group was too poor, you hired your fighting done. That way you didn't have those embarrassing halts to the bloody business. You went to a different sort of zecolletro, the Tatt-Habor. You hired a cell of tattolits to do your fighting. These Tatts were where we shoved our bad boys, the ones that were more trouble than clan or family could handle. The ones who liked hurting, the ones who got sexual pleasure from setting fires, the oversized who seemed born to be bullies, the undersized who wanted vengeance on the world for their lack of inches, the rebels, the too bright, the disrupters. And there were the boys who went on their own for who knows what reasons to the training halls of the Tatt-Habor. Once they were Tatt, they had no family, no clan, no nokarif. Their whole world was their particular cell, their only loyalty was to that cell, the cell's only loyalty was to its employer. There were no rules for tattolits. No. I'm wrong. There was one rule. Win. However you could. Whatever you had to do." She gave Lipitero a quick twist of her lips, a parody of a smile. "One thing the Ykx did for us when they made the Gate and came through, they killed off the tattolits. Had to." She sighed. "End of lecture. Almost. One last thing. Something the Poet thought." She had a softer smile, a raised hand for Pegwai. "He knew a lot he wouldn't talk about to anyone but his family. Most everyone thought he was a fool. He wasn't. He had the tact not to question me," dry laugh, "he wouldn't have got much. I knew less than half he did about my own people. As long as I kept out of sight and didn't interfere, he let me listen while he talked with his . . . his informants. One thing Telka and the Holavish are doing—they're trying to put together a new Tatt-Habor. So far, it keeps falling apart on them." She leaned across the table toward Chulji. "You're saying the Sea Min have a Tatt-Habor?"

Chulji worked his mouthparts, his antennas drooped. "I don't know, Ti. It's only old stories I don't remember all that much of. Let me think." Under the table his feet and feet-hands did a clattering dance on the floorboards. "Aaah, Triffakezaram said she didn't stay long under the water, she wasn't all that welcome there. And she didn't like them much either, except for their poets—she was a bit daft on poets." He opened and closed his dactyls, twitched all over. "I remember this. Gunja have practice matches. Triff told us about one . . . aaah . . . how did it go? Like a kind of lethal dance, she said. Closing and fleeing, weaving about each other, one against one, one against three, one against more and more until one dies the play death. And then the dance is over. One of the few times they weren't terribly boring she said. Most of the time they sit around playing with their weapons and talking fight with other gunja. You can understand one word in ten, she said, and that's not because they speak a kind of Min that's very different from Land Min, though they do. That's because nine words out of the ten are terms they've got for some fancy way of holding a hand or a tentacle or whatever, that sort of thing. Very, very boring, she said. Other times, they're not so bad. They have poetry contests, she said, when the prize goes to the one who can improvise the finest couplet on some topic someone throws at them. The more couplets, the better they are, the higher the esteem given the speaker. She went on and on about that till I stopped listening. Verrry boring." He twitched his mouthparts in a Skirrik grin and stopped talking.

Timka rubbed at her forehead. "Not so bad as it

might be, I see what Triff meant; if what she told you
is accurate, they're related to the tattolins all right, but
not nearly so murderous. Bad enough, though." She
faced Maggí. "There it is. With Telka trying to set up
a Tatt-Habor in the mountains, it's not odd she heard
of Sea Min gunja and she's probably been exchanging
messengers with them for some time now. No problem, then, setting up an ambush for us. Most likely the
gunja were delighted to go after a real enemy for
once. Reminds me, Chul, did Triff give you any notion how many fighters in a gunja cell?"

His crimson tripartite eyes flickered as he searched
his memories. "She said they were supposed to have
two score to each cell . . . aaah . . . she said the rest
of the Sea Min liked them only a little better than they
did her; that was why she spent more time with the
gunja than she did with the others, that and their
shuping poetry contests. She said they were having a
hard time getting boys to join them. Thing is, Ti, I
heard this more than ten years ago and Triffakezaram
was telling things that happened to her more than fifty
before that. What it's like down there now. . . ." He
shook his head, antennas twitching. "I haven't a guess."

Maggí made an impatient sound. "Two score," she
said. "Better than I hoped. what's a Pochiparn?"

"Sorry, I forgot." Chulji pulled himself into a more
compact form, shivered all over. "Gunja pets, sort of.
They use them to attack ships or . . . or forts, things
like that. Triff said that was part of novice training.
They were supposed to go out and get a baby Poch for
their cadre. Yes, yes, I know, what's it like? Aaah . . .
sort of like a combination between a rabid wolf and a
wounded shark with a dozen arms, each one of them
longer than this ship. Once it's turned loose it eats or
pulls apart everything it can get its suckers on. Triff
said the older and bigger it got, the nastier its temper
got. Not something you'd want to face on a calm sea
where you can't run for the horizon. It's pretty fast,
Triff said, but a ship with a good following wind can

lose it. So they come at you when it's calm or quartering the wind and swimming down deep where you can't see them. Aaah, a Pochiparn's an air breather, it has to surface every half hour or so. You couldn't see the blow from a ship, even the mainmast, but Timka and me flying watch, we're bound to spot it. We'll most likely be able to give you at least a ten minute warning—they wouldn't blow closer than that to the ship—and the direction it's coming from."

"Lovely," Maggí said. "Skeen, Petro, any ideas?"

"Submarine warfare." Skeen grimaced. "Give us a while to talk things out and see what we have to work with."

Lipitero tapped a fingerclaw against the bowl of her glass, a sharp little sound that pulled eyes around to her. "How long are we likely to have for getting ready?"

"They'll want deep water," Maggí said thoughtfully. "One day, a day and a half at most, though that might be stretching it some."

"Not very long."

"No. Ti, you and Chul take a look at the deck passengers, will you? I want to know how much I should worry about them. Hal, stay with me a moment, I want to talk to you about what you'll be doing in this melee to come. All of you, I'm rolling the dice and counting on you to weight the throw in my favor."

Skeen set the darter on the table, laid the little cutter beside it. "And a pair of boot knives." She was talking to herself, the cabin was empty; Lipitero was down in the forward hold digging among her gear for whatever it was she had there; she'd been mute since they left Maggí. She touched the darter, sighed. "I suppose I'd better let Pegwai use you. Left-handed I can't hit a horse more than a bodylength off. Wrong sighting eye, and I can't seem to change or compensate. Mala Fortuna, you owe me." She kicked a chair away from the table, sat and waited.

Lipitero came in with a long leather case, set it beside the second chair and settled herself at the little table under the window. "The Mate and some of the crew are breaking out crossbows and enough bolts to thistle a dozen cells of gunja." She reached out, touched the darter. "An interesting weapon. Does it work on Min? They throw off poisons so easily."

"You keep darting them until they're too dazed to shift." Skeen nudged the cutter with her forefinger. "And a pair of boot knives," she repeated, this time to a hearer other than the walls. She pushed the metal cylinder about some more, glancing at Lipitero and away.

Lipitero tapped a clawnail against her chest. Through the silk of her robe came a faint tink of metal. "The hover field's batteries are powered up; I've got an hour's lift without glide, five hours with. I have a short-range, short time stunner, you remember, the one I used on Angelsin. Not much use in these circumstances because the range can't be increased. There's a short-range cutter too, mounted on a swivel; reach— one body length." She flattened her hands on the table, the claws out like crystal scimitars, delicately drawn against the dark wood. "We're talkers and evaders, we Ykx," she murmured. "We watch and we tease apart the strands of motive and we jerk on them to our advantage. We only fight when we can't run; we've surprised more than a few who pushed us into corners. Used to be that seldom happened, here or on the other side. Coraish Gather went lazy and careless. Coraish Gather is dead and Sydo Gather is facing extinction. It's this world, I think. There's something about it that perverts our energies. . . ." She drew her claws along the table top, cutting fine grooves in the tough wood. "That interferes with our fertility. Not just ours. You've seen how empty Mistommerk is; it should have folk three deep by now with all the Waves trying to outbreed and annihilate each other. But that hasn't happened. I was talking to Chulji a while back, one of those days when he came in to keep me company." Her eyes flickered about the room, opening and closing, shifting right to left; it made Skeen dizzy to watch her. "The last hatching in his Skirrik family, seven out of the ten eggs didn't." She made a soft sad little sound, half a sigh, half a moan. "He said the Old Ones have been working at it. They think it's something subtle, probably a complicated synergism." She laced her fingers and rested her hands under the spring of her ribs. "If you want to know why I'm blathering like this, I might be an anomaly but I'm enough like the rest to find this . . ." her lips curled into a tight smile, ". . . to feel a twist in my gut, when I contemplate what I'm going to be doing with this." She bent to the side, caught hold of the leather case she'd brought with her. Long, narrow, heavy from the way she handled it. She set it on the table, traced a complex curve on a square set in the side; when it cracked open, she lifted the lid. Skeen came round the table to look over her shoulder. In the case was a black cube whose sides were so smooth they made dark mirrors, night itself compressed into six squares. A cylinder machined to a like perfection projected from one side, a little longer than Skeen's forearm; pewter gray lines curved through the black, might have been elegant decoration or powerlines; with Ykx artifacts it was hard to tell which was art and what artifice.

"Impressive," she said. "What does it do?"

"It eats mountains."

"Huh, tell me another."

"Seriously. You've seen Coraish. Ask yourself how we made it." Lipitero pushed her chair back, got to her feet, twisting aside to avoid Skeen. When she spoke again, her voice had a gentle remoteness that lifted the hairs along Skeen's spine; it was too much like the voice of the Mala. "You can set the beam any length you want up to a hundred meters. You can change the shape of the beam, make it a broad blade and slice out blocks of stone, you can narrow it and

carve fine detail, you can bend the end into a scoop
and stir it around, churning stone into a fine slurry.
Visualize it, Skeen, see what this thing will do when
you use it against flesh instead of stone." She shivered. "You want a closer look?"

Skeen touched a side of the cube. It felt soft like
fine silk. "I won't trigger it by accident?"

"No."

Slipping her single hand under the cube, Skeen tried
lifting it. The weight astonished her. "You can't glide
with this."

"No. I can manage about ten meters at full press of
the hover field." Skeen turned her head; Lipitero's
voice was chill, expressionless, her scarred face full of
misery. "I have been thinking," Lipitero said. "When
Ti or Chulji spots the Pochiparn, I will manage it to
that observation platform on the mainmast. As soon
as the beast gets close enough, I can cut it into collops
before it knows it's dead." She closed her eyes. "And
most likely slice a few Sea Min with it." She shuddered, opened her eyes, a forced smile tightening her
mouth. "Discourage them, don't you think?"

"They have objections, they should mind their own
business." Skeen tried once again to lift the excavator.
"With two hands, maybe." She moved away from the
table, stood cuddling her stump. "You're stronger than
you look."

"I have to be, don't I."

Day on day on day the ship crept across a seething
sea, a sea that hummed and hissed against the sides,
an empty sea; horizon to horizon beneath a coppery
sky shimmering with heat, but for the ship nothing
stirred, nothing, neither dolphin nor flier, not even a
cloud. Day on day on day, they waited, ready for an
attack which did not come.

On the ship each waited in his own way.

The passengers in the deckwell honed the edges of
the halberds Maggí passed out to them, practiced throw-

ing the short-hafted spears, loosening arm and body
without releasing the wood. Grim but cheerful, they
waited, talking about this and that, mostly shared memories; the women with children (especially older boys)
patiently repeated old arguments; the children were to
go below when the warning was given, shut but not
locked into the forward hold; those older boys had
their own bobtail spears and were to defend the younger ones if things went badly on deck. They wanted to
stay where the excitement was, where the glory was,
but their parents saw no glory in the slaughter of
children and refused to hear their pleas.

Day on day on day of tension-filled fruitless watch
and wait.

The Aggitj prowled along the rails, staring down
into the cuprous blue-green, willing the Sea Min to
appear, urgently needing release for the energy pent
up in them. The Boy took little note of the passage of
time or the jitters of the others on the ship, his full
attention was required to soothe Ders and keep him to
some semblance of sanity. The youngest of the Aggitj
was a bomb waiting to explode. The Boy kept him as
far away from passengers and crew as he could; Hal
and Hart helped him and in this sharing were themselves helped to endure that hot endless wait.

The sky was coppery with the heat, the air sultry,
thick as gelatin, thick as the tension on board the ship.

Lipitero sat quietly on the quarterdeck, her robe
pulled close about her, the cased excavator by her
knee. Now and then Skeen walked past her on her
restless prowls about the ship. The Ykx's face was
hidden by the robe's cowl, the silver fur on the back of
her hands was blotched dark with sweat, patches of
dampness spread under her arms and along her spine
where the silk of her robe clung to her body, but she
never moved. After a while, Skeen began to wonder if
she'd turned to stone there, but she didn't break the
Ykx's concentration to ask.

Skeen and Pegwai practiced against each other with

staffs on the first day. On the second, Skeen fit the darter's holster and the lanyard to a leather strap that Pegwai could wear as a shoulder sling, then watched him practice with the darter using ice darts without the drug. Pick them off one at a time, she told him, you're good enough. You'll get more that way and the reservoir will last longer. She cut a slot in the end of her staff and set the limber resin knife into it, the deadly watercolor waterclear blade able to cut a thought in half. When it was bound in place she did no more practicing with that staff; it was too dangerous now, nothing would stop that blade, not leather, wood or even light mail. Let them come, let the bastards come, Lipitero will slice them with the excavator, I'll slice them with my bladed staff. Let them come and learn the stupidity of facing fighters they have scorned out of their ignorance, their willful ignorance. Come, Djabo curse you with warts and boils, come will you before I chew my nails off up to my elbows.

The sun rose on the fifth day, swimming in heat haze; the wind dropped until it was barely strong enough to give the ship steering way. Chulji-sea eagle labored up to soar in wide circles above the laboring ship. Timka-sea eagle spiraled wearily down, blurred into cat-weasel and loped along to the cabin she shared with Skeen and Lipitero.

Skeen sat at the window, staring out at the endless unchanging empty sea. She looked around when Timka came in, naked Pallah now, having shed her fur for Pallah hands. "Nothing yet?"

"Nothing." Timka yawned, pulled herself into one of the top bunks and stretched out to sleep.

Skeen listened to the quiet breathing, punctuated by an occasional squeaky snore, until it became a rasp grinding her nerves raw. She went out and walked along the rail, eyes narrowed against the glare, staring at the same emptiness she'd seen from her window, until she noticed she was very much in the way as the

crew labored to nurse forward speed from the fitful
wind. She climbed to the quarterdeck, settled beside
Lipitero and Pegwai, watching Maggí pace, read the
flutter of reef points, take in the thousand implications
in the condition of the ship and call out a steady
stream of invective and orders, her deep voice hoarse
with the exercise.

Even up here where what wind there was had a free
flow, the heat was punishing. Sweat lay on her skin
and rotted there, collected in her head hair and slid in
streams down her face and neck. Pegwai's breathing
was slow and even; he didn't sweat all that much, his
folk were adapted to this sort of climate, they'd developed alternative body states to cope with changing
temperatures. It slowed them down, but they stayed
comfortable. She gazed at him with envy and irritation. Since she and Lipitero were drenched and miserable, it seemed decidedly unfair he should suffer so
little. She scraped her hands across her face, gloomed
at the oily muck she collected. "Salt water baths are
an abomination."

Pegwai chuckled.

"Hah! Any more of that, I bite."

The morning steamed on. Subdued voices from the
deck passengers. The shouts from the crew and their
work chants seemed muted, lifeless. The wind dropped
yet more, the sails began to wrinkle and sag. The
cook's helper brought a bucket of fresh water to Maggí.
She continued her driven pacing, slopping water on
her face and arms, dabbing at her not-hair. The silvery
filaments writhed and crackled with small explosions
of cold fire, otherwise lay flat against her skull.

Afternoon. Idling in the water. Crew lounging about,
half asleep, drained by the heat and the morning's
labors. Deck passengers soddenly asleep, most of them.
Alertness at its lowest ebb since Efli Baq. Those few
awake breathing through their mouths. The air had

little virtue. Unless they took in great gulps of it, they
felt they were suffocating.

Timka came out of the shadows below and stood
blinking in the reddish hazy light. Her light robe sagged
about her; under it her flesh shifted and rippled as if
the breathless heat made it uncertain of any form.
Heavy eyed and slow footed, she climbed the stairs.
Maggí glanced at her, went back to staring at the sails,
grimly silent, waiting with the same exhausted sag for
something to happen. Anything.

The lassitude broke apart.

With a wild scream, Chulji plummeted through the
rigging, snapped out, shifted to Skirrik the moment he
touched down. Still tottering, he waved an arm about
forty-five degrees east of the ship's bowsprit. "There,"
he squeaked, "The blow, the blow, about five, six
stads off."

The crew jolted to life, ran for the crossbow chest,
snatched up bundles of bolts and scrambled into the
shrouds; they were at their posts before they were
fully awake.

The quiet, drowsing deckwell got suddenly busy,
some passengers chasing down children and herding
them to the hold prepared for them, others on their
feet, flexing arms, doing kneebends, swinging spears
and halberds; a chaos but an orderly one, each individual movement fitting neatly into a defensive whole.

Lipitero stripped off her sweaty robe, clicked open
the case and lifted out the excavator. She danced claw
tips over the top of the cube and it deformed, extrud-
ing handgrips, dropping the main weight into a teardrop hanging off the shooting tube. The hover field
glowed a rich orange about her; with a straining wavering whine, slowly at first then more quickly, it
carried her to the top of the mainmast. She stepped
onto the small circular platform there, eased herself
down onto it, wrapped her legs about the mast, rested
the weapon on her thigh. Tense and filled with a
heavy distaste for what she had to do, she waited.

Timka cast off her robe, shifted to sea eagle and went winging away. Chulji followed her.

Maggí leaned on the forerail of the quarterdeck, eyes moving constantly. She'd worked out her tactics during the tedious wait for this moment and given her orders. Now she watched to see if there was slippage between theory and practice.

Skeen pushed a last time at the damp hair straggling into her eyes and got to her feet. She stood waiting for Pegwai. "Five, six stads. How much time does that give us before this mess starts?"

He grunted, shook out the skirts of his scholar's habit. "Given a good wind, the Kiskar would make that in ten minutes. Swimming?" He shrugged. "No point your coming down too. I'll meet you on deck with your Min slicer."

The sea eagles came screaming back, circled round Lipitero, pointed the line for her. She eased around until she was facing between them, steadied the excavator, called a warning to them, touched on a blade of light that was a meter wide and a hundred meters long; a deep harsh humming filled the emptiness between sea and sky. She played the beam through the water. Steam sprayed up and out, a hissing that screamed around the thrum of the excavator; the water boiled and shivered, turned pink with the blood of the Pochiparn, foamed and blanched with the colorless colloid that ran through Min flesh. When she saw the shadows of the Min swimmers flicker and disappear, diving deep, she shut down the beam and began working on the fairly complex problem of changing the form, length and properties of the light blade.

Tentacled shapes came shooting from the water like squameri seeds pinched between thumb and forefinger; they swarmed up and over the rail with a lithe, undulating movement, shifting in mid-leap to their land-fighting forms—bipedal, hairless, translucent cyanic flesh more slippery than oiled porcelain and far

tougher. They were clumsy out of water, but terribly
hard to kill, trained to shift to an alternate form whenever their prey managed a damaging cut or got a shaft
in a dangerous place. With the shift, the bolt would
drop away, the wound would close over. A second
shift and they were more dangerous than before. They
went after the defenders, tentacles flailing, caught them
and squeezed, a slow crushing death. Those of high
rank carried cutting weapons adapted to their tentacles; none had projectile weapons of any sort, their
eyesight out of the water wasn't all that good. The
fighting ground being limited to the ship's decks and
the shrouds, they had only to press and press until
they cornered crew, passengers, and the renegade Min
they'd been bought to kill, to slash and squeeze them
till only gunja were left alive.

In the shrouds and on the decks, crew shot and
reloaded, a rain of bolts that managed some damage
in spite of the fluid shifts of the gunja; most of these
flickered through the double change and lost the bolts
without losing a step. Kneeling behind the forerail of
the quarterdeck, Pegwai chose his targets, put a handful of darts in each, overloading their systems with the
drug before they could shift it away. As they got
among crew and passengers, he had to be more careful, the darts wouldn't kill, but the Fish would if a
fighter collapsed before one of them. The Aggitj raced
along the rail, working with saber and spear, agile and
serious for once, doing a dance they'd learned from
birth on the dueling grounds of the ancient holds. Boy
and Beast scooted about after them, keeping low,
spitting their poison at Min legs, tentacles, whatever
they could reach without damaging defenders; they
spat and Min melted into a sticky slime. As soon as
Lipitero shut the blade off, Timka plummeted to the
quarterdeck, shifted to the cat-weasel the instant her
feet touched wood. She loped to the maindeck and
wriggled through the fighting to Skeen's side; the Pass-
Through was striding about, using her bladed staff

with deadly effect, cutting the attackers to such small
pieces she got the S'yer more often than not, though
when she missed, the undead gobbets of flesh oozed
together, forming a new gunj. Ti-cat took care of
those, slashing through the S'yers with a fierce satisfaction. Each one down was one less to come at her
again; unlike Lipitero she wasn't bothered by the killing; the dead had passed beyond pain and anger, she
hadn't. More Min came. And more. When she had a
moment to think, Timka knew it had to be more than
one cell attacking. Min and more Min, swarming over
the rails. Pegwai refilled the reservoir of the darter
and went on taking out as many as he could hit.
Beside him Houms and the best shots among the crew
picked off more, distracting those they didn't manage
to kill so the Aggitj, Maggí, the crew, the deck passengers, Skeen and Timka—whoever happened to be
nearest—could finish the job. Poison exhausted, the
Boy found one of the jagged stone Sea Min knives and
scurried about, slashing at Min legs with it. He was
kicked and grabbed at, but he was old in surviving and
wriggled away before the tentacle could get a firm
hold on him. Fluids from the dead and dissolving Min
turned the deck into a mud slide, the Min sliding in
the leavings of their flesh as badly as the Nemin did.
Cursing, grunting, panting, screaming hate and pain,
hissing, thuds, wild shrieks from both sides, the struggle went on and on, neither side gaining an edge. . . .

Until Lipitero up above finally finished her adjust-
ments on the excavator, shortening the beam so she
wouldn't punch holes in the ship, refining it until it
was a rod of light a hair thick; she set it on millisecond
bursts, eased out to the edge of the platform, hooked
her feet into the ropes to steady herself and began
picking off Sea Min, working around the edges of the
struggle, triggering the burst only when she had a clear
shot. Each Min she hit exploded like a tuber a cook
had forgotten to prick.

One. Two. Five.

They were gunja drilled to blood and sacrifice; they endured and ignored all death, even the agony as Chalarosh poison dissolved their still living bodies, but when hot dripping bits of their brothers splattered over them, they faltered. The death struck and struck. They saw nothing, heard nothing. They died.

Nine.

They began to mill, moaning with fear and indecision. Their leaders were down, they moved in the residue of their own; invisible death came from nowhere, one cell had lost two thirds of its members, the other, half. Another exploded.

Eleven.

They broke and went overside into the sea.

The deck stilled.

Maggí rubbed at a weal on one arm where a Min tentacle had caught her. She nudged the comatose body of a darted Min with her bare toe, spat with disgust. "Houms," she called. Her not-hair writhed about her head, lines of weariness dragged down the corners of her mouth. She swung around. "Baliard, Tritz, Ishal, Za Grann. . . ." Her crew—one by one she named them. Battered and bloody they gathered around her, those that could walk.

Ti-cat watched for a moment, disturbed by the smell of the blood (that was the cat speaking in her); she glanced up. Chulji was aloft again, watching to make sure the decimated cells didn't reform and return. He glided in slow circles, wings outstretched. She could feel his weariness in her own bones. She wasn't so tired right now (that was the cat too, she was always surprised by the amount of energy the cat had), but she would be the moment she shifted. She ran up to the quarterdeck, swished her tail at Pegwai. He was refilling the darter's reservoir again from the bucket of fresh water Maggí had provided; he stopped what he was doing and watched her shift through several forms, losing cuts, bruises, Min fluids and splotches of blood somewhere in the transformation. She finished as Pallah, pulled her robe on and jerked the belt tight. She was clean, almost cool, as neat as if she'd just come from a long thorough bath.

Pegwai chuckled. "Don't get too close to Skeen, Ti. She's not going to appreciate the contrast." He sighed, "I've never really envied Min before."

She smiled at him, too weary to respond with more than a nod. She went down to find Skeen.

Three of the crew were dead; others were carrying the last of these up to the quarterdeck where they'd be out of the muck. Maggí was standing over the cook's helper, a Pallah boy barely past puberty; his arm was out of its socket. Maggí put it back in, the boy screamed and fainted. She stepped aside and let two sailors take him below. The cook was in sickbay receiving the injured; he'd see to the boy. She looked after the bearers, saw Timka, beckoned her over. She scraped her hand across her face, looked down at herself, then examined Timka clean and cool. "Min," she said, exasperation in her voice. Then she shook herself, "Ti, I could use some help in sickbay. Up to you." She swung her arm to take in the deck. "I've got to do something about this mess."

"Yes, of course. I'll fetch Skeen."

"Skeen? Ah, yes. If she will."

Skeen had her hip hitched on the rail; she was leaning into the shrouds staring at the sluggish water brushing slowly past, her eyes were heavy and she looked as exhausted as any of the rest. She was covered with blood and Min fluids, there was a small cut up near her hairline, an angry abrasion on the back of her hand, small round scabs like bloody freckles scattered across it. The staff with the knife embedded in the end lay rocking slowly against the rail, smeared with colloid and blood for half its length.

"Skeen?"

Skeen yawned, moved slightly so she could see Timka. "Min," she said, exasperation in her voice.

"That's three of you. No imagination, you Nemin."

Timka stopped talking, lifted her head, startled. "Am I dreaming, or was that a breath of wind?"

Skeen slid off the rail, looked up. "Hai, Petro," she yelled. "It blowing up there?"

The Ykx's voice came drifting down to them. "Yessss, better by the minute."

"You coming down?"

"In a little. I like it up here. Cool."

"Hah. If I had two hands, I'd be up there too." Skeen yawned again. "You wanting something, Ti?"

"Maggí needs help in sickbay, I'm going. You?"

Skeen looked at her hand and the handless arm, she plucked absently at the eddersil tunic. "Me and my clothes need a bath. You go down, I'll wash." She looked at her sleeves and sighed. "And borrow one of Petro's robes. This sort of thing keeps up, I'm going to need a change of clothes."

The children were out of the hold, helping tend the wounded among the passengers, fetching buckets of sea water so their elders could scrub the muck off the wounded and out of the well.

The ropes were creaking as the winds strengthened, the sails booming out. Houms was bellowing orders to the weary crew; half of them were working the ship, the other half were rolling the darted Sea Min overside and scrubbing the residue off the deck planks.

Maggí inspected all that with satisfaction, nodded as she saw Skeen and Timka go below. She crossed to the well. "Indu Annaji, any dead?"

A hefty Balayar woman looked up from the head she was bandaging; she was a series of soft squares, square head, square body, arms and legs jointed rectangular solids. "Lifefire's blessing, no," she boomed. Her laughter was as large and solid as her body, as infectious as measles. "Ykx's blessing, I should say, say it loud and clear. Pop pop spit, like boiling mush." She laughed again, sobered. "We'll take care of our wounds, Captain, but when you're not so busy, some tea and hot broth would go down easy."

"I hear you, Annaji. When I can spare the cook from the wounded, you'll get that and more."

As the sun dropped lower and lower in the western sky and the wind continued to freshen, the ship was purged of its filth and corpses (not the crew dead, they were sewn into canvas and waited in a corner of the quarterdeck for the proper time and the proper distance from the Min dead; they waited until the decks were clean and Maggí had time and energy to give them a proper send-off, though with the heat being what it was and dead flesh being what it was, they couldn't wait too long). Skeen had about exhausted her meager supply of antibiotics on the worst of the wounded, Timka and Pegwai had cut and sewn and bandaged until their eyes were crossing with weariness. The cook went back to his galley when Pegwai came down; he got busy with his pots and fires. The galley was a hell all its own in that heat, but he was used to it and glad to get away from the miseries of the sickbay.

Up at the masthead, Lipitero stirred, stretched, moving with some care. As the wind blew stronger, the sway of the mast was increasing, and she was getting dizzy. She adjusted the hover field to let her down slowly, she got a good grip on the excavator, slipped off the platform and drifted to the quarterdeck.

She glanced at the canvas bundles, sighed, and turned her back on them. She resorbed the handgrips and reformed the cube, tucked the excavator into its case and clicked the lid home. She reached down, scooped up the robe and squatted looking at it. In the bustle of the battle, the crew had tramped across it, it was still damp with her sweat, a filthy rag. She draped it over her arm, caught hold of the case and rose to her feet. She moved to the forerail, rested the case on it, and looked out over the ship. A scratch crew was working

the ship, the others, she presumed, either wounded or
getting some rest. In the deckwell the passengers were
gathered about several lanterns eating a hot meal,
talking (she couldn't make out individual words, but
the tone made her smile a little, she heard fatigue and
satisfaction mixed), children laughing and excited, in-
dulged by their parents in a way they seldom enjoyed,
enjoying it as fully as they could because they knew
how brief the license would be. She lingered watching
the strange children play—only a few children—five or
six, a leaven in the adult loaf like the children in Sydo
Gather. The whole inside of her ached as she watched;
she hungered for her own then, she needed them
around her, the smells and sounds, the warmth of
other Ykx, Ykx voices, Ykx laughter, Ykx . . . well
. . . vibrations. She was alone and it was like death;
for the first time she truly understood those Ykx penned
alone by the Chalarosh, she understood their willing
themselves to die; the pain of that total separation
from her kind struck so deep, only the hope of finally
ending that pain made it endurable. She reminded
herself of her reasons for being here, shook off the
malaise and went below.

From being becalmed, the Goum Kiskar blew into a
ferocious storm and blew out again in less than an
hour, then settled to a fitful progress across the remaining stretch of the Halijara. After the storm, more
cleaning up. Work on sails and rigging, pump out the
deckwell. Bumps and bruises among the passengers,
one broken leg, several broken heads. By the day
after the storm, the lightly wounded were back on
their feet thanks to Skeen's drugs and Pegwai's nee-
dles and Timka's tending, able to do some of the
lighter work and let some of their fellows snatch a
little rest. And the badly hurt were resting comfortably without the fever that killed more than the original
wounds. Maggí came down several times to visit the
sickbay; she walked from one pallet to another, kneel-

ing beside each to tease the man gently, to pat him a
little, rising to move to the next. She nodded to Timka
as she left, and went to find Lipitero.

Quarterdeck. Early afternoon. Hot and steamy, a brisk
wind, Goum Kiskar slicing through glittering water.
Lipitero standing unrobed, the wind playing through
her crimped silver-gray fur, her heavily metaled harness glowing richly gold in the sunlight filtering through
the sails and shrouds.

MAGGÍ: You're opening the Gate for Skeen.

LIPITERO: Yes. Or why would I be here.

MAGGÍ: That's a question I've wondered about.

LIPITERO: No doubt.

MAGGÍ: There aren't many Ykx left on Mistommerk.

LIPITERO: We don't make ourselves obtrusive.

MAGGÍ: That's no answer. Ah, forget that, if you
    wanted to answer you would have. Skeen isn't talk-
    ing either, so I have to guess. There's something on
    the far side the Ykx want. Or need. It's my guess
    you're passing through to get it and coming back
    with it. You'll need transport?"

LIPITERO: It's not something I want to talk about.

MAGGÍ: I suppose your reasons don't matter all that
    much. There's something I want you to do for me.

LIPITERO: I'll listen, Maggí. I owe you.

MAGGÍ: I was in sickbay just now. Petro, three years
    ago the pirates round Tail End were hungrier than

usual and hitting anything that floated past. We had
a bad time with them, I had six crew wounded in
that fight. One in the belly; you know this world,
you know what that meant. He was begging us to
kill him by the time we made the next port. Houms
offered, but I couldn't let him do my job. Two
others died from the fever. Of the three that lived,
two are still with me, one never got well enough to
work again, he's living in Karolsey. I go to see him
most times I'm there. He was cook's help, Petro, a
baby. He's not twenty yet, and he's an old man. I'm
always expecting to find him dead each time I drop
anchor there. I think about that, then I think about
Skeen and her hand, how close she was to dying and
how fast she recovered once she used her own medicines. I think about that other time and I go down
and see the wounded from this fight. I feel cool
heads, I see clean wounds, I see a man hurt worse
than Tefote was already up and mending sail. And
what's the difference, Petro, what's the whole difference? Skeen's pharmacopoeia. Petro, I want those
drugs. Not just a stock, but a continuing supply. I
don't want to do Lifefire's grace on more of my
friends, I don't want to see another boy go from
puberty to senility with nothing between.

LIPITERO: Shouldn't you be talking with Skeen about
that? What do I know about the far side?

MAGGÍ: I like Skeen, but I know Skeen. She's im-
pulsive, generous. If I was in a tight place, I can
think of few others I'd rather have at my back. But I
wouldn't want to depend on her, not for something
that meant she'd have to meet a schedule, not for
something that was supposed to continue for a long
time. Oh, I could probably get her to agree to be
my supplier, and she'd come through once, maybe
twice, then she'd slide away. She'd have the best
excuses, but the end would be the same. No, if it

can be done, you're the one to do it, Petro. Get
Skeen's help if you want, but remember what I said.
Don't do it for me, do it for the Ykx. Think of the
market for these drugs. Me, but I'm only one. There
are hundreds—no thousands—who would be as eager as I am to have a way to fight the killing fevers.
Say nothing now, just think about it.

**MORE GROUND (OCEAN) TO GET ACROSS.
DO I GO FOR TEDIOUS DETAIL OR SKIM
LIGHTLY ALONG THE PEAKS? CONSIDER HOW
LITTLE SUBSTANCE INTERVALS OF PEACE
OFFER TO THE TELLER OF QUEST TALES (OR
ANY OTHER SORT). OUR HEROES SLIP-SLIDE
ALONG SLEEPING AND EATING AND PASSING
THE TEDIOUS HOURS WITH TALES OF THEIR
OWN FROM MORE ADVENTUROUS TIMES. HM,
THIS SOUNDS LIKE A LEAD-IN TO SOME STORY
TELLING. NO, I THINK NOT. I'M RATHER
TIRED OF THAT PLOY. I THINK I'LL TRY THE
NARRATIVE SUMMARY BIT INSTEAD.**

There is a kind of peace that comes after a killer
storm, more exhaustion than peace, the time before
the survivors gather themselves and start again. As the
days pass, Timka begins to think they are in such a
period, that the Kalakal Ravvayad have exhausted
their resources for the moment with that abortive attack in Sikuro, that Telka has wasted her last out-
Mountain resources with the gunja defeat and will wait
for Skeen and Timka to come to her. The Goum
Kiskar drops anchor in the harbor at Karolsey. They
visit the ancient poet Nanojan Sogan. They drop passengers, take on new after warning them there could
be trouble ahead. They drop some cargo, take on
more. Skeen talks Maggí into breaking away from her
usual route up the Tail and darting across the short
stretch of open sea between Tail End and the outer
Bers and Bretels of the Spray, Maggí, reluctant because of her daughter and the crew who are as important to her, putting aside that reluctance because she'd

have Timka and Chulji flying watch and Lipitero ready
to use the clumsy but effective excavator.

The voyage along the Spray is one feast after another. Pegwai Dih turns out to have cousins and col-
laterals in nearly every port they visit, whether that's
on a tiny Ber, a larger Bretel, or one of the heart
islands they call the Leskets. He introduces Maggí as
one to be valued and is seduced by the warmth and
welcome and the wonderful food into telling over and
over the story of the quest, of Skeen and Timka, the
tragic death of the loyal Aggitj Domi, the terrible
circumstances of the Boy. He cajoles Lipitero to come
exhibit herself to folk who treat her with the most
delicate of courtesies and an unabashed delight in
possessing though only for the moment one of the
wonders of Mistommerk, a magical mythical creature
whose alien beauty will inspire their artists and musicians for seasons to come.

Feast to feast, rumor running before them, they
progress along the Spray. But even pleasant things
must end. They reach the end of the Spray, the island
group Lisshin Tula and one of its Bretels, Tiya Muka.
This is a middle-sized island inside a crazy maze of
waterways around Bers that are little more than dots
of rock, though some of them soar more than two
hundred meters from the agitated surface of the Tenga
Bourhh. It is a smuggler's haven whose splendid harbor is inaccessible to ships without a local pilot to
guide them through the confusion of the Bers and
none get a pilot without being "known." Maggí knows
and is "known" and slides into port and a friendly
welcome from Hannahar Tech who is the self-appointed
Headman of the eclectic collection of Wavers living on
Tiya Muka.

Skeen strolled out of the bathhouse rubbing vigorously at her hair, a heavy toweling robe tied about
her, flapping about her long legs as she climbed through
the blooming har trees, savoring their delicate rather

astringent scent and the crunch of coarse sand underfoot. She came out atop a steep slope of broken rock above a secluded inlet, a part of the harbor where no houses were built by edict of Hannahar Tech who jealously protected his favorite vistas. She settled on a boulder windworn smooth. No wind this day, just a silken soft flow of air up from water so saturated with color the blueness was an assault on her eyes. She gave a last rub at her head, dropped the towel beside her, shook her spiky hair out from her head, sighed with pleassure. I could get to like this. The placid scene stretching out before her brought memories of the time when she was a skinny desperate teener, recently escaped from the fish cannery and trying to claw her way off a world that would kill her if she didn't because she wasn't going to be caught again. Ever. She listened to the water lapping in a slow steady rhythm against the barnacled rocks below her. If I didn't have to stay here forever. A little lapping water goes a long way. She closed her eyes, leaned against the twisted, rock-hard dead tree behind her, remembering that other time, that other vast green park with its ornamental water and ornamental beasts, so violent a contrast with everything she'd known she was in a state of churning rage the whole time she was there; it was a lacerating memory in one way, pleasurable in another; that park and the monstrous house that sat in the middle of it marked her first real triumph, the place where she managed to get her life into her own hands. Bona Fortuna and some fancy footwork got her over the wall, her hard-won skills and a massive dose of patience eased her into the house. She broke into the house brain and stumbled onto information about the High Hipe who owned the house that bought her a small ancient ship and a pilot to fly it for her; he was supposed to dispose of her when she was far enough from Tors, but she worked a deal with him too and got her first lessons in ship handling and navigation. It was years later that she acquired Pi-

carefy. . . . She uncoiled, heeled a rock down the
slope, starting a small slide that didn't quite reach the
water. Fuckin' stupid world! How much longer, how
much longer, how can I stand the waiting, the fuckin'
stinkin' endless slog getting nowhere? She looked round
for the towel. It was time, more than time to be
getting back to the Inn, more than time to start goos-
ing Maggí into finding them transport out of here.

A flutter of wings behind her. She jumped away,
turning as she came down. "Djabo! Chul, don't do
that. You'll give me a heart attack or something."

Chulji worked his mouthparts in a Skirrik grin.
"Wanted to talk to you."

"Walk with me then." She scooped up the towel
and draped it over her shoulder. "I don't want to stay
here any longer."

The path was too narrow at first to let them walk
together. Skeen went along it toward the town, almost
loping in her drive to get on her way again.

"Eh, Skeen, slow down will you? How can I talk if
you gallop like that?"

"Sorry. What is it, Chul? Thing is, I'm a bit fidgety
today."

"I noticed." He scrambled down beside her and
walked along for several paces without saying anything. Finally he clattered his pincers and pulled his
top pair of shoulders up near his earholes. "Skeen,
I've been thinking."

She looked down at him, and smothered a grin; he
was so earnest, so very young. "A good habit to get
into," she said gravely.

"T'spp, t'spp, no need to be sarcastic. What I want
to say, from here on I'd be baggage, so I'm going to
stay with Maggí. She needs me and she's promised to
get a discount for me at some jet mines she knows. It's
a good job and everyone's friendly. So what do you
think?"

"Jet. That reminds me, meet me on the Kiskar after
supper tonight. I've got something I want you to have.

You know you couldn't find a better place. Don't be an idiot, Chul."

"What I want to say, I didn't want to look like I was scuttling out on you."

She put a hand on his shoulder. "I don't see it that way, Chul. Maggí needs you, she's made enemies helping us; it's only right you stay with her and help protect her from their malice. It'll take a load off my mind, believe me. Though you shouldn't tell her that, just look after her, hmmm?" She felt his shoulder swell under her hand, saw the pride and relief in his ugly-sweet bug face, and had to fight the urge to pat his shoulder as an unexpected gush of maternal sentimentality flooded through her. Fortunately that didn't last more than an instant and was gone before she embarrassed both of them. "Get along now and tell her you accept. And don't forget, meet me on the ship after supper."

Skeen opened the box and set it on the table close to the stickum so the bits of jet shone richly black against the cream velvet lining.

Chulji took up the pieces one by one, examined them with reverence and care, saying nothing until he'd looked over each piece, his antennas shivering the whole time.

"The slave dealer had those, Nochsyon Tod. I thought perhaps you might know where they belonged. I didn't feel like leaving them with him." Skeen started to gesture with her stump, made an impatient sound and changed to her left hand. "Whatever, they're yours, I'd have given them to you before, but, well, things happened and I got distracted."

Chulji set the final triangle of jet into the hollow in the velvet. "This is old, Skeen, it's from the first days here. Someone must have broken into a grave shrine. That," he touched a delicate tracery with the tip of his dactyl, "that's the Ur-nest sigil. One of the first nests organized after the Passing. He who earned this jet, he wasn't hatched there but in one of the branchings, the symbology is so old, I can't read it, it'd take a scholar. Ah! Skeen, I can't take this, it wouldn't be . . ." he made a complicated skritching sound, sections of which went beyond the range of her hearing, "um . . . there's no way I can translate that, except I couldn't . . . um . . . take the responsibility for it." He clicked the lid shut. "If you don't mind, you could give this to Pegwai to give to Scholar Dissarahnet at the Tanul Lumat She'll know how to take care of it." His antennas went rigid, his squeaky voice deepened suddenly. "And she'll do something about Tod and the Lifefire cursed thief who desecrated our dead."

Skeen suppressed a twinge and was rather happy the Min Skirrik boy knew nothing about her other-side profession. "Too bad; I thought you might be able to use those bits to earn yourself some points with your folk."

Chulji giggled, a bubbly squeaking that made Skeen's teeth ache. "Might do, ah yes, might. You tell Pegwai to tell Dissarahnet I was the one told you what to do. Aunt Scholar will see the family gets the news."

The Aggitj and the Boy surrounded Skeen as she climbed from the ship's boat onto the wharf belonging to Tech's Inn. "We heard Chulji is taking a job with Maggí Solitaire." Hal stepped aside, then matched his steps to hers as she started up the winding track to the Inn that sprawled across the flat above. "That he's not going on with us."

"Yes." She thought of explaining but a look at Hal's serious face prompted a question instead. "Why?"

"We've been thinking."

Skeen waited for him to go on, but he didn't, just climbed beside her, staring at the ground. "Yes?" she prompted.

"We've been thinking this is a good place for us to stop too. We've been thinking us going on with you isn't going to be much help. You're better off, you and

Timka, if you kind of sneak in, her sister can't be looking everywhere all the time." He stopped. They'd reached the flat and the Inn's veranda was just ahead. "And there are things we got to do."

Skeen looked sharply at him; his face was grave and troubled, but only, as far as she could tell, because he didn't know what she was going to say. "Well, come in and have a last drink with me," she said; she touched his arm, smiled. "Remember what I told you when we started this thing. No strings on me, none on you."

Inside, she found a table close to the fire but far enough from the other patrons to provide a measure of privacy. After the Balayar girl finished giggling with the Aggitj and brought them stoups of Tech's homebrew, Skeen looked round at the unsmiling faces. "Lighten up, friends, it isn't the end of the world." She drank, drew the back of her hand across her mouth. "So. Things to do. Mind telling me?"

Ders leaned forward eagerly, but subsided when the Boy touched his arm and murmured to him, speaking so softly Skeen couldn't hear him; whatever it was, it quieted Ders. Hal gave the Boy an approving nod, planted his elbows on the table. "We talked it over," he said, "a lot." The other Aggitj muttered agreement; the Boy grinned, showing his poison fangs. "We decided we're going to Rood Meol. We're going hunting, Skeen. We're going to seech out the Kalakal's Heart and kill him, then we're going after Ravvayad and after that if we're still around, we're slipping into the Backland, the Boy, us and any Sualasual still around, and we're going to kill our uncle if we can, and his Rossam and the soldi he keeps around because the other ashanku and him are always fighting and we're going to take his Hold, make it ours. That's it." He straightened his back, grinned at her, lifted his tankard in an informal toast to the end of it all. The others lifted theirs and drank with him.

Skeen smiled, joined the toast and drank with them. This was suicide, she knew it; she thought briefly about trying to argue them out of their plans, but what could she do? Take them with her? That was just as dangerous, maybe more, what with Telka and the Holavish. Besides, it wasn't her job to take care of them. Hal and Hart were old enough to know what they were doing; Ders wasn't, Ders probably never would be, but they'd take care of him while they could. "Keep your heads down," she said. "Bona Fortuna smile on you." How much they've changed, she thought, the dew's rubbed off. Well, I never fixated before on ignorance as innocence however charming, and this is not the time to start that idiocy. Bona Fortuna indeed, though I'm afraid you'll know the Mala better.

He came in smiling and genial, a small man covered with honey-amber fur that darkened in a mask about his eyes and over his dainty pointed ears. He looked round at them from the blue foil eyes of a high-bred cat. "Maggí Soiltaire."

"Usoq."

He pricked his ears at Skeen. "Torska."

"Sujipyo."

"I know you, I think. Harmony Pit? Ship Picarefy?"

"You got me." She frowned, then her face cleared. "I'd just come in with an Oud-tua load. You bought a pot and some skeeders off me direct and helped me," she smiled at pleasant memories and gave him a speculative look, "celebrate."

"Yes." His whiskers twitched and the blue eyes narrowed to sleepy slits. He bowed to Pegwai. "Scholar." After Pegwai returned his greeting, he said, "You'll be wanting the Lumat. Ah, we can do that, Pouliļoulou and me. My ship, a sweet thing, though not over large. The one thing she lacks is canvas, that sweet silken canvas the Lumat weavers make and is so hard, so hard to come by." With another twinkle and twitch he bowed to the robed, cowled Lipitero. "Ma dama, rumors of your coming have run before you, I swoon with awe in your magical presence." He rolled his eyes, put his hand over his heart, swayed and turned briskly to Timka. "Timka Essora, there's more than me praying you can curb your pestilent sister. She's spurred the Stammarka Nagamar into shutting their waters to everyone—even me who am the mildest and most harmless of travelers. Have you any idea what that means? And how many snots are out there on the Tenga Bourhh snooping into things that're none of their business? Hah! Even Atsila Vana's got guard ships out. Ah, the bribes it takes to slip the least thing by them. I don't dare have a Min on board, they've pressed the Skirrik into warding for them. They want no Min anywhere near them. Lifefire bless and reward you, Essora, if you will take that sister of yours to the far side and get her out of our hair."

"Well, Usoq, I see the years haven't changed you. Your tongue still flaps at both ends." Maggí's dry tones brought him round, woke a broad grin on his round face.

"Nor you, Maggí Solitaire. You were a wonderful woman then and a warm armful now. Ah, Maggí, if only you knew how I dreamed of you on the few cold nights we have." He widened his eyes in an exaggerated, soulful gaze and heaved a prolonged sigh.

"Oh, sit down, will you." Maggí tapped the gong and three serving girls brought in a huge bowl of steaming punch that filled the room with hot lemony sweetness. They set it on a bed of coals prepared in one corner of the room; two of them ladled punch into tankards for those around the long table, while the third trimmed the candles and made sure all of them were burning properly. The windows were open and the night was cool enough to make the hot drink welcome.

Usoq pulled a chair up to the end of the table, drank a long draft from his tankard and sighed with pleasure. "Tech's Mix is always superb."

"My friends want to reach Oruda as quickly and with as little fuss as possible."

"One wonders when you were so noisy coming along the Spray. Ah, well, no doubt you had your reasons and it's none of my business. See, Maggí Solitaire, I say it for you." He pushed the tankard aside, brought out a stained, much folded map and spread it on the table. "Come round," he said. "I'll make more sense if you see what I'm talking about. Maggí, fetch that candelabra with you, this is getting hard to read; I suppose I ought to get the Lumat to give me another." He shot a sly glance at Pegwai. "Eh, Scholar, if you look careful, you'll see a maze of corrections; your mapmakers need to do a resurvey of the coast along there." He smoothed a plump square hand over the map.

"Since you're in a hurry and the Funor Ashon cranky about letting travelers through their lands, I doubt you'll want me to land you here." He put a stubby forefinger on the deep inlet south of the Skirrik mountains and west of the Stammarka Morass. "Consider, though. You can acquire some horses, haha. Don't ask me about that, Skeen, you have your little ways of doing what you have to do. There's a fairly well-used track along here at the edge of the foothills, a boundary of sorts between the Funor on the Plain and the dwellers in the mountains. Min and outcasts. Once you get here," he stabbed the finger at a small black dot on the river, "You wouldn't have to wait long for a ship going upriver to the Lakes. A day or two at most."

Skeen and Pegwai exchanged glances; Pegwai shook his head. "The Funor have working com-links."

"That's out, then. The Funor don't like us, Usoq; for our health we'd better keep our heads down around them."

"Hm." He raised his brows as he twisted round and looked from blank face to blanker. He sighed and traced the long looping line of the Rekkah, up from

the Nagamar watertown past Istryamozhe, through the
mountains and across the Funor Plain, tapped his finger on the dot that represented Oruda. "This is how
you came. Right? Ah, yes. Everyone uses that way,
coming and going. It's the safest way, slow going
upriver but you're sure to get there. Funor wouldn't
bother you on the river. You want? No? Last resort?
Right. You're waiting for me to cross my hands and
declaim behold the miracle; behold, my friends, mira-
cles come expensive. Ah, yes. Ah, yes. A hundred
gold each, banked with Tech before we start."

Maggí snorted. "Dream on, little man; before I let
them pay that, I'd take them up the Rekkah myself.
Work your tricks however you want, but not on me or
my friends."

"Now, Maggí Solitaire, is that playing the game? I
ask you, will you come between a man and his profit?
Shame, Maggí, shame." He spread his hands, hunched
up his shoulders. "Like I told you, life's got difficult
lately. My expenses, Maggí, you wouldn't believe how
they've exploded on me. If I do this thing the way
your friends want, I could lose my sweeting, my joy,
my Pouliloulou which is my all in all and my living
besides." He shivered all over, the fur in his mask
stood up as if someone had shot electricity through his
face. "I have to cover myself, you understand that.
You must. What if someone asked you to do something that most likely would scuttle Goum Kiskar, eh?
All right, all right, say three hundred with a suit of
Lumat sails."

"Say one hundred gold and a suit of Lumat sails.
And that's worth more than your first offer, Usoq old
friend. You know the price of Lumat canvas." Maggí
turned to Pegwai. "If you can provide them for this
pirate, my friend? I know how long I had to wait and
the contortions I had to go through to get mine. But I
also know it was worth everything I had to do to get
my name on the list."

Pegwai shook his head. "List I can't manage. One

suit for a single-master—if that's your Pouliloulou moored beside the Goum Kiskar—yes, I can call in some favors. Yamakalelbiseh is a friend, he's head-man of the Chala weavers." He rubbed his hand across his mouth, stared out the window across the room for several breaths before he spoke again. "You'll want surety for the sails. Not knowing how much my word can be trusted. Hm. I am willing to do this: I will write an undertaking on the funds of Sibetsig Dih for the cost of a suit of Lumat sails for a single-masted coaster, good for six months after this night, the first call day being two months hence." He dropped his hand, smiled tightly at Usoq. "Thus, if I fail, you'll get your price anyway. If I produce the sail contract, I'll have plenty of time to cancel the undertaking."

"Call day, one month."

"That's not negotiable."

"You have a low suspicious mind, Pegwai Dih. Usoq's an honorable man, ask anyone, ask Maggí Solitaire who will tell you the truth if you press her. Forty-five days."

"Fifty-five. Not another sooner."

"Ouw ouw, how can a man live? So I have a great heart, I won't be minching. Fifty-five days it is." He turned to Maggí. "Two hundred gold and it's a bargain, you don't know what I'll be taking my darling into."

"A hundred gold would buy ten Pouliloulous, exquisite though she is and sweet to the hand, I'll grant you that. And you'll be having some of the best fighters on Mistommerk defending her when my friends come on board."

"How can you put a price on heart's blood, Maggí Solitaire? Sweat and the skin off my hands and years of my life. One ninety."

Skeen and Pegwai walked to a window and stood looking out over the harbor. Timka curled up on a windowseat and dozed. Lipitero settled into a chair and watched intently as the bargaining went on. This

was for her life. She knew enough to conceal her
tension from Usoq, pulled the cowl forward until its
shadows hid her face, tucked her betraying hands inside the robe and locked them about the straps of her
harness. After a short while, though, she grew fascinated with the complex dance between these two; they
knew the steps and trod them with a skill that amazed
her. When it was finally over, she had the feeling that
each had ended just about where he and she had
intended. I could no more do that than Usoq could fly
off the roof of this Inn, she thought, for all we Ykx are
supposed to be universal negotiators. I'm an anomaly
in more ways than I knew.

"Now that you've stripped me of my pride, Maggí
Solitaire, now that you have squeezed all the juice out
of me, let us talk about how we can accomplish this
thing. Scholar, you and the Pass-Through come see."

They bent over the map and watched as he talked.

"This is the south branch of the Rekkah. And this is
the Stammarka Morass. Now that's supposed to be
impassable for several reasons. For one, it's too shallow, your Lumat maps say it, for anything but those
rotten reed boats the Nagamar throw together. T'ain't
so, Scholar, no, indeed, though I'd appreciate it if you
didn't bother reporting that bit of news. Eh?"

"Can't promise that, Captain, what I can promise is
to bury the information so deep in dullness, no one
will bother with it. That do?"

"I'd rather not have it mentioned at all; if you've
got this Lifefire cursed need to report everything, then
swear on your mother's womb, you'll see it don't get
recorded for another score of years. By that time I'll
either be dead or retired, then who cares who knows
what."

"Ah. Right. That I can arrange, Scholar's Seal. My
word on it."

"Appreciate. You know what I said, the Stammarka
Nagamar shutting off the Morass, that's true enough,
but maybe I exaggerated a trifle. It's touchy, yes, and

expensive in this 'n that, and that expense is over and above passage fee, Maggí Solitaire."

"You're pushing damn hard, my friend, I thought we had ourselves a fast deal."

"So we do, but I balk here, Maggí. Pay or no play."

"How many more of these balking points you going to throw at us? I'm teetering on saying forget the whole thing."

"Ow ow, Maggí, Usoq's an honorable man, you know that. No more, my word on it."

"No more now. What about when my friends are committed, when they're deep in the Morass with you standing alone between them and the mud and a thousand irritated Nagamar? I don't like the smell of this balking nonsense, Usoq. Seems to me you've changed more than I thought."

"All right, all right, suck in the smoke, Maggí, though it hurts like a knife in my heart, I'll swallow the expense. You're a hard woman, Maggí Solitaire. By the way, that's the second reason most everyone thinks the South Rekkah is a junk river, no use to anyone. The Nagamar. A real nasty bunch to outsiders, but I've managed to do a favor here and there and they let me slide through now and then if I don't push it. Ahhh, there is this . . . it's been a couple of months since I was there last and the Nagamar were starting to act like they forgot what a favor is. That miserable Min woman and her airhead followers—it's their fault, stirring up the Nagamar, sneaking in where they've got no business. Well, well, I hope they like what happened, I know for a fact that a bunch of them left dripping tailfeathers. Might have had a hand in that myself, might not, still, it's chancy for any outsider going there now. Thing is, Pass-Through, you won't be where Funor can get their hands on you. And you don't need to say anything should you want not, but I'm assuming you're making for the Gate. Well, it'll only take 'leven days to get you up to Spalit if you'd like getting off there. Now if you compare that with the thirty some it'll take going up the West Rekkah to Oruda, you'll see one of the benefits of the route, dangers aside, and you'll be at least five days closer to the Gate. Now, I don't want to tell you your business, but there's a lot of river traffic between Spalit and Dum Besar, should you want to go that way, get you that much closer, and faster than you can make it riding. Well, that's it. I'm willing. Up to you where I take you."

Skeen scowled at the map. "Pegwai Dih has to get back to Oruda, not Spalit."

"No problem, Pass-Through, better for me if I take the long way back, 'cross the lakes and down the West Rekkah. Got no problem with the Funor, no, and Ferryman at the Fork, he'll winch the cables down and let me past. All included in the price, so let your hair fall, Maggí Solitaire. Usoq said he'd swallow the expenses and he means it."

Timka stood on the deck of the Pouliloulou watching Maggí Solitaire say her farewells to her daughter. Behind her, Skeen was fiddling aimlessly about the piles of gear, her back turned to that scene, deliberately refusing to see Maggí lose the command of herself she'd maintained without break before, on the verge of crying, hugging the girl over and over, holding her by the sleeve of her tunic, talking earnestly to her, loosing the sleeve, hand darting to touch not-hair, cheek, to touch and touch as if she feared she'd never touch her child again. Timka felt her own small pangs of envy, but these were drowned by the pain she felt in Skeen; she was unhappy with knowledge she hadn't asked for, would rather not have, couldn't use, too raw and fresh to ignore. She wrinkled her nose, tapped impatiently at the rail, then went to find out from Usoq what they could do with the small mountain of gear they'd acquired in their travels. Pegwai kept adding notebooks to his and samples of anything small and portable he found interesting and thought the

Lumat might not have. Lipitero's share was heavier and more enigmatic. Timka found herself wondering how on Mistommerk they were going to transport all that to the Gate.

With Usoq directing them but not lifting anything heavier than a finger, Pegwai, Lipitero and Timka carried the gear down and stowed it in holds that were built as finely as a kehlwood chest and better than rooms in many grand houses, and (as they found later) much better than the cramped airless cabin they were supposed to share. Usoq's interest vividly presented. Passengers were far down on his list of values.

As the lading of the boat continued, Timka drifted out to stand in the bow watching the tide rise near its ordinary high. Rannah was finally being rowed out to the Pouliloulou and Maggí was pacing back and forth back and forth along the end of the pier, more than ever like a powerful dangerous big cat. She was too far for Timka to make out more than a sketch of her features, but her anxiety and love for her child was graven in every line of her body. Timka sighed. Now that Chulji was leaving them, she felt more alone than she'd ever been, even when she was alone in Dum Besar. When she was living with the Poet she always knew she could go back when she really wanted to. Carema would take her in, defend her, so would a lot of friends she'd made in that house. Now, she couldn't feel sure of that. She'd come to realize she'd been away too long, that nothing she thought she knew about her folk might be real, might be depended on. Alone. Exile, maybe permanent, exile in a place far more alien than Dum Besar. The closer she got to the Mountains, the more demanding the urge became to go back, to fight Telka and her Holavish. She needed her kind almost as much as Lipitero did hers and if she was finally severed from them it might just open a wound an eon wouldn't heal. Fight Telka, free the unhappy from her dominance; just thinking about that charged her with energy and drive, like that she felt when she went to cat-weasel, only ten times stronger. Yet even as she thought and felt, she knew with chilling certainty how foolish such a notion was.

Chulji-eagle broke into her angst with a cawing shriek. He was gliding in taut circles over the boat. Laughter that was almost crying exploded out of her; she stripped and shifted and went winging up to join him in a last air dance, a celebration of their kind-ship and friendship and a promise of sorts to meet again.

Crossing the Mother of Storms in Terwel Mo's Meyeberri, warm and reasonably comfortable in a tight, fairly roomy cabin was one thing; crossing it in a boat half that size with a choice between a smelly crowded cabin and a sea-swept deck was something else. Lipitero, Pegwai, Usoq, they refused to let Skeen on deck except in the rare calms; without two hands to grab and hold on, she could too easily be washed overboard and Usoq wouldn't have his deck cluttered with lifelines. If we have to run, he said, what a mess that would be, my crew'd be tripping over you and poor little Pouliloulou would maybe flounder and miss her reach. No, no and no—no lifelines on my decks. Skeen fumed and fussed and wielded a bitter tongue, but she stayed below; she couldn't argue with them when she knew quite well they were right. The Pouliloulou rode close to the water, smooth and sweet, slipping through blows that would have battered a larger ship, but that didn't make her a comfortable ship for those unaccustomed to her complex and sudden shifts and motions. Usoq and his crew—two tough resilient Balayar girls who seemed to have eyes in their toes and fingers and nerve connections to the nerve lines of the boat—played the Pouliloulou like some giant musical instrument; they moved about the ship like slim brown ghosts and a sealman whose golden fur was sleek with damp.

Twilight. Near calm. Skeen out exercising with obsessive energy near the mast. Pegwai aft talking with

Lipitero, stylus busy in the notebook fluttering on his knee. The crew and Usoq below, giggles coming from the hutch he shared with them. Rannah fidgeting near the rail, wanting to go listen to Pegwai's questions, not yet daring to intrude on them.

Timka touched Rannah's arm. "Tell me something."

"If I can, Timka 'a." She smiled shyly; she was a friendly but rather formal child and gratifyingly in awe of the four adults, a polite gentle child who'd never suffered physical hurt, though Timka now and then wondered how she'd dealt with the long absences of her wandering mother. She made Timka feel protective, she had the same effect (perhaps even more intense) on Pegwai and Skeen. How could her mother thrust her into such dangerous business as this?

"Why did Maggí send you along with us? We could all get killed any day."

Rannah's not-hair wriggled, then smoothed out. "You've done pretty well so far at keeping alive."

"Domi."

Rannah nodded. Her thin face crumpled with sudden sadness, brightened as suddenly. "Mama figures I'll be safer with you all than with her. She figures if there are more gunja out looking for trouble, they'll be hunting the Goum Kiskar, rather than this. . . ." She swept a hand about at the crowded boat. Her face crumpled again, this time with worry. "Mama says she's going to be careful, she says she's going to work the Spray for a while and not go out in deep waters, she says the Sea Min don't come into the shallows. She says with Scholar Dih's introductions, you know, on the way here, and all that, she should do pretty well, though she has got to get back to her own waters eventually. She says with Skeen and Lipitero and Pegwai Dih and you looking after me, I'm about as safe as anyone can be. She says Usoq might be a worm, but he's a competent worm and if anybody can get me safe to the Tanul Lumat, he can."

Timka patted the girl's shoulder. "Your Mama's

pretty competent herself. She'll be fine." She flicked
her fingers toward the stern. "Now, go do what you're
itching to do. Don't worry, Pegwai won't mind. Nor
Lipitero. If she was saying anything she didn't want
you to hear, she wouldn't be talking to a Lumat Scholar,
she'd be talking to her friend Peg. Scoot."

Rannah flushed with embarrassment, then flashed
Timka a grin very like her mother's; not-hair wriggling
with her eagerness, she made her way back to the pair
and settled close by Pegwai's knee.

Timka smiled after her, then watched Skeen some
more. That made her nervous, so she stripped, shifted
and flew off as a sea eagle to practice her version of
exercising to exorcise the demons plaguing her.

Pouliloulou slipped into the Stammarka Morass three
hours after midnight on the ninth day out from Tiya
Muka.

Dark. Secret. Silent. Stinking. Patches of reeds, tall,
their frizzled tops reaching halfway up the mast. Patches
of brush, tide marks of mud on the lower parts, branches
where most of the small teardrop leaves were fallen
away leaving a nubbly nudity up to the growing tips.
Sand spits dark with algae, sand spits glowing pale
through the muddy water. Pouliloulou seemed to gather
herself, dust off her metaphorical hands, to hunch
down and slip with ease along the wandering channels;
her sails (not Lumat silk canvas but not to be despised
either) caught the whispering winds and she slipped
like a noisy shadow into a world of silence and secrecy.

Fair or not, Timka left Skeen to simmer in her
confinement and sought the slightly wider spaces of
the deck. Don't go shifting, Usoq said to her when the
coast was a low dark line showing against high-piled
moon-silvered clouds. The Nagamar aren't Skirrik; they
won't know what you are if you don't shake your hips
in their faces. All bets are off if they learn I've sneaked
a Min into the Morass. Even Maggí Solitaire wouldn't
blame me for dumping you. I don't care how itchy you

get, no shifting. She settled herself in the bow and
gulped in a few experimental breaths of the hot heavy
air; not much better than ordinary breathing. Three
hours after midnight and the fringes of the Morass
were warmer than Tiya Muka at noon. She sighed,
regretting Usoq's strictures; a bird could fly in cleaner,
cooler air. So I live like Nemin for the moment. She
wrinkled her nose. Poor limited things, stuck with one
shape all their lives.

For nearly an hour the Pouliloulou twisted and turned
through the reeds, until she reached the transition
areas where the trees began, tall furry things, dripping
with fungus; she nosed into a broader channel, water
that shone a greenish silver in the moonlight. Under
the trees on either side glints where the moon reached
the water, silver spangles on a silken gown, slipped
out and away from them as they moved farther and
farther into the Morass. Timka heard splashes, rustles,
a few eerie cries from bird, beast or reptile, she couldn't
tell which, strange minor ululations that held within
their brief existence all she'd ever felt of sorrow, loneliness, wanting, need. Small sounds that only served to
make the night's heavy silence yet more intense. Trees
and water, even the cloud-broken sky had an ominous
feel, as if the Morass was waiting for them, mouth
open, and they were sliding willy-nilly into that mouth.
Usoq's a worm, Rannah had said, quoting her mother,
but a competent worm. Lifefire grant that was true
and he knew what he was doing.

She'd felt something like this before when she slipped
into Tod's House, a combination of apprehension and
excitement that was disturbing but . . . ah, it could
become addicting, she thought. She frowned at the
water hissing past the bow. A passenger. Passive. Con-
strained. She'd waked out of passivity not so gradually
as she traveled with Skeen, shaken out of it as much
by Skeen's defects as her virtues. Perhaps more. Because Skeen wouldn't, Timka had to assume responsibility for herself. In emergencies she could count on

the Pass-Through, but day to day, Skeen just wasn't
there; she slid through the fingers like mercury. At first
this was frightening and annoying, but Timka nodded
at the water, acknowledging that she liked being responsible for herself. She liked it so much she found it
very hard to lie back now and let Usoq do all the
work. She didn't trust him that much, only to the
extent his self-interest merged with theirs. She thought
a lot about Skeen and the world on the far side of the
Gate, trying to get a better grasp of it from the chaotic
chunk of Skeen's memories settling into her own
head. Very little made any kind of coherent sense.
She had few points of reference to help her; what she
did get was a better understanding of why Skeen was
the way she was. She'd been broken repeatedly as a
child and badly mended. She functioned well enough
as long as she limited the complexity of her life, kept
to a minimum the connections she had with others.
Underneath her surface friendliness and that impressive competence, there was a pool of fear and self-
loathing that frightened Timka when she caught glimpses
of it—frightened her and gave her a queasy relief.
Lifefire's blessing, this isn't me.

In the middle of these musings one of the crew girls
came to the bow, waited politely until Timka moved
out of her way. The girl crawled out along the stubby
bowsprit, hooked her feet in the ropes and began
chanting enigmatic syllables, not numbers, no language
Timka knew, a soft but carrying sound that slipped
back to Usoq at the wheel. Pouliloulou fled on up the
channel, water glinting out and out under the trees,
the glints smaller and smaller as the moon dropped
into and through the clouds, the darkness thicker and
heavier, the air thicker, harder to breath. As if the
Pouliloulou plowed through gel instead of air, doing
this with the delicate grace she used cutting through
the water.

On and on, noisy shadow slicing through the water.
On and on into that deadly silence. Timka got tired of

the tension and began thinking about going below. She drowsed by the rail wondering vaguely how broad the belt of wetlands was, how long they were going to be stuck in the steam and stink and the purported danger. Usoq, she thought, running up his price with claims of jeopardy. The rise and fall of Vohdi's soft chant merged with the boat's song, the chorus of small creaks and groans. Timka dropped deeper into her drowse.

A watervine slapped around the rail beside Timka; a few seconds later wet gleaming figures came up and over the rail, Nagamar females, fighter class, five of them. Silent except for the water dripping off their leathery scales. Menacing. Usoq snapped an order; the crew girl Cepo slipped off the bowsprit and joined Vohdi dropping anchors overside fore and aft, then they glided along the far rail to crouch beside the wheel. Usoq touched one then the other on the head, walked round the wheel and went to confront the intruders.

He saw Timka by the rail and hissed with impatience and fear. "Get below," he shrilled. "Get, woman, you're in the way here, get, get."

Timka rose slowly to her feet, yawned and strolled below. She stopped in the shadows of the passage, dropped to her knees; she wanted to keep a wary eye on Usoq; if he tried anything, at least the Company would have a few moments' warning.

Moonlight gleamed on long long fingers flickering through angry signs. Usoq replied, his pudgy fingers dancing through dexterous combinations, his pudgy body bent over his hands, radiating his eagerness to convince. He finished, waited. One of the warrior women made a chattering angry sound and went into signs that needed little translation. The Nagamar was telling Usoq to turn himself and his boat about and get out so fast he set his tail on fire, and if he didn't he could feed the needlefish in the mud below. Usoq hunched himself up yet more and went into a series of

swift signs, protesting the order, or so Timka thought,
trying to persuade her to listen to his offers. He worked
body as well as hands. Like a puppy wagging his tail,
Timka thought, but she quickly cut off that disparag-
ing thought. Whatever it takes. Go, little worm, talk
her round.

When the Nagamar started signing again, she was
calmer, her hands slipping with easy fluidity through
her silent speech. She paused, looked thoughtful, began signing again.

Usoq relaxed. He watched intently, picked up the
thread the moment she dropped it. Bargaining begins,
Timka thought. She relaxed too. She continued watching, fascinated, as the silent dispute went on, a dispute
now over the fee for passage. Odd, in its way; like the
arrangement the Sea Min and their Land Min cousins
had with the Captains crossing the Halijara. A way
of the world she hadn't suspected for all she prided
herself on knowing more of the world than most.
Individuals and groups found ways of dealing with each
other that had nothing to do with official pronounce-
ments. She yawned. The ominous night had turned
simply oppressive. She took a last look at the bargain-
ers. Close to the end, yes, there's satisfaction in each
of those bodies. The four other Nagamar had grown
restless; they were moving about the boat, hadn't shown
signs of coming below yet, but that might happen at
any moment. She got to her feet, moving as silently as
she could, unwilling to pull their notice her way before
they came on their own. She ghosted along the passage to the cabin door, eased it open and slipped
inside.

Skeen sat up. "Anything happening?"

Timka settled onto the floor, her back against the
wall. "Usoq's friends. Not so friendly. He's working
out the passage fee right now."

Pegwai leaned forward. "Not so friendly?"

"Started out that way. Usoq calmed them down."
She smiled at Rannah. "Competent worm."

Rannah ducked her head. She looked tired. She should have been asleep, but the closeness in the cabin and her general excitement at getting this far into the Morass had kept sleep away from her; no doubt there'd been a lot of tension in that room too, tension Timka had walked out on. The girl sat on her pallet, watching the other faces with a shy avidity. A scholar in the bud. Maggí was right, Lumat is where that one belongs. By the time she's Pegwai's age there won't be a hair's worth of difference between them.

Lipitero was looking tired also; she was wearing one of her robes of concealment, though the cowl was pushed back. Her fur was sticky with sweat, standing out from her head and neck in damp peaks; she was breathing with some difficulty, but not in serious trouble, at least, not yet. The glow from the single small lamp sank deep in her crystal eyes, its fire burning down there in tiny gold-red shimmers. She said nothing, content to let the others ask the questions.

Skeen rubbed at her stump. "They coming down here?"

"I wouldn't be surprised. Calmer they might be, but they still aren't all that happy letting this boat cross the Morass."

"How many?"

"Five. Fighter caste."

Skeen sighed, took out the darter, checked the drug and water level, handed it to Pegwai. "In case," she said. "No use asking for trouble, better to be ready than sorry."

Pegwai pushed the sleeves of his robe down over his hands and sat with them in his lap, the darter hidden by the thick folds of cloth. "Eleven days from the coast to Spalit," he mused. "If I remember the map correctly, it'll take five of those days to cross the Morass. That's a minimum, granting the wind keeps steady."

Timka sighed. "And granting the Nagamar don't change their tiny minds."

They sat in silence after that, the lamp filling the room with the smell of burning oil. Wet fur from Lipitero, thick and musky. Tart lemony odors from Pegwai. A harsher darker smell from Skeen who was sweating as copiously as Lipitero. A faint herbal scent from Rannah, mostly overpowered by the other smells in the room. Timka couldn't smell herself. She thought about that for a while, wondering what her body was contributing to the melange. Surreptitiously she sniffed at her wrist, wiped her hand in her armpit and sniffed it, but she couldn't smell herself. That bothered her. The others were so powerfully present to the nose, she had to be too, but there was no way for her to know how the others were receiving her. She began wondering how they thought of her. How did Skeen see her? She closed her eyes and riffled through Skeen's memories but there was nothing about her there. Maybe that was telling her something, maybe Skeen didn't give a curse about her, couldn't be bothered about what she was like. No, that wasn't true. Unless I've been totally wrong about her. She shook her head.

Skeen chuckled. "Not so bad as that."

Timka bit her lip to hold back the questions she couldn't possibly ask. "No," she said finally. "It's just that I don't like waiting without knowing what's happening."

"Me, I'll put off knowing just as long as I can. Give me peace and ignorance and I'll wallow in both."

"You don't mean that. Not you."

"Well, in a way I do. Long as the Nagamar are up on deck, I'm fairly sure we've got no problems Usoq can't handle. Let one of them stick her nose down here, then it's toss the coin and hope it comes down Bona not Mala."

Skeen's last word was still lingering when the door burst open. The Nagamar female who'd done the bargaining above stood in the doorway, a feral menacing figure. She looked from face to face, lingering on each, lingering longest on Lipitero's, startled to see an

Ykx. Her eyes flicked over Rannah, she wasn't interested in an Aggitj child, went back to Lipitero. With a
series of gestures she ordered the Ykx to strip. As
Lipitero came to her feet, the Nagamar stepped back
into the passage and produced a shrill whistle that
shattered eardrums and brought Usoq running. Her
hands fluttered through angular signs, a command for
him to explain. Lipitero stripped off the robe and
stood hunched over in the low-ceiled cabin, clutching
at a bunk post with one fur-backed hand. Her metaled harness glistened and glowed in the shifting light
from the small lamp, her crystal eyes held fire again.
Usoq cleared his throat. "Ykx," he said and rein-
forced the word with a flutter of his hands. Another
whistle, demanding, angry. Long fingers closed into a
knot, hand whipped side to side. "No," he said, his
voice shrill with fear, "no Min. No, Ykx." His hands
moved emphatically, broke off when she made a
slicing incisive move of her bladed hand. She beckoned Lipitero over. Skeen hunched over, rubbing at
her stump; she'd contrived an arm sheath for her boot
knife, the one with the metal blade. Her fingers were
close to its hilt as she scratched aimlessly at the gray
film over the end of her arm. Pegwai shifted position a
little, making sure he had a clear shot at the Nagamar.
Usoq saw both and grew measurably shiftier. His
eyes darted from Timka to Skeen, skidded hastily
from Skeen's cool measuring eyes, skittered to Pegwai,
swung off him almost as quickly, came back to the
confrontation between the Nagamar female and the
Ykx.

The Nagamar was running her overlong fingers along
the Ykx harness, plucked painfully at the hair on
Lipitero's arms. For a long moment, Lipitero endured
this, then she stepped back, pushed the Nagamar's
hand aside. She produced a chirping tweetling sound
that rose beyond the hearing of all but the Aggitj girl.
Rannah looked startled, grimaced with pain, pressed
her arms over her ears, crossed her forearms over her

not-hair. The Nagamar hissed with anger and surprise, leaped back, crouched, squealed at her in a similar series of sounds.

Lipitero spoke slowly after that, fumbling for the little Namarish she knew, began moving her hands, stiffly, slowly, through her meager assemblage of signs.

Timka watched, tucked back in the shadows at the end of the bunk, ready to shift if she had to; once she did, they had to be sure they got all the Nagamar, if they didn't, they could have the entire Morass on their back within hours . . . well, a day or two anyway. She stayed tense for several minutes, but the Nagamar changed her attitude so fast it was almost comic, would have been comic if she hadn't felt so much like vomiting.

The Nagamar female whistled again, a series of ear-splitting blasts. The other Nagamar came tumbling down the passage and circled about her in a slippery gleaming mob, bringing with them the smell of mud and vegetation and their own bitter tang, flat webbed feet splatting noisily on the planks, long long fingers fluttering, voices whistling and chirping, dipping in and out of audibility. They signed at her, stroked her, pulled at the straps of her harness, generally making total nuisances of themselves. Finally the squad leader whistled them into order and sent them tail dragging and reluctant back onto the deck. She touched Lipitero a few more times, waggled her head, mimed extreme wonder, then shooed Usoq before her back topside.

"I feel like a plucked fowl," Lipitero murmured, a plaintive note in her muted voice. She glanced along the passage to make sure no one had heard, then retreated into the cabin and dropped heavily onto one of the bunks. "Hai, Peg, you think this is going to keep on the whole time we're in this place?"

"Seems likely." He scratched at his nose, stared into the shadows. After a few sighs and some thought, he said, "I'd talk to Usoq as soon as you can get hold of him, see if he can negotiate some relief for you. Look but don't touch. Even keep them off the boat, let them watch from the water or the trees. Them, hm. I've a suspicion the news is going to fly and Nagamar will be swarming around like flies about a carcass if you don't mind the unlovely comparison." He leaned over, handed the darter back to Skeen. "Usoq knows his business. Skeen?"

"Yup. I'll throw in ten gold if he needs sweetening. Probably won't, you know. He isn't going to want the Pouliloulou weighed down with Nagamar and you might point out how much good having you on board is going to do for him in Nagamar eyes. Make life a lot easier. Were I you, I'd bargain for two flights—you can fly in this air? Good. Morning and evening, you go up, show yourself off. Other times, you're down here, no touch no see. And yes, let him handle that Nagamar female, a bit of time he'll have her licking honey off his toes." Skeen tapped her fingers on her thigh, grinned at Rannah, a quick twist of her wide mouth. "A competent worm, oh, yes."

Lipitero glanced at the door, grimaced. "I'd rather not go up there."

Skeen clicked her tongue against her teeth, a soft irritated sound. "Can't you feel it? We're moving again. He won't leave the wheel. He's got to make time now, he knows it, the farther he can get before the flood, Nagamar I mean, the shorter he'll have to endure that kind of notice. Um . . . I'd offer to bargain for you, but I don't think that I'd have the same . . . um . . . clout with him. I can try. . . ."

Lipitero shuddered, sighed. "No. . . . Toss me my robe, please Rannah? I might as well make the point early that I'll show what I want when." She caught the bundle the Aggitj girl lobbed to her, pulled it on. She stood a moment smoothing it down over her body, then she pulled the cowl up over her head and moved away down the passage.

Timka moved out of the shadows and dropped onto a bunk. "Poor Petro, but I can't regret it. No one's going to look hard at me and wonder what I am.

Which is just as well, given that fighter's attitude
toward Min." She exaggerated a shiver. "I wouldn't
want her after me, hooo!"

Skeen chuckled. "Poor little Min."

"Phffft to you, Pass-Through."

Midmorning in the days that followed, Lipitero rode
the lift field up, extended her flight skins and soared
over the Morass, turning in slow spirals so the Nagamar
adults and children could get a good look at her. She
stayed up there for over an hour (she admitted to the
rest of the Company that it was a lot cooler and
smelled better up there) then drifted blown-leaf back
to the boat and vanished below deck. Midafternoon,
she repeated the performance. The original squad of
Nagamar swam the waters about the Pouliloulou, keeping off the curious who would have swarmed and
swamped the boat given the chance. The crowds increased each day, their whistles, chirrups, grunts and
clicks as thick in the air as the damp. The noise never
stopped, night and day, day and night, a punctuated
muttering, long wavering whistles breaking from the
background noise, sinking into it. Timka felt eyes on
her always, day and night, night and day. Each breath
she took was blown into her out of the lungs in the
murmurous trees, she could taste the burning sweet-
sour flavor in the air, in the food. She couldn't escape
them even in her sleep, she dreamed of eyes on her, of
mouths breathing on her, she wanted to take wing and
speed away, but she couldn't. She was Nemin for the
space of the Morass, Nemin because she owed debts
to Usoq, to Skeen, to Maggí and through Maggí to
Rannah. To Lipitero. She watched Lipitero fly and
hated her for a moment until she talked herself out of
it. Five days, she thought.

Four days. Three. Two. The land around them was
rising very gradually, beginning to dry out, weeds and
brush were replacing reeds, the trees grew closer together and were changing from the furry wet-footed

growth in the Morass to more ordinary trees, the fungus was drier and grayer, sparser. The water was brighter, more translucent, gathering into channels; the channel they slipped along acquired definition as it acquired recognizable banks. The noise from the trees grew more demanding and at the same time more wistful as if the Nagamar thronging there wanted to weave a cage about the magical creature who'd come to their place, but suspected they could not. Usoq was increasingly nervous. This was a perilous time; if the Nagamar decided to hold onto Lipitero there was nothing he could do; on the other hand, if he capitulated to their demands, he had no illusions about what Skeen, Pegwai and Timka would do to him. And Maggí, once Rannah was safe at the Lumat.

Leaving Vohdi at the helm (the South Rekkah was a lot more forgiving here) Usoq came to the cabin a few minutes before Lipitero was scheduled to start her afternoon flight. Rannah was on deck, talking to the youngest of the Nagamar guards, putting into practice interviewing skills she'd picked up watching Pegwai, enjoying herself thoroughly. Timka was curled up more than half asleep in one of the top bunks. She roused as he came in, rolled onto her stomach and lay watching him.

He pulled the door shut, frowned, opened it again and stood in the doorway and beckoned to Lipitero. As soon as she reached him, he caught hold of her arm, leaned toward her and whispered. "Ykx, I'm telling you, don't come back. When you go up this time, keep going."

Skeen unfolded from the bunk where she was sitting, brushed past Usoq and settled herself with her back against the far wall of the passage, her long legs crossed; she pulled on a drowsy mindless look, murmured, "How long till we're out of the Morass?"

"Tomorrow afternoon. If they don't try stopping us."

"If Petro doesn't keep going, how soon will they try something?"

"Lifefire knows, any time the whim strikes them." He gave Lipitero a sour look. "They aren't going to like it if she runs out on them, but that's still better than having her here."

Skeen patted a yawn, coughed. "So she leaves. She'll need to wait for us. Where?"

Usoq fidgeted, glanced along the passageway toward the hatch. "Does that matter? I ought to get back, that crazy bitch will be down here stiff with suspicion."

"It matters. More than Nagamar'd love getting hold of an Ykx. She can't spend the whole time in the air. Give us a place she can reach but likely no one else."

"Ah ah ah, no . . ." he danced from foot to foot like a boy needing urgently to find a handy tree. "Look, there's an island about a day and a half on, mostly rocks, bad currents both sides, far as I know, no one goes there. That do?"

Skeen raised her brows, Lipitero nodded. "If it doesn't I suppose she'll have to look for herself."

Usoq took off along the passage, scurrying away as if afraid another moment would bring more difficulties.

Skeen got to her feet, moved inside the cabin, stooping so her head wouldn't bang against the timbers. "Want the darter? Just in case?"

Lipitero was digging into her pack. She brought out one of her robes. She folded it small, tucked it into her harness. "No, you might need it a lot more than me. If they turn mean."

"Um . . . mind a suggestion?"

"Never."

"Push it a little. Wait for this flight, start an hour later. Be darker then. Um . . . sniff the air, see how it feels, you could be a bit edgy. Let the Nagamar know you're a bit tired of showing yourself off like this, lay a trail for disappearing. Might tip the scale to us. Just a hint though, and not if it doesn't feel right."

Lipitero found a small pouch, filled it from her

cache of dried fruit and nuts, tied the pouch to her
harness so it dangled beside her thigh. "I hear. You
know, Skeen, I'll be pleased to pass the Gate." Her
fur roughed, she shuddered. "I don't like this . . . this
covetousness. It was bad enough in Cida Fennakin,
but it was the sort of thing you expected from Angelsin
and her kind. You can deal with being a commodity.
This is different. I feel like I've got fingermarks, no,
eyemarks, all over me. I want to scrub myself for
hours to get rid of this. . . ." She twitched again,
settled on the floor beside her pack.

Timka rubbed at her eyes, curled up and went to
sleep again. Nothing she could do; it was simpler to
sleep and let the time pass.

Lipitero fidgeted about the deck ignoring the Nagamar
squad leader who started getting edgy when the time
for Lipitero's rise came and passed. As the afternoon
slid on, the Nagamar started getting shrill. Finally
Lipitero shrugged, threw off the robe she'd been wearing and rode the lift field high enough to catch some
wind and began her long loops over the river. The
loops stretched gradually longer until the last one broke
and the Ykx vanished into the frizzled clouds.

The squad leader waited till the sun was coloring
the western sky, then she laid hands on Usoq and
warbled at him. He writhed in her grip, signed one-
handed and gabbled out a flow of Trade-Min, word
tripping over word; to Skeen (who was sitting unnoticed, she hoped, with her back against the mast) it
was mostly nonsense, half-disclaimers, broken protests,
other things, perhaps words to remind the Nagamar of
other times, old debts, whatever. It sounded like babble, but it worked, the squad leader let go of his arm,
not exactly calmed down, but her anger was no longer
focused on the furry little man. She tromped about the
deck hissing to herself, stopping to glare at Skeen and
Pegwai. Around and around, out to the bow to gaze
unhappily into the gaudy clouds. Around and around,

stopping by Rannah and the young guard. She kicked
the guard off the boat, pulled Rannah to her feet and
dragged her over to Usoq. She pushed the Aggitj girl
against him and began snapping through angry signs.
Skeen got quietly to her feet and moved so Usoq
could see her and she could see the girl. She unsnapped the holster. "Peg," she murmured, "watch
the crew girls. They'll be dangerous if they see him
going down." She felt at the darter, switched to spray.
Djabo's weepy eyes, why can't I teach these fuckin'
eyes of mine to aim straight: . . .

Usoq patted Rannah on the shoulder. "Calm, calm,
there's no problem here. No, no, no problem here.
Rannah love, tell the kurshup here what you know
about the Ykx, why she's not here, tell her and me I'll
translate."

More patting, more flickers of his hands telling the
squad leader what he was saying. Skeen watched the
lean musuclar shoulders of the woman, saw their con-
tours soften a little and knew he was translating accu-
rately. As she'd suspected, the Nagamar knew more
Trade-Min than she admitted to. Clever little man.

Rannah blinked, turned to stare at the darkening
clouds. "Oh. She didn't come back?" She swung round
to gaze wide-eyed at the Nagamar. "I didn't notice, I
was talking to Kisri, you saw me. You want me to
guess, I'd say she didn't like all these people staring at
her. She said she felt like a bird in a cage. I think she
must have decided enough was enough and took off,
but I don't know that." She stopped talking, stood
looking as dewy and innocent as a downy chick. Skeen
disciplined a smile away. Maggí's daughter, yes, indeed.

Usoq finished his translation, paused a moment,
then added some more. At the same time he nudged
Rannah with his elbow, urging her away. The squad
leader ignored her and started a silent elbow-swinging
wrangle with him while Rannah ambled over to Skeen
and Pegwai.

Skeen rested her shoulders against the mast and slid

down it till she was sitting. Rannah dropped beside her. The girl touched Skeen's wrist, tilted her head, her whole body a single wordless question.

Skeen winked at her. "The veritable daughter of Maggí Solitaire," she murmured. "You do learn fast."

Rannah grinned happily. She lifted her bowside shoulder, dropped it. "Not coming back?" she murmured, taking pains to move her lips as little as possible. "What will they do?"

"No. I don't know. Um . . . in a minute or two, go down and let Ti know what's happening. Peg and I had better stay in sight for a while longer."

The night slipped down on them. The squad leader paced around the deck a while, went overside into the water, came flashing back a short while later, paced some more, her movements angular and filled with irritation. Skeen stayed on deck until moonrise, watching two more of those departures and returns, then she went below, leaving Usoq at the wheel and the crew girls taking turns bringing him food and scrambling to follow his orders as they worked to ride the edge between racing and recklessness.

Morning. No Ykx rising. Moaning mourning whistles from the trees. Louder. Louder. Grieving. Demanding. The Nagamar squad leader crouched in the shadow of the sails, watching, suspicious, unhappy. Skeen came on deck briefly, looked around, winced at the volume of sound directed at the ship, the number of dark silent forms in trees on either side, and went back down.

The Morass began changing, the change increasing as they fled battered by the sound, Usoq and the crew working harder as the winds grew more erratic while clouds gathered overhead, graying the day, underlining and intensifying the dolor of the griefsong coming from under the trees.

Skeen fidgeted with a bit of wood but couldn't concentrate on it; the sound was muffled down here but that didn't seem to help much. As if her skin had been flayed off, her flesh and nerve ends left bare. She cut carelessly at the wood, swore as the knife slipped and nicked her thumb.

Pegwai looked up from his notebook. "Try sleeping."

"Hah! Tell me how. Then tell me how much longer that's going on."

"Timka seems to manage well enough."

"Her? She could sleep in the crater of an erupting volcano." She slipped the knife back into the arm sheath, dropped the scrap of wood and kicked it recklessly away, narrowly missing Rannah who was squatting beside Pegwai, watching him write, making her own entries into her own notebook. Skeen bit her lip, waved her hand in a half apology. She stretched out on the bunk, pulled a blanket over her ears and tried to ignore that miserable idiot sound.

She fell into a half-doze and a succession of dreams, enough to wear her out emotionally and physically, dreams that had her sweating and moaning, working arms and legs, throwing her head about. Pegwai shook her awake a little past noon. "I'm waking you so you can get some rest," he said dryly, "and give us some peace."

She sat up carefully, her head felt swollen and sore, her eyes inflamed. "Gahh, Djabo's sorry face, I've got morning after without the fun of the night before." She pressed her forearms against her temples. "Ehhh, what a head!"

"Come up on deck a while. Some fresh air for your head, some hot soup for your stomach, you'll feel better."

"Yeah, mother." She lifted her head, looked startled. "The noise, it's just about gone."

"We're just about out of the Morass." He held out his hand. "Come, you're hungry, that's most of it."

'Any trouble with the Nagamar while I was sleeping?" She caught hold of his hand and let him pull her onto her feet.

"I'd have waked you, do you doubt that? There were a few moments when things looked tense; nothing came of it though. The Nagamar have their own peculiar honor. They won't harm anyone they've given shelter to, whether that's tacit toleration or the whole formal game." Pegwai let her stumble out in front of him and precede him up the passageway. He stood beside her at the mast, looking forward along the ship to the storm visible ahead, the curtains of rain like silver veils falling so heavily it obscured the landscape ahead so completely Skeen couldn't tell what kind of terrain they were moving into. She moved into the bow, turned and looked back along the boat. No Nagamar aboard. She walked back along the rail, staring down into the water as she moved, holding onto the rail with her single hand to fight the pull of vertigo. The water was much cleaner here, sandy bottom, pale, almost white. She could see the dark shapes of fish and other waterdwellers drifting backward as the boat blew past them. No Nagamar in the water. She scanned the trees. No groaning mourners in the trees. She drew in a breath, let it out in an explosive puff, threw out her arms and danced in an unsteady circle, a small triumph, had to be small, no space and the deck wasn't that steady underfoot. She went back to Pegwai, moving more sedately. "No Nagamar," she murmured.

Pegwai stared ahead. "Yes." His voice merged with the wind, she had to listen hard to hear him. "They left an hour ago after a long argument with Usoq. I don't know what it was about, I tried a bit of prying, but he talked over and around me until he had me chasing my tail."

"Trouble?"

"Ahhh, ask me again when Petro's back with us."

"I see. Temptation?"

"What do you think?"

"We don't turn our backs on him ever and we sleep in shifts."

He stopped talking as one of the crew girls ran past;

the wind was erratic, it kept changing direction and force, managing the sails took hard work and close attention. He squinted at the black clouds piling up ahead. "We're coming up fast on that rain. You find a spot out of the way, I'll go fetch that soup."

Skeen looked into the empty bowl, set it down beside her. "You were right. I needed that."

Pegwai glanced at the sky again, surprised himself with a gentle belch. "Pardon. Hmmm, yes, even a day like this looks brighter with hot food inside you. Which reminds me. Remembering what happened in Fennakin, you think we need worry about Usoq and the food he provides us?"

She yawned. "I'm not awake yet, I think. Eat in shifts? I suppose."

A fistful of warm rain splatted down on them. They collected their dishes, went for a leisurely circle around the boat, both of them relaxed, enjoying the quiet, the occasional flurries of rain, the interval between crises, then they went below.

The Pouliloulou plunged into the storm and flounced through it, giving the passengers so rough a ride Skeen was sick over the rail and Timka went wan and flaccid, wondering if she was after all going to suffer a Chorinya of some kind. Both of them snarled at Pegwai whenever he showed his placid Balayar face. Unfair, oh, unfair for him to be enjoying himself, not just enduring the swoops and jolts, the yaws and twists, but enjoying himself. Skeen told him in descriptive detail how obscene his grin was, Timka twitched a cat-weasel head onto her shoulder and hissed loathing at him. He scooped up Rannah (who was a bit pale, no more) and took her topside, telling her in far too audible a voice, a voice too audibly amused, to leave those soreheads with their miseries, the air was a lot better on deck. They came through the storm into a grassy waste-land, clouds still thick and low over banks that were

tangles of briars and a few stunted grayish trees, though
part of that grayness might have been the clouds that
seemed to suck color from everything and everyone.
Washboard knolls rose in packed waves beyond the
banks, covered mostly with sparse bleached-out grass,
old growth from last year. Skeen had left this part of
the world toward the end of summer and was returning to it in time to catch the dregs of winter; even this
far south there was a chill in the air once the sun went
down, a damp cold that settled into the bones. Timka
dealt with it by shifting to cat-weasel and spending
most of her time nose to tail in one of the upper
bunks. Pegwai hauled out a pair of knitted trousers
and a soft wool undershirt. Skeen dug out Angelsin's
fur-lined cloak, cut nearly a meter off the bottom and
had Rannah hem it for her. And so the second day out
of the Morass slid by.

Shortly after nightfall Skeen was standing in the
bow, staring ahead, worrying (though she'd deny it
ferociously if challenged) about Lipitero. The river
island was on the edge of the cultivated land; according to Usoq they'd reach it soon after dawn tomorrow.
She'd deny too that she'd expected Lipitero to come
sliding onto deck most of the day; the Ykx surely
knew they were getting close. All day she'd watched
the boiling gray sky, but she saw only a scattering of
birds dipping in and out of the clouds. She cursed the
clouds and cursed the missing hand that meant she was
useless about the boat, couldn't even work to use up
excess energy and pass the time away. Couldn't sleep,
too many nightmares when she did manage to doze a
little; she was sick of nightmares and the ruts her mind
trudged over and over. What she could do was keep
away from the others as much as possible. Her nerves
were too naked to endure the abrasion of much con-
tact with them and she didn't like how she felt when
she was nasty with Pegwai or Timka and she didn't
want to start on Rannah. She knew herself well enough
to know she'd savage the child with as little restraint

as she would the adults. A hand touched her arm. She jerked away, her heart clenched and thudded, she swung around ready to claw, caught hold of herself and stood shivering, glaring at Timka. "What is it?" She heard the snarl in her voice and wasn't sorry for it. If Timka wouldn't take the hint, she could take what came.

"Min," Timka said. "Up there. Over us. More ahead."

"Ah." Skeen raked her hand through her hair until it stood in spikes about her face while she struggled to put the pieces of her head together. "Ah. . . ." She bent at the waist and leaned closer to Timka so she could get a better look at her face. "They know about you yet?"

"I don't. . . . No. Unless Telka's there or one of her top Holavish. And I'd feel them if they were."

"How soon before they know?"

"If they don't swing this way, maybe no more than a half hour. If they do, any minute."

"They know it's you?"

"Might. Once they get close enough. Someone like me and who else would be coming this way?"

"All right. I hear. These like the little birdboys that followed me out of Spalit time when?"

Timka closed her eyes and concentrated, her features squeezing down into fine curved lines. She was shivering from the cold, she'd thrown on one of her loose cotton robes, her feet were bare; she'd come the moment she'd felt the touch. Skeen watched her a moment then turned to scan the darkness overhead. If there were bird Min up there, they were above the clouds.

Timka came out of her trance, cleared her throat. "Holavish," she said. "Fighters, I think, not scouts. Well, some scouts but most not."

Skeen glanced at her ringchron, then past Timka at the crewgirl at the helm. "Let's go below." She grinned. "It's time Peg shared a little of the miseries."

*   *   *

Morning.

Clouds high, raveled dirty wool. Patches of remote and chilly sky. Angular black silhouettes of large birds of prey, drifting in broad slow circles high over the boat. Beyond the range of crossbows. Also beyond the reach of Skeen's darter.

Brisk wind, drier, the smell of it smoky and herbal, taint of animal droppings heavy on it.

Small herds of deer-like beasts with palmate horns grazing on the rippling ridges. Rodents bustling about low hutches mounded close to the waterline, tending tuber gardens they planted haphazardly in the mud, the vines crawling everywhere, new leaves uncurling, the old hanging in limp folds. Fingerlength bugs like a cross between ant and centipede rushed about in chaotic swarms along broad runways, their bodies brushed amid the pebbles.

The river looped east as the land changed again. Beyond the west bank the ridges grew higher and stonier, turned into low rounded hills with few trees but much thorny brush and low writhing bushes with dark purple red bark and small stiff round leaves. The east side was different, the land was much flatter, with patches of cultivation, large herds of ruminants in fenced pastures, now and then a wheel for raising water from the river, smaller horse herds, some woolies on the wild lands with shepherds on the slopes beside them.

The Pouliloulou clawed steadily upstream, Vohdi at the wheel, Cepo sleeping and Usoq below somewhere. The wind was blowing off the east pastures; as the boat followed the curve of the river, she shifted balance and began to lose way, but as long as the wind was steady and the curve easy, the boat was rigged so the girl could handle it alone. Timka watched as she worked cranks with one hand, kept the wheel steady with the other, seemed to have one eye on the sails and the other on the river ahead and all the while her lips were pursed for a happy lilting whistle, her dark eyes were crinkled with pleasure and her whole body seemed to dance. Rannah crouched by Timka's knee, watching also, fascinated. "It's like Rak'yagel on a horse," she murmured. When Timka bent down, brows raised, she said, "Back home there was this old man, a Pallah, he took care of the animals for us. There are wild horses up in the mountains around our place. Sometimes they came down and tried to raid our herds, so he made some traps. He caught this stallion in one of them. Big and black as the heart of night, not pretty, rough and covered with scars, but wonderful. I don't know how to explain it. Anyway he tamed the stallion and used him to sire some of our best horses, but even when the stallion was old and, oh, you know, seeing Rak'yagel riding him it was like seeing a storm riding a storm. It was kind of beautiful and kind of terrible and it made me, I don't know, want to do things—not just ordinary things, something kind of wonderful like that."

Usoq came on deck carrying a broad, flat stone; it was grayish white and looked like someone had put it together from cement and reeds. He settled it in a boxy object close to the steering gear, stood and dusted his hands. "You feeling helpful, you two," he said, "you could give me a hand bringing up some things. 'Course now I wouldn't want to be spoiling your morning for you. Though maybe those might." He waved a hand at the bird Min over them. "I'd like to get together some little surprises for them, case they come to visit."

"Why not." Timka pushed away from the rail and followed him down.

They brought up a brazier and a sack of charcoal bits, a small cauldron half-filled with a tarry substance that looked rather like brownish black glass, five crossbows (which Usoq cocked and set carefully down beside the box) and a wicker box filled with crossbow bolts that had straggly collars of firemoss bound behind the points.

"Nasty," Timka said. "And this?" She dug a finger-nail into the resin in the pot.

"Little secret of mine." Usoq set the brazier on the stone inside the box, piled charcoal in it and used a firepot and pitchy splinters to start the charcoal burning. He set the cauldron on the grill and stepped back, dusting his hands and giving the bird Min overhead a feral grin. "A half-hour thereabouts, those fuckers better think twice and then some before trying on anything with me. They burn fiercer 'n pitch once you get the fire going." He looked a little startled as he remembered suddenly he was talking to a Min, but didn't bother with disclaimers, being intelligent enough to refrain from making bad worse.

Rannah made a soft, disgusted sound and walked off, thin shoulders rounded, her not-hair flattened to her skull.

A half hour later Skeen came yawning up, Pegwai stumbling behind her. She sniffed, wrinkled her nose. "What's that stink?"

Timka turned round. "Usoq's secret weapon. For the Min up there, if they decide to atttack us. Fire arrows. That goo in the pot is supposed to make the fire hot enough to kindle Min flesh." She shivered, sounded gloomier than she liked. Though these were her enemies, they were also kin of sorts. Burning was a hellish death for a Min. Even thinking about it made her sick to her stomach.

Pegwai moved back to stand beside Usoq who was stirring his mess so it wouldn't burn, Skeen joined Timka in the bow.

She glanced up, "More of them this morning, if I can still count," hitched a hip on the rail. "Usoq say anything about when we see this island where Petro's supposed to be waiting?"

"No, he's been fiddling with the glop, that's all. And Vohdi never talks, you know that."

"Where's Rannah?"

"You didn't see her? She was upset. Usoq said something about Min burning like pitch pine and she didn't much like it, so she went below."

"Poor kid, I doubt she's seen a hand raised in anger before this trip. She's getting a good dose of horrors, isn't she." Skeen rubbed the tip of her forefinger along the blade of her long nose. "I've been thinking. Maybe we should leave the boat, you and me and Petro when we pick her up. That'd take the pressure off Peg and her and even old worm back there. There's enough cover out there, your friends might have trouble picking us up again. No, Peg and I didn't see her, but we were in the galley for a time before we came up here. Getting something to eat. And if we managed to get over the Mountains into the Backlands, we might be able to sneak around the backside of Telka's army and slide through the Gate before she knew what was happening."

Timka stared at her. "You're forgetting something, aren't you?"

"You've said it yourself I don't know how many times, your outreach is a lot longer than most other Min. Maybe if we took them by surprise, went fast enough and were sneaky enough about it, we could lose them. With you on watch, able to spot where they're going before they got close enough to pin us, we could stay loose. Remember, those boys looking for you that first time when we were in the Spitting Split, they couldn't find you."

Timka gazed down at her hands. She knew well enough what was behind this. Skeen was restless, nervous, getting more nervous every day. She'd been patient for a long space now, ever since Sikuro. There was the fight with the Sea Min, but that was over three months ago. Nothing she could do but ride Goum Kiskar, then Pouliloulou, and try to exercise her jitters away. With that hand gone, she was useless about the ship, couldn't help with the small repairs like Rannah and Pegwai did sometimes, not much interested in the countryside. No one to talk to, Usoq was as trustworthy as water-smoothed stone, the kind apt to turn underfoot at the most awkward moments. And getting closer and closer to discovering the answer to the question plaguing her, whether or not she'd been betrayed by ship and lover. If that proved to be wrong, if the man had a good and honorable reason, Timka got the feeling Skeen would be disconcerted and far more upset than she would be to find her suspicions were true. Timka didn't understand that. It seemed terribly perverse to, well, need such punishment, as if it validated something about Skeen she couldn't live without. She thought about Skeen's scheme; it was remotely possible it could work, but she couldn't see much point to it. Skeen couldn't really think it was possible to creep up on Telka and surprise her. No, it was more likely that terrifying recklessness she'd shown more than once in these treks back and forth across Mistommerk. Plotting and scheming and wariness and high alertness until it got too much for her and she went flying off in a wild leap into nowhere . . . that, Timka had to admit, she always managed to pull off, mostly because of her earlier plotting and the help of her friends. She thought some more about the plan. It might work, except. . . . She gazed at the sky a moment, then squeezed her eyes shut and probed. Except that there was someone important up there. Not Telka, a male, almost as good as Telka though, Lifefire singe her S'yer. She sighed, opened her eyes. "It might have worked, Skeen, but there's someone up there whose reach is near as long as mine. No, I don't know him; I recognized the . . . well, call it the feel of his aura."

"One of the fighters no doubt. Shit. I suppose it's just as well. Petro isn't really built to ride a racehorse." She looked up, shading her eyes with her remaining hand. "They going to track us the whole way? Or they going to try hitting us again?"

Timka make an irritated sound. "How can I know? Ask yourself, unless we do something radically stupid, why should they? We're coming to them. No Ever-Hunger to throw them off this time."

"Um . . . remind me to tell you something in a bit."

"Well, one last point, then I'm finished. I'm not about to turn saintly and offer to go away and lead them off. Letting Telka pull me to squealing bits a pinch at a time doesn't appeal to me. Which brings up something that's been bothering me. We turned back a double cell of gunja, but we had the Aggitj, the Boy, Chulji, Maggí and the rest on her ship. Eighty Min. According to the Poet, Telka has ten times that many fighters she can call on. Against three of us. Even with Petro's excavator which I admit could probably take out a good percentage of those, still, the odds aren't encouraging."

"You don't look all that worried."

"I'll start if you tell me you haven't got a plan."

"Mmmh." Skeen glanced up, then along the boat. "Yes." The wind was a loud whine, the water piling past the bow threw up a steady murmur that blended pleasantly with the creaks, thrums and snaps from the rigging and sails. "Lipitero, the Sydo Remmyo and I worked out something . . . you aren't going to like it."

"You terrify me. Go ahead."

"Um . . . we decided it was likely the attack would come close to the Gate." She frowned. "We didn't think about this tracking business."

"I couldn't say for certain, but I think you can forget that. The closer we get to the Gate, the more our choices narrow, the easier it is for her to get set up to wait for us. Go on."

"If it starts to seem like we'll be rolled over, Lipitero is going to release the Ever-Hunger."

Timka swallowed, appalled. She opened her mouth, closed it. "But . . . Skeen! It won't stop with the Holavish. It'll eat the Mountains clean. The other Min, they don't deserve that, they don't . . . they . . . ahhh!"

"It's not that bad." Skeen hitched a hip onto the

rail, wrapped her handless arm in the ropes. "Even
Pegwai doesn't know this. The day after we left the
lake, a dozen Ykx started cross country, keeping away
from settlements and flying mostly at night, heading
for the place where the two Suurs are only five hundred or so stads apart, the north waters of the Okits
Okeano, then across the Backlands. Petro thinks they're
settled in already, waiting for us to arrive."

"Do I have to ask? Yes, all right. Settled in where?
Lifefire, Skeen, twelve Ykx perching on a mountain,
the news would be back already half around the world."

Skeen scratched at her nose. "Seems there's a set of
Gather caves not far from the Gate. The Ykx closed it
up when they moved away. This was after the other
Waves started coming as life got pretty confused around
the Gate."

Timka shook her head. "All the stories the old ones
told us, all of them, nothing about a Gather near the
Gate. They said the Ykx came through the Gate and
scattered; leaves before the wind, they said."

"It was a while back, remember. People forget.
Especially what they want to forget. Those first Waves,
a confused time, lots of things got lost."

"I wonder if it'll be different this ti—" Her eyes
snapped shut, she bent slightly at the waist, though
she wasn't much aware of that as she slipped into
intense concentration. Dimly she heard Skeen calling
her name, asking her . . . asking her. . . . "Trouble. I
think. . . ." She straightened, stripped off the light
robe she was wearing, shifted to the largest most pred-
atory of her bird forms, the sea eagle, and went pow-
ering up toward the Min over them, spiraling up and
up, ignoring them except to turn on any of the fliers
that tried to come at her; her self-confidence grew
with each pass; the months on the trek had taught her
even more than she'd guessed. She couldn't remember
learning these moves, but they came as naturally as
the sweep of her wings; maybe it was watching Skeen
move, maybe it came from the memories she'd ab-

sorbed from Skeen, maybe it was a combination of a
lot of things. She was astounded by how easy it seemed,
felt her soul expanding to the point she felt momentarily like a god of the skies. Which was absurd. Of
course it was. Tend to business, Ti-bird. She looked
along the river ahead of the boat. Two bends, then the
river widened, split about three small islands, two of
them only dots of rock, the third like a smiling mouth,
long and narrow and slightly curved with rocks and
several uprooted trees piled together at the upstream end. A thick cloud of bird Min circled over
that pile, diving at it, dropping things on it; she saw
puffs of smoke and bits of flame that leaped and died
from a lack of fuel. The objects were aimed at a
dragged-together shelter, but bursts of a familiar gold
glow deflected them. Lipitero. Under attack. She
counted the Min ahead. Nearly a score of them. Too
many. She hesitated a moment wondering if she could
drop down and let the Ykx know she was on the point
of rescue, but a bit of thought convinced her there was
no way Petro could tell her from the other Min and
she wasn't likely to hold her fire just because some
bird squawked at her. Those other Min were keeping
their distance; she must have done some fast effective
damage to keep them that far away from her. Timka
slipped round, losing a little height, tried to gauge how
far the boat had to come before it reached the island.
She moved her wings slightly, holding herself steady in
the air and watched the gleaming sails with the dark
splinter underneath creep along the wrinkled line of
water. Quarter of an hour. Maybe a few minutes more.
She flipped round again, climbed higher until she was
over them all, her tags circling around at a cautious
distance from her. With a scream of rage and defiance
she drove herself at her top speed into and through
the cloud of attackers, hitting them with body, claws,
tearing beak, then swung about and went driving in a
long breathless slant for the boat.

*   *   *

As Skeen watched Timka climb (someone or something goosed her good, she thought, look at her, like she had a rocket in her tail), Usoq yelled. Cepo came scrambling from belowdecks, snatched up a crossbow and a bolt. She dipped the bolt in the bubbling resin, held it ready to the fires, waiting for the Captain's word. "Pass-Through," he squalled, "ehhh, what t'hell that about?"

Skeen was watching Timka maneuver, clicking her tongue with approval as Ti-bird sent a Min rolling when he flew too close to her; the darter was out, set to spray, held in her left hand, no use as long as the Min stayed as high as they were, but if they came at the boat, they'd get a surprise. "Don't know," she yelled back. "She said something about trouble and took off."

"The Island's just ahead, they going after the Ykx?"

"Could be."

A fizzy snarling sound, a cat's curse, and Usoq was poking bolts into the cauldron point first, pulling them out points and collars covered with the hot resin. He handed them to Cepo who leaned them in a neat sticky row against the side of the firebox. The boat swung away from the main knot of the Min, diping east again, cutting yet farther into the cultivated lands, then it rounded a rocky knoll and started west. One more bend, as far as Skeen could tell. She yipped with pleasure as Timka veered round and went rocketing through the mass of fliers, slashing at them, knocking them off the wind, scattering them. She swung round again and came plunging toward the ship.

She shifted as soon as her talons touched the deck, scooped up the robe, tied it round her. More than a little breathlessly, she said, "They've cornered Lipitero. They're attacking her. She's holding them off for the moment. I don't know if she's hurt or how badly, but the quicker we get there the better. I don't know. . . ." She looked round at the straining sails, relaxed enough to smile a little. "Though how you stop and ground-hitch a boat. . . ."

The boat rounded the next bend and Timka saw the islands immediately ahead, two dots like droppings of a giant bird, the long mouth island beyond. The Min above it were swinging in tight circles, squawking with noisy jagged rage. They weren't attacking Lipitero now. At least she'd managed that much, though she'd feel happier if she knew more about the kind of weapons they had, something more than stones, certainly more than stones, something that made fire. Usoq was going to fight fire with fire. No doubt he knew more than he was saying about how Min flew and fought. Should I ask—no—he'd throw words at me, I'm too tired for that. Words hard as stones. Lifefire, I wish . . . Telka, how many have to die? How many Min will you burn to reach me? Will you share the blame with me if the Ever-Hunger gets away from the Ykx and cleans the mountains of life?

Usoq began shouting orders as the nose of the Pouliloulou reached the thready point of the long island. Vohdi brushed past her, began working frantically at ropes. As if the sails danced and bowed to the cadence of Usoq's voice, they came folding down, heavily graceful. The boat reached the mid section of the island before it coasted to a stop and began to drift backward. A final shout; Vodhi in the bow, Cepo at the stern released anchors. They caught and the boat swayed between the two cables. The crewgirls dashed to the wheel area, snatched up two of the crossbows and stood, each of them holding bolts ready to light the resin the moment Usoq gave the order.

As soon as the boat was stopped, Skeen looked at the rail, cursed and thrust the darter back in its holster. She didn't snap it shut, the lanyard was clipped in place, and swung over the rail into the water. Half swimming, half striding she surged up onto the stony soil and ran toward the pile of boulders and twisted

trees at the north end of the island. Timka hesitated a
moment, the cat-weasel hated water, the eagle was
vulnerable so close to land. With an impatient sound,
she stripped off the robe once again, blurred into the
cat-weasel and flowed like gray smoke over the rail.

Skeen was almost at the crude shelter when she
caught up. She leaped onto one of the taller boulders
and perched there watching the Min, her mouth wide
in a taunting grin—come on you shupping imbeciles,
come on, like all the rest of you came, find what they
found.

The Min continued their angry circling beyond the
reach of Skeen's darter; apparently it was beyond the
range of whatever weapons they carried because they
hurled nothing down but wordless noisy curses.

Skeen reached cautiously toward the shelter, pulled
her hand back a lot faster than she put it out as the
faint gold flicker bit at her. "Hai, Petro, ease off. It's
me. Skeen. Timka's sitting on a rock here licking her
chops and waiting for one of those clothheads to come
close enough so she can get her teeth in him. You all
right. That fuckin' Usoq, he should have known. Eh?"

"Took   your time." The voice was hoarse, painful.
"Watch those [sound: wobblyhiss, some clicks, par-
tially inaudible]"

"Gotcha." Skeen rolled onto her back, shaded her
eyes with the stump of her forearm. She grinned. "I
think they're finally learning a little, Petro. They're
sure not about to get any closer."

Rustles, a few rattles, some scrapings and the shriek
of wood being pulled over rough rock. A mutter.
Smell of burning wood. Lipitero pulled herself painfully from the shelter. One of her legs was crudely
splinted with wood sliced from one of the smaller
branches, tied on with strips of the robe she'd brought
with her. Her fur was singed in several places, there
was a suppurating burn on one shoulder; the pain
must have been unendurable. Her eyes were sunken,
dull; there was a gray film over the dark nubbly skin

on her nose; even where it wasn't burned off, her fur had lost most of its gloss and was twisted into peaks.

Skeen rolled onto her feet, took a look at her and whistled. "You look like I feel after a three-day drunk."

"Damn your smart remarks, Skeen." Lipitero levered herself onto an elbow and struggled to bring her legs around. She stopped, lay panting, her pointed ears pinned against her head. "Haven't had a sip of water f' two days."

"Ti, grow some hands and get over here." Skeen unclipped the darter, set it on one of the boulders, dropped to her knees beside Lipitero. "Petro, this is going to hurt. . . ." She slid her handless arm under Lipitero's legs, her other around the Ykx's shoulders. With a grunt of effort, pushing off with her powerful leg muscles, she lifted the wounded woman onto her shoulder and started trotting toward the ship.

Again Timka hesitated. It wasn't the time to try something she'd been wondering about, but she couldn't resist showing off for her kind wheeling above. She concentrated, tried to remember some of the desperation of the fight in the Aggitj's room the night Domi was killed, then shifted. She looked at herself with satisfaction, laughed aloud and shook a clawed fist at them. She had the Pallah shape, but her fingers were stubbier with the cat-weasel's retractable claws and she had the cat-weasel's thick coat of gray and amber fur. She leaped from the boulder, scooped up the darter and ran after Skeen. This body was intoxicating; she had that superabundant energy and a lot of the cat's musculature, her senses were so acute she was nearly leaping out of her skin at the least unexpected sound. She bounded past Skeen, hit the water with a growl of intense disgust, pulled herself over the rail, swung around in time to take hold of Lipitero and lift her on board. She gave the Ykx to Pegwai who came silently up behind her, turned to help Skeen on board but backed off as the Pass-Through snarled at her. With a shiver of relief she shifted to her standard

Pallah form—and nearly collapsed from exhaustion. Apparently she was going to pay heavily when she used that shift. She could remember, though, with a terrifying vividness how she'd felt when she made that change. There were powerful tugs fighting whatever good sense she had, telling her to go back to it, to feel again that surge of power, that—well, say it, Ti—that was demonic if you looked at it one way, god-like if you saw it another. Even though she knew a little longer in that state might have depleted her to the point of death. With a weary sigh she pulled on her robe, tied the tie and looked around.

The crewgirls were raising sail with the same energetic skill they showed in everything they did; Usoq was leaning on the wheel, watching his boat and the sky with an equal intentness. She steadied herself with one hand and bent her neck slowly because she was dizzy and her head ached.

The Min were still a disturbed swarm buzzing about high above them, showing no sign they intended to attack any time soon.

She eased her head up again, raised her brows at Usoq.

He grinned. "Burned a couple last time I was round these parts. Put your bunch and me together, looks like they don't want to bite." Cepo came trotting past him and stood by the anchor winch. "Vohdi, ready?"

Her voice came back with a happy lilt even in the single word. "Ready, So."

"Raise 'em."

The Pouliloulou skimmed along the South Rekkah, with Timka, Skeen and Pegwai standing guard turn on turn, but the Min didn't attack. Most of them disappeared. Four stayed behind to follow them and make sure they didn't sneak off the ship and try losing themselves among the Pallah and the stray Min who were sprinkled about, salt to season the blander Nemin. Usoq drenched the coals and let the resin cauldron cool, but he kept the setup ready on deck, just in case one of the fliers succumbed to a brainstorm. The first night after the island brought more clouds streaming in, scumbling around; it didn't rain that night, but the morning was as dark as a night at moon's full and by afternoon the mast tip almost touched the clouds. By nightfall the winds were so strong and erratic, Usoq hove to and rode out the storm with bare poles and double anchors.

After she'd downed a few sips of water, Lipitero blinked wearily at the anxious faces hanging over her, managed a crooked smile, then sighed and fainted. Skeen worked over her for some time, cleaning the wounds, injecting her with the last of her antibiotics, spraying the gray film over the worst of the burns. Teeth clenched, struggling against nausea, Rannah helped her. When the work was done, the Aggitj girl sighed, bent down and stroked her fingers over the soft silvery down on Lipitero's cheek. "Will she be all right?"

Skeen twitched, bit down on her lip and swallowed the ugly comments that leaped to her tongue; no point in spewing her choler and anxiety on the girl's head. "Probably," she said.

Pegwai came in with a cup of the soup he'd been brewing in the galley. He looked at Lipitero, then Skeen. "She should have this."

Skeen smiled wearily. "Smells good. Is there more of it?"

"A pot still simmering."

"Safe?"

"Usoq and the girls are busy. For the moment. Later, I don't know, I suppose we go back to staggered meals."

"Well, then, old friend, you see what you have to do." Skeen took the hot mug from him and moved back to Lipitero. "Take this, Rannah. When I lift her, you hold it to her lips and give her small sips." She began rummaging in her pack, brought out the drug disc; she set it on the bed and turned the knob until she had what she wanted, pressed the disc to the inside of Lipitero's elbow and activated it. Lipitero stirred, blinked open her eyes. Skeen put the disc away, slipped her arm under the Ykx's shoulders and raised her. "Pegwai's cooked up some marvelous soup, Petro. Just you relax and drink. It'll make you feel more like yourself."

The Pouliloulou slid into Spalit before dawn on the third day after Petro was taken off the island, sails reefed until the wind drove them barely faster than the current sought to push them, creeping along in fog so thick it was impossible to see more than a meter beyond the bow; both crewgirls were back on duty, moving more slowly, some of their vigor gone, having had only snatches of sleep on those three days. When Vohdi shouted wharves ahead, Usoq eased the boat toward the shore and brought her alongside the first with the sound of wood rubbing on wood but no more than that. The girls had mooring cables over the bitts in the next moments, the ship tidied to quiescence, and were back waiting for Usoq's orders before Skeen had time to yawn twice and scratch her head.

"No hurry, none at all," Usoq said with a lazy amiability that didn't quite cover the rancor boiling under his surface. He was hating them pretty thoroughly at the moment, wanting control of the Ykx, not daring to try for her. "We'll be overnighting here. Too much the Rekkah's been for us, too much," he smoothed his hand along the flank of the nearest crewgirl. "We need our sleep and meals we haven't cooked. Eh, Vohdi? And clean slippery sheets to slide between, ah, it's a healing just thinking about such things."

"No doubt." Skeen yawned again and went below to fetch the others.

*　　*　　*

The fog persisted all day, a dreary dripping day with the sun a faint cold glow that produced little light and less heat. Late in the afternoon Skeen left the taproom of the Spitting Split and wandered out to the riverfront. She settled on the end of a wharf, legs dangling over the edge, her feet dissolving in the fog. She couldn't see the water, but she could hear it, the melancholy sound suited her mood; the eruption of irritation that had plagued her the last few days had drained away, leaving her limp as boiled spinach in mind and body. She swung the feet she could see as dark blurs and brooded into the knotted fog.

Suddenly the end was so close she could see it. Suddenly. Three days upriver to Dum Besar. A day, a night and a day across the Plain, one more day through the Mountains to the Gate. A week. One fuckin' week and we'll all be dead or through to the other side. Ahhh, Djabo, I don't know, I don't know, I don't know what I . . . want. Tibo, why? Do I really want to know why? Ahhh, want, that's nothing. I don't want to know, I HAVE to know. Can't run away from this one, can you Skeen old girl? No room for running.

She struggled to switch her thinking to another track; since the Gate closed on her, she'd concentrated on reopening it, almost everything she'd done was directed to that end. There was still an effort to be made, but it was time, more than time, to start thinking about what she'd have to do once she passed back to the other side. I wonder if the Junks are still waiting for me. Does time here run at the same rate? No way I can tell till I'm back and see how many days passed there. Forget that. Waiting Junks. Nah. Gate's one way for most folk. Look what happened to me. Old Yoech must have been hanging about when another Pass-Through made the jump. Who knows why, it's the only way he could have come back. The Junks chase us, we disappear and never show up again, why waste their time hanging around. Satellites? No, I've been through that before, the sun's acting up too

much, there's that much on my side. Three of us to get
back into Chukunsa. Ti's no problem—she can just
grow wings and fly in. Hm. Petro? Don't know, she's
got a lot of instrumentation in that harness. We'll both
be walking. How are we going to transport all this . . .
this stuff we've collected? Take a horse through with
us? That's a possibility. To sell the jewelry and artifacts, I'll have to get them into Chukunsa. Tchah!
Easy enough for me to walk out, nothing on me to
ring bells. Tibo's told me often enough not to jump
without looking where my feet come down. Djabo's
drippy nose, it's a mess. Hmm. Can't take it through
the gates. Over the wall? Hah! Here's a thought.
What's the use having a shapechanger around if she
can't solve these little difficulties. Ti can carry quite a
lot if she has time to rest and doesn't have to go too
far. Another thought. She can go places no Junk could
reach. Hm. Hide the jewels and things somewhere
along the chasm walls. Once Petro and I've got a base,
Timka can fly the stuff in. Have to work out the
details. Might be a good idea to leave most of the stuff
stashed until I locate a buyer. Mmm. Some kind of
papers for Petro and Ti. Don't need much to get off
Kildun Aalda, it's getting down again somewhere else.
If I prostrate myself before her, will Bona Fortuna
have a ship ready to go from Aalda port scheduled to
touch at a freebase? I don't want to hang around once
I've sold the jewels, bound to be questions. . . .

"Skeen." The voice came out of the fog behind her,
quiet and a little melancholy, startling her because she
hadn't heard footsteps.

"Peg?" She started to get up.

"No. Stay there."

She heard a soft grunt as he lowered himself, the
thud of his knees on the planks, the pop of his joints,
the whisper of his robe. His hands brushed her shoulders, were heavier on them as he smoothed his palms
from her neck to her arms and back again. Heavy but
gentle, back and forth.

"You're very tense," he said. He squeezed her shoulder muscles, his fingers digging painfully into her.

"Hah." There were a lot of things she could say. Too many. So she said nothing.

His hands stroked her neck, his thumbs rubbed behind her ears. Up and down. Hypnotic. They tightened on her throat, smooth fleshy noose. She couldn't breath, she didn't struggle, she let it happen. Gentle easeful blackness.

When she woke, she was back in the Inn, in her bed. Pegwai sat near the fire, watching the dying flames crawl across the coals.

"Peg?" Her voice was hoarse, her throat sore.

He turned his head. "It's been a while."

"No privacy."

"That too."

"Too?"

"You understand me."

Skeen sighed, winced. "You make me feel too much. It . . . bothers me. I couldn't cope with that and everything else going on. Peg, can you understand? I want smaller pleasures. I don't want to feel so much."

"You're not coming back here. To Mistommerk, I mean. Once you're on the other side."

"Peg, I don't belong here, I'm used to . . . oh, a life that's more, what, more enabled, ahhh, faster, not better—" The last two words came hastily, trailed off as he made an impatient gesture. "Say this, with a different kind of comfort, a different kind of problem. Look at me fumbling for words, but I can't really explain because you don't know both worlds. It's like trying to explain blue to a blind man. Oh shit, anything I say is wrong. No, I won't be back."

"Let me stay with you. A last time."

"Djabo." Skeen moved restlessly on the bed, the too familiar darting burn flashing from groin to nipples. She tried a smile. "I don't know if Maggí or I should trust you with her daughter."

"Skeen!"

"I didn't mean it." She brushed her hand across her breasts, bit back a groan. "Trying for psychic pain, icing on the cake, ahh, gods, yes, Peg, yes. . . ."

Lipitero sucked in a breath as Skeen came across the room toward them, scratched and battered, one eye half closed. Before the Ykx could speak, Timka's hand closed on her arm. "Don't say anything, I'll explain later."

Timka poured out a cup of tea. "This isn't as hot as it might be; if you want, I'll have the girl get us more."

Skeen pulled out a chair and sat. She reached out a long arm, brought back the cup. "Never mind, it's the caffein I want, not the heat."

"They get off all right?"

"No sign of trouble. I talked with Nossik," a jog of her elbow indicated the man behind the bar idly wiping at it with a folded cloth, "he put me onto one Brampon who has a boat and is willing to sail it upriver to Dum Besar for the paltry sum of a gold for each of us. I didn't much feel like arguing but for the look of the thing I beat him down to one gold ten silver. Brampon and Nossik agree that the fog's going to hang about for a while yet, but it should thin out some in the afternoon; he says it doesn't bother him, he navigates by the feel of it most times anyway; I have a notion he travels a lot in weather like this," she grinned, "if you know what I mean."

"Travel with Skeen and see the halfworld."

'Just about. I mentioned we might have a bit of trouble and he should look out for hostile Min between then and whenever we left. He didn't seem much worried by that."

"You think they'd go after him?"

"Me, I would. Break some bones and burn the boat. Discourage the other boatmen, leave us stranded here. We want to travel, it's on foot or horseback; in either case, it'd slow us down considerably, leave us far more vulnerable, give them more chances to attack us." She drained the cup, passed it across the table for Timka to refill.

Timka hefted the pot, shook it, waved one of the serving girls over to the table and ordered more tea. When the girl was gone, she frowned at Skeen. "You don't look very worried."

"No?" Skeen stretched, patted a yawn. "It's not me that's flying around up there. Brampon knows how to take care of himself. If he doesn't, too bad." She yawned again and settled to staring drowsily at the fire that crackled cheerily in the fireplace a short distance away from the table.

"Conceited, aren't you."

Skeen chuckled. "Truthful."

The serving girl came back with the pot. While Timka filled Skeen's cup, one for the silent brooding Lipitero, finishing with her own, Skeen ordered a large breakfast for herself. Watching her, Timka wasn't too surprised to see the edginess that barbed her tongue and put harsh angles into her movements was dissolved away. Despite what she'd learned from the dreams she'd siphoned out of Skeen, she couldn't understand that combination of pain and pleasure, though she could make some guesses about what lay behind it. Ah, well, that didn't matter as long as it didn't get in the way of what they had to do. She sighed. "When are we leaving?"

Skeen glanced at her ringchron. "Another hour."

"Plenty of time."

"I hate to sweat. What about our shadows, they still up there?"

"All four of them. One flew off to the east a while, but he's back."

"Nosing around the Pouliloulou?"

"Checking to make sure they haven't mixed up their Min."

Skeen leaned forward, interest vivid in her face. "They can't tell Min from Min from up there?"

"Not them."

"You?"

"Depends."

"Telka?"

"We'd know each other as far as we could reach."

"Hm. Oh well, might as well go with Brampon now that I've made the arrangements."

HERE'S WHERE WE SKIP AHEAD AGAIN,
COVERING GROUND THEY CREPT ACROSS
WITH THE USEFUL DEVICE OF THE NARRATIVE
SUMMARY. UP THE LAZY RIVER WITH
BRAMPON, THROUGH AN ALTERNATION OF
FOG AND TEMPEST, THE FOUR MIN
FOLLOWING WITH DOGGED PERSISTENCE
AND NO IMAGINATION. THE TRIP WAS
UNCOMFORTABLE, OF COURSE, IT WAS AN
OPEN BOAT, THEY GOT WET AND STAYED
WET, GOT COLD AND STAYED COLD, ATE
TOUGH LEATHERY POCKET BREAD, CHEESE
AND DRIED MEAT, DRANK FROM THE RIVER
(NOT SKEEN, SHE WAS BLUNT ABOUT HER
DISLIKE OF THE THOUGHT) AND A BARREL
OF ALE FROM NOSSIK'S CELLARS. BRAMPON
DROPPED THEM AT A DESERTED LANDING
NORTH OF THE CITY AND HENCEFORTH IS
GONE ENTIRELY FROM THE STORY, NEVER
HAVING MADE MUCH OF AN ENTRANCE INTO
IT. AT ONE OF THE ESTATES BEYOND THE
GROVE WHERE SKEEN AND TELKA NOT SO
MUCH MET AS COLLIDED, THEY ACQUIRED A
LIGHT CART, A FAST TEAM AND SUFFICIENT
HARNESS TO CONNECT THE TWO BY (a) A
QUICK NIGHT RAID ON A BARN (b) A STOCK
AUCTION THEY CHANCED TO STUMBLE
ACROSS—WELL, IT COULD HAPPEN (c) THE
EXPENDITURE OF THE LAST OF SKEEN'S GOLD
AND SOME HARD BARGAINING. YOU
CHOOSE THE ONE THAT APPEALS TO YOU AND

COLOR IN THE DETAILS WITH YOUR OWN
IMAGINATION. TIMKA DOES THE DRIVING
AS THEY START TOWARD THE MOUNTAINS;
NOT ONLY IS SKEEN MINUS A HAND, SHE IS
MINUS THE LEAST FRAGMENT OF
KNOWLEDGE ABOUT HOW TO HANDLE A
TEAM. LIPITERO IS EQUALLY USELESS, SO
TIMKA HAS TO SCRATCH UP ANCIENT
MEMORIES, STRUGGLE WITH THE STRAPS AND
BUCKLES AND CONVINCE A PAIR OF
HIGH-SPIRITED BEASTS THEY WANT TO GO
HOW AND WHERE SHE DIRECTS THEM. BEING
MIN IS A HELP HERE. WHEN THEY GET TO
FEELING TOO INDEPENDENT, SHE FREEZES
THEM IN PLACE UNTIL THEY GO MORE
WILLINGLY. SO THERE IT IS, THE LAST RUSH
BEGINS.

While they bounded along rutted dirt lanes (the cart
was a light, well-built vehicle with graceful hand-
turned spokes in the wheels and an iron tire shrunk
onto the rim, but its springs would be flattered if
you called them primitive), Skeen dozed, ignoring the bumps and lurches, and Lipitero brooded.
  While Timka slept, exhausted by her labors, Skeen
and Lipitero stood two-hour watches; they'd planned
no more than a four-hour stop to let the beasts rest
and graze; there was really no point in pushing too
hard, they weren't racing anything but impatience.
Telka and her army were in place, waiting for them;
they could have rested longer, but as Timka said, why
make Telka impatient and bring her after them too far
from the Gate. Skeen took the first watch, woke
Lipitero and lay down to snatch some more sleep.

Lipitero watched and brooded; toward the end of her
second hour, she got firewood from the cart and started
water boiling for tea.

When she had breakfast ready, she woke Skeen and
Timka.

"I've been thinking," Lipitero said, raising her voice
over the rattle of the cart and the horse noises. She
pointed at the Min visible intermittently through the
ragged clouds. "They should be told about the Ever-
Hunger."

"Waste of breath," Skeen said. "They won't believe
you."

The leather cushions on the driver's seat squeaked
as Timka slid around so she could see Lipitero. The
horses slowed to an amble, but didn't quite dare stop
completely. "I'm afraid Skeen's right," she said, hesi-
tating over the words as if she didn't want to believe
them, as if she wanted Lipitero to convince her otherwise. "They've got too many lives invested to dare
believe you."

'No doubt," Lipitero said. "But they've lived all
their lives with the Hunger waiting for them. That
must count for something. It's not so hard to believe,
is it? Ykx penned the beast. Isn't it reasonable that an
Ykx can release it?"

Skeen wriggled along the cart bottom until her head
caught on the low side; she stared into the sky watching
the dark shapes form and dissolve as they flew in and
out of open patches. Her smile was unpleasantly like a
smirk. "First catch your hare."

Timka snorted. "If you're going to be like that,
Pass-Through, I'm sure we both prefer your silence."
She glanced at the Min, then at Lipitero. "I could go
up and challenge them?"

"You could. No. They'll be more apt to listen if I
go."

Skeen stirred. "Keep your batteries at full charge,

you're going to need them. No thermals to ease the drain, not on a day like this."

Lipitero fidgeted with the ties to her robe, staring past the horses at the mountains hazily visible ahead of them. Finally she nodded, two short sharp jerks of her head. She got carefully to her feet, took off the robe of concealment and let it fall. She smiled. "I have missed soaring," she said and shot Skeen a glance full of mischief, "Lovely to have a splendidly ethical excuse to do what one wants." She chuckled at the grimace Skeen contrived, then powered the lift field and went soaring up.

The fliers retreated, consternation and agitation visible in every feather.

Lipitero didn't attempt to pursue them, simply rose until the glow globe about her touched cloud. "Min of these Mountains," she cried, and her voice was a giant's shout that boomed across the Plain.

Timka gaped. Skeen sighed. "More waste of energy. She's done something to the shunt field that makes it amplify her voice." She moved uneasily, scanned the pastures about them and saw far too many Pallah in them for her comfort. "We stick out like warts here."

"Hush, I want to hear this."

"How can you miss it?"

"See me," the great voice continued, "I am Ykx. Hear me. You have attacked me and died for it, yet I have been merciful. I am merciful still; my honor commands me to give warning. If I am attacked again by one or one thousand, I will not hold my hand. Behold, I am Ykx. Believe me and beware. If I am attacked again by one or one thousand, I cry doom on the Min of the Mountains. If I am attacked again, I will loose the Ever-Hunger. I swear it by Gather and by Blood. I will loose the Hunger on you and you will know terror all your days and horror all your nights. I am Ykx. Hear me." She spread her flight skins; the cold gray light of the sun, the warm gold light of the lift field shone on her shimmering silver-gray fur. For one last breath, she hung there under the clouds, then she dropped swiftly into the cart.

As soon as she was down, Timka slapped the reins on the team's haunches and gave them a needle that sent them into a long lope which made things highly uncomfortable for everyone in the cart.

Sometime later when the team had settled back to a steady walk and talking was possible, Lipitero smiled with satisfaction. "Am I right, Ti? Two of them have left us. At least I got that much reaction from them. Do you think it means anything?"

Timka twisted round. "Can you loose the Hunger from here?"

"Why?"

"If you can't, you've just issued a call for Telka and the Holavish to take you out before you do get close enough."

"Ungh. I didn't think of that. Yes, Ti, I can loose it from here. Matter of fact, given proper atmospherics, the Sydo Ykx could loose it from Sydo Gather. They couldn't corral it again from there. That's why they sent the others. Mmmh, I can prod the Hunger a bit without actually loosing it. They'll feel it stirring. That help?

"It might keep them off our necks for a while longer, might even start some arguments. Will it stop them? No. Because it's not just Telka, though she's one of the drivers. The Holavish want the old days back, the old ways. The weaker converts might hold back, but the true believers don't care how much destruction they cause. Death or glory, death and glory, it's the same thing. I don't understand that. I don't want to understand that."

Skeen stirred, stretched. "It happens," she said drowsily. "You Min've got no monopoly on airheads."

"That's a very helpful comment, Skeen. Got any more of them?"

"My, we're snappish today."

Timka clamped her teeth on her lip, holding back the words crowding her tongue. She focused on the bobbing heads of the horses and settled for interior monologue. So you're the only one allowed unreasonable irritation; so you're the only one allowed to scratch at whoever's nearest you; so you're the only one who can get edgy and show it. The litany went on and on until she'd worked through her anger and was merely tired and disheartened.

Around an hour after Lipitero's speech, a small swarm of Min came winging from the west. They were agitated and angry, fear hanging round them like a bitter fog; Timka probed with as much energy as she could spare, but she got nothing more definite from them. She thought about warning Skeen that the newcomers might try some sort of attack, but they continued their agitated loops with no sign they intended anything more intrusive than a stringent watch with possibilities of a raid to snatch the Ykx if she and Skeen gave them the slightest chance of bringing it off. She glanced over her shoulder. Lipitero was curled in a tight knot and seemed to be sleeping, Skeen was definitely asleep, her face slack, her mouth dropped open. Ah, well, time to make a fuss when the Holavish showed signs of doing something drastic.

Later still, it started raining, a cold steady drizzle. The horses plodded on, the cart creaked along, lurching over ruts and sinking perilously in the glutinous red mud; Skeen and Lipitero huddled under an old sail Skeen bought from Brampon, Timka took off her blouse and skirt and grew a coat of sleek fur. The talent she'd discovered in herself was proving useful for more than battles and rescue missions. On and on, deep into the night, deep into the Mountains. When the track got so rough it was dangerous to continue without more light, Timka tied the team to a stout tree, taking no chances the watching Min would try to spook them; she joined Skeen and Lipitero under the sail which Skeen had converted into a crude tent. Lipitero was building a small fire with the last of the dry wood. She fanned the smoke out of her face, nodded to Timka and moved aside to let her help with the meal.

They ate, then sat huddled in blankets watching the fire die, listening to the patter of rain on the canvas.

Lipitero cleared her throat but it was a moment before she spoke. "How far is the Gate from here?"

Skeen scratched at the film over her stump. "Three, four hours. No more than that."

"The Gate will take about half an hour to power up. When do you want me to activate it?"

"Does the Gate have to be working when you release the Hunger?"

"Yes."

"Ti, what about your Holavish army? If they're here, they're hiding."

"They're all around us now. I almost can't think for them pressing on me. The main body is ahead, though."

"What the hell they waiting for? By the way, how many?"

"Like leaves on the trees, mmmm, I can't say exactly, maybe four to five hundred. What are they waiting for? The Ever-Hunger is raging, you can't feel it? Ah, I remember, you're not as attuned to it as us. Petro? No? I can feel the barrier creaking as it lunges against it. That's . . . terrifying. You don't know how hard it is to keep going toward that thing, even when I know Petro will protect us from it. Them out there, they don't have a hope of avoiding it. They're working themselves up to the attack, but they're not ready yet. Another thing, not that it counts for much except as another stone in the balance pan, it's raining. Hard to fly in the rain. They're waiting for it to stop." She passed a hand over the short plushy fur on her face. "I could give you maybe a minute's warning before they come at us."

"Every little bit helps. Petro, if they haven't at-

tacked by morning, and we'd better keep watch to
make sure they don't try surprising us, activate the
Gate as soon as we move out of camp. Let me think
. . . um . . . there's a recent burn-over about an hour
from the Fountain Glade. Flattish land, some sapling
thickets, a lot of open space. Were I their warleader
that's the place I'd choose; their numbers will count
for a lot more in that kind of terrain. Can't be sure
that's the place—it might be, that's all. Ti gives the
word, you turn the Hunger loose. Be a good idea to
have the excavator ready. Will the rain damage it?"

"No. Now?"

"Out in the rain again, sorry." Skeen sighed, looked
up at the sagging canvas over them. "And it's time I
got my slicer ready. I should have done it before but I
didn't want to cut off a foot or something." She
shrugged off the blanket and crawled into the rain.

The morning came dull and gray, the drizzle diminished to a light mist. Timka gave the horses more
grain, helped Lipitero fold the canvas and tuck it
down tightly over the gear; there was a curdle of
despair in her stomach, her hands were unsteady, sounds
roared in her ears as the Holavish pressed their hate at
her, raptor and predator, the many-shaped Min army—
out there, around them, hating Lipitero, hating Skeen,
most of all hating her, that hatred hardened and sharpened by their own terrors. And behind them, beyond
them, the Ever-Hunger silent-howled its need. As her
fumbling hands worked, she cried silently—believe
Lipitero, Holavish, believe the Ykx, sister. Believe the
Hunger will be loosed on you. Let us go, let us leave.
You'll be rid of me that way, rid of us as surely as if
you ripped out my S'yer and burned it. Over and over
she flung the silent plea to them as if by will alone she
could drive the truth through their malice, through the
complex of needs that impelled them to their own
destruction, maybe the destruction of all life here.

Skeen returned from her prowl through the trees.

"They're keeping back." She moved her shoulders. "I can feel them out there." She looked up at the thin mist shrouding the treetops. "This should burn off before long. We'd better get started."

Timka stripped and shifted to the Pallah cat-weasel; she had to freeze the horses several times before they'd accept her anywhere near them, but she finally got them started. Skeen stood in the body of the cart behind her, holding onto the back of the driver's seat. The whippy knife that looked like flexible glass was bound into a slot in the end of a staff of polished hardwood, she held the staff securely in the elbow crease of her right arm; the flap on the darter's holster was tucked behind the belt, the lanyard was clipped in place, the slide on spray, not singleshot. There weren't even ruts to follow now, they were threading through trees and brush, picking a route around the bulge of the last mountain before they reached the narrow rambling valley where the Gate was. Timka fought her discomfort and struggled to keep track of the Min around them, like following an ocean current, water flowing in water, an ocean of Min flowing and flooding around her. A bit over two hours after dawn when they were close to the burnoff Skeen remembered, she felt the flow surge forward, the blast of determination from the dominants. "Skeen," she whispered, "it's starting."

"Petro, turn the beast loose. Now!"

"Ti, you're sure they're going to do it?"

"Yes, yes, the fools, yes, if you could feel them like I could, Lifefire, yes."

Lipitero squeezed gently at the lock, tightening and releasing it in the code pattern that would reduce to almost nothing the field that kept the Hunger penned. "It's done. Ten minutes and it's here."

Timka glared at the swaying grass ahead of them. The Pallah cat's pale blood was burning. She pulled her tongue over her lips and felt herself salivating; her enlarged, mobile ears twitched, not that she heard any physical sounds. . . ..

The Min will crystallized. . . .

"IT COMES," she cried. She stood, slapped the reins hard on the team's haunches, yowled a hunting cry that sent them into a blind panic. They ran full out, eyes wild, the cart bounding behind them. Petro braced the excavator on the cart's side, touched on the light blade; it was a meter wide, ten meters long and barely more than an atom thick. She swung it in a great arc, slicing through vegetation, stone, flesh. She felt no resistance beyond the weight of the instrument, but saplings fell and beast Min shrieked. On the other side of the cart, Skeen set herself to ride its leaps and lurches like a surfer in rough water. She swung the darter in a matching arc, her aim point about a meter off the ground, pulsing out sprays of darts whenever she saw something to shoot at. Timka leaped about between them, plucking fliers like ripe plums whenever they got close enough to be dangerous.

The team began to slow. Three times, someone among the Holavish with a little more sense than the others tried to stop the careering of the cart by freezing the horses, but Timka undid their efforts the moment they acted and the run went on; she even found time to steer the groaning beasts around the worst obstacles, pricking them right, turning them left as the terrain demanded. She danced on the seat and yowled, had to restrain herself from leaping down among the Min and slashing with handclaws and feetclaws until she drowned in Min flesh and Min fluids.

She heard a deep thrumming like horses running, coming out of the West, a great herd of them spread horizon to horizon, running wild. From her precarious perch on the seat she saw Min at the rear of the horde break and run.

Earth and sky throbbed with the beat of the beast.

The darter ran dry. Skeen shoved it into the holster and reached for the bladed staff.

The horses screamed and dropped. The cart rocked wildly, then settled as the weight of the beasts anchored it. In the next instant the flesh began melting off their bones until the harness straps held a set of bones and a few wisps of hair.

Everywhere Min screamed.

Lipitero shut off the excavator and set it down. "Skeen, Ti, get over here. Close to me. You're all right for a few minutes but no more."

Life emptied out of the Min around them, then their flesh spun away. The SOUND filled the space between earth and heaven, it vibrated in their various bloods and bones. Timka shuddered with loathing and terror and guilt. The SOUND wasn't eating her, but it was inside her, she'd never be free of it, never clean again. . . .

After an eternity that might have been five breaths or ten, the sound diminished, flowed away from them moving south and west, lapping up the life that had run from it.

Lipitero closed down the shunt, fiddled with her harness again. "There," she said. "The Ykx at Fellarax will begin herding the Hunger back into its pen."

Skeen stood slowly, looked around. "The thing's thorough, you'll have to give it that." She vaulted over the side and went to look at the heaps of horse bones. "So much for horsepower. Come on, Ti, shift and help me cut the harness loose."

Timka snarled, a soft deadly sound.

Skeen set her hand on her hip, waved her stump. "Come on, use your head, Ti. We've got to get out of here and we need the cart, or can you turn yourself into a mule and haul the gear for us?"

It took several minutes of interior struggle, but Timka finally threw off the Pallah cat-weasel and reverted to the standard Pallah form. Listlessly she dragged on her robe, pulled the tie tight and tumbled herself over the side. "You should have left me cat," she muttered. "I'm about as much use as a sick cow this way."

"You'll manage. Get a move on, I need your hands. Djabo's nimble digits, I'll be biting my elbows before I get to the Tank Farm."

With a lot of grunting and cursing but no real difficulties, Skeen and Timka pulled the cart through the drying smears of dead Min, Lipitero walking beside them with Skeen's darter, its reservoir refilled from the water bag. In less than an hour they reached the eerie motionless glade where the Gate was. Skeen retrieved the cached swords and other items from the hollow in the tree, and dug the Min jewelry from the rodent nest in the rockpile beside one of the Gate posts. She set these things in the cart, then scowled at the swirls of dust that filled the space between the posts. "I think it's wide enough," she said finally. "Ti?"

Timka blinked at her, but didn't seem to see her. The bright green gaze was absent, turned inward. She pulled the ties loose; with a kind of whole body shrug she threw the robe off, shifted to her earlier, simpler form, the cat-weasel, and loped toward the Gate. She gathered herself and leaped through the dustclouds.

"Oh, fuck." Skeen snatched the darter from Lipitero and ran after the Min.

Two cats were kicking up more dust in a snarling vicious battle, banging from ruin to ruin, wrestling, clawing, heads striking like serpents. They were covered with that cream-yellow dust; impossible to tell who was which. Skeen swore and darted them both, darted them again when they looked like they were starting to shift.

She heard a scraping noise behind her, whirled, went to help Lipitero ease the cart through the Gate and wheel it into a rutted pot-holed street. The Ykx looked round the ruins and the dry-bones valley. "Wonderful."

"Patience, my friend. Things get more interesting after we get out of here." Taking Timka's shabby robe, she went to the cats and flicked some of the dust off them. Now that they were lying still, it was easier to tell the difference between them. Telka-cat was a shade or two darker, had a blunter muzzle (more cat than weasel), and small round ears; she was chunkier than Ti-cat and somehow not so lethal. Skeen wrapped her hand in the loose skin at her nape and began dragging her toward the Gate. Lipitero started to help, but Skeen waved her away. "Keep watch," she said. "No telling what's hanging about here."

She muscled the cat through the Gate, took a last look around. Nothing had changed. The air hung still and silent, not a leaf was moving. No insect or bird noises. Trees like painted images. Short thick grass, not a blade moving. From the west the faint sound of water falling. "Well, Mistommerk, it's been interesting." With a flourish of her single hand, she stepped back through the Gate. "Any problems, Petro?"

"Not even a hungry gnat."

"You'd better shut down the Gate. I don't know what kind of sensors the Junks might have scattered about here." She walked to the cart and stood scratching her back against a corner as she frowned at Timka. "Too bad I had to dart Ti. That sister of hers just about gave me a hernia and now her." She wiped at the sweat beading on her brow, swore, then bent to lift the comatose Ti-cat.

"Still the same sweet temper," Tibo said.

Skeen swung around so fast she staggered; she steadied herself, slipped the knife from her arm sheath and started for the man standing in the ragged gap between two of the higher walls.

"Get a hitch on it, love." He raised the stunner he'd been holding casually against his thigh. "Just to make sure you listen."

She straightened, looked at the knife, slid it back into its sheath. "Tibo you baster, where's Picarefy?"

Tibo stood in the opening, the stunner steady on her, lithe compact little man, his walnut brown skin gleaming in the white searing light of the sun, his black eyes laughing at her. "Safe. That's the point of the exercise."

"What? Never mind. Where is she? That's the only thing I want to hear."

"Marigold Pit."

She gazed at him a long moment, then sighed, tension draining out of her so completely she barely found the energy to keep standing. "Why?" It was a question she dreaded asking, its answer something she dreaded even more.

"Abel Cidder."

"What! Where?"

"I was working on Sessamarenn the Aviote. He'd hinted he wanted to finance a backcountry dig outside channels. We were in the Golden Wheel, in one of the privacy alcoves, a high hole, he said it reminded him of his perch back home; we had the field up and tight and were doing some of the preliminary chat, both of us looking down at the main floor. Abel Cidder came in with a Junk, the Brolmahn no less. They were talking, friendly as tronchai in a cold winter."

Skeen ran her hand through damp sweaty hair. "I thought a lot of things, but never Abel Cidder." She ran her tongue over dry lips. "We're going to have to do something about him."

"You'd get a lot to agree with you. So, after Cidder went upstairs with the Brolmahn, I chatted a bit more with Sessamarenn; it felt like I was sitting bare ass on a zarb mound, but old Sam's no fool. If I ran out right after Cidder showed, well, you see what I mean. We finished the meal with each understanding the other pretty well, about where I expected when I sat down with him, so I must have handled myself well enough. I tell you this, there was just one thing in my head. Picarefy. Cidder had the clout to confiscate her if he nosed her out. The name change and the papers were good enough for the Junks but once Cidder started sniffing through reports which we both know he does,

may his nose get the tichzenrotte and fall off, he'd
have us cold. I caught a jit to the shuttle port, my gut
in knots. When the shuttle ferried me up with no
trouble and there were no sett buoys anchoring her, I
relaxed a little, but I knew there might be no time
left. I didn't dare go back down, not even to leave you
a message. I didn't know where you were and there
was no time to hunt for you and going through Picarefy's
com, well, I didn't know who might be listening. I
explained the situation to Picarefy; we agreed you
could take care of yourself well enough while we were
gone, that I'd get back soon as I could manage it and
collect you once I'd calmed you down enough so you'd
listen. Marigold was the closest Pit. I left her at Ambo's.
Cream was in and hungry. I hired him to bring me
back and hang around looking like he was planning to
buy something. He's not one of Cidder's pets, not like
us." Tibo grinned. "Cidder only persecutes the very
best." He sobered. "I figured you'd be ready to roast
me over a slow fire, but I didn't expect you to vanish.
I've spent the last five months going slowly crazy,
Skeen. I even broke into Records to see if they'd
shoved you into a work camp, sweating blood the
whole time afraid they'd killed you. You know what I
found, a record of a saayungka chase that ended in
this valley and a lot of notes about mysterious disap-
pearances here. Folk who melted into air and never
showed up again. This is the third time I've come
here; I've just about wiped out my stash in bribes.
Yours too, I'm afraid."

"Cidder still in Chukunsa?"

"No. Seems he left the day after you disappeared."

"I've been thinking evil thoughts about you, Tibo."

"Still?"

"No. I believe you. Thanks. If I'd lost Picarefy . . .
um . . . and you, of course, I don't know what. . . ."

He tucked the stunner away. "Ah, love, I know my
place, I do."

Lipitero came round the cart, handed the darter to

Skeen. In Trade-Min it took Skeen a second to understand, she said, "Looks to me like this one is no
danger to us."

"No. He's a friend of mine. Djabo's hairy tongue,
Petro, you're going to have to learn synspeech." She
looked down at the cat's body. "When Ti wakes up,
maybe she can handle that. Her sister gave me the
Trade-Min, let's hope this language business works
both ways."

Tibo came cautiously over to them. "Who's that?"

The abrupt switch from language to language was
making Skeen feel a bit dizzy; she was thirsty and near
exhaustion, her head ached and she had some major
shifts of attitude to negotiate; she caught hold of her
temper's tail and said with more than her usual patience, "Her name is Lipitero. I wouldn't be here
without her help. You might say she's our boss for the
next few months. I've got one whiz of a story to tell
you when we have some free time. By the way, how
did you get out here? I hope not walking."

"Nope. You've beaten the odds before so I expected you to show sooner or later and I thought I
might need some speed when you did. Got a scoot up
there," he nodded at the next mountain over from Tol
Chorok, "in a place with some shade and water."

"How long will it take you to get there and bring it
back?"

"Bring it back?" He looked from the cart to Lipitero,
raised his brows. "Why not come with me, both of
you?"

"Because there's three of us and there's a cartload
of things I don't want to leave behind."

"Skeen, it's a scoot, not a freighter." He nudged
Timka with his boot toe. "This cat the third? I know
you can go weird about animals, don't think I've forgotten that python you infested Picarefy with. This
beast doesn't look even half as friendly as Py and he
tried to eat me. I'm sure she's a lovely pet, but by the
gods, Skeen. . . ."

"Don't let Ti hear you calling her a pet. She resents it."

"I'm missing something?"

"Fuckin' right you are, love." She grinned at him. "Just wait till you see what it is."

Tibo set the scoot down on the dust flats outside the ruin and helped Skeen pull the cart out to it. He eyed the swords with approbation and hefted Lipitero's gear with apprehension, but loaded it anyway, hoping to have an excuse to leave the cat behind; Skeen read it in his bland face and sly sidewise glances. As soon as she saw the scoot, she knew it could carry the two of them plus the baggage and nothing more. Lipitero was going to have to follow on her own. No problem. With the heat being what it was, there'd be plenty of thermals she could ride, minimizing the amount of assist she would need and the danger of her being picked up on Junk sensors. Timka was even less trouble. She could use her own wings. Skeen grinned at the thought; she was looking forward to seeing Tibo's face when Ti shifted.

Timka stirred as they were carrying her out to the scoot. Her body twitched, she moved her head, produced a breathy growl.

"Ease her down. Gently, Tibo, you're not throwing one of your cousins through a routine. Petro, fetch her a clean robe, will you?" Skeen went to the cart for one of the waterskins, leaving a nervous Tibo squatting beside Timka, his hand on his stunner.

Skeen squeezed a few drops into Ti-cat's mouth. "Come on, Ti, it's hot out here. Wake up and get rid of that fur, you'll feel a lot better."

Ti-cat took another mouthfull of water, then lurched onto her feet. She stood a moment, twitching all over, moving head, shoulders, haunches, legs, as if she checked them out to make sure they were working. A last shudder, then she shifted. She glared at Tibo, snatched the robe from Lipitero and slipped into it.

Tibo pulled his hand across his mouth, opened his eyes wide, shook his head. "I don't believe it. I see it and I don't believe it."

Skeen giggled. "I know. That's how I felt the first time I saw it happen." She turned to Timka. "Think you can do a language transfer? From me to you and Petro? It'd make life easier for all of us."

Timka pushed her tangled black curls back from her face, looked around, grimaced. "You and Petro kneel, if you don't mind; it'll work better if I touch both of you." She knelt between them facing the opposite direction, stroked her fingers up Skeen's face, feeling into her, stroked fingers up Lipitero's face, feeling into her; she pulled, felt Lipitero quiver under her fingertips. When the transfer was finished, she sat on her heels and sighed with weariness.

Lipitero was rubbing at her temples and frowning.

Skeen got to her feet. "This is one time it's really better to give than receive. The worst ache will be gone in an hour or so, Petro. Can you still soar?"

Lipitero started to nod, grimaced and decided to try out her painfully acquired language. "Yiss I can, it takes little strenth."

"Ti?"

"Give me the direction, I'll put on feathers and find a windstream that'll carry me faster than that thing."

"Let's go then. The sooner we get offworld, the happier I'll be."

As the scoot skimmed along a dozen meters above Kildun Aalda's surface, Skeen lay back in her seat, closed her eyes and let herself go limp. Her judgment was vindicated and that pleased her well enough, but she had this peculiar feeling of uncertainty when she should have been relaxed and content. As if she hung by her thumbs over an ocean of boiling oil and her thumbs were giving way. Tibo had changed . . . no, that's wrong . . . no, he's what he'd always been . . . I've changed . . . no, that's not it. . . . She finally decided that during the time on Mistommerk she'd built Tibo into something more than he was. She'd need to relearn the man, the capable flamboyant little man who needed people a lot more than she ever would. She brooded over the Mephistophelian figure she'd created in her mind and was fascinated by it, by how much more dangerous and unstable and interesting her invented Tibo had become. She smiled ruefully, secretly. I'm going to miss that Tibo. She thought about Lipitero soaring over them. Another job starting, maybe harder than getting that Gate open. Rallen and the Ykx. Rallen, Rallen, where are you, Rallen?